Elizabeth Parsons Ware Packard

The Great Drama

The Millennial Harbinger. Vol. 1

Elizabeth Parsons Ware Packard

The Great Drama
The Millennial Harbinger. Vol. 1

ISBN/EAN: 9783744741842

Printed in Europe, USA, Canada, Australia, Japan

Cover: Foto ©Andreas Hilbeck / pixelio.de

More available books at **www.hansebooks.com**

THE GREAT DRAMA:

OR,

THE MILLENNIAL HARBINGER.

BY

MRS. E. P. W. PACKARD.

WRITTEN IN 1862, UNDER THE INSPECTION OF ANDREW McFARLAND, M.D.,
LATE SUPERINTENDENT OF THE INSANE ASYLUM
AT JACKSONVILLE, ILLINOIS.

VOL. I.

PUBLISHED BY THE AUTHORESS.

———

HARTFORD:
THE CASE, LOCKWOOD & BRAINARD COMPANY.
1878.

To secure our complete emancipation from the subjective principles to which the common law of marriage holds us liable, is one of the chief objects of this book.

Modification of this principle is not what we seek, but its entire abolition; so that the marriage law shall not impose any civil disabilities upon the wife which it does not impose upon the husband. Or, in other words, we desire our government to so emancipate us from our present legal position of slaves, as to make our legal position to correspond to our social position as companions or partners of our husbands.

And until this end is achieved, let us unceasingly work for it, knowing that our "Divine Republic" can never be inaugurated until this equality of rights is secured to married women.

(3)

INDEX TO THE SERIES OF BOOKS

COMPRISING

THE GREAT DRAMA:

OR,

THE MILLENNIAL HARBINGER.

PREFACE.

PROVIDENCE capacitated me for the authorship of "The Great Drama: or, The Millennial Harbinger," by placing me where I was almost as completely isolated from all worldly influences as if I had passed beyond the river of death. In other words, I was entombed in an insane asylum; placed there, by my reverend husband, while in a perfectly sane condition, to destroy the moral influence of my independent thinking and teaching in a Bible class, which he thought was imperiling the fallibility of the Presbyterian church creed!

Yes, I have been kidnapped and imprisoned for three long years, under the American flag of religious toleration, simply because I maintained the right of private judgment in religious matters. I have risked and lost my all of earthly good for my honest convictions. Yet, after all, instead of now recanting to secure my personal liberty and thus attempting to redeem my blasted reputation for sanity and intelligence, I have fearlessly maintained my right not only to think as I please, but also to write as I please, in the production of the following book, even while in the absolute power of a most intolerant, bigoted despotism!

Here I was cut off from all written communication with the outside world, not even allowed to correspond with my own children. Thus I was completely severed from all the cares and responsibilities attending the family relation. For more than two years I had thus rested from all worldly cares and responsibilities, and during this time I had schooled myself

(5)

into such a state of quiet submission that my soul had attained to a condition of trustful quietness and peace.

My health was as nearly perfect as I think it is possible for any one to be, having abandoned the use of drugs thirty years before, using no stimulants, not even tea or coffee, consequently had never been sick during this time. I had confined myself exclusively to a vegetarian and fruit diet for the previous eighteen months, and had limited myself to only two meals a day, and took a full sponge-bath daily, and spent ten hours of the twenty-four in sound, quiet, and refreshing sleep.

My immediate surroundings had not only been made more tolerable, by the removal of some of the more furious and dangerous patients to another ward, but I was allowed a room to myself, and it was furnished too in a comfortable and tasteful manner. These alleviations were the result of an interview which Dr. McFarland, the superintendent, had allowed me with the trustees, who were thus convinced that it was the *use* of my reason rather than the *loss* of it which had occasioned my persecution. Dr. McFarland's opinion coinciding with their own, proposed that I make a written defense of my opinions, adding, " and I will publish it myself."

"Well done, Dr. McFarland! if you are going to give me such liberty, it may possibly prepare the way for my liberation."

The paper was faithfully furnished by the doctor, and I, with the most elastic feelings which this hope of deliverance inspired, went to work to prepare my document for the printer. But before twenty-four hours had elapsed since this liberty license was granted to my hitherto prison-bound intellect, the vision of a big book began to dawn upon my mind, accompanied with the most delightful feeling of satisfaction with my undertaking. The next time the doctor called I said to him:

"Doctor, it seems to me I must write a book—a big book."

The thoughts and their arrangement are all new and original, as suggested to my mind by this sort of mental vision. What shall I do, doctor?"

"Write it out just as you see it."

He then furnished me with stationery, and gave directions to the attendants to let no one disturb me, and let me do just as I pleased. I commenced writing out this mental vision, and in six weeks I penciled the substance of "The Great Drama: or, The Millennial Harbinger," which, when written out for the press, covered two thousand five hundred pages of note paper. Can I not truly say my train of thought was engineered by the "Lightning Express?"

My spiritual freedom was unbounded. I was trammeled by no oligarchy of creeds, sects, or customs of society. I was palsied by no fear to offend, no desire to please, no dependence upon the judgment of others. This asylum was indeed the birth-place of my "spiritual freedom," where *the God within* was enthroned as the only monarch of this realm of human freedom.

Thus panoplied for my work, the inspirations of truth found an unobstructed communication of thought, through my healthy brain and organism, thus capacitating me to write a book, which, if read with a tithe of the pleasure I experienced in writing it, cannot but become a most welcome guest in every household, not only in America, but throughout the world.

Mrs. E. P. W. PACKARD.

Chicago, Ill., January, 1878.

(1496 Prairie Avenue.)

INTRODUCTION.

In introducing "The Great Drama: or, The Millennial Harbinger," to the public, I desire to inform the reader that the style of the book is wholly original, as I never heard of the "railroad style" of writing until I used it myself. But as my mind is constituted on the "high-pressure" principle, it seems a very natural style for me; and since my thoughts naturally come by flashes through my instincts, I can appropriately say my trains of thought are engineered by the "Lightning Express."

. I am the "conductor" of two trains of cars across the continent; one the Christian, and the other the Calvinistic, and as they move in opposite directions, my "switches" are necessary to avoid "collisions." My main track is "nature," her laws and tendencies—which I call Christianity. My opposing track is a perversion of "nature," or evil and its tendencies—which I call Calvinism. Into the two trains which I conduct over these respective routes I gather all the good and evil found in every department of American society, both Church and State. I expose the evil, or Calvinism, found in American institutions and customs, and "freight" it on to its terminus—"the bottomless pit." I defend the good, or Christianity, found in them, and "express" it also to its terminus—the seat of the Divine Republic, which is the "kingdom of heaven," established in America—the model government for the world.

The reader will please bear in mind that this book was

(8)

written in 1862, during the war, and has not been changed to adapt itself to the present time. I therefore speak of Abraham Lincoln, who was then the President of the United States, as a personification of the American government.

And in my highly figurative and symbolical style I speak of Doctor Andrew McFarland, the superintendent of the insane asylum, as my personified "Christ"—as a natural man, developing the legitimate tendencies of Christianity. (Although in this case I found the "clouds" concealing him so very heavy and black that if a "Christ" *can* be found here, none need despair!) Manliness I call God-likeness— and a perfectly-developed, natural man, a "God," or a Christ-like man.

I speak of Rev. Theophilus Packard, my legal husband, as my personified "Calvin,"—as a regenerated man, developing the legitimate tendencies of Calvinism. A perverted man I call a "devil;" and a perverted woman I call a "fallen angel." I speak of good and evil as "God and devil," and thus I claim there is a "God and devil" in every human being, and that the devil is destined to become God's subject; so that in the great battle-field of every human soul Christ is ultimately to come off the victorious conqueror, by the repentance of each and every human soul. Thus a "Christ" is to be developed from every natural man.

I speak of myself as a personification of a "natural woman," illustrating, by a kind of autobiography of my own life, the legitimate tendencies of her instinctive nature. I speak of the "Great Drama" as "my book," since it was written in a prison cell, where I had access to no books except Webster's large dictionary and the Bible. With these exceptions, my education and experiences were the only library from which I could extract the thoughts of my book.

I speak of "woman" as a personification of the "Holy Ghost," in whom is concentrated the spiritual forces of God's universe; and a perfectly-developed natural woman as a "Holy Ghost," or a spiritual woman. And as every natural man is to become a "Christ," by repentance, so is every natural woman to become a "Holy Ghost," by repentance. I speak of the "marriage of the Lamb" as the complete emancipation of woman from her hitherto subjected condition, when our man-government will extend to her identity, equal protection with themselves; then the "spiritual" power of woman will be married to the "intellectual" power of man, thus inaugurating the "spiritual reign of Christ," on earth. I speak of "husband" as the "protector" of woman's identity, whether married or single.

The simple and artless style in which I clothe my thoughts is not only symbolic of the "flying train," but it also adapts the book to the comprehension of the common people for whom it was written. It is a book of simple facts and opinions; not a logical one. I leave the logic for my readers to supply. Were it appropriate to this "railroad style" of writing, I could give good and sound reasons for all the opinions I have expressed. As for the facts from which I draw my illustrations, they are simply truths, needing no defense, since truth is self-sustaining.

There is, of necessity, some repetition of the same thoughts on my different routes across the American continent; but these thoughts are as variously illustrated as the scenery varies on the different tracks; or, in other words, the same principles of Christianity and Calvinism are brought to our observation in some new form, from which we procure our "miscellaneous freight." But, of course, our "wheat and stock cars" are run on all our routes.

Now, my dear reader, as the "Lightning Express" dashes on, allowing you only a "glance and a glimpse" of the passing panorama of thoughts chasing after each other in seemingly promiscuous, wild confusion, be not alarmed! since no

" collisions" take place under our skillful "engineer's" superintendence; and he also gives us a little time to individualize some of our thoughts at our "switches." And, besides, if you do not fancy our "emancipation car" for the transportation of thought, you are at full liberty to abandon it at any "station" for the stage-coach or the one-horse wagon, where you can dwell on one view or thought to your heart's content. But for ourselves we have a decided preference for a "glance and a glimpse" at an extensive region of thought, knowing that such notes may serve as gems of future development, when our passengers are all safely landed in the "depot" of individuality, where perfect freedom of thought and expression is enjoyed in this quiet resting-place for all our weary passengers.

This book has been in readiness for the press sixteen years. When I was first liberated from my asylum-prison I could not print it for want of money. Afterwards, for want of courage.

I found that I was so far in advance of my contemporaries, in my conception of truth, that I feared another imprisonment might be the result of a premature publication of "The Great Drama." Therefore prudence suggested that its publication be delayed until my sanity had become more fully recognized through the publication of books of a less radical nature ; hoping also that, ere long, I might find a class of contemporaries whose liberality might shield my personal liberty in risking the publication of original thoughts expressed in an original style! Thank God! I feel that that time has fully come; for I now so often hear the radicalism of my book echoed, both from the American pulpit and press, that a much longer delay may expose its author to the charge of being herself the echo, instead of the originator, of the thoughts of "The Great Drama."

And, besides, I would most thankfully acknowledge, that

by the liberal patronage the public has bestowed upon my other books I have earned money enough to print it myself. I have sold thirty-six thousand of my own books, by single sales, by my own personal efforts. And now I have not courage enough to keep it hid any longer; for there is a " vow" recorded in the archives of high heaven, that "'The Great Drama' shall be published if the Lord will but grant me deliverance"! I am delivered—my " vow" stands recorded there! The fulfillment of this " vow" can be postponed no longer. For I now fear God's chastening rod more than I do the public criticisms attending its publication.

"THE GRAND CENTRAL DEPOT."

"THE GRAND CENTRAL DEPOT."

From this " Grand Central Depot " all our different trains start to gather up the Calvinism and Christianity lying at the various " depots " on their respective routes or tracks. The " freight " stored at this " depot " consists of the great fundamental principles or truths which the eleven succeeding " trains " illustrate and enforce.

The " commentary " accompanying it is given as an illustration of the position I profess to assume and advocate, viz., that the office of a commentator is no exclusive ecclesiastical right or privilege conferred on the aristocratic few, but is, on the contrary, the common, universal right of a common, universal humanity. The priest has no more right to give his interpretation or opinion respecting the Bible than I have. Neither have I any more right to dictate to him what his opinions should be, than he has to dictate to me what my opinions ought to be. I have a right to my own opinions, although diametrically opposed to his, and he has the same right to his opinions, although diametrically opposed to my own.

I have no right to the claim of infallibility in my own opinions ; neither has he any right to this claim.

I am not responsible to any human being for my opinions ; neither is any human being responsible to me for theirs.

The only claims which my opinions have upon another's reason and conscience are, the claims which reason and common-sense demand in their defense. The only claims which the ecclesiastic has upon my reason and conscience in support

(15)

of his opinions are, the claims which reason and common-sense demand in their defense.

I claim that common-sense is the common platform on which a common religion must be advocated and maintained.

I am responsible solely to God alone for my opinions; so is every other developed human being alone responsible to God for his opinions.

'T is bigotry which says, My opinions are right and my brother's are wrong. 'T is Christianity which says, " Judge ye not of your own selves what is right."

There is but one human being in the universe who has any authority over my opinions and conscience: and that being is Mrs. E. P. W. Packard. The inspirations of the Divinity within me, as indicated by my own reason and conscience, are authoritative over me; but are of no sort of authority for any other being in the universe.

I claim that a Bible-class should be conducted on these freedom principles—that each member should be allowed to be true and honest to the inspirations within his own soul, untrammeled by human creeds or educational influences.

The opinions of each honest member would be as likely to be as various on any given question, as the countenances of the class are various. Thus each member would find in the other some new view of truth presented for his own mind's inspection. Thus each human being would become a brilliant source of light and truth, reflected from the Sun of truth, through the inspirations of his own individual reason and conscience.

I don't want my Bible-class to give me Scott's, or Henry's, or Clark's, or Doddridge's, or Barnes's, or any other human being's opinions on the point under discussion, but their own individual opinion as reflected through their own minds—I can read the published opinions of others for myself—I want a new and better source of truth—the opinion of the common minds of the common people. They are God's mirrors, untarnished by human dogmas and human creeds to a far less degree than the creed-bound theologian.

Thus being self-reliant and independent, can every son and daughter of the human family bask in the exercise of that complete " liberty wherewith Christ makes his people free "— free to do and judge for themselves what is right for them to think and do—without this impious interference of a self-elected judge over a brother or a sister's conscience and opinions.

God is the sole judge of his whole family—he has never delegated this office to any one of his children to dictate to another child. Should one of my children venture to domineer over another child of equal rights and privileges, I should regard it as an insult to my authority, demanding my manifest condemnation. So will God surely condemn those members of his family who assume to lord it over the opinions and conscience of another.

I have been true to the inspirations of the Divinity within me, in uttering, without restraint, my own opinions of truth and duty—and that individual who dares to blaspheme these utterances, dares to blaspheme God himself. And it is blasphemy to call these opinions, insane opinions, and if a brother or a sister feels inclined, as he peruses this volume, to yield to the tempter at his side, who is striving to induce you to feel that another cannot differ from you in opinion without being insane on that point, as you value your own immortal soul's welfare, I entreat, yea, warn you, to resist this blasphemous insinuation, lest you be found among the number of those who could not find peace, though you sought it carefully and with tears—for blasphemy against the Holy Ghost cannot be forgiven, but must suffer the penalty God has assigned to it, as its just punishment. And Oh! as you love happiness as well as I do, don't bring upon yourselves that measure of misery you have meted out to me, by calling me insane.

CALVINISM AND CHRISTIANITY COMPARED.

Calvinism and Christianity are antagonistic systems, and uphold antagonistic authorities.

Christianity upholds God's authority; Calvinism upholds the devil's authority.

The kingdom of Christ and the kingdom of Satan can no longer exist in one and the same family or government. The time has come when the tares and the wheat must be separated, for the harvest of the world is fully ripe.

I am gathering the wheat—the truths of Christianity—into God's granary; my husband is gathering the tares—the lies of Calvinism—and binding them in bundles to be burned.

He is a consistent Calvinist; I am a consistent Christian.

Calvin was a bigot, an intolerant despot, a murderer.

Christ was a kind, liberal, charitable, and tolerant friend and protector to all, and the Saviour of all.

Calvin trespassed upon the rights of others; Christ protected the rights of all.

Calvin hated, with a deadly hate, his Christian brother; Christ loved, with a saving power, even his enemies.

Calvinism is treason to God's government; Christianity is loyalty to God's government.

Christ's teachings and Calvin's teachings were antagonistic.

Christ taught there is but one God; Calvin taught there are three Gods.

Christ taught that he was the Son of God; Calvin taught that he was God himself.

Christ taught that the Son could not be as old as his Father; Calvin taught that they could be of the same age.

Christ taught that he, himself, was a subordinate being, subject to God's authority, and that he acted with delegated power, as the world's Saviour; and that when this end was fully achieved he should deliver up this, his delegated authority, to his Father, and he, himself, be subject to him, and God would then be " all and in all." Calvin taught that he was God himself, and acted by his own self-derived authority.

Christ taught that God was the Father of all the human family, and as such, purposes and designs the best good of all his children, and he taught that he had omnipotent power to carry out and accomplish all the benevolent purposes of his Fatherly nature. Calvin taught that the largest part of the human family were the children of the devil, and that he had omnipotent power to thwart God's purposes concerning such, and could insure to them eternal destruction, in spite of God's intentions and purposes to redeem the whole of the human family from destruction.

Christ taught that every sin would receive its just punishment, that is, must either be individually repented of, or its penalty must be endured by the wrong-doer himself; that the law of justice is inexorable; that the only way to escape punishment is to escape the cause of punishment. Calvin taught that the favorites in God's family would be exonerated from this law of justice, simply because they believed that Christ died for sinners.

Christ taught that punishment would continue so long as transgression continued: that whenever repentance took place, pardon ensued; and that all would some time repent, because he had purposed to save all, in this way, alone: and he taught that death and hell would finally be destroyed; and of course, if the effect ceased, the cause must have ceased.

Calvin taught that the greater part of God's family would transcend God's ability to discipline into subjection to God's authority, and obedience to his commands, and that, failing in his ability so to do, he was determined to show his power over them, by keeping them in endless, hopeless torment, and thus, fiend-like, manifest his despotic authority, by torturing for ever his helpless victims.

Calvin taught that the day of probation terminated with the death of our natural bodies. Christ taught that there were no limits to God's mercy—that he was unchangeable, "the same yesterday, to-day, and for ever"—and therefore repentance would always remain a condition of pardon—that free agency is an indispensable law of our moral nature, over which the death of our natural body has no influence—that this natural law of our physical being has no more influence or control over the laws of our moral nature than the natural law of eating or sleeping has over them; or, in other words, the putting off of our natural body has no more power to change the laws of our moral nature, than a change of clothing has to change the character.

Christ taught that our natures are holy—that all their God-given instincts and laws are but a type of his own nature, which we cannot violate with impunity—that to disregard nature's claims is to disregard God's claims. And he has shown us what these claims are, by living a natural life himself, on earth, for our example. He has shown us that sin consists in violating the laws of our God-like nature, thus depraving or perverting it from its original tendencies—that he came to restore human nature from its present perverted condition, to its original natural state of innocence.

Calvin taught that our natures are sinful—that to live a natural life is to live a sinful life. He taught that human nature is our worst foe, which we must conquer into subjection to his perverted standard of faith and practice, or be lost eternally !

Christ taught that to be baptized, we must go down into the water, and come up out of the water, as he did. Calvin taught that to be baptized, we must stand up in a house and be sprinkled !

Christ taught that to feel right we must first do right—that our feelings grow out of our actions, as directly as the plant does from the seed. The seed is the act, the feeling is the perfected fruit. We cannot generate a kind feeling, until we have sowed a kind seed in a kind act. The thought or impulse which prompted the act is not the feeling, any more than sowing the seed is the fruit—for if this impulse is not carried out into an act, it is like letting the seed lie in the granary, instead of planting it; so, of course, there is no fruit. But a kind impulse carried out into a kind act secures, invariably, a kind feeling; and a wicked impulse carried out into a bad act secures, invariably, a bad or wrong feeling. So by our fruits we are to be judged, not by our thoughts or impulses. I can never tell how a liar feels until I lie myself, and then I cannot help but know how he feels; and to feel like a thief I must first steal; and to love my enemy I must first do him good—bestow upon him a kind act, and God will bestow upon me a kind feeling towards him; and he cannot create a kind feeling in any other than in his own appointed way—the way of obedience, or right doing. This is living faith which works by love, or kind impulses.

Calvin taught that to do right we must first feel right—that a filial feeling could be cherished independent of a filial act, that the act was only the expression of the feeling. Thus a child could in reality feel filial towards his parent, while disobeying his commands. This is dead faith which is too lazy to work at all, except by a feeling of hate. And when his faith is tested by his fruits, it will be found to have no fruit at all, because there was no feeling at all—only blind impulse. The seed has been in the granary, instead of the ground, and no fruit grows without planting an act from which to grow.

Christ taught us to work out our own salvation, by doing right, and thus feeling right, as he does. Calvin taught us to do nothing but sin, and trust Christ to work out our salvation for us; that if we did our duty we were in danger of trusting to our own works, instead of Christ, to save us.

Christ taught us to overcome evil with good; to call out into active use all the kindly emotions of our God-like nature, and thus forestall or supplant the evil impulses,—or, in other words, to starve or choke out the evil by giving it no chance to act wrong,—and cultivate the good by employing all our energies in doing right.

Calvin taught us to overcome evil with evil—to attack evil to destroy it, and thus excite it into action, as a self-defensive act; thus its own action feeds its life or feeling, and it grows as rapidly as tares will when once planted; he acts wrong, and he therefore cannot help feeling wrong. He teaches that the first step towards becoming better, is, to believe we are very bad, and if we are too honest to say we are bad when we feel that we are not, it is the darkest sign of guilt; thus. the upright, sincere soul feels driven to become bad, so that he can make an honest confession of his guilt, in order to secure the confidence of his Christian brethren that he is converted!

Christ taught that to clothe ourselves with his righteous- ness, is, to do like him—be like him by doing right in every- thing.

Calvin taught that to clothe ourselves with Christ's right cousness, is, to act contrary to the dictates of human nature, and utterly repudiate obedience as a meritorious act, or, as a reason why we should be acquitted and justified in God's sight, and depend wholly upon the merits of Christ, entirely independent of our own,—or, in other words, to continue in an unnatural state, depending upon a sovereign act of God to appropriate the vicarious sufferings of Christ for our benefit, independent of our accountability.

Calvin taught that the "elect" were all that would or could be saved, and that these were God's children, and all others were the devil's children.

Christ taught that all were God's dear children; that all had good and evil in them, but that all the evil in them he came to destroy, and that for this purpose he had elected some of his children, and capacitated them, by peculiar sufferings and trials, to be co-workers with him for the good of the many—like as if a father should bestow peculiar advantages upon one child, that he might be fitted to be the educator of his other children.

This is the " economy of grace." I believe that with this company of sanctified ones, who have come out of great tribulation, such as he endured on earth, he will make such assaults upon Satan's kingdom as will insure its entire overthrow and destruction; and I believe that this reign of Christ on the earth, with his elect co-workers, is about to be inaugurated, and that these troublous times are only the day of preparation for a better state than has ever been experienced on earth. These clouds which precede this bright millennial day will soon be dispersed by the sun of righteousness, and that a kingdom is about to be established which shall never be destroyed. Then will the great work of redeeming a lost world commence with accumulated power and efficiency. Christ, with his chosen band of purified ones, will then make practical the beneficent, self-sacrificing principles of his unselfish government; so that no inveterate foe to his government and reign, not even the stoutest Calvinist, will be able then to resist, effectually, any one of his benevolent plans to save the whole class of Calvinists from endless torment, by leading them to bow to his scepter, and become kind and tolerant towards others, as Christ and his followers are towards them. I believe that all who have died unsanctified will live again upon the earth, where their surroundings will be so favorable that they will be able to live natural lives, and in this manner take the first step to a higher, spiritual life; for God says, with no exception, " First the natural, then the spiritual."

And the poor deluded Calvinist who has been led to despise
nature, will not be found to have committed a sin too great
for his Benevolent Sovereign to pardon, on the ground of late
repentance. I believe that some incorrigible Calvinists may
compel God to punish them one thousand years, in what to
them is endless torment, before they will be willing to renounce Calvin's creed and adopt Christ's creed,—"to do
unto others as they would wish to be done by,"—in its stead.

But since no man ever lived more than one thousand years
in one body on earth, so I think one thousand years of punishment will be as long time as will be necessary to subdue
the most inveterate Calvinist.

Christ gives entire spiritual liberty to all his moral agents;
the bad as well as the good are equally free to do as they
please. Evil is left as free to destroy itself, as good is free to
defend itself, or save its life from destruction. It is one of
the inalienable rights of "evil to slay the wicked," or commit
suicide of itself, as it is for goodness, or God, to never die.
God is eternal and can never die. Evil had a beginning and
must have an end, for it has death in its very nature as its
inalienable right, just as surely as God or goodness has life
in its very nature as its own inalienable right. But for the
highest development of goodness there must be suffering to
germinate it, like as plants all have to germinate amid putre-
factions; but after this germinating process has once taken
place, it can thrive and grow in more congenial elements.
The acorn has in its nut the future ship, but the ship has not
begun to be built until the acorn is planted where evil or
putrefaction can germinate it. So the angel lies with folded
wings within each human form until evil has slain its own
love-life, and by this fermentation process liberated the angel
from its confinement, so that it can have ample room for the
growth and expansion of its hitherto occult but native powers.
Thus evil, or Calvinism, is an indispensable accompaniment of

Christianity in its birth-throes of development. But, thanks to God, when this process is completed we shall no longer need this slave to help us up higher. No, we can now do our own work, and emancipate all our slaves into full liberty to kill themselves as quickly as possible.

Calvin gives no liberty except to the evil principle, but confines the good as its subject. It holds all the power to legislate, to domineer, to dictate, to usurp, to compel entire, unresisting submission to its despotic authority, like as Calhoun taught the principles of secession, or domineering usurpation of Northern rights to Southern control and dictation, and now having subjected the freedom principle to slavery's control, he is using his own inalienable right to destroy himself, as the South are now doing as fast as they can; and the North thus emancipated from its subjection to evil, can now stand on their new-born liberty principles, and be content to let our slave, who has thus rendered us such an indispensable service, go freely into his own grave which he had dug for the republic. We can well afford to do as Christ does—let secession principles be free, as we wish to be, knowing that they are allowed to dig their own graves, and lay down in them freely of their own accord, without any of our interference to prevent it; for American soil is free soil, and we can well afford to have the secession principle make its own grave in it, to rise no more; for the natural death of evil is eternal—it can never rise again. Let the Northern secessionists be free to follow the Southern into the same grave of oblivion; for unless they are free to show to which side they belong, by a frank, open, and untrammeled expression of their heart utterances, we may be in danger of electing traitors to freedom into our future state offices, as we have long been doing.

Christ says the "tree is known by its fruit;" and also he directs us to let "both grow together until the harvest," and

2

then, when all fruit is perfected, we can better tell to which heap to assign it,—whether to the tare heap of secession or slavery, to be burned with eternal fire,—or to the wheat heap of liberty, to be gathered into the granary offices of future statesmen.

Calvin says the tree is not known by its fruits, its acts, but by its thoughts or motives ; so that a man can talk secession principles and defend them, and still be loyal and sound in motive for freedom ! You must not judge people by what they say and do, but by their motives ; for a man can say and do things in opposition to freedom, and still in motive and heart be true to its principles ! Therefore be sure and let this principle be thoroughly established and acted upon, or we shall, if it is not, be apt to elect sound men instead of traitors into our future offices in government !

Christ tolerates all religions and all sects under his benign reign of universal freedom. The Mohammedan can come to America and advocate his Mohammedanism, and build his " long house," and gather into it as many wives as King Solomon, if he chooses to do so, and no one has the least right delegated him from God to interfere in the least with his own inalienable right to his own opinion and his own conscience, even if it differs from the common opinion on the American continent; for our continent is free to tolerate all religions, as each man's individual opinion and conscience dictates to him, so far as his individual practice extends. And if our principles and practice which conflict with this Mohammedan's are not based on truths, such as reason and common-sense can defend, let them fall before this Mohammedan's, if his are better fortified with reason, based in unalterable truth, than ours are,—for every man's work must be tried to see of what sort it is ; and if our national customs and practices and religion have so much dry hay and Calvinistic stubble mixed with them that they cannot stand on their own intrinsic merits before the greater light of Mohammedanism, let them be burned up,—or rather let their fictitious principle, its Calvinism,—be destroyed, thus separating the precious from the vile, without trespassing on the principles of God's government in its defense.

Calvin tolerates no religion but what is in fellowship with his own views of truth and duty, thus making himself the standard of faith and practice, and God, and his government and authority, his subject, or agent, in carrying his principles into practice. He says to the Mohammedan, " We are a free people—are free to let others think as they please ; we are in favor of entire freedom of opinion and conscience, so long as you don't choose to think or practice different from what we think is correct and right. All other views in conflict with our own we regard as errors, which we feel conscience-bound to expose and condemn. So if you, Mr. Mohammedan, cannot be convinced of your errors, and repent, and conform to our customs and our usages, we shall raise such a merciless storm of persecution against you that your ' long house ' will be in danger of being burned."

" But what does this mean ? " says the Mohammedan. " We heard that this was a free country ; that this government protected its subjects in the lawful exercise of their inalienable rights ; and now you say that unless I give up my religion, my inalienable rights of property will be in danger of being most egregiously trespassed upon ! Does your government shield and defend such an interference with my right of opinion and rights of conscience ? "

" Yes, our human government feels compelled to defend the morals of community, and it enjoins on us the duty of directing our children into the paths of virtue, chastity, and purity ; and we consider this your ' long-house ' as a kind of pest-house of moral contamination, which our duty to the rising generation compels us to destroy ; but we are sorry to have to do so; we had much rather you would devote it to some other use, and thus supersede the necessity of our destroying it for you. You are at full liberty to be a Mohammedan—to think as you please—for this is a free country; but you must act right, or we shall be bound to interfere with your vile practice."

"Vile practice! why this is my religion. Is religion a vile thing? I would sooner give up my life than to give up my religion; and, in fact, I will defend it to the last, or I shall forfeit my title to a home in my future paradise. What do you mean by your tolerating liberty principles? Why, indeed, you are not as tolerant in your practical application of your freedom principles even as we are in Turkey; for we even tolerate your missionaries there in advocating a religion entirely hostile to our established religion, such as the government sanctions. I am sure our Mohammedan religion is the religion of freedom, instead of your Christian religion, if this is a specimen of the freedom of opinion and conscience which it enforces. This is precisely the principle of the Pope—unless your opinions and practice are like what we think is right, we shall persecute you until you will renounce it, and recant your religion, and become a Christian.

"I am sure a religion which is thus intolerant and bigoted in its application to individual rights, is no better, at least, than my own. I shall be very loth to make so poor an exchange. I don't think it is right to burn up your house because your religion allows you but one wife, even if you do burn up mine because mine allows me to have several. If you think monogamy is God-law, why you must keep to your one wife, and never secretly deprive another man of his due, or trespass on his daughter's or wife's inalienable right to their honor and virtue.

"But since I think I have a right, secured to me by God himself, to openly marry, provide for, and take care of more than one woman, as my legal wives, I am sure I have the same right to be true to my principles as you have to be true to yours—and you have no more right to trespass upon my identity to maintain your principles, than I have to trespass upon yours to maintain mine. I compel no woman to marry me against her will or wish. I leave her free to let me provide for her or not, just as she chooses.

"I trespass on no one's inalienable rights in the practice of my religion ; and now who gives you a right to trespass upon mine to maintain your own ? I am sure God has never given you this right, for he has directed each individual to be first . true to himself in judging for himself what is his duty to do, and then, to respect his brother's rights as he does his own.

"Now, would you like to have me compel you to marry and support several wives, as I do, or have you treated as a heathen, unless you did ? Has not God given you a right to judge for yourself how many wives you might have ; or has he told me I must be your conscience in this respect ? My common-sense and reason teach me, that all this sort of interference is wrong—is a direct trespass on God's authority and family government over his children, and that the only duty we, as individuals, owe to ourselves and society, is, to defend our practice by reasonable and sound arguments, based on nature, reason, and the Bible, and in this way to let our light shine out for the enlightenment of society. For example—

"If you think monogamy is right, prepare a defense of this your castle, by surrounding it with impregnable arguments, based in reason, nature, common-sense, and the Bible, and *thus* defend the practice, and act up to it like an honest man ; and then you have done all that it is your duty to do ᵒ make this practice current in society. And I am bound ᵒ defend my polygamy in the same manner ; and if by this open, honorable course, some women choose to come to me for protection, in spite of your arguments to the contrary, I am doing no wrong to them, to you, nor to my conscience to take them all under my protective wing, any more than you are doing wrong to give protection to only one.

"And you ought to fellowship me as a Christian brother, so long as I am true to my principles, and true to my conscience; for God fellowships me so long as I am thus an honest man, or else he is a different being from what he was in David's and Solomon's day, for he said David, expressly, was a man after his own heart, which it seems is very protective in its nature towards defenceless woman, for David was a ' woman lover.' And as for Solomon, he says himself he was the ' wisest man' that ever lived; and he had the largest number of wives of any man I ever heard of, and who knows but that this was the wise thing the Lord referred to in bestowing upon him this compliment? *I* am inclined to think it was, and I am going to strive to merit such a kind of compliment from God, myself, and you have no right to interfere with my rights of conscience. Indeed, you cannot do so without becoming a traitor, baser than Judas was, to your own professed principles of spiritual liberty to all mankind.

"Yes, brother, you may devote all your husbanding to one woman, and I will not molest your rights of conscience in so doing, for I am not the keeper of your conscience—that is your own express guardianship; and to God, and not to me, are you responsible for the use you make of your conscience. And I, too, brother, have the same right guaranteed to me, and from the same source.

"But whose practice is right and whose is wrong, or whether both are right or both are wrong, is a point to be settled individually with God himself, who is the only qualified judge of another's conscience, whose training and educational influences may have been altogether different from our own.

"And if, in the final settlement, you have been found to be

true to your monogamy principles, in your whole life practice, you may hope to be approved of as being a consistent,
honest man. And so with me; if I have cared for, and
attended to, all the wants and wishes of my 'long house'
full of wives, as my conscientious principles dictate, I, too,
may be found to have been an equally honest, consistent,
true man.

"But if your monogamy depends upon trespassing upon
the inalienable rights of those who differ from you in opinion
on that point, in order to be supported, I think the sooner it
falls prostrate before the greater light in your midst, the
better: for you are only 'treasuring up wrath against the
day of wrath,' to thus practice high treason against the government of the God of the universe."

"Yes, Mr. Mohammedan, I've heard all your sophisms
and subterfuges in support of your unchristian practice; and
all I have to say to you at present, is, that I sincerely pity
you, poor deluded man! and will engage to make your case
a special subject of prayer, in our conference meetings, hoping the Lord will yet open your eyes to see your sins in their
true light, and thus be brought to repent and forsake them
before the day of mercy closes upon you for ever. But, sir,
as your friend, let me give you one more caution, which is
this:

"We have insane asylums in all the free states, where we
imprison all whom any individual chooses to call insane, on
the ground that their principles lead them into a practice at
variance with the established customs of society; therefore,
it would be wise for you to be on your guard, lest you are
kidnapped ere you are aware of your danger, and are put
where you cannot again escape into the liberty of being as
kind to your wives as you please, for no man can come near
his wife in that institution, and so long as you won't recant
your principles, there is no hope of escape from this prison
of endless, hopeless torment."

"What! brother Christian! is my personal liberty put in jeopardy by my adherence to my conscientious principles, as well as my property?"

"Oh, it is not for conscience' sake we imprison you,—it is only because these principles lead to a corrupt practice, which we, for the sake of appearances, call insanity, instead of Christianity, for we are a Christian people, and we should be ashamed to persecute Christianity under its own name, so we christen it insanity, and it is all passed over as an act of charity bestowed upon the insane person, and all for his own good, exclusively!"

"Horrible! Sophisms! Subterfuges! I should think it was your Christianity which has to resort to these artifices for its support, instead of my practical common-sense religion! If your Christianity has to be supported in this way, because it cannot be in any other manner, I think I had better send over to Turkey the Macedonian cry, 'Come over and help us;' for we have lit upon the darkest corner of the earth, so far as the true light of Christianity is concerned, for they cannot even allow a difference of opinion to exist here without jeopardizing the personal liberty of the thinker for life, for this independent thought."

"Oh, no! Mr. Mohammedan, you are wild! You are getting insane! I see more and more the need of my timely caution. This *is* a free country. Can't you understand me? All have a right to think as they please. 'Tis only for their being insane that we imprison hopelessly—not for opinions."

"I find it is very hard for me to see with the eyes you have; it must be we take different views of the same subject. How is it; does your rule work both ways? Can I be allowed to call you insane because you don't think as I do? for you see, you differ from me just as much as I do from you, and is this difference insanity on your part, as well as on mine?"

"Pshaw! what a foolish question!"

" But, brother, it is of importance to me, a new-comer, that I get correct practical knowledge of your practical principles, lest I stumble on some of these dark mountains of ignorance, and be tripped into some of your charity prisons, without knowing the cause of this interference with my identity. I thought that, so long as I molested no one, and interfered with no one's rights but my own, that my identity was protected to me by the government : but by your account of the practical operation of your laws, my inalienable rights receive no protection at all from them, by the slander of insanity being allowed to make a nonentity of me, so far as the rights of a citizen are concerned."

" Oh, never fear! Mr. Mohammedan, you know this is a Christian government, and one principle of Christianity is, one's dying for another's sins, as Christ, its great founder, did ; and now if you are called to die a spiritual martyrdom, by being treated as if you were insane, it is only dying for the good of the people, as Christ did. The community will, in this way alone, be safe from your contaminating influence, and we think it best to be Christian in our practice, and let this one man die, instead of this great community being left to become Mohammedans."

" Oh, brother, my heart is sick with these utterances of your bigotry and intolerance!—I may as well flee at once to a land of freedom, for I see even that privilege will not be left me here long. And I will tell to the world that America is, at heart, a bigot, a despot of the first degree ; that all reason and common-sense, to say nothing of humanity and brotherly love, seem to have utterly fled from the continent ; and the quicker foreigners flee from it, the better—never to return."

" Oh! no! no! Mr. Mohammedan, we can't have you traduce us in that style, our character is at stake, 'tis better that you die in one of our insane asylums, rather than have

2*

our reputation and character for freedom die in public estimation! The good of posterity demands that our country retain its fair name untarnished. So I see you compel us to put upon you the stigma of insanity, lest others heed your tale, as being a true one, and our name thus get upon its fair escutcheon a blot. And for fear of what might happen, we have concluded to lodge you there, for awhile, at least, so that the taint of insanity can become indelibly branded in, so that your testimony ever after may be subject to being impeached, whenever the defense of the cause of Christ demands it; for the cause of Christ—the cause of freedom—must be maintained at all hazards!"

"Ah! but what will become of my wives and children in my 'long house,' when I, who have sworn to befriend and provide for them according to the best of my ability, am taken from them?"

"As for that matter, your wives and children will be turned upon the county for support, after the avails of your 'long house' have been expended in paying your asylum bills, and when this is consumed, you, with them, will be then a state or county pauper. This is the charity we feel bound to extend, in support of our charity institutions—I mean our taxes by which we thus support you, are our benevolent contributions to the cause of Christ!"

"Well, I must only add, if this is supporting Christ's cause, it is using the devil's funds to do it with; and if he finds any more loyal subjects than you are, I'm sure the devil is better served by your freedom principles than Christ is."

Christ allows each individual to have the sole and entire superintendence of his own conscience himself, and he allows no one to superintend the conscience of another. To trammel the rights of conscience is to trammel God himself, for conscience is God's secretary, subject to no dictation except from God himself. Supposing Seward, instead of acting as the Secretary of Government, as he has sworn to do, should allow any one to dictate his messages whom he chose to let do it, independent of the government's authority; and should report these as valid governmental documents? Should we not say he had trespassed on the government's rights by thus consenting to this usurpation of governmental rights, and, by so doing, had become a traitor to the government?

Will not Christ condemn us as traitors to his government over us, if we treat his authority over us in the same manner?

No one has any right to dictate to Seward, as the government's secretary, except the government itself. No one has any right to dictate to the conscience of any human being, except God himself, and whoever attempts to do so, is a rebel against God's government over his creatures, and this usurper will be entitled to be treated as a traitor to God's government for so doing. And he who resists this trespass on God's authority over him is the only true, loyal subject of God's government. And as the most invincible attacks upon the Godhead within us, are made under the subterfuge of insanity, so the successful resistance of this most potent force, in maintaining one's rights of conscience inviolate, notwithstanding, will be considered as the highest proof of loyalty.

Christ has not only empowered his subjects with authority thus to defend their consciences, but he will admit none into his realm who will not thus defend his authority and government.

Thus Christianity is loyalty to Christ's government, or, in other words, it is simply protecting your own conscience inviolate. We are personating his cause only while we are doing this thing. To serve our conscience is the way in which we are required to serve God. Thus the only way to serve God acceptably is, to serve ourselves, by protecting the Divinity *within us;* and to do this thing is as much as any American can do for Christ while under this Calvinistic eclipse which is so terribly obscuring our Christianity in the present crisis of affairs.

True Christianity is based on the No. 1 principle entirely. Until a being can take care of his own principles and his own conscience, he ought not to be delegated to take care of others; and I know of no being who does this thing as it ought to be done, but God himself, and his oldest Son; and therefore they are the only beings to whom we have any right to submit our principles or our conscience as dictators.

Supposing our government could not maintain its own inalienable rights to its existence, who would wish to be subject to its dictation?

I say if the government cannot defend and protect its own rights, it cannot defend or protect mine. Its Christianity requires it to be true to itself, and thus capacitate itself to be true to its subjects. These are Christ's teachings.

But Calvin teaches us that all this care of our own interests is selfishness; that to be Christian we must sacrifice ourselves to the good of others; that instead of keeping their own vineyard, they must keep others' vineyards for them. Thus their principle of benevolence requires them to usurp the rights of others, and subject them to their control for their good!

I don't think it is for the good of another to be deprived of the care of their own souls. Neither do I think any single being is capable of taking proper care of more than one soul; and I think God is of the same opinion; or he would have given more than the care of one soul to some individual besides himself. But since he has not given to one individual but one soul to care for, I think he holds no one individual responsible but for one soul, and that is, his nearest neighbor—himself.

We are to teach others how to take care of their own souls by taking *exemplary* care of our own, not by being his soul or his conscience for him, as Calvin directs.

Calvin says, I am the standard; you must conform to my views of truth and duty, or you are wrong; you are not capable of taking care of your own souls; you need theological teachers to tell you how to do it. And the how to do it, is, to give up your own reason and conscience to their dictation. Mind you, don't trust to your own reason and conscience, for those faculties are all perverted by the fall of Adam, so you must trust to our reason and conscience, for ours was not perverted by the fall of Adam,—or, if it was, we are converted, so that Christ's image now is reflected through us; and although he has told you to judge for yourselves what is right for you to do, still we think it is better for you to trust us rather than yourselves! We have attained to a higher type of benevolence than he did, since we volunteer to take care of your souls for you, while he simply told you to take care of them for yourselves! You know Christianity is a progressive principle! It carries a man out of himself into others, thus cursing his own soul to save others!

But as for myself, I do wish the Calvinists would let me take the care of my own soul entirely upon myself,—or, at least, wait until their services are called for; for my feelings tell me that it is a breach of etiquette to be so very officious in looking after my exclusive interests.

And, besides, I think I can take better care of my own soul than you can, for I have nothing else to do. My Father made me the guardian of my interests, and I don't like to relinquish my part to the care of an usurper. Besides, I think your own interests seem to need the attention so freely volunteered to me. If I am not mistaken, Satan has got a good grip-hold of you already, for this domineering, usurping, bigoted spirit are his own signals, or "coat-of-arms."

Yes, Calvin's practice is the practice of pollution, that of trespass on others' rights, thus corrupting and destroying himself. So that instead of quietly doing as God has commanded him to do—to take care of his own soul—he just ruins it, in his fiendish attempts to destroy others. And it is destroying others to deprive them of the rights of conscience.

Christ says it is never right to do wrong under any circumstances.

Calvin says it is right to do wrong to promote the cause of Christ; that to trespass on another's identity is not doing wrong, when the defence of creeds demands it, as a means of creed defence—that self-defence—the defence of the Deity within us—is a minor consideration to the defence of human dogmas! We can crush the soul-life of a human being—his conscience—and be guiltless, if, by so doing, our church-creed can be protected from the liability of being found to be a fallible document!

Christ teaches that truthism is the only infallible creed in the universe, and that the truths of science, history, and nature are as really truth as the Bible is.

Calvin teaches that the Bible is the only creed-book—that science, history, and nature are phantoms, which will be liable to vanish before the greater light of the Bible. I believe he regards God as the author of Bible-truth—but scientific truth, historical truth, and natural truth, I don't know but he thinks the devil is the author of these truths!

But I, like the Mohammedan, find it very hard to see subjects in the same light he does, for want of consistency in his logic.

He says the devil is a liar; and he admits, too, that America was discovered by Columbus. Now, if the devil is the author of all truth, outside of the Bible, then he was out of his element when he inspired the historian to write this truth.

So he must tell the truth sometimes at this rate; for I believe it is just as much, in reality, a truth that Columbus discovered America, as it is that Christ died for sinners, and, therefore, both truths are equally entitled to my belief. I don't pretend to say which truth is the most important, for I don't know, which is. I know all truth is binding upon my conscience as a subject of faith, since I believe all truth emanates from God, the source of truth, as truly as that all light emanates from the sun, the source of light.

And I believe that all falsehoods emanate from the devil, and no light or truth comes from him at all—for, "there is no truth in him." He sometimes gets truth for his companion, and then, on his Calvinistic principles, he calls her himself. But it is only by the law of usurpation that he has any claim upon his wife's identity. Let him pretend to love her ever so well—it makes no difference in the fact that she is from heaven and he is from hell. And when the harvest comes, he can no longer hold on to the wheat, by his usurped claim; for the prime owner calls for truth as his own child, which he lent to the devil for her highest good. He could not transmute her into falsehood, for there were no lies in her, any more than there were no truths in him.

Mongrels are no part of God's work. They are a Calvinistic production. And Calvinism is all the devil's work, entirely. It is a perversion of a good principle into a bad or false application.

Thus its professions being so holy, just, and true, it has beguiled many an honest soul into its mazes and dark labyrinths of speculation, until it has so blinded the simple soul, as to lead it to lose its reckoning entirely. And thus it plunges on in its blindfolded condition, until its own light, the light of conscience, is extinguished entirely.

It then follows an "*ignus fatuus*" as its guide, and is soon as conscientiously wrong in its practice, as it is blindfolded in its theories. He really thinks a person cannot be right in carrying out into practice the simplest truths of nature, simply because he does not see with his eyes. He really thinks all are blind, but himself; and he insists, that unless they will put out the eyes of their own reason, and supply its place with a blind credulity, they are impious rebels to divine authority! They tell us that "God's ways are past finding out," so we must come to the study of God's works with reason's eye extinct, or blinded, lest we make God a being like unto us, and his claims the claims of reason and conscience!

Oh! what a terrible thing it must be to degrade the great God into a reasonable being, like unto ourselves! subject to the same impulses and passions as ourselves! This sacrilegious skepticism must be manfully met and put down, for God's honor demands it! Only think of God's loving like a human parent! and what is almost blasphemy to love a woman, as his wife!

Why, they are actually making God as one of our men—like him in his attributes and nature. It is actually as ridiculous as it would be to call an acorn an oak!

Oh! Mr. Calvinist, truth is a bother to you; it is the most invincible evil you can find in the universe; really, an acorn is no more an oak than a human being is a God. The acorn has to die and rise again a hundred times after it has once germinated before it can bear much resemblance to an oak tree a hundred years old.

And does a human being die and live again as many lives as the germinated oak sees of winters and springs?

But the oak does not die; it only has the appearance of death. The root holds the life while the winter frosts are passing over it, so that it may be shielded from injury, until spring invites it out again upon its spreading branches. Neither does man die when he is resting awhile out of sight in his wintry grave, invigorating his powers for another season of growth and expansion in his next body.

It is thus man dies and rises again to a new life, more and more in harmony with the Divine—the acme and sum of human progression. Thus " as in Adam we all die, so in Christ shall we all be made alive." That is, since we all had to die as Adam did to germinate our first life, so in likeness to Christ we shall all live an eternal, God-like existence.

CALVINISM AND CHRISTIANITY FURTHER COMPARED.

Calvinistic family training requires the parents to be despots, ruling their children with a rod of iron; independent, arbitrary authority, regardless of reason, justice, or equity, making might the law supreme.

Christian family training requires the parents to rule their children with love and kindness, embodying their might or force in the potent influences which reason, justice, and right give to their commands. Such parents are a personification of the Deity to their children, thus leading them by the same principles by which God is training the great human family for a state of unalloyed happiness. God as personified in Christ is the Christian parent's model, guide, standard, law.

Calvinistic teaching makes the teacher the tyrant, the despot of the school-room; a being to be shunned by the pupils as their most implacable, unrelenting, overpowering enemy, or conqueror, making it the first and chief business of his profession to bring his scholars under complete subjection to his arbitrary power.

Christian teaching makes the teacher the sun and center of all genial, kindly influences of the school-room, from whom is constantly radiating smiles of encouragement to the diligent student, genial and kindly aids to the dull and desponding, and unremitted kindness to the wayward; and displaying his greatness and dignity only as he carries up the intellect and the heart of his pupils by the attraction of his own.

Calvinistic institutions enforce their claims by compelling the orphan to receive their patronage at the expense of the holiest feelings of the maternal nature, and requires the criminal and the insane to share their benefactions at the price of their personal liberty, and all else that they hold dear on earth, submitting their identity of being entirely to the arbitrary control of laws framed by those who are entirely ignorant of the wants and desires of those for whom they make them, since experience has taught them nothing on this point by which to judge. Could the Calvinistic lawmaker be the only one subjected to his own laws, the injustice of the code might be thereby mitigated. These Calvinistic institutions curse, make worse, degrade, and ruin the manhood, through the agency of the most malign instrumentalities, bestowed by the Calvinistic perversion of the benevolent principle.

Christian institutions enforce their claims through the free agency of their pensioner, never compelling him to receive, as a favor, what they would spurn as an insult, but, recognizing the dignity of their claimant's parentage, they guard against the least trespass upon the inherent, inalienable rights and privileges which a higher Supreme Sovereign has bestowed upon his subjects, and such as cannot be interfered with or abrogated with impunity. Christian institutions bless, reform, elevate, save the subject through the agency of benevolent means, bestowed for a benevolent purpose.

· Calvinistic governments protect the oppressor of humanity. They are a terror to the good and a shield to the wicked.

Christian government protects oppressed humanity, in whatever form, color, or relation it exists. None are too low for its clemency to reach, none too high to be beyond its benignant influences. Christian governments are a "terror to the evil-doer, and a praise of them that do well."

Calvinistic marriage requires the free agency of the junior partner of the firm to be entirely subject to the senior partner's dictation. He is not only the boss of the firm, but the firm itself. It is the union of the serpent and the dove, where the sagacity of the serpent is employed, not to shield the purity of the dove, but rather to charm its weak, resistless nature into resistless subjection to its satanic control.

Christian marriage recognizes the individual rights and the personal identity of both parties. It appoints the man, the "lord of creation," to be the senior partner, to whom all family questions must ultimately be referred for final settlement without appeal. It places woman as the junior partner, and claims that her influence as a partner be respected in his decisions, allowing her arguments to be tested by love's magnet, and all her inalienable rights are carefully and sacredly protected to her. She, confidingly and lovingly, leans upon her senior partner's superior reason and judgment, not only as her rock, but also as her refuge. He sustains the same relation to her that Christ does to the church. He is her saviour and protector. It is the union of the lion and the lamb,—the lion, strong, not to destroy, but to defend and protect the weak, confiding lamb. He is a gentle-man,— gentle to shield his mate, as well as strong to protect and defend her.

Calvinism teaches that regeneration consists in a change of our nature, not only from bad to good, but also, character, as of a lion to a lamb.

Christianity teaches that to be regenerated, we must be born again ; that a change of organization can only be effected by a change of bodies ; and that this change of body can only be effected by our dying, and being thus liberated from our defective physical organization. We can then expect to be born of other parents, whose conformity to Nature's laws may have produced a more natural or less perverted organization of a new physical body. Thus, being born again under more favorable auspices, they have a better chance of living a natural life, approximating nearer to our model, Christ. Thus, regeneration, instead of being a change of nature, is only a perfection of our own nature.

Calvin taught that the resurrection consisted in our rising in the same identical body in which we died ; that this body slept in a torpid condition, like an entombed toad in a rock, until the resurrection trump called them to judgment.

Christ taught no such suspension of being or life, but rather a constantly successive life, in various, different forms and organizations. He taught that they that have done good, or improved to the best of their ability the surroundings Providence had assigned them, might expect their next life and bodily surroundings would be more favorable to a higher life, on a higher plane, than their former one had been, thus raised " to a resurrection of life." But they that had done evil, or had misimproved or abused their privileges or the advantages of this life, would, as a just punishment, be raised to live in bodies whose surroundings were less favorable than before. Thus these would be raised to a " resurrection of damnation."

Calvin taught that we must forgive without repentance on the part of the offender. Calvinistic repentance would require our government to forgive the South, and restore them to all their constitutional privileges, now forfeited, without their acknowledging they had done wrong, or giving us any pledge of not repeating the game at any future day. This forgiveness would dictate this indolent, selfish, perverted form of forgiveness, as a substitute for the thorough and efficient course of bringing the offenders to the gospel terms of forgiveness—*practical repentance.*

Christ taught that repentance was the only term of forgiveness; that to forgive without repentance, is death to the offender, by severing the strongest cord by which he was held to repentance. Thus restored to favor and shielded from harm, he strengthens himself in his iniquities, until they secure his own destruction. He thus tempts them on to the greater usurpation of our inalienable rights.

The Calvinistic heaven consists in blissful inaction—selfish rest—merely using the small organ of tune to sing in selfish joy, while sitting on their hard seats witnessing the torments of lost souls,—among whom are found wives, husbands, parents, children, brothers, sisters, friends, lovers, neighbors, and countrymen! They rest not day nor night, although their throat and lungs, it would seem, must be weary of singing one song eternally long!

The Christian heaven is the rest of action,—combining the most exquisite use of each and every faculty, instinct, feeling, and affection with which our God-like natures are endowed, and, like their author, are all cheerfully, voluntarily, and instinctively employed in benevolent, self-sacrificing efforts to raise up from the depths of despair the tortured souls with which the prison of hell is tenanted, sent there by heeding the " doctrines of devils," which the Calvinistic preacher had authoritatively and most positively assured them are the doctrines of the Bible—of God.

The Calvinistic mark is, a hater. He despises the opposite sex, and is a despot over his dependents. They are found among the women-haters and the men-haters and the negro-haters of society.

The Christian mark is, a lover. He loves and adores the opposite sex, and is the protector of his dependents. They are found among the men-lovers, the women-lovers, and the philanthropists of society.

The Calvinistic theology confines the Deity to the male

sex, and as God is to them simply a lord or a tyrant, so does each man, invariably, become, unless influenced by the female part of our dual natures.

The Christian theology represents God as combining both natures, individually distinct, in one perfect whole, since man, made in God's image, is not perfect, alone. His nature is incomplete without its counterpart, and there can no son be given to a man, alone. Therefore the Holy Ghost must be the wife of God, and Christ, the Son, the offspring of this holy union. So that our Catholic brethren have not deviated, so very far, from a God-revealed truth, in worshiping God, through the " Holy Mother," as the bigoted Calvinist had taught us he had. Again, nature teaches us the same truth, in that the son instinctively worships the Deity through his mother, who, to him, is a personified Deity, a friend. And so the daughter instinctively looks up to the father as her personified Deity, a protector.

Calvinism teaches the individuality of man, and the nonentity of woman,—that the wife is only the parasite, or an echo, of the husband's mind, will, or purpose.

Christianity teaches both to be equally endowed with God-like natures, and individually accountable, only, to their sovereign. Each individual conscience is an infallible guide for their own individual acts, but no guide for another's actions. 'Tis trespass—high treason—to attempt to lord it over the conscience of a brother or a sister. God, the Father, is the only capacitated judge of his own children's actions, and he demands, as his own exclusive right, the right to punish them. No child is allowed to punish another child, or one sinner to punish another sinner. 'Tis high treason thus to usurp the father's authority over his own family, for it is in direct disobedience to his express command, " Vengeance is mine, I will repay, saith the Lord."

He delegated this authority, while the race was " under

age," in the time of the Jewish dispensation, when corporeal punishment was necessary, as an appropriate means of disciplining and developing the manhood. But, when the manhood became fully developed, the Christian dispensation took the place of the Jewish, when the penal code was abrogated, and God demanded that, since his family were now " of age," they should govern themselves, as Christ, the eldest son, did, who had received a perfect training, and was now a model for the other children. And, since he never trespassed upon the individuality of a human being, and never punished one, so we never should, if we profess to be Christians. "Judge ye not of your own selves what is right," was his invariable, practical rule.

The potent influence of his silent example rendered him, everywhere, and in every place, a "terror to the evil doer, and a praise of them who did well." Thus this embodying spiritual, omnipotent power, superseded the need of any physical restraints, which circumscribed, in the least degree, the entire spiritual freedom of his fellow beings.

Christian, go thou and do likewise! and thus make Christ's government paramount to all other governments. The earth is now experiencing the birth-throes of spiritual, individual freedom. Its long-looked-for messenger!

Calvinism teaches that the spiritual world is a future state—that it can only be entered through the gate of death—that while a tenant of the body, we can have no communication with it, whatever—that our retribution is mainly experienced there, and postponed until our entrance there, at the death of our natural bodies.

Christianity teaches that the spiritual world is all about us—that where there is a spirit life, it lives in the spirit world—that our natural life is but the counterpart or shadow of our spirit life—that every emotion and feeling is in the spirit world—that the manifestation of that emotion or feeling is in the natural world, and that death produces no change of this order, except that the death of this form of life is but the birth-place of a new form of life, subject to the same laws as before—that this new form or resurrection is but a type of the same spirit, culminated into a superior, or inferior body to the last, just as the spirit's nature demanded—different bodies have the same spirit, the bodies varying in beauty and ugliness just in adaptation to the spirit's demands.

Calvinism teaches that every birth is the birth of a new spirit—that this single earth life is its only natural life, and when it dies it enters the spirit world, not to return—that it there lives on in a disembodied state.

Christianity teaches that there is nothing new under the sun; that every new form is only another manifestation of an old thing; that since the race of men, before the flood, were created, no other human beings have been created. These comprise the whole race of men, and, that God has been at work upon them ever since, to perfect them by planting and transplanting them, in forms as various as the individual forms are various. That the great giants, animal-men of the flood, have, by this process of cultivation, now become much more delicate and refined, tending towards an entirely, spiritual form, which is only a perfected animal form, such as Christ appeared in on earth.

This animal nature was completely sublimated into the spirit nature, or, in other words, the spirit controlled the animal completely. The animal, sensual nature was entirely subject to the moral or spiritual control. This is being entirely regenerated—like Christ.

Those who have attained this point of entire sanctification, are still held in reserve, as Christ's body-guard, to attend him in his conquests of the world. They are now, have always been, and will ever continue to be, engaged in this benevolent work, so long as any soul is not completely sanctified, or made wholly like Christ. These are those who have been found in every age of the world, who have dared to stand up for Jesus, from Abraham down to William Lloyd Garrison. Garrison is one of the Abrahams of this age; but not alone, as the first Abraham was, for, now, their name is legion. Legions of angels attend the later triumphs of Christ, the world's conqueror. Ten thousand times ten thousand now wait upon him, ready to do his bidding, as indicated by their consciences. How large the number who dare to stand up for Jesus, in this evil and adulterous age, where sin or Calvinism is culminating!

Such, too, have suffered with him during this dark eclipse—so dark, that one cannot see another, but all must grope about, single file, and alone, for no one can find his fellow. But since our elder brother trod dark Gethsemane, alone, so must God's other children tread the same path to glory. The faith that survives this dark eclipse of our Father's face, must have attained the giant form of the antediluvian stature, or it might fail to carry us safely through. This test once past, with the crucifixion which succeeds it, we shall rise above earth, and all its woes, so far as their power to harm us is concerned. We can unlock prison doors with spirit power, and escape out of the power of our crucifiers to harm us; because the power to sin in us is entirely destroyed; so, of course, no misery can reach us, being above its power to harm us.

Thus we live in heaven, on earth,—"Yea, if I make my bed in hell, thou art there." Yes, heaven is in hell, as well as on earth. And all are in this world, all about us. Where misery is, there is a hell. Where happiness is, there is a heaven.

So, fear not, Christian, to die; for it is only to give you a better body, that you are taken off to a secret room, for

3

awhile, to change the clothing of your spirit, that it may be arrayed in a costume fitting its developed powers. You need a new garment to fit your present developed form, for you have outgrown your dress.

The dying which the Bible recognizes, is, the dying of the animal control of the spirit nature. This dying is but languishing into a new and higher life. Dying is but going home to Jesus. It is to be like him, to die unto sin, and to live unto God, or perfect obedience to all the laws of our holy nature.

Christ teaches, that there is no such thing as a disembodied spirit—that all life has form—and that the form is adapted to the spirit life within. The mineral, vegetable, animal, human, and divine life, are all embodied life. When life escapes one form, 'tis only to assume another form. The grave of one is the birth-place of another, and when the old life has been entirely disengaged or delivered or withdrawn from the old form, the body sinks into its original, gaseous elements, ready for another transformation. But the spirit life, at first nourished amid the corruptions and decaying of its old dying, worn-out form, is soon seen emerging into more expanding elements, where it develops its native powers in exact proportion and counterpart resemblance to the spirit—its occupant.

When the spirit body has found its appointed functions, as the spirit's servant, and the seed is perfected, it dies again, to perform another similar revolution, ever striving to perfect its ultimate good seed, early housed and laid up for a future harvest of spiritual fruit in God's garden.

Christ was himself the first perfected seed. Never did his human nature become entirely sublimated into the divine until that point when he exclaimed, in parting with human nature's last hold upon him—his dread of suffering—"It is finished!" The divine will had swallowed up the human will, or desire to escape human suffering. His love for God's will became so absorbing that he could say, as some of his perfected followers have since said,—" I love my sufferings, because it is the will of God I should suffer, and, since he made them, they are welcome as an expression of his perfect good-will and pleasure concerning me."

When the divine will rises superior to every other human will, desire, or affection, then, and only till then, is he perfected seed for God's great future harvest. But it is not disembodied at this stage of its progress. The human spirit being sublimated, or at-one-ment with the divine, is none the less a tenant of a body. It has only changed its relationship to the spirit, from guest to that of servant. As the Jews saw Christ ascend into heaven in his glorified body, so have we often seen him return again, in the perfected nature of every true man.

Christ multiplies himself in every perfected man, who lives out the holy instincts of his divine nature without restraint or embarrassment from his human nature. And as we have had a " model man," of God's own forming, sent for men's help to become like God himself, so I think, since God is not partial to his sons, that he will send us a " model woman," some time, for the aid of his daughters in becoming like their God-mother—the Holy Ghost.

We have had many myriads of angels sent among us, varying in rank from the seraph to the highest archangel. Still, we wait for God himself, multiplied in a woman's form, as a representative of his better half. Till such a personage appears, let us, true women—God's angels—follow our blind instincts, in perfecting our womanly natures, until a safer guide, or model, is given us.

It won't do for us to be Christ or man-like, exclusively, for we have a different sphere assigned us by God, and he, of course, has adapted our natures to our lunar spheres. If we

can only shine with borrowed light from the "lords of creation," let us not complain, for you know we have nature's law
of compensation to fall back upon for our relief and encouragement, to submit, with becoming meekness, to our humiliating position in this respect. Let us let them rule the day,
knowing that God has appointed us to rule the night, and
they will be all the more willing to yield to this law of the
universe, if we don't oppose it by trying to rule them in the
day-time. You know that opposition only makes them more
lordly than God made them to be; therefore, don't let us
enhance our humiliation by a vain attempt to better our condition by the use of means which only renders it worse.

I don't believe God's wife interferes with her husband's
plans. I presume she believes he is competent to make his
own plans without her help, or, if he wants it, I think he will
be the first to know it, and if he seeks her as a counselor, she
will feel all the more flattered by the compliment than she
would have felt had he even accepted her voluntary advice.

Let us bear in mind that their superior intelligence leads
them to take a more comprehensive view of things than it is
possible for us to take. Therefore, we must be willing to
trust to their judgment rather than our own in these matters.
Don't let us embarrass them by casting a cloud or eclipse
over their shining disk by the interference of our well-meant
but ill-timed suggestions. Let us remember that the end, or
accomplishment of a plan, presents quite a different view
from what the beginning, or development, presents.

And, besides, these plans are their own business, and we
are not responsible for their failures, nor are we to usurp
the credit for their success. Besides, I think if we are faithful to our train of shining stars, I don't think we shall find
much time to superintend the sun's revolution. While he
gives us the light of the candle and the light of the fire, in
his own absence from us, let us use them for the children's

benefit, trusting that he will not forget to provide for the wants of his numerous offspring, even if he has a large and important business to transact with other luminaries.

Sister angels, permit me to make one more friendly suggestion, which is this: You know we think a great deal of our influence and reputation, and we are extremely anxious for appreciation. Therefore, let us be exceedingly cautious about getting into bad company with fallen angels, or Calvinistic women, by adopting any of their habits or customs, in practice. You know a man is known by the company he keeps, and if we choose to be found familiar with their habits, they will be very apt to think we have associated with them secretly, somewhere, and thus bring useless suspicion upon us. And it would be quite a misfortune for us to have our husbands get jealous of us; for we hate to be watched, just as if we did not know how to take care of ourselves.

We feel in our merriest moods when we are trusted by our husbands, and confided in, as being not only competent to take care of ourselves, but also our children, and our household duties. Oh! how this confidence does stimulate us to exert ourselves, to the utmost, to show, by our works, that we merit this, their confidence, in our abilities to fulfill the duties our sphere assigns us. We should feel extremely mortified to find, by his superintendence of our duties, that he did not consider us competent, as we supposed he did, when he chose us out of the many others, as the one whom he considered competent, for the post he had chosen us to fill. Let us prove ourselves, by our own deeds, deserving of this unlimited confidence, in our practical womanly virtues, and we may be sure of securing it, if our husbands are true Christ-like men. But if they are consistent Calvinists, woe be to you! For, I can assure you, upon the best authority—that of experience—that the more you try to please such devils, the more you can't!

Calvinism teaches that our natures are finite in their capacities—that but a moiety of our present faculties, instincts, and emotions, and affections will survive the grave. I believe tune is the only organ they immortalize, and as for the affections, I believe they suffer ossification, or they could not be capacitated to witness the scenes of anguish they depict, as exhibited in close proximity to their mansions of rest, unmoved to pity and help. I think Abraham must be far off from them, out of speaking distance, at least, so that they will need a messenger to send communications by—for, if birds of a feather flock together, they cannot be in his region—they will have a long road to travel, to get to him, perhaps several successive lives to live, before they get a body so perfected that Abraham would not be contaminated by their company.

Never fear, brother Calvinist! God has time enough to work in. He is in no hurry. He can wait for your snail-like progress towards the heavenly regions. But he must be sure you are going in the right direction; that is all the force he needs to exert over your free-agency. Progress being his immutable law, you have no chance to escape from becoming a true mirror, to reflect his image from, perfectly.

Pardon us, brother and sister Calvinists, if we go on before you. We will tell them you are coming after, though you could not walk quite so fast as us, for having nearly lost the use of your feet, by standing still so long! However, as you regain their use, by action, you can hope to accelerate your progress by and by. But do, for our sakes, come on as fast as possible, for we cannot be completely merry, until your safe arrival. Then, then we will have an universal jubilee.

Christianity teaches that all the faculties, feelings, instincts, and affections of our God-given natures are infinite—a type of God himself—but that we are in a progressive state, tending, by the centripetal power of attraction towards this sun of the universe.

But when we shall get there, or how long we shall be compelled to move in our circumscribed orbit, we know not. We only know that " we shall be like him, for we shall see him as he is," in our individual God-like organization, so perfected, that we can see God, through it, just as he is. For we shall become like him before we shall see him as he is, for only till then is his work complete in us. Then, " as face answereth to face in water so does the heart of man to man."

And thus is every true or developed man an incarnate God, and every truly developed spiritual woman is a living " Temple of the Holy Ghost."

But since there is but one sun and its single mate the moon, but stars innumerable, and as they all shine with light reflected from the central luminary: so God, with his mate, the moon, Ghost, are the parents of countless children, among whom the first-born son, Christ, the morning star, shines most conspicuous.

He, our elder brother, is the first to rise, to hail the coming of the king of day, whose kingly splendor seems to extinguish even the light of the morning-star. Still, it does not. Each star is in its proper place, shining to its full capacity, true to its heaven-appointed laws.

And although its glories seem to be eclipsed by the superior splendor of the king of day, yet, it is only that he may hold each star in its proper orbit; that he performs this, his revolution, not to eclipse the minor splendor of the modest star. He only rules one-half the time, and leaves his great family the other half to the moon's gentle sway, when the children shine the brightest, under her gentle influence. 'Tis thus that each in its proper circle moves, securely guarded from interference through the perfectly balanced forces of centripetal love and centrifugal force, to give us one grand illustration or representation of his great family government, both for our admiration and imitation.

God's paternal character is the one wherein His brightest glories shine out in their most resplendent luster—"like as a father pitieth his children, so the Lord pitieth them that are His." Here is sympathy—the crowning virtue of humanity—encircling the great pulsating heart of the universe. Yes, he, the Master soul of the universe, pities them that are his. Who are his? All the beings which he has made in his own image. The whole race of men are all and each and every human being his own dear children, by birth and by adoption. He has redeemed all who are under the power of sin. Those who are not need no redemption, no forgiveness. The brothers of the prodigal son needed no redemption, no forgiveness, for they had never wandered from their father's superintendence and control. They were justified on the ground of practical obedience—"neither have I at any time transgressed thy commandment, and yet thou hast not killed for me the fatted calf." "Son, all that I have is thine." But it was the prodigal alone who needed and claimed forgiveness on the ground of repentance.

The Christian dispensation is now giving place to the spiritual reign of Christ. And let the birth of the angel messenger,—individual, spiritual freedom of all,—be hailed as the harbinger of the millennium! And so may the age of righteous retribution terminate in this short, total eclipse of manhood—thus marking, with unmistakable clearness, the point between midnight darkness and noonday effulgence.

The moral nature of the race is now fully developed. They know right from wrong, good from evil, and now has come the time when the " spiritual " armory is demanded, to give vitality to the " moral " faculties—when the spiritual attract the moral and intellectual towards the Sun of the universe. Or, to use another figure, the lion is to be influenced by the lamb's gentle, confiding nature, and thus tamed of his native ferocity, into the kind, gentle protector. Or, without a figure, woman is to assume the sphere assigned her by God,—that of being man's helpmeet, in gathering the ripening harvest into God's granary.

So, don't be disheartened, my friend, Henry Ward Beecher, as you seemed to be, when you prepared your sermon in the *Independent*, of August 2, 1862. You were then looking at the world from the nadir of the eclipse. Let me remind you, brother Henry, that it is not midnight, as you seem to apprehend. 'Tis only an eclipse at noonday. Evil is culminating, but good is not in the rear. The race has come to be " of age." Good and evil, both, have now attained manly strength and proportion. And, if the good attain to freedom, the evil must be free, too.

Remember, brother Henry, that you have committed yourself in favor of " universal suffrage," freedom to all, and now, it won't do for you to trespass upon the devil's rights. Our brother devil's inalienable rights are as sacred to him as are the rights of any other subject of God's government, and God will not allow any of the rights of his subjects to be invaded or trampled upon with impunity. He careth for the human foxes, and the fox nature which he has bestowed upon them, is a part of his own, well-done work. A good, harmless fox is a mirror, through which God's image is reflected, and his cunning nature is given him for this purpose. But a mischievous, or a Calvinistic fox is the devil's mirror. But when we invade God's territory by attempting to substitute a hen's nature in the place of the fox's nature, we become traitors to God's government.

Our superior intelligence is, by this act, sunken to a level lower than that of the innocent, cunning fox. Our superior intelligence is bestowed upon us, not for the fox's injury,

but for the artless hen's protection against his artful cunning. Intelligence which does not bear the stamp of benevolence upon it is devil-like, not God-like.

Besides, brother, in a pitched battle we must give the
devil fair play, or our victory is tarnished by injustice. The
devil and God are now in death grapple, and although, for
the time being, the devil seems to hold God under, yet I
believe that the " triumph of the wicked is short," and that
God is yet to emerge from the smoke and din of battle, an
unscathed, triumphant, universal conqueror.

I hope the devil will now be willing to take his proper
place as subject instead of sovereign of God's empire.

Yes, Mr. Calvinism has been sadly worsted this time.
But, out of benevolent pity to him in his humiliating defeat,
let us remember that he is our brother, to be redeemed from
all evil. And let us " do unto him as we would wish to be
done by," in exchange of circumstances.

Again. The humiliation which God employs as a means
of sanctification to his children is not such as Calvin, or the
devil, employs as an instrumentality to accomplish his purpose. God's humiliation elevates his subject by placing him
on a higher plane of manhood. It raises him from a state
of mulish obstinacy into one of lamblike docility. This is not
degradation, it is exaltation.

Calvin's humiliation degrades its subject by stifling the
noble aspirations of his lordly nature. It dethrones the
divinity within him. Blasting and mildew and a loathsome
stench follow in the track of its Juggernaut car of progress,
corrupting with a deadly miasma the whole surrounding
region, leaving their rotten carcasses of manhood unburied,
uncared for, save by the more humane vulture and hyena.

Christ teaches us that his cause is the cause of individual
human rights; that a defense of human rights is a defense
of his cause.

Calvin teaches that God's cause is the subjection of human rights to his own perverted standard of right; that he and his clan are the peculiar favorites of heaven—" the elect "—the mighty aristocracy, through whom the blessings of heaven are to be showered down upon the common people; that the common people need their light to guide them into correct views of truth and duty; that the light that is in the reason and conscience of the common people is all darkness, because their natures have not been regenerated like their own. Therefore, to do the common people good, they—the elect—the converted ones—must lord it over these humans, as if they were mere automatons, or minds "dead in trespasses and sins."

Whereas the "dead" ones are the converted ones, who have so regenerated their holy, God-like natures as to completely metamorphose themselves into incarnate devils, from whom naught but falsities, and damning heresies, and practices the most unchristian and inhuman proceed. And the live ones are the living and breathing mass of common minds, who, true to themselves, are striving to retain the very identity these Calvinists are striving to usurp from them. Their instincts teach them that they have an inalienable right to be the sole judges of their own acts, so far as human authority is concerned; that God not only allows them to superintend themselves, but also requires them to do so, or they will be regarded by him as traitors to his government.

Those are "dead in sin" who are dead to this great principle of individual human rights, and alive only to the satanic principle of my right to rule over others.

The great principle of individual sovereignty, independent of all human dictation, whatever, is the very foundation principle of God's government, as Christ, his representative, promulgated and enforced.

The defenders of Christ's government make the higher law supreme in their practice, and the lower law subordinate in its application to their individual practice. They claim that no human law which is in conflict with a divine law is of any force as a moral obligation on them to obey; that they are as much bound to resist such enactments as they are bound to save their own souls; that all the penalties annexed to secure obedience to it, however heavy or momentous, do not add a single iota of force to the moral obligation to obey it, so far as conscience is concerned.

But the defenders of Calvinism make human laws or human governments the law or standard of their individual practice. The mere fact that the practice is a legal one is sufficient to satisfy their conscience, if it has life enough left to oppose it. They consider the penalties by which these immoral enactments are enforced as punishments due the offender, instead of being, as they really are, persecuting enactments, by which the conscience of the subject is to be brought under subjection to human dictation. In this manner they claim that the divine law may be subject to the human law, instead of making all human laws subject to the divine, as Christianity dictates they always should be.

The defenders of Christ's government make all human creeds and constitutions subordinate to the dictates of truth, as it is progressively developed by the advancing age. Thus, what was good and suitable for a past age, is no standard for the present age or race of men, any more than the clothing which was well-adapted and appropriate for the boy of twelve years is not adapted nor appropriate for the man of thirty years. So our Constitution, which was adapted to the development of the liberty principle as our pilgrim fathers found it, is very inappropriate, and not adapted to the present development of the liberty principle which is now struggling for birth, by bursting the trammels by which this straight-jacket constitution holds the individual liberty principle in subjection to human enactments.

Spiritual truth is also confined in the same unnatural manner, by the human creeds and dogmas of the ecclesiastical forms and usages of the church, but which is, like the liberty principle, struggling to burst from its confinement, to bask in the atmosphere of entire spiritual liberty. These shackles must and will be broken, for Nature will have its own way in perfecting its own fruit, and although obstacles temporarily impede its onward, upward progress, it will ultimately overcome them, as surely as the accumulating waters above the dam will, in time, increase in momentum of sufficient force to break the dam and clear itself from all obstructions to its ultimate progress. The moral elements will no more be held back by dams, or constitutions, or creeds, than will the physical elements be held in subjection to human control. The time has come when this great, strong dam across the stream of truth and liberty must be broken. The constitution of the American government must give place to the free, unobstructed reign of righteousness on this continent; for Christ will reign on this American continent king of this nation, as he is now the king of his individual subjects in it.

His subjects are those who will not allow any law or practice to obstruct the free reign of individual conscience over each and every individual human soul. So his government of " universal liberty to all," is to be established upon the ruins of this American republic.

Our republican principles are but a stepping-stone to the higher and more efficient form of a monarchical or kingly government, where God, the King, reigns supreme over all. And his throne is within all human souls.

Our mongrel government, or reign of good and evil united, is, ere long, to be supplanted by the reign of goodness, independent of its subjection to evil in any form. This reign of anti-Christ, or this opposition to good by the evil, is to be overthrown; and the government is to be left free to do right, without opposition. Then, and only till then, is Christ's kingdom established on this American continent,— or, in other words, only till then will the kingdom of heaven be established on a permanent basis on the ruins of our republican or anti-Christian government.

Our republican government is anti-Christian when it persists in giving equal liberty and privileges to the evil as well as the good, even after God plainly demands the separation of these two principles, and the assignment of each to its original place,—that of goodness reigning over badness, or, in other words, of evil being made subject to good. The good, or God, is to hold the reins of government, and evil, or the devil, is to be his subject.

The President has hitherto been allowed to be nothing but a mere automaton, or a great Nebuchadnezzar image, only acting within the prescribed limits of the Constitution, like a machine, without heart or soul, a will or purpose, or even reason or conscience. One man could work this machinery of government about as well as another, since his own individual manliness was left no scope or room for exercise outside of this straight-jacket.

But Lincoln is too big a man to get into this jacket, so he has ventured, as the only *dernier resort*, to act according to his own reason and common-sense, after he found he could exercise no reason or common-sense so long as he was trying to lie upon a " bed which was too short for a man to stretch himself upon, and the coverings too narrow for a man to wrap himself in."

Yes, a full-grown man, with the reason and common-sense and conscience of our good, upright, and honest President Lincoln, has found it impossible to keep himself within the prescribed limits of the old Constitution, which the country has entirely outgrown, although fully purposing to do so before making the experiment; but finding the exigencies of the case to demand expansion, he, like an honest man, has ventured to use the reason and conscience God has given to him, as a guide for his own acts, independent of the Constitution.

Thus he has ventured to honor God above the American government, and, as a result, they that honor God shall be honored by him, ultimately. For the present, he, like all martyrs for the truth, is suffering all kinds of persecution for conscience' sake; but ere long, the blessings of persecution will be his crown of rejoicing, if he holds out to the end, in making his own reason and his own conscience his guide for his own actions, instead of the Constitution, where its mandates conflict with his own manliness.

Abraham Lincoln is an example worthy of all imitation, to all American citizens, in so far as he has made the laws of his own manly nature paramount to the laws or constitution of the American government. May the light of his manliness, in that he honors God's government above human governments, be as the polar star to guide all this American people into the same glorious path to honor and heavenly felicity!

And may our "Ship of State" which is now contending with the bleak winds of contending armies, and driven about by the gusts of passion and prejudice, apparently without chart or compass, be soon anchored in the haven of peace, being guided there by the helm of true manliness, whose only compass is the will of God, as it is dictated through each individual American conscience!

Christ, with his host of redeemed ones as his body-guard, is holding himself in readiness to be enthroned on the crumbling ruins of this anti-Christian government; where he, as King, will be endowed with ability to protect each individual conscience from the usurpation of other sovereigns of equal powers with his own.

He will also restore Reason to its proper throne in the seat of each individual intellect; to be sovereign supervisor of each thought, feeling, impulse, desire, and affection; thus reigning in each individual act as the "Lord of lords and the King of kings" to every individual subject of his reasonable and intelligent government.

Christ's government—the government of the individual sovereignty—is thus to become the mediatorial government, by which each sovereign of the universe is to thus pay his allegiance to the Great Sovereign over all; thus making "God all and in all" over his great human family.

The twelve tribes of Israel will then be returned to Jerusalem, where the new temple is to be built as a model for the expectant world's imitation.

These twelve tribes are the whole class of thoughts, instincts, and affections with which our God-like natures are endowed; and their return to Jerusalem is their return to their native, original tendencies; or, in other words, returning from an artificial, perverted life into a natural, or Christian life of unperverted nature. And this new temple is the God-like Reason of every human soul, to which all these tribes resort to pay their intelligent homage to the Maker of all things. The Shekinah is the female spiritual of the universe.

A COMMENTARY.

Psalm ix. 17. "The wicked shall be turned into hell and all the nations that forget God."

All that sin, who forget or disregard the dictates of their own consciences, shall experience misery or punishment, in exact proportion to their guilt, either in this body or in some other body. They will remain in this unhappy condition, until they become penitent; and as repentance has always been a condition of pardon, I believe that under the government of an unchangeable God, it always will continue to be, so long as sin is permitted to exist.

Matthew, xviii. 13. "And if so be that he find it, verily I say unto you, he rejoiceth more of that sheep, than of the ninety and nine which went not astray."

All parts of us are not perverted or depraved; in this parable only one out of a hundred was lost or gone astray from the right path. That which we have not perverted we need not repent of, only that which we have misused is wrong in us; but like the ninety and nine just persons, they need no repentance. Christ came not to call the righteous to repentance; for they that are doing right, in that respect, need no repentance; but he came to call sinners to repentance, or that part of us which is unnatural he came to restore to a natural state, and thus saves it from securing its own destruction.

Matt. xxv. 46. "These shall go away into everlasting punishment."

Those who persist in a sinful course will be made to see their guilt in so aggravated a light, as to feel that their punishment must be everlasting, in order to meet the demands of their guilty consciences. Thus they will be made to experience what, *to them,* is endless torment, since they can see no hope of deliverance.

Prov. xiv. 32. "The wicked is driven away in his wickedness; but the righteous hath hope in his death."

While in a state of rebellion and sin the sinner is driven from, or deprived of, peace and happiness; but those who do right are sustained by a hope that, when all evil in them is destroyed, they will be uniformly and unceasingly happy.

Luke, xvi. 23. "And in hell he lifted up his eyes, being in torments."

While receiving his punishment, in that miserable condition, he looks about in every direction to see if he can find any alleviation of his torment.

Dan. xii. 2. "And many of them that sleep in the dust of the earth shall awake; some to everlasting life, and some to shame and everlasting contempt."

Those who are in a stupid, unconscious, moral condition, shall be quickened, and brought to a state wherein they shall be conscious of their true condition or character; some shall rejoice to see that their course of rectitude has brought them to a state of happiness, and others will see that their neglect of known duty has only fitted them to be subjects of shame and contempt; and the just punishment which is due them for their neglect of duty will, to them, seem everlasting, since their conscious guilt seems overwhelming. He here describes their state as it seems to them from the standpoint of their own bitter experience.

John, v. 29. "They that have done good unto the resurrection of life; and they that have done evil unto the resurrection of damnation."

The practice of virtue or goodness naturally tends to increase and perpetuate it, so that they which have done good will rise to still higher degrees of vitality, and will, by its practice, continue in a state of eternal progression. But evil is directly contrary in its tendency. The practice of it tends to exhaust, debilitate, and ultimately to destroy itself; so that they that do evil become less and less capacitated to enjoy its pleasures, from exhaustion, until at last nothing but satiety and disgust are experienced.

II. Thess. i. 9. " Who shall be punished with everlasting destruction from the presence of the Lord, and the glory of his power."

Their punishment will continue until their power to do evil is entirely destroyed, separated in the meantime from all sources of enjoyment. The destruction of the evil is so complete that it is called everlasting destruction—or a destruction from which it can never rise again to all eternity. This destruction may take place in a short space of time, since fire is a very destructive element, and makes very quick work when well under way, in destroying all which is destructible. Chicago, for instance, can be destroyed by fire in a much shorter space of time than it takes to build it, and still it is eternally destroyed—that is, the same identical city can never be built again, because fire is an element which eternally destroys what it undertakes, or what is destructible.

Prov. i. 26. " I also will laugh at your calamity; I will mock when your fear cometh."

This seems like the utterance of a retaliatory spirit; but it is not. It is only a just punishment—a retributive providence, designed wholly for their good. His apparent indifference towards them, and utter lack of sympathy for them in their sufferings, and his even seeming to make light of their anguish, is only used as a means to break their stubborn will into submission to his rightful authority over them. A false tenderness, or an unreasonable and untimely manifestation of sympathy is sometimes the greatest calamity which could befall us in our rebellious state.

Mark, xvi. 16. " He that believeth and is baptized shall be saved; but he that believeth not shall be damned."

He that believeth the Bible, and manifests his sincerity by obedience, shall be saved from the punishment due the transgressor. But he that doubts God's testimony, and, risks the consequence of transgression, will secure to himself the punishment due the transgressor. He is thus damned, or doomed to suffer, so long as punishment is necessary to bring him into a penitent condition. His highest good demands this his just punishment, as an indispensable necessity to bring him to repentance.

Matt. v. 22. "Whosoever shall say, Thou fool, shall be in danger of hell fire."

To call a rational, moral agent a fool, or an unaccountable, irrational person, and treat him as such, is one of the greatest indignities and insults which can be offered to a human being, and awakens the most painful kind of feelings in the injured one: so that to have the punishment commensurate to the offense, the highest degree of suffering must be inflicted upon the transgressor; and this, to our conception, is the sensation caused by burning in fire.

Matt. xii. 32. "And whosoever speaketh a word against the Son of Man it shall be forgiven him, but whosoever speaketh against the Holy Ghost it shall not be forgiven him, neither in this world nor in the world to come."

Calling the Son of Man an insane person is not so aggravated an offense as to call the work of the Holy Ghost insanity; for the Holy Ghost is of a more spiritual nature, and therefore more sensitive to spiritual abuse and insult; and if the personification of the Holy Ghost is a woman, then, since a woman is not only a more spiritual, but also a more defenceless being than a man is, it must, of course, be a much more heinous offense thus to treat a woman than a man, as Christ says it is. This offense, therefore, is of so much more aggravated a form of abuse, that it cannot be forgiven, but instead of repentance being allowed as an atonement for it, it cannot answer the demands of justice for this heinous offense, and therefore it must receive its full punishment, being an unpardonable offense. And since this is a sin for which repentance cannot atone, it must endure the punishment for it until the power of the sufferer to commit such another offense is eternally destroyed. This trifling with humanity, and treating it, in a female form, as if its humanity were extinct, may require, as a just retribution, the total extinction of humanity in the transgressor. Their human form may, at death, be exchanged for a beast's form, since they treated humanity like beasts. Only as an animal is an insane person cared for, totally regardless of their claims as human, sensitive, spiritual beings; and since this treatment naturally tends to the extinction of the moral faculties, so this attempt to destroy the Godhead in another may be punished by its total extinction, for a time, in themselves, as a punishment commensurate to the offense.

Mark, ix. 45, 46. "Into the fire that never shall be quenched, where their worm dieth not, and the fire is not quenched."

We must be separated from iniquity—dissevered from it, otherwise misery will be inseparably united to our destiny; for as long as sin, the cause, exists, so long will misery, the effect, follow. The fire is unquenchable, and the worm is undying, so long as fuel and food are furnished to sustain them. Therefore we are exhorted to cut off the offending member, and peace and pardon ensues.

I. Peter, iv. 18. "If the righteous scarcely be saved, where shall the ungodly and the sinner appear?"

If the righteous suffer so much from persecution, what must the sinner endure, when he is called to receive the same measure which he has bestowed upon the innocent, as a punishment, added to his own guilt as a trangressor?

Matt. xvi. 26. " Gain the whole world, and lose his own soul."

If, for the sake of present gratification, we sacrifice our own manliness, we may lose our noble nature, and degrade it to that of a brute's, and become as insensible to moral influences as they are : thus lose our own soul, or extinguish its nobleness, by abuse. This temporary extinction of the Godhead within us is only a just punishment for our abusing it. Possessing the world is not sinful, but gaining it by unlawful means is what is detrimental to the interests of the soul.

I. Cor. xi. 29. " He that eateth and drinketh unworthily, eateth and drinketh damnation to himself."

If we attend to the duties and ordinances of the Gospel simply as a form, without the spirit of obedience in our hearts, these very acts of hypocrisy will be punished as sinful acts. This is a kind of self-immolated penance for transgression, sought as a refuge from the stings of a guilty conscience. Thus employed, they only enhance the guilt they were intended to assuage : therefore they are damned or doomed to suffer for so doing.

Luke, xiii. 23. "Are there few that be saved?"

From Christ's reply it seems that to many the door of heaven will be shut against them for ever, apparently. The *few* who are saved, by faith, is small in number, compared with those who reap the bitter fruits of disobedience, by being shut out from all happiness for a time, with no tangible hope of deliverance. The *few* who are saved from sinning, by faith in God's testimony, are the elect, whom God has chosen to fit them to be co-workers with him in securing the salvation of the many. Like as if a parent should bestow upon one of his children superior advantages, for the purpose of using him as the instructor of his other children. He only shuts the door of instruction to the many, until their chosen teachers are qualified for their office. This is the " economy of grace."

II. Cor. iv. 3. " But if our Gospel be hid, it is hid to them that are lost."

Sin is blinding. To pursue a course of iniquity is to shut out the light of truth, and extinguish the light of reason. The rays of gospel truth cannot penetrate the understanding of him whose reason has become extinct, through the influence of wrong doing. He is lost to the influence of truth, so long as he continues impenitent; but when he repents, his reason is restored to him, so that he can now discern the claims of the Gospel upon him. This doing right opens the understanding to the apprehension of the simple truth; while doing wrong closes it, effectually, against it. Thus " the wicked walk in darkness and know not at what they stumble, but the righteous holdeth on his way."

Rev. xx. 14.—" And death and hell were cast into the lake of fire. This is the second death."

Fire consumes everything destructible. Death and hell are evils, therefore destructible. Fire is suffering. So, through the influence of suffering, the evils of our fallen natures are consumed. Thus we die the first death in a natural way. But when we resist this law of our Maker by murmuring, or by trying to escape it by doing wrong, we incur increased suffering by our guilty means of avoiding it, and thereby we have to die a second death. This second death is the punishment of willfully wrong acts. "They that *would not* that I should reign over them, bring them hither and burn them." So we must be purified by suffering or fire. The result of right action is often unmerited abuse; for God has so permitted it as a means of our sanctification; and if we expect to escape this abuse by wrong-doing, we are only preparing for ourselves the agonies of the second death. Death and hell, being destroyed, may mean that the death-penalty and punishment, both, are to be annihilated in that community where moral power has acquired its manhood strength and can stand alone, self-reliant, independent of penalties, for its existence. Just as a child naturally outgrows his educational influences, and with them the penalties of disobedience, which, in his infancy and childhood, were necessary to him as helps to his virtues. But when his virtues have acquired manly strength he no longer needs restraints and penalties, but can be trusted to take care of himself, independent of any dictation or control from others. He now has in his own breast the only monitor needed for virtuous action, viz., the dictates of an enlightened conscience.

Rom. ii. 11, 12. "For there is no respect of persons with God. For as many as have sinned without law shall also perish without law; and as many as have sinned in the law shall be judged by the law."

It is not persons that God judges, but their acts; and the acts give a character to the person, instead of the person giving a character to the acts. Ignorantly wrong acts will be corrected and destroyed without punishment, but willfully wrong acts will have to be convicted and punished as guilty acts.

Matt. x. 28. "And fear not them which kill the body, but are not able to kill the soul: but rather fear him which is able to destroy both soul and body in hell."

The persecutors of the good have no power to harm the soul or spirit of their victim so long as they hold fast their own integrity, since no power can harm our souls except our own voluntary agency. And this free agency is upheld in us only while we fear to disregard God's claims, as dictated to us by his secretary, our conscience. For if we disregard his claim he has power to take from us our reason, whereby our humanity or our soul is destroyed, and we become insensible to the exercise of any pleasurable emotions. Thus the violation of God's physical and moral laws tends to incapacitate both the soul and body for happiness, and fit it only for a state of unmitigated misery, or hell.

Psalm xi. 5. "The Lord trieth the righteous: but the wicked and him that loveth violence, his soul hateth."

Discipline is an evidence of love towards a child. It strengthens and develops the capacities of the soul, and thus qualifies it for a higher plane of enjoyment. This is the obedient child's portion. But he hates rebellion and disobedience, and love compels him to punish it to a degree proportionate to the offense. "Upon the wicked he shall rain snares, fire and brimstone, and an horrible tempest." All these destructive agents are employed, not to destroy the sinner, but his sins, and this tempest will continue until all his love of sin is destroyed; then, and only then, is he prepared to profit by the discipline of his Father's hand. Love compels our Father to assume this stern manner, as a means of bringing the willful child to repentance.

Psalm vii. 11. "God judgeth the righteous, and God is angry with the wicked every day."

Goodness is indispensable to a judge. Thus God is the only capacitated judge of character. Those whose sincere purpose is to do right, have, therefore, no cause for fear before this righteous judge. But the sinner, while he shuns the paths of truth and righteousness, is constantly exposed

4

to suffer the just penalty of disobedience. Thus, he feels the just indignation of his offended Father. This act, to the guilty sinner, seems like the manifestation of an angry or revengeful feeling, when it is only the expression of love in just the manner his highest good demands. So long as his rebellion continues, so long does he compel his Father to chastise him.

Isaiah, iii. 11. "Woe unto the wicked! It shall be ill with him: for the reward of his hands shall be given him."

It is a most sad and melancholy condition to expose ourselves to the punishment of immutable, inflexible justice. There is no escape from the penalties of a broken law. He must receive his just due, for if love and mercy will not lead him to repentance, justice is compelled to step in and enforce the demands of a just law. It is only another manifestation of love towards his children, to promote their highest good.

Rev. xxii. 11. "He that is unjust, let him be unjust still: ....and he that is holy, let him be holy still."

To be "still" in a certain state, does not imply that it will be always so. If the trustees should decide at their next meeting that Mrs. Packard should remain here "still," I should not therefore feel that my state was hopeless, but should as confidently believe I should be delivered as ever; and that just as soon as if they had not so decided. This act I should look upon as a part of the great scheme which God had planned for my escape. So God's saying at a certain stage of man's redemption, let his present state continue, so that each one may receive according to his deserts, I do not therefore feel justified in believing that this discipline would not ultimately change his purpose of disobedience, so that he could, as a result, repent and become holy. The temporary result of holiness is trial,—of wickedness, is punishment;

and this holiness will sustain the trial unharmed, and this wickedness will bear the punishment until subdued into a yielding state, so that they can be made holy by obedience. The principles of God's government warrant such results; for goodness is to live, and wickedness is to be destroyed or annihilated, since it has no inherent life. God, by his wise discretion, will overcome it, and bring it into a state of voluntary renunciation.

Psalm cxxxix. 8. "If I ascend into heaven thou art there : if I make my bed in hell, behold thou art there."

Goodness or love is omnipresent. He is present with his obedient children to increase their happiness, and he is present with his disobedient ones, to see that none but just punishment is bestowed upon them for their good. He is in constant effort to make their rebellious condition just as tolerable as their highest good will permit it to be.

Matthew, xiii. 30. " Gather ye together first the tares and bind them in bundles to burn them : but gather the wheat into my barn."

In the development of character, good and evil have equal opportunities for growth. But when they have ripened, and their distinctive characters are fully developed then, the separation is to take place. Evil is to be concentrated, and it is to work out its own destruction. When this takes place, good is to be shielded and protected from any further exposure.

Psalm xvi. 10. " For thou wilt not leave my soul in hell ; neither wilt thou suffer thy Holy One to see corruption."

While the righteous are being tried and purified, their hearts are sustained by hope of ultimate deliverance. But the sinner feels that his torment will be endless. But since the Holy One exists in every human soul, however depraved, this part of him will survive the destruction of the evil in him, for God will not suffer himself to see corruption.

Romans, ii. 9. " Tribulation and anguish upon every soul of man that doeth evil."

Sin and misery are inseparable. Doing evil secures tribulation and anguish to the transgressor ; and there can be no escape from it, any more than they can escape from feeling pain, by the touch of fire. The law of recompense is immutable. Punishments and rewards are the result of established laws.

Heb. ii. 15. " And deliver them who through fear of death were all their lifetime subject to bondage."

If their deliverance comes at all, it must of course come after their lifetime ; for they are all their lifetime subject to bondage. Therefore, probation does not terminate with this life, but is continued on as the circumstances of their new life render it appropriate to their condition. But very few are delivered from bondage, or attain unto a state of entire sanctification in this life. Some do, and then, like Christ, pass into a state of unalloyed blessedness—or, in other words, they rise unto a state of life or happiness just fitted to their sanctified condition.

Others rise to battle it again with sin and temptation in a new form, and if they triumph over sin under this new trial, they are then delivered unto a resurrection, in their next life of happiness, as the result of holiness. So, like the oak-tree, we die and live again each fall and spring, to find some seasons very propitious for a strong and vigorous growth, and others, in consequence of drought, or some combination of misfortunes, hardly hold their own as good as when the season of growth commenced for this year. Still, on the whole, the oak progresses in size, and will, in time, attain to the gigantic proportions of its nature. So man is, by each successive life, becoming more and more like unto his glorious model—God himself—as his immortal nature aspires unto.

I. Tim. iv. 10. "Who is the Saviour of all men, especially of those that believe."

Gospel salvation saves from sin, and those are especially saved who are saved from sinning, and the greatest security against sinning is a belief in the testimony of God's word, viz., that sin will be punished, and holiness be rewarded. Therefore, the confiding, trusting child will not disobey, knowing the punishment is sure to come if he does, since he believes his father never lies. But the doubting, disbelieving child ventures to disobey, trusting he may in some way escape the penalty. But he cannot. So he has to be saved by repentance, caused by punishment; while the obedient child is saved without repentance; for his faith saved him from sinning, so as to render repentance necessary. The brothers of the prodigal son did not have to repent to gain their father's blessing, for they had at no time trangressed his commandment, and therefore, of course, had nothing to repent of. But the prodigal had done wrong, and he, of course, had to return to the paths of obedience, before he could find his father's blessing, which his disobedience had forfeited, until his repentance restored it to him. So all the prodigals, or lost ones, in God's great family, are to return to their father's house, and by repentance are to secure his forgiveness and forfeited favor. But those who are saved from sinning are, like the prodigal's brothers, justified on the ground of obedience—not of repentance—for 'tis only the wrong-doer who needs repentance, not the righteous or right-doer. For the righteous to repent of doing right would

be doing wrong.   So he is justified on the ground of obedience, the result of his living faith in God's word.

The above commentary is here given as a specimen of my
independent, common-sense investigations of Bible truth,
as I apprehended it.   I have copied the above from notes
I have taken since I have been in this asylum; and as they
contain the sum of many of the original views and principles
contained in the succeeding volumes, I thought this the most
appropriate place for them.

"THE CELESTIAL TRAIN,"

A SPIRITUAL IMPRESSION.

PREFACE.

The "Celestial Train" contains a few "glances and glimpses" at some of the great natural laws towards which our progressive natures are evidently tending. It carries us into the higher unexplored regions of thought where we take a few notes of the state of society where "natural laws" are all culminated into the "Divine Code." And since the law of liberty or spiritual freedom is the great law of gravitation in this territory, my thoughts are licensed to unfold themselves in a state of entire freedom, untrammeled by creeds, sects, or customs of society.

The reader must bear in mind that our "Lightning Express" goes so very rapidly over the territory through which it passes, that it gives us no time for the special observation of any particular object; but on the contrary, view succeeds view so hastily, that it hardly allows us one moment to note the present view before the succeeding one calls for our notice, or it is lost for ever on this trip of observation. It is only at the "switches" it allows us time to individualize our thoughts at all.

4*   (81)

THE " TICKETED PASSENGERS " ON BOARD THE " CELES-
TIAL TRAIN " ARE FOUND IN THE FOLLOWING

LIST OF PASSENGERS.

Gen. George Washington, ex-President.

Mrs. Martha Washington, his wife.

Dr. Andrew McFarland, Jacksonville, Ill.

Mrs. E. P. W. Packard, and four of her children, viz.,
Theophilus, Isaac, Samuel, and Elizabeth, Chicago, Ill.

Mr. Chedister, Hospital Carpenter, Jacksonville.

Oliver Cromwell, the Usurper.

King Charles Stewart.

Rev. John Calvin, the Bigot.

Jeremiah, the Prophet.

Peter, the Apostle.

Noah, the Antediluvian.

Jonah, the Ninevite.

Abraham Lincoln, President of United States.

Senator Morton, Indiana.

Gen. McClellan, Officer of the Army.

Dr. Woods, Pres. Theological Seminary, Andover, Mass.

Prof. Parks, Theological Seminary, Andover, Mass.

Mrs. Marian Severance, South Deerfield, Mass.

Dea. Spring, Manteno, Ill.

Methuselah, the Oldest Man.

Floyd, the Traitor.

Rev. H. W. Beecher, Brooklyn, L. I.

The Southern Slaveholders.

Rev. Theophilus Packard, Manteno, Ill.

Widow Dixon, Manteno, Ill.

Pres. Lincoln's Cabinet, Washington, D. C.

Mr. Miller, a Calvinistic Husband.

Mrs. Wood, an Asylum Patient.

Paul, the Apostle.

Rev. Mr. Bedell, Philadelphia.
Trustees of Insane Asylum, Illinois.
David Crockett.
Dea. Albert Peck, Shelburne, Mass.
Samson, the Strongest Man.
Goliath of Gath, the Giant.
King David, the Psalmist.
O. S. Fowler, the Phrenologist.
Copernicus, the Astronomer.
Dr. Hitchcock, President Amherst College, Mass.
Prof. Snell, Amherst College, Mass.
Joshua, the Judge of Israel.
Martin Luther, the Reformer.
Legree, Sambo, and Quimbo, " Uncle Tom's Cabin."
Michael Servetus, Scientific Theologian.

THE "BILL OF FREIGHT" ON BOARD THE "CELESTIAL TRAIN" IS FOUND IN THE FOLLOWING

LIST OF THOUGHTS.

Washington's Statue.
Echo, an illustration of spirit medium.
I, as Washington's medium.
The tares and wheat in our government stack.
Christ-like men women-defenders.
Washington's echo.
The marriage law a despotism.
Insanity the devil's shield.
The insane of the spirit world.
Will Christ's government uphold insane asylums?
Shall we have bodies when we reign with Christ?

Is reason to be needed in spirit life ?
The stigma of insanity.
Christian and Calvinistic sisters' dialogue.
No standard of insanity.
The Calvinism of our government.
Evil slays itself.
To kill Calvinism is to resuscitate the government.
First the useful, then the ornamental.
Ministers keep a Sunday suit.
Reform no one.
Separation of the sexes is Calvinistic.
Go-a-headitiveness.
Fruits and vegetables our natural food.
The Orthodox Creed.
My ark of refuge.
Hot love.
Brother George, can we love only one up there ?
Woman's right to choose her husband.
How government can be dispensed with.
Human punishments unchristian.
The insane spurn restraint.
Naturalness is called insanity.
Calvinistic lies about God's character.
Insane asylums manufacture devils.
The devils are to be redeemed.
Dr. McFarland's honorable love token.
Faith in the nobleness of manhood.
Woman overburdened.
Woman desires offspring.
A husband's daggers.
Government's conservative feet and toes.
Woman craves appreciation.
Christ's government will protect the married women.
A Calvinistic theological seminary.

Thinking for ourselves.
Wishing one dead.
Calvinistic benefactions.
'Tis duty to free ourselves from an oppressive husband.
The man who ought never to have a wife.
An invincible purpose removes stumps.
A husband's daggers illustrated.
Dangers from spiritual illumination.
Should be as free after marriage as before.
Women-haters need to be grafted.
Kissing tainted with Calvinism.
A Christian dance.
Never compromise.
Time necessary to great achievements.
Christian sophisms.
Lincoln in his lion's den.
The traitors slay themselves.
It is our duty to hate evil.
Easier to cover evils than to cure them.
Calvinistic cure for evil.
Too much punishment, too little protection.
How to cure insanity.
Friends should take care of their insane friends.
Our insane laws.
Beelzebub's den.
Woman-crushing process.
Dangerous to be a married woman in Illinois.
Dr. McFarland's Calvinistic side.
Censorship on letters is wrong.
A breaking up time.
A division of labor, but no drones.
Should not bear what we can help.
Intelligence a power in woman.
Nature is God's best book.

How the sun stood still.

Use the only test of virtue.

Rebels not neighbors, but robbers.

Right is might.

I am imprisoned for thinking.

Spiritual health rests on natural health.

Human nature is a holy nature.

A part of God cannot be lost.

Government should protect the soul's rights.

United States president must stand on his own acts.

Woman's talisman.

Punishment is reformatory.

Dying does not affect the character.

How a woman-hater was made.

Government should den up the wolves.

Advice to the president.

I am somebody.

'Tis liberty lunatics fight for.

Disloyalty to Christ don't pay.

Calvinism punishes the innocent for " their good."

America has an idea of trying Christ's government.

All must be free to do wrong as well as right.

Freedom of opinion no humbug.

Mysteries about Dr. McFarland.

Characteristic mark of an asylum patient.

The sanest people called insane.

Christian Sabbath.

Never right to do wrong.

Never wrong to do right.

Contrast between Christ's and Calvin's preaching.

"THE CELESTIAL TRAIN."

A SPIRITUAL IMPRESSION.

Last night, Sept. 17, 1862, about midnight, as I should judge, I was awakened, gradually, by the singing of two patients in the lower halls, mine being the eighth hall, the highest of all. They seemed to be in different wards, but answering to each other like an echo. One could be heard very distinctly; the response, or echo, faintly, still distinct enough to perceive it to be a perfect echo.

I think they must have been singing some time before I was awakened to a conscious state, for I have an indistinct recollection of its noise as a disturbance. I seemed struggling to suppress a kind of faint desire, like to an ejaculatory prayer, "Oh! I do wish you would be quiet, so that I need not be awakened entirely to a conscious state, for I am sleeping so sweetly!"

Still my prayer was unheeded, and in spite of my struggles not to wake up, I did open my eyes to an entire consciousness, and found myself lying straight upon my back, and the night being quite warm, I had one limb and foot entirely exposed upon the outside of the bed. As I stretched out my toes and felt the foot-board, the figure instantly flashed before my mind of "Washington's statue" in marble, in the Boston State-house, where he is represented with one limb exposed outside his drapery, with his foot resting upon the pedestal.

This figure was instantly caught up and associated with the music when the echo impressed my mind with vivid distinctness. The whole being only one breath of music in length. It was the same thing over and over, over and over again and again, without the least variation of time, order, or expression. This monotony, though long, was not wearisome, for my mind instantly caught at it as an illustration of spirit mediums, of perfect development; one being a perfect or complete echo of the other. "There," said I, " is Washington, and I, his medium, transcribing his dictations for his beloved country's welfare."

He, from his higher spiritual position is viewing our country's destiny, through his perfected, spiritual spectacles, and, seeing the mighty responsibilities devolved upon this generation, to give to it its future character and position, his great, benevolent soul is drawn out in all its sympathetic tenderness towards those valiant, loyal spirits, who, on earth, are in sympathy with his holy aspirations for our triumph, in this, our mighty struggle, to separate the Calvinistic from the Christian principles of our government and institutions.

" Yes," said I, " brother George, I will be your willing medium for this holy purpose. The wheat must be separated from the tares, and the tares must be burned. Yes, George, I will do what my single hand can do, under the direction of thy pure spirit's influence, to transcribe thy thoughts, as the country's long looked-for 'leader,' to lead them on to a glorious victory over all their devilish practices, growing out of Calvin's ' doctrine of devils,' which have well nigh choked out the whole harvest of perfected wheat, which is already reaped and strewed out in single heads all over the great harvest field."

Yes, so insidious has the Calvin devil been in sowing his tares amongst it, that each head, even, has its tare associate; and, while standing side by side, had an equal chance at germination, growth, and perfection of their totally different natures. But now, as they lay strewn upon the field for separation, the wheat is, many times, found buried beneath the more luxuriant tare partner, and is thus hidden from observation.

Still, as the work of the frugal husbandman progresses, he finds and secures each single head in his bundle. Not one escapes his frugal, cautious husbandry.

Thus carefully secured in bundles and bound by his inflexible cord of consolidation, they can brave the wind's and tempest's power. Strong in union, they baffle the tempest's power to unbind and scatter their single heads to the breeze. And, as they stand in single bundles, made still more compact by being bound in one great stack, they—the government, the great stack of assorted wheat—now take undisputed possession of the great field, securely and dauntlessly looks on, while the great Husbandman gathers together the tares, in rough, promiscuous form, into a heap of stubble for the flames to consume.

But, for the more conspicuous display of his bonfire to the country about, he defers applying the torch until the sun is down. And then under the reign of the gentle moon, the tares are consumed by the fire of love, lit by the daughters of the land as they accompany their brothers out to witness the conflagration. But, in their gleeful joy to emulate each other's flame in brilliancy, they, careless of themselves, and their more combustible garments, in their unselfish ambition to kindle the highest flame of love, expose themselves to being burnt with the tares; and, were it not for their gallant brothers' protection, and more watchful care, they might, some of them, be burned to death by accident.

Thanks to the instinctive manliness of Christ-like men, who rush to the help of the defenseless, regardless of their own danger. Yes, they need but to know that a sister is in danger, and help is certain as the decrees of God.

" Brother George, you would not have let me lie here, two and a half years, under this heap of tares, without coming to my rescue, did you but know of facts as they exist. You did not know that the enemy held me in his own, undisputed possession, without one to take my part."

No, of all the sons of men, not one has yet appeared in my defense, as the protector of an injured, helpless woman. There is one, and only one consideration, on which I can extend to them gospel forgiveness ; and that is, on the terms of gospel repentance. This is, to never let another angel sister lie uncared for, unshielded, unprotected either by law or practice—a helpless victim in the power of consistent Calvinism. Oh! do send some men or some law to their rescue! Don't let their faith in manhood be so severely tested as mine has been, for I fear even the love and confidence of a true woman would suffer harm thereby, in leading them to doubt the sincerity of your manly professions of honor and nobleness.

" George Washington, a perfected son of God—like Christ, your elder brother, is not this the echo of your noble heart? Would you not fly to the rescue of injured woman? Would you not expose yourself to extend help to the tortured victim, writhing under the hands of despotism ? "

Yes, brother, I know you would. And who knows but that it is through the influence of your noble spirit's power that Dr. McFarland's eyes are beginning to be opened to facts as they exist? Who knows but that it is through the influence of your gallant heart that Dr. McFarland has allowed me the right to speak in self-defense? Where should I now have been, and through what thorny paths might I now have been wending my solitary way, had he sent me home last September, as he proposed to do, by recommending me to the trustees as a discharge candidate!

Oh, my sensitive heart shrinks with instinctive horror at

the thought of again grappling, single-handed and alone, with personified despotism, in the human form of a bigoted priest, who holds my destiny for both worlds by the mighty power of unlimited despotism, shielded by Calvinistic marriage laws!

Thanks to God! my great deliverer, that I am shielded from this most horrible fate, even though it be at the price of home and all its clustering joys, and the loss of my most precious of all jewels—my six children, and the loss of what, to me, is dearer than my natural life—my personal liberty.

Yes, a prison in hell, among maniacs for my companions, is far more preferable. For here, my sympathetic nature finds sympathy from sister spirits who share my fate. Yes, here I find them in large companies, among whom are abused wives, abused daughters, abused mothers, abused sisters, whose Calvinistic friends have cast them off, as beneath their notice or regard; and this asylum here stands with open hands, ready to receive any applicant who can present any claim, whether true or false, to what Calvinistic, perverted humanity may choose to christen insanity!—the devil's shield! the christian's inquisition of the nineteenth century!

Oh, insanity! insanity! thy name is legion! for it includes the whole catalogue of impulses, feelings, affections, under forms as various as the human family's individualism.

"Brother George, do they have insane asylums where you are? If not, I should like to join you."

But if they do, I will risk it, for I am sure the first among its insane patients will be found Christ, the Son of God, and with him some from all the civilized nations, who bear any striking characteristic resemblance to his image; such as Abraham, Jeremiah, and the apostles and christian martyrs of all ages.

Yes, to the insane asylums of the spirit world will I go, to find my spirit companions; for I know freedom awaits me there, for the angels rolled away the stone from the door of Christ's insane asylum, and he came forth to talk with them for a short time, and then ascended out of the reach of his enemies' power to harm him more, henceforth to be their king—no more their subject. I, in entire confidence in his simple promise, am expecting to "reign with him," for I have "suffered with him."

"Brother George, when we come with Christ, to reign with him on this earth in our glorified bodies, such as he ascended in, do you think he will establish insane asylums for his followers? Or will he let them have their liberty to do as they please, leaving their benevolent natures full scope for development, in plans as various as their organization, for others' good? Or will he circumscribe them to set forms, to church creeds, to societies and institutions where individuality is lost in organizations? I should like to know how it is, for I have an instinctive horror of confinement. I want space, room, expansion, unlimited freedom.

"I do not want to be obliged to toe the mark, as I have had to here, with the insane asylum switch held over my head, as I have had here, at every deviation from the chalk line.

"By the way, George, how is it,—are we going to have bodies when we come to reign with Christ? I have been told that we should not have bodies then; but it is a puzzle to me how they can feed us without mouths!—how we can see without eyes!—and how they can dress us, and take us out to walk on the streets of their chief city, without bodies and feet! You know how troublesome it is to understand these things while our reason is not dethroned; and our common-sense will conflict so with these things, or views, as I ought to say.

"Have we got to lose our reason, and become insane, to understand these things? In other words, is insanity a test of loyalty in Christ's government? Or can we understand his directions, and does he govern us through our reason? I am very particular on this point, for I do not feel willing to uphold an unreasonable government. For, of all things in the world, I have the greatest dread of insanity; and I am not willing, voluntarily, to uphold an insane government, lest, by abusing my reason, even by winking at, or countenancing unreasonable acts, God should dim this faculty, so that I should have the mirror of himself within me besmeared with specks and filth."

I have always had the greatest reverence for this faculty, and I have taught my children to have also. And now, if your government there is Calvinistic, I have made a great mistake on this point.

And, besides, if it is there as it is here, one loses their moral influence among many, if they have once been thought to be insane, by having been made to suffer a term of imprisonment in the insane asylum—and the longer the term the greater the disgrace. Whenever, after it is once ascertained to be a fact that they have suffered a term there, there seems to be no getting away from the stigma attending it.

If you go to a new country, somebody is sure to tell on you. And when the suspicion is once aroused, there is no hope of you. You cannot even speak a word of your own, indicative of your individuality, without somebody saying, "See, she is insane!" We have to be looking for some strong tree to grow upon, afterwards; and this parasite life does not suit my disposition at all.

I do not always like to be obliged to tell who the author of all my ideas is, for I somehow want people to feel that I can think as well as some other folks. And, besides, it is such a tax upon my memory to remember names and dates. I believe I must be under seven on these bumps!

And then, if I do have the lion-heartedness to speak my

own thoughts, somebody is ready to exclaim : " Oh, don't you think Mrs. Packard's insanity is coming on again ?" Or, " She must be getting worse," if before I was hopelessly insane ! " I heard her say, myself, that she thought all the devils would be saved, as well as all other human beings !"

" Well, we must not heed what she says, for she will speak out sometimes, for she says her tongue is her own, and if she used it, she should not use it to speak lies with ! Just as if, telling other's opinions instead of her own were telling lies ! Oh, she has got such strange notions, I don't wonder her husband wanted to get rid of her, as he tried to, for life. But he couldn't find any place to keep her entirely hidden from observation. She would somehow break cage, and get out into the world again ; and before you knew it, the next thing would be, to hear of something Mrs. Packard had said or written to somebody.

" Again, she annoyed people so much, where she was, she being, as she used to say, ' a terror to evil doers,' or as her insanity taught her to say, a ' thorn in the Calvinistic side of things.' No Calvinist was ever at home in her company, and you know her society had to be very select to avoid them, they are so common.

" I could not help pitying her the other day, when we met her in company, and she had been saying something which she seemed to think was very important, and we all smiled ; and she seemed to think we were laughing at her ; but we did not mean she should see us, and out of pity to her, we apologized, pretending it was something else. But she seemed to doubt it, after all, for she was pretty careful after that to keep her thoughts to herself.

" I heard the other day, one of her ' fallen angels,' as she calls them, talking with another very charitable, good, kind, christian woman, about her. The christian lady remarked:

" ' I don't see but that Mrs. Packard is all right. I don't see any insanity about her.'

" The Calvinist replied, ' Well, I do. I have seen enough to satisfy me she is insane—and besides, we know she is, or they would not have kept her there in the asylum—and then, after seeing her all that time, discharge her as " hopelessly insane," unless she was so. For, you know, superintendents in insane asylums know who are insane and who are not. That's their business, you know, and business or professional men understand their own business better than common people, who have never taken lessons on that subject.'

" ' Well,' the christian lady replied, ' I don't care what Dr. McFarland did say about her, I have just as good a right to my opinion as Dr. McFarland has to his—and it is my honest opinion that he has made a great mistake, this time, in her case, in calling Mrs. Packard an insane person—and, as for myself, I shall not pin my opinion on to his coat sleeve, if he is a great man. God made my mind as well as his, and I am accountable to God, not to Dr. McFarland, for the use I make of it. And I shall dare to be true to my conscience, and do by Mrs. Packard as I should wish to be done by, in exchange of circumstances. I think she has been slandered, by being called insane, when she is not—and I mean to defend her from it.'

" ' I shall do no such thing. I believe her to be an insane person, because Dr. McFarland *said she was ;* and he is such a great man, I cannot set up my opinion against his. If you choose to be so self-conceited as to think you know more than he does, I don't think much of your sense, that's all. Besides, you know, there are various forms of insanity—and I heard he remarked, that hers was one of those occult forms, which required peculiar skill and discernment, such as experience alone could furnish. Hers is one of those cases where one in a thousand would not detect or even think of, unless you had known her to have been insane.

" 'At any rate, I shall believe what she says that suits me, and what does not I shall call insanity, and let it pass for what it's worth. I do say, that a person who has once been insane, cannot be trusted afterwards. Her conclusions and suggestions must be jealously watched and guarded against, lest you imbibe some of her insane notions yourself, and thus share her fate.'

" ' Well,' replied the christian, ' if insanity is of so hidden a character that it cannot be detected by any common-sense person, I am sure it ought not to be punished with capital punishment—for, that insanity which cannot be detected by irregular conduct is not worthy the name—and, if ever there was a lady-like, christian deportment, more uniformly and invariably manifested, than Mrs. Packard manifests under *all* circumstances, I am yet to know. In fact—she is the sanest person I ever met !' "

Thus, Brother George, you see what diametrically opposite conclusions are drawn from the same subject. You see we have no standard by which to judge of accountability. The sanest people in the world are thus rendered liable to be deprived of their accountability at the whim or caprice of a fallible brother or sister who are themselves lost to reason on this point.

Oh, George, I am sick of this world as things now are. My chief comfort lies in the fact that life is short, and therefore I hope to quit it before long, and enter the society of kindred spirits, from whom I need not fear abuse, only love worthy objects. Yes, Brother George, I do want to go off to some other country out of the reach of hearing such balderdash as that Calvinistic sister uttered ; for the very word insane is like a stench in my nostrils.

Now, if Christ does rule his empire with reason, right, justice, and charity towards all, I should like to become a citizen, and let old, boasted, free America go to pot! I do say, things have got to a fine pass down here, when a person cannot *think* their own thoughts without incurring the risk of a life-long imprisonment for it, as I am enduring, for nothing but claiming a right to my own thoughts.

I tell you, George, our government has become so Calvinistic since you left the presidential chair, that I don't think it is worth fighting for, to save it. For my part, I, nor my children, are under no obligation to it for protecting our inalienable rights. I feel more like reporting them to England and France, and getting them to come and help destroy it from off the face of the earth.

The government does not protect the oppressed. It does protect the oppressor. I doubt whether there is a government on the face of the earth where greater injustice is shielded, by government, than has been shielded in my case. Even the most despotic governments in the world allow the right of self-defense to its worst criminals, while our government denies it *wholly to me* who have invariably been one of its most loyal, useful citizens, and now permits me to be imprisoned, hopelessly, without judge or jury, for simply thinking differently from my husband on points in theology!

American government! are you not doomed to destruction by a just God? And will not all the oppressed ones in our land say, Amen?

Indeed, the intelligent ones will; and I do believe that all the true men, and women too, in this country will respond to the sentiment uttered by Mr. Chedister, our cabinet-maker, here, in my room, yesterday, viz., that he hoped the trustees would get justice done them, for the course they were taking with me, by perpetuating my imprisonment after they knew that it was only for opinion's sake that I had been treated as insane.

Every loyal citizen must say that, if our government don't make an example of its officers who deliberately and know-

5

ingly imprison its loyal citizens for opinion's sake, by punishing them as traitors to our Constitution, the government may well be buried, since its life is extinct.

I, for one, intend to do my duty to get the character of our government tested by this case. I shall report the action of the trustees on my case at the December meeting, 1862, and solicit justice at the hands of the government of America. If they support the trustees in this act of religious persecution, they ought to be supported on their bier to the tomb! And you, Brother George, will rejoice to be one of the government's pall-bearers, won't you?

The mourners at such a funeral will be only the Calvinists!—the disloyal!

Your advice to these Calvinistic trustees, I am sure, would be, "Agree with thine adversary quickly, while thou art in the way with him; lest at any time the adversary deliver thee to the officer, and thou be cast into prison. Verily I say unto thee, thou shalt by no means come out thence till thou hast paid the uttermost farthing."

However, we, Christians, believe in freedom to all the good and bad, the gods and the devils. The devils have just as good a right to hang themselves as the gods have to let them. The Hamans, with their wives' help, can build their gallows, while the Mordecais can wait the time of their promotion, until they swing themselves on it.

George, isn't it a blessing to us, with our tender, loving, sympathizing natures, that we don't have this ugly, hateful business of punishing to do? God knew how we should hate it, and so he has arranged it so that "evil" does the "slaying" of the wicked. The devils like this mean business. It just suits their nature. So all are suited with this wise arrangement. The devils are allowed a great deal of liberty, under God's government,—liberty not only to kill themselves, but each other also.

But have we not reason to rejoice that they cannot kill God, or goodness, in any form? that their attempts to do so only rebound back on to themselves? "Evil slays the wicked." I am quite in love with the principles of Christ's government. The more I know of it, the better I like it. Indeed, I am about ready, already, to renounce all other governments for his alone,—that is, I am determined to recognize allegiance to no laws or government which conflict with his government. But, George, as the world now is so alive with Calvinists it requires no small degree of labor and lion-like bravery to stand muster now. I have to shoot them at every turn. I begin to think they are swarming, they are so thick. However, the old hive is less burdened by this process, if we are more so.

That is, only let the Calvinists be seen and known in their own true colors, and the vitality of our constitutional principles will be resurrected, to destroy them. To kill Calvinism is to save, or resuscitate, our government.

I'll shoot a Calvinist as soon as I would the devil! And the more of Calvinism I can shoot, the more of Christianity I can protect. I do hope and pray that Calvinism, and all its legion train of insanities, will, ere long, be buried in the soil which gave it birth. Or, in other words, I hope that Calvinism may be made to fill the grave which it has dug for Christianity.

General Washington—Commander-in-chief of our armies—God's vicegerent and Christ's forerunner! Say, must not our great government stack be taken to pieces, and each bundle unbound, and each head of wheat be severed from its fellow, in order that the chaff, which was unfortunately bound up with it, may be driven away by the breezes of heaven? Must not the threshing-floor be swept and garnished before the winnowing of the grain? Can the pure seed-wheat for another harvest be prepared by any process short of this?

Has not the cockle of the present harvest given us trouble enough to warn us that indolent, careless haste, in preparing seed, is not a labor-saving process ?

Had we better not mine a little longer, to be sure that we have got ore enough to build the feet and toes of our image, without mixing up the deficiency with miry clay ?

Let the splendid image of our present government be both our model and warning. A model as to the display of its golden head, but a warning as to the practical inutility of its feet. We want a government whose feet can be used to walk with, without jeopardizing the whole image by its first progressive step.

Oh! the Calvinism, the conservatism of our splendid government !

Is it not splendid ? Is it not useless ? Useless splendor! Can we not afford to sacrifice its splendor for practical utility ? But, if possible, let us have a splendidly *practical* government. But if one is not compatible with the other, let not utility be sacrificed to display. First, the useful, then the ornamental.

Let the military splendor of its army be employed in protecting the practical husbandry of its supporters—not in calling them from their useful toil to protect it. But so true and loyal are we, its subjects, that we will both labor and fight for it, if need be, rather than suffer its power to defend us to be destroyed.

But, General, you know how loyal we are ; but the trouble is, we don't know how to show it. We want you, from your superior position of observation, to dictate our movements. We stand ready to do everything, and almost anything except wickedness, to defend it. But we do not like to do wrong under any circumstances. To do wrong that good may come is too Calvinistic.

But these Calvinistic principles are so subtle, we are in

danger of confounding them with synonymous symphonics. Remember his garb and Christian name has, for a long time, held us entirely at his mercy. Instead of coming in his own hideous name as a charming serpent, he took the name of Christ, and with Cromwell's sanctity, he demands the death of King Charles Stuart, as heaven's decreed instrumentality for the advancement of his holy cause of truth and right-eousness on earth. And his sanctity and prayers deluded us. We did not suspect that Christ was not his real name, for it sounds and looks very much like Calvin, you know. And in our characteristic haste we stumbled at a name.

But I think we have learned a valuable lesson by our fall, so that we shall be more cautious in future about appear-ances, knowing their deceitful character, from bitter expe-rience. Henceforth we shall ask an additional test of character from our religious teachers. They must not only honor God with their lips, but we shall see to it that they treat their wives right at home, too. For we begin to find out that priests keep a Sunday suit, and are sometimes found looking quite shabby at home, meddling with what does not belong to them. Their study gowns sometimes bear marks of dough upon them.

But don't let us be too hard upon them—perhaps they volunteered to knead the dough to save their poor, sick wives the labor of doing it themselves. Or, perhaps, they had a love fit come over them, and in an attempt to steal a kiss from the baker, they came too near the kneading board. You know we can't tell how they get their marks, for we can't see into their kitchens ourselves; and since they do not keep servants, lest they tell on them, we must be content to let them keep kitchen scenes from our observation.

However, I guess some of them do hold the baby very willingly, sometimes, so that their wives can polish their linen. So we must not blame them for what they do do right. We must not fall into the faults we are complaining of, that of calling things by their wrong names. Don't let us call self-sacrificing, disinterested benevolence by the horrid name of selfishness!!

Pardon my episode, General, you know we women are very apt to bring in home scenes into our talk; that being our province of government, we are very apt to draw our illustrations from familiar scenes there enacted.

But to return to the subject. What are we to do to save our country and government from becoming an utter wreck?

You won't tell us, as Jeremiah did, in building his wall, to each man build up opposite his own house, will you? That would be dull business. No excitement to relieve the monotony of wearisome toil. We had much rather be in company, for then we could recreate ourselves by jocose talk and story-telling, and it would be so much pleasanter, you know. And if the wall is not built up quite so quick, we shall have secured some pleasure with our toil, and that will balance the delay of the enterprise.

But, on the whole, General, I don't know, upon second thought, but that your suggestion would be the best after all. For this rubbish and dirt about our houses and doors don't look well, and it is also an inconvenience to the public travel. And the quicker it is done the better on the whole, and then we can have a general jubilee or sociable, in gentlemanly style, with the ladies with us, in some of our nice, new, clean houses.

This coarse, vulgar talk with men alone isn't of much account after all; 'tis too Calvinistic. It always takes the women to give the polish, you know.

So I think we will straighten up our own home first, and then we can help our neighbors, if they need our help.

But I should not like to offer them any service before my own home was in good repair, lest they should tell me to look to my own home first.

General, the allusion to ladies suggests a thought which I should like to present for your consideration. Is it your custom, in your province, the spiritual world, to separate the sexes? Did God make them to associate together, or not? It has been a question with some, down here, whom I believe they call Calvinists, by name and practice both, to separate them in schools, colleges, churches, the lawyer's bar and the judge's bench, congress and legislation, etc. This class seem to think that women are going out of their proper sphere to go to the polls, although they can go to church or prayer-meetings together, and don't seem to feel any harm in it; only they act a little shy of them, they don't come quite so near together as I like. I want my partner so near that I can feel him, not going on before me, so that I have to run, and get all out of breath, to catch up with him. I am not one of the lagging sort, and I don't like to be seen in the rear. And, besides, it looks so squaw-like to be tagging on so, behind my husband—Indian file.

If they are in such a terrible hurry, I do wish they would let me hold on to their arm, so as to keep up easier. Never mind, we will let these Calvinistic men see that we *can* stand on our own feet, without their help, too, to keep us from falling.

And I am not certain but that we shall outrun them yet, after all. They may yet be the ones to call out, "Stop, wife! hold on! I can't keep up with *you!*"

"Never mind, husband, you are a man, and I guess you can get along alone. However, if you really need my help, I'll come back for you, for I remember how I used to feel, to see you running away from me, so hard; and I do go in for the principle, that the sexes ought not to be separated under any circumstances, and unless my practice corresponds with my preaching, it is not much use in preaching now-a days." Things have come to a strange pass, down here.

You can't make folks believe a word you say, unless you act it right out to them before their eyes. "*Do it!*" is all that will satisfy them. I think their go-a-headitiveness is under a state of unusual excitement.

Some people do seem to go most too fast, and run into a stump, before they know it. Yet, on the whole, I like this go-a-headitiveness, if you do get a thump once in awhile by it. It's sure to call attention to the stump, and then it is more likely to be dug up and be removed out of the way of other travelers. So, if our precipitancy can be turned to others' good, it seems to make up for the pain we suffered from the bump.

I suppose you don't have stumps in your region; they are mostly confined to new settlements, you know. But since we have such a great debt to pay, I think the sooner they are dug up the better; for our husbandry is our great dependence.

We can't live fighting always. It don't pay. The men have now been so long at it that the women begin to talk about breaking up the greensward themselves, only they take off our ox-team to feed the soldiers with; so we can't do that.

By the way, you don't eat such things up there, do you? We have to be pretty quick about it here, or the old carcass will stink before it is all eaten up. I wonder if the Hottentots are obliged to eat their human carcasses so soon? I often think, I don't wonder people's breath smells so bad sometimes—Calvinistic people, I mean—when I think what a narrow chance they run!

I do hope you will get your fruit-trees well on the way before my time comes to join you, for I think fruit is so luscious, and makes such good blood. Besides, I always seek good authority for my practice, and, as I see the subject, I think God intended fruits and vegetables for man's food.

For that is the only kind he prepared for our first parents, and I suppose he knew what was best for them, because he had just made their stomachs, and he knew what was best for them.

And I think God pampered Peter's conscience when he let down the great sheet of animals and told him to "slay and eat." You know when our children get off from the track we can't bring them right straight back; we have to give in a little to them.

Is it not astonishing how people, with God for their father, should ever eat the carcasses of great fat hogs, those filthy creatures that Christ sent the devils into?

By the way, perhaps this is the reason why there are so many swinish men now-a-days—Calvinists, I mean. Some of them act so much like hogs that you can hardly tell them apart, only these hogs have two legs and the other kind have four. But I don't think there is much advantage gained in the difference; for the old fat hog can wallow along, dragging his four legs after him, about as fast as the old Calvinist can on his two.

Some people pretend to say that we partake of the same nature, in disposition, as the animal we feed upon. If so, I should rather be like a lamb, or a cow, than like a hog. He is too conservative an animal to suit me. The flying food suits my nature better than either. My spirits move in feathers, when not too tired from hard work. The sailing nature of the flying fish does very well, and since Christ ate fish, so I do.

The fact is, I have walked so long alone, I've got tired of it; and now, for awhile, I've tried running, but I ran right into an insane hospital, and there I had to stop running. No, that isn't so,—I never ran so fast in all my life as since I have been confined within these brick walls by bolts, bars, and

5*

keys. I've already run almost out of hearing of orthodoxy in my race after the truth!

The orthodox creed is so meager as to the truth, that I don't wonder that it is called milk, fit only for babies' food. I ain't a baby now; I'm a full grown woman, and can hunt up my own food, too. But I have to go outside the orthodox creed to do it, though.

I can tell you, General, I think 'tis a favor to me that this ark of refuge, with a Noah in it to protect me from the wild animals, is provided, where I can think, and think aloud, too, without being pelted with the insane switch, as I was on the outside. I've got so out of conceit with the Calvinistic elements of old earth, that I ain't sorry to see it submerged in the waters of strife, for it does need washing—'tis so dirty.

This cold bath, so cold as to chill all the love elements of home and country, almost, cannot but neutralize some of the fictitious elements, and bring out to view the real substance, if there is anything left but Calvinism. I've found something besides Calvinism inside here, and, more than that, I intend to bring it out to view, too. I ain't afraid to tell what a Saviour I have found!

I am so much in favor of action that I even venture to use my wings in flying out of the window of my ark of refuge, to see if the waters ain't so assuaged on the earth that I can venture on it on my own feet. But my letters bring back no indications of life—love-life—as yet. I must wait another seven days to see if any response is to be made for publishing money.

If I can find an olive branch I will bring it back to old Noah, and he will then believe my statements respecting the state of things, I think. Perhaps the tangible proof of regard and attention I receive through the sale of my book will convince him that I am not the isolated being he took me to be, by my friends having been so shy of me so long.

But he slanders both me and them to think so, for every-body does love me that ever saw me, except my husband, and he says himself that he loves me better than any other lady he ever saw. But that is precious little, I can tell you. And he has such old Calvinistic ways of showing it, I think he and Calvin must have looked so much alike that you could not tell them apart.

I think Servetus and I could understand this kind of practical love. No school like experience in love matters. I do wonder if Servetus felt such hot love as I do? I don't think he did, for in those days they didn't know how to show it, except by some tangible proof—a stake which could be seen and felt. But now-a-days love has become so much more spiritual and refined, we are more sensitive, we can feel the persecution on the spirit without the appearance being made manifest, as then.

So Brother Servetus, I think I must carry the palm; for, on this principle, I am sure you will acknowledge that I have experienced hotter love from my husband than you did from your brother Calvin. And, besides, he is so much longer at it, in consuming the spirit of a woman than the body of a man, by the slow torture of twenty-one years.

Is not such love stronger than death? Poor fellow! he cannot help it; for who can love right without a heart?

I guess he will get one when he gets a better body, some time. You know God can put a heart into a man that has not got any, for he can do everything.

My other friends would have been glad to have come to me, but they have kept the doors closed very close about me for my special benefit. They thought it would be best for my insanity to cut off outside communications. It was not because the superintendent wanted to monopolize the love of his sane patient. It was only because he thought "her good" required it!

Benevolence is a very large bump in our superintendent's head, and we knowing ones have learned how to make allowance for the organization and temperament of different people.

Now I am in the region of the affections, I should like to inquire into your love matters, up there. But I must drop the General to do so. It is so cold,—and say, " Brother George, can they love only one up there ?" It makes a great fuss down here if a woman loves more than one man, and I cannot stand it, for all the world. I do have to love every man I see, although I have my preferences, of course. I must own up (for I don't believe in lying about love matters any more than about anything else) that I don't love the Calvinistic brothers with quite so hot love as I do the Christian brothers.

But, oh, the Christian brothers, I love them most as well as I do my eldest brother, Jesus Christ ; and the family resemblance is so striking in some that I can see Christ's image almost perfectly. And, oh, how I do love them !

Some have told me, but I don't know how true it is, that my husband shut me up here for fear I would run off with some man ! But, to tell the truth, that man doesn't understand me. It is the last thing in the world I should think of doing, to run after a man ! I altogether prefer to have them run after me.

But there is one point where my singular propensity is manifested. I say that I think it is just as right for a woman to tell a man that she loves him, and would like to become his wife, if he has no objection, as it is for a man to say to a woman, " I love you. Will you marry me ? "

If anything, the woman has the preference to choose first, for she has a more circumscribed orbit to choose from, in selecting her protector, than a man has, and this might be some compensation. However, our old, prudish notions and customs make it seem, at first, to be indelicate and unwomanly. But I think it is only the effect of habit.

And, besides, has not a woman as much fortitude to sustain a denial as a man has? But I should rather the man who refused my request to become my protector, wouldn't tell of it, for fear it might injure my market. But it need not; only we have so much Calvinism left amongst our institutions here yet, that even love matters are tainted with it.

If you can believe it, there is despotism in love here. Only think, some men love their wives with such a despotic love that they are hardly willing a man should look at them. It most makes them mad to find another man has the same good opinion of his wife as he has himself. I should think they would be flattered by the fact rather than otherwise. I am sure I should not want a man that nobody else wanted. I shouldn't care how many else wanted him, if I only could get him myself.

Oh! Brother George, I do wish I could be free to love men, and not hurt the feelings of anybody in doing so. God and Christ are men, and I like them so well, I should like to show it by loving somebody like them; and more than that, I want to be loved by somebody just as purely and ardently.

Well, Brother George, I guess (I am a Yankee, you know) that you will by this time begin to think that my philanthropy is confined chiefly to the No. 1 principle.

Well, you are good at guessing. It is even so. I do think if each one would attend to his own business alone, the need of a great governmental power would be abrogated. The law is only meant to protect the good; and if all would just let others' matters alone, and not interfere with their rights, lawyers, judges, and courts could be dispensed with; and, of course, we should not need to have war any more, for there would be nothing to war about.

It is these incessant restraints and checks which so vex men. They were not made to be governed. They were made to govern themselves. And when one brother undertakes to punish another brother for what he thinks is wrong action, he usurps the authority of our common parent, and leads the oppressed brother to inquire :

" Who made you my overseer ? Did father tell you to take care of me in his absence ; or, have you usurped authority? I shall tell pa of you when he comes home, and I know you'll catch it ; for I heard him say, myself, the children must all be kind to each other, and be very careful about trespassing on each other's rights. He told me what to do, and it is none of your business whether I do it or not ; that's my look-out. I tell you, brother, this meddling with my duties won't pay ; you see if it does when pa looks into the matter. If he did not give you' work enough to do while he is absent, or you have got your stint done, you might be reading the war news, instead of overseeing me."

Brother, it is not christian for one sinner to punish another sinner. It is a Calvinistic principle, for it is an usurpation of God's authority—as sovereign—and he says, " Vengeance is mine, I will repay."

Punishing the children is the father's work, not the children's.

But the worst feature of our government, brother, is, they don't protect our sisters. The brothers domineer over us a great deal too much. I don't think our good father ever gave them any right to tease us so. If he has, he is a Calvinistic God, and we don't like him much. Our priests tell us they are like him. But I doubt it. I think they slander him awfully. They say he is going to put some of us children into an insane asylum, and keep us there, longer than Dr. McFarland does—a great deal ! But though the torment in Dr. McFarland's asylum is " endless," while we are there—for he is exceedingly careful not to let us have the least hope or prospect of our ever getting out, until the very day our friends come for us—yet in many cases it is not life-long or endless. But they all have to be made to feel, like as Jonah did, while in the whale's belly, " the earth with her bars was about me for ever," although the " for ever " is, in all cases, more than three days and three nights, a great deal.

Oh! this endless torment *is* dreadful! People ought to be great criminals—awfully guilty—to be made the victims of such torment! If our superintendent would only tell us how long a term was assigned to his afflicted patients, as a just punishment, due for enduring the greatest earthly affliction, we could bear this endless torment more patiently! But no—their good forbids this alleviation!

I am glad criminals in our penitentiaries don't have to suffer endless torment for doing wrong, as the insane have to for doing right.

Oh! Brother George, if you have any influence at headquarters, do, I entreat you, use it in destroying these insane asylums; for they are the culmination of the Calvinistic principle—the *punishing of the innocent!* Oh! George, do tell them that the lovers of their race and country have just as good a right to their liberty, as the traitors, or the haters of mankind, and we will engage to be a great deal better citizens than some of them are, if you will only unlock our doors, and let us be free—free to do good—that is all the freedom we ask for, and this all the use we will make of it.

These asylums will make excellent hospitals for the sick and wounded soldiers, and we should make first-rate nurses for them, if we could only be left to do as we please. We have studied and read medical books, and that is not all, we have been to school to our instincts, so long, that we have become quite adepts in the natural sciences. 'Tis thus we excel in certain points, so much.

We are not Calvinistic enough, or artificial enough, to suit our contemporaries. It is our naturalness, or sanity, that is called insanity in us. It is only a mistake in words, or terms.   'Tis only the little word " in " before sane, that makes all this trouble. Just look into the matter, and you'll see, and I hope convince our President, that it is only in christening us wrongly—that we want our false names changed to the real, true name—sane, instead of insane.

We are such stanch advocates of the simple truth, that we enter our protest against going under false colors. Yes, we protest under oath, if you desire it, that it is just as great a slander to call us insane, as it is to call a christian a Calvinist.

But, George, these slanders about my Father's character trouble me more than the slanders about myself. And I am determined to take his part, and defend his true character.   Do you think I shall ever be made to believe all the lies the Calvinists tell of him, when I know 'tis false and slanderous, and I can prove it, too?   They say he is such a tyrant and cruel despot, that none can please him, or even come near him, except Christ goes before him to carry the shield of protection! Just as if he would not extend his scepter to his queen without being asked to look !

I know I will let my children come to my room without all this parade, and he says he has made us just like himself—only he's a great deal better, and knows more, and has had longer experience. Still, even I should not keep punishing one child all his lifetime to make him mind me. If one thing wouldn't do, I'd try another thing, and so I'd keep on trying, until I beat him, or conquered his stubbornness.

I wouldn't be beat by him, and put him into a fire, and keep it burning hot, and go off and leave him all alone, so that I could not hear him scream ; or, what is worse, hear his first cry for mercy. I should only be so glad to attend to it, that I would not risk myself out of whispering hearing distance, lest his penitential tear escape my notice. No, I wouldn't do so, for I couldn't, because I should pity him so much. And I believe that God pities more than I do.

And this isn't the worst of it. He never gives them any chance to repent, or holds out the least hope of forgiveness to them, if they do, because they didn't repent before he began to punish them! Just as if punishment was not meant for their good, instead of being, as the Calvinists tell us, to show them his great power over them.

I should think, if my father couldn't show me how great he was in any better way than that, I should not be likely to care very much for him, or his professed love for me or my welfare.

I should feel like cursing and damning him, as our maniacs, here, do; and I can't blame them for it, for they only speak out what I should feel. And I don't see how speaking out a thing is so much worse than thinking or feeling out a thing, only these Calvinists make such a fuss about cursing and swearing, as if it was such a terrible thing.

But I go in for the swearer. In my opinion, he is not so great a sinner, in God's sight, as the priest is who slanders God so much that he can't help damning him to the lowest hell—that is, the Calvinist's God. He is such a fiend, I think 'tis none too good for him, and I would go in for keeping him in the hell he had prepared for his children, as the maniac does, who only speaks out his honest feelings, in view of this detestable being whom the Calvinists call—God!

The maniacs don't pretend to love a being they can't love if they would, and wouldn't if they could, as the Calvinists do! I have not so great a dread of the Calvinistic God, as I have of the Calvinist's God-maker. I had rather risk my chance of mercy in his hands, than in the hands of his creator.

How absurd to think of his keeping a child in an endless

torment asylum for life. But this is not so bad as his maker does, to keep his wife there.

I'm pretty sure all the patrons of the institution are Calvinists. No Christian could, or would, put a friend into a place like this, to be tormented. If he ever bore the Christian mark, this act must obliterate it, entirely. Satan knew what he was about, when he got up this asylum business. He understands how and where to manufacture devils, and he does " right smart " business at it, here, in this mint.

It's my opinion, unless some dauntless spirit exposes the real, true character of our Calvinistic clergy, before long, the devil will find the market glutted with his coin—supernumerary devils!

However, I've heard it said that the worst devils were once the best saints; so, perhaps this machinery may react, and turn out saints, yet, instead of all devils—or, rather, turn devils into saints. I do go in for the principle that all the devils will be redeemed, and restored to allegiance to the " King of kings and the Lord of lords." For, if they are not, we have an omnipotent devil, as well as an omnipotent God.

But I say, God is omnipotent, and the devil is his subject; and all God's subjects are to be in subjection to his authority, and are to be ruled with love. And, since death and hell are to be destroyed, there is to be no place left for punishing, and of course there is to be a time when there will be none to punish—not even one devil!

It is already ascertained that the sweetest wine makes the sourest vinegar; and since progress is the law of the day, perhaps we shall yet find out that the sourest things can be made into the sweetest. I have some such latent hope; and on it I am building my castle—the most splendid castle you ever saw! that of seeing Dr. McFarland turned back into a true man, again. The Beelzebub may yet be the ——!

But, George, since my Calvinistic or devilish husband has put me under this important personage, is it not best for me to " hope all things," and " endure all things," with such a hope to sustain me?

Who knows but that I shall find another husband yet, perhaps in the very hell he put me in to get rid of me himself? Dr. McFarland has begun to make love to me already; you see he grants me one honorable token,—the right of self-defence; and perhaps he will find that I can defend myself, and him, too, yet! And, you know, there is no knowing where one will end, when they begin right! And such honorable tokens to a true woman! They who learn the alpha are apt to learn the omega!

God has made a promise to forsaken children, but I cannot find any to the forsaken wife. I guess he did not think, when he wrote the Bible, how bad a man could become. I do not believe it could ever have entered his loving heart that a man would ever forsake his wife, and, what is worse yet, imprison her where she could not defend herself, or protect or defend her own offspring.

Never mind, God knows what he is about. Calvin thinks his sagacity will carry him safely through the breakers he has got himself into; but I think God holds the scales, and that justice is a more potent principle than sagacity. Therefore I am not concerned if there are not any promises to the forsaken wife: there is a God who can make some, and who can keep them, too.

I have unbounded faith in the nobleness of manhood, and God is so much like them, or rather, so much more like them, that I can trust him, and not fear, " though the earth be removed, and the heavens pass away with a great noise." I believe it is only to get rid of the Calvinism, so that a " new heaven and a new earth " can be established, wherein righteousness, not wickedness, shall reign.

And I must bear my share of the trouble in this moving business,—and moving always comes pretty hard on the women's temper. But since fretting always makes things worse, rather than better, I think it is best to keep pretty quiet, till we get settled in our new home ; and then we can talk and laugh over our annoyances, and make fun over them, and so harm nobody. It is strange how things do get mislaid in moving! It does seem as though there must be robbers about sometimes,—that is, before we find them.

Even in this asylum, where the machinery is so much like clock-work, things do get lost sometimes. There seems to be some devil haunting about my papers and stationery, so that I am obliged to keep a sharp lookout to hold on to them ! But notwithstanding all my care, I have been robbed several times, and once I lost my whole book into the bargain ! But either God, or I, or somebody else, sent a justice after the robber, and he had to fork over !

However, the master-mason is allowed pretty free use of his workman's tools,—rather too much liberty, I sometimes think. But, never mind, if he will only destroy the asylum, it matters little to me how he does it. Either way that suits him best, suits me best ; only be sure the work is done up thorough. I go in for completeness in destruction, as well as in construction. Still, I do prefer he would save himself.

But, when asylums, prisons, slavery, government, and all, are destroyed at once, *en masse*, it does make a great smash-up. This moving of the heavens and earth at the same time, does turn things quite upside down. And if it does not turn our tempers into acidity before we get through, it will not be the fault of circumstances.

But let us, sister angels, try to be as patient as possible during this moving-time, hoping that all our troubles will be left with the old homestead, and all our joys removed with us to the new one. I guess if we are very patient, our husbands will let us have servants there (freed slaves!), and then our nerves will be stronger, and we can be more merry companions for our husbands, and be more patient with the children.

When the old Calvinistic carcass is snugly buried out of sight and hearing, then, perhaps our christian government will make some women's rights laws, so that we need not do so much work, and be subjected to so many annoyances as we have been. Perhaps they will divide our cares and multiply our joys, by requiring of us only what God does,—the bearing of the children, while the men bear the toil.

You know, brother, that these Calvinistic men have let us bear both: generous, kind-hearted, unselfish souls! But a little too much of a good thing is no great favor, after all. At least, I do not feel so much like thanking them for it, after I get all I want, or know what to do with.

But the truth is, my husband is not one of these generous givers in respect to children; he was afraid we couldn't afford it. Our salary, you know, was small; never over six hundred a year, and for many of our first years of married life, only three hundred and seventy-five. But I used to tell him we could " trust Providence and keep the powder dry, too ; " for I was so strong and healthy I could take care of more children, and educate them besides, even fit them for college, with no extra help. My uninterrupted health, and constant flow of cheerful good nature, did capacitate me for such responsibilities, without increasing his burdens too much either.

But, no ; he held the purse, and he knew best how to calculate upon its depth. So I had nothing to do but to yield. Wasn't it a fortunate thing, that I was not of the obstinate sort, for what could I have done in such a case, had I been mad about it ?

I used to think in my own mind, but I didn't dare to

breathe such a thing to him, that I should like to leave twelve sons to become patriarchs on earth, after I left it, and one "tamer,"—a sister. You know how boys always need a tamer. Indeed, I considered myself very fortunate to get five sons and one tamer.

The fact is, I couldn't suit him anyway in the world, and, if I do say it, I speak the truth, for I will not tell lies about myself, any more than anybody else. I have been as good a wife to him as ever a man had, and he didn't even know it! And you can't make him believe it, either. He will have his own way of thinking, and so will I have mine ; and that is, I'll not trouble him any more, in this body, but let him have things his own way, now.

I wonder how he likes his bachelor-hall life! It's my opinion his home don't look quite so cozy as it did when Elizabeth was at her post ; neither do I think he always finds the nicest and most delicate food on his table now, that he found on any table, as he used often to tell me he did, when he came home from exchanges. He likes good food, and he likes to see a clean house, and he had both when I was his housekeeper.

Brother George, there is one thing more I should like to inquire into a little. Do Christian husbands look daggers at their wives, up there, when they speak something they do not like to have them say before others, or, do they cast love darts from their eyes, when they summon up courage to speak out above a whisper ?

I am very curious to know how it is, for I have a great horror of those daggers. They make such a sore place in my heart, that it don't get well for a long time. My Isaac tells me not to notice them. He says, " Pa only opens his eyes at you, that's all ! Eyes can't hurt you. He looks at me with his eyes wide open, sometimes, and I don't mind it. I just keep right on talking just the same. His eyes don't hurt *me !* "

But Isaac is a boy—he don't know the hazard the wife runs to keep right on talking. He don't know, nor think, what is to come of it, if she does, when he gets his study gown on, alone with her! He don't know how the insane asylum switch hurts, for he has never been in one, as I have. He don't know what a dreadful place it is, and I hope and pray he never will, for I expect before he gets a wife to cast him into one of them to get rid of him herself, that our humane President will have put this outlay of public treasure to a better use than it is at present—as an American inquisition.

But the trouble is, he is so tremendous slow about doing things, especially when he has to step out of the old tracks to do it.

But, come to think of it, it is those clay feet that bother him so much. I sometimes think he might as well have no feet at all, as to have such as cannot be used to walk into reform movements with. He needn't be so careful of his toes! if he should chance to hit a pebble-stone and break one of them off, there is no great harm done; for since he lives in a progressive age, he could, with the means which his golden head furnishes him, get one put on again; and if he employs the best kind of artisan, as he can well afford to do, he may get one as natural as life.

You know we can get eyes and noses and teeth to look as well and even better than the original; and I don't think he need to think so much about his feet, and with shoes and stockings on, who would know or care whether he had five toes or even three toes?

It might make him lame for awhile. But what of that? Lame men do great business, sometimes; especially when they have a great head for the feet to serve, like Senator Morton of Indiana.

And, besides, our people would gladly make him a present

of an elegant cane to walk with, while he is lame. They are even eager for a chance to show their loyalty to him, by aiding him in his progressive movements. But they don't like to urge him forward. They had much rather he would be self-moved and voluntary, and then he would not be so likely to run back in his traces again.*

But I don't think there is so much danger of the retrograde movement, as there is of his not running the risk of this exposure. He is too afraid to move at all.

This "stand-still policy," I think, General McClellan has played out pretty well. We don't call for a repetition of that movement again. I guess the President, himself, begins to see that this "stand-still policy" don't pay now-a-days.

However, he has got long legs, they say, and you know such folks get over the ground very fast when you once get them started. They seem to, somehow, get on very rapidly, without seeming to make much fuss about it, either. That is, I mean, they don't seem to get tired out so soon as Van Burenites do. I go in for tall men, even if I do have to look up to them.

But we, short women, can do something at the pedestrian line, even without a man's arm to lean upon. We lean on Jesus and go ahead. We ain't so bothered about what others will think of us while we can see Jesus smile upon us and our movements. Even the appreciation of this one man satisfies my approbativeness for the present, that is, till I get my work done, which he told me to do. If I suit him well, and he praises me, I think others will, too, after awhile. But now I must work and wait.

The labor and the wages don't always come together. Some pay-masters don't pay up until the work is all done. But some give an earnest when they think it is needed to stimulate the laborer to greater efforts.

---

* This was written while the people were calling for the emancipation of the slaves.

Still, I don't believe but that he likes to employ those best who don't think so much about the pay all the time they are at work. I guess he can be trusted to attend to his own business without my prompting and dunning him. At least, I, for one, am going to risk it, and you'll see how I come out. I ain't afraid of coming out at the "little end of the horn," either.

You see if anybody else ever puts me into an insane asylum again! that is, if Lincoln ever gives them a chance to do so, by taking me out of this, for speaking my opinions. Jesus told me to do so, and I have dared to do it; and you see I don't go round a thing for fear of touching it, either.

But the truth is, I have been schooled into these things. I have had to get possession of my free territory by storm and conquest; and you know, Washington, that what has cost us a great deal to obtain is very dear to us, and all the more precious for the pains it has cost us to obtain it. The insane asylum bugbear has now been met, and if I haven't conquered him, it ain't because I haven't tried to floor him! My fear of this animal is not of a very reverential kind; that is, I shall think what I please and speak what I please and write what I please in spite of all the insane asylums in America; and if God don't make use of me as an instrument for their destruction, it won't be because I haven't asked him to do so, or coveted this honor,—I mean the honor shall be due me, whether I get it or not.

Honor isn't what I'm after, though,—'tis the destruction of Calvinism and all its legion train of insanities. The honor of being the devil's deadly foe is enough to satisfy my present ambitious aspirings.

I'm pretty sure I've secured a liberal share of contempt already from the Calvinists. I ain't very popular among the devils, at least!

But these daggers, George! I have digressed again from

6

my subject. I don't know as you can understand what I mean; for I don't think Martha threw daggers at you from her eyes. I guess she was proud of you when you spoke, and looked her approbation from her pure eyes. Therefore, for want of experience on your part, I must be a little more definite, to make you understand my meaning. A verbal description of the form and use of this spiritual weapon may therefore be necessary.

They are horrid things! I assure you, to throw at women; and the fact is, they are always followed with gold or silver ones, if not, in some cases, with the coarse, rough, broad-axe. But thanks to the selfishness of human nature generally, men don't like to kill their wives in cold blood often, for fear of the halter about their own necks. If it wasn't for this, how many precious lives might be sacrificed prematurely!

But it is not so great a mercy to us, after all, as you may imagine it to be. For my part, I had much rather be killed outright than be twenty-one years about it—dying by inches.

Calvin is a god compared with those Calvinistic husbands, for he was not many days roasting Servetus; and these husbands are all their lifetime at it on their wives. If one fire can't be kept constantly burning, they know how to light secret fires, so that they are indefatigably at it.

My husband was always fond of having his meat well cooked, and his pies well baked. He liked to see the lovely brown on the piecrust and the turkey, although my fancy was for rare beef and delicate-looking piecrust. But, by conforming to his tastes in these matters, as I always tried to do, since I prefer others' pleasure to my own, I got to like it better than my own, after all. Yes, if you visit me at your new country up there, I can tell you I won't set unbaked piecrust before you, nor a white turkey for you to eat.

So you see we can suck some honey out of even a wasp, if

we only let them have their own way, and not interfere with their wishes, or propensities for freedom,—entire, unlimited freedom.

Oh! how I do wish they didn't have so much liberty to torture their poor, defenseless, helpless wives, so much! This life-long martyrdom is too long, by half, at least. I don't wish to turn the tables and torture them the other half; but I do want to get rid of my tormentor, without losing my children, and home, into the bargain.

Brother George, don't you think Christ will protect the rights of married women when he comes? Will he let these devils rule spiritual women as our laws do? If he does, his practice must contradict his preaching. I do say, George, that there is no class of human beings on earth who are so much in need of governmental protection, and no class who have so little protection, by the government, as the wives of Calvinists.

They are often roasted even brown by their protectors! No, persecutors!

I know it is so; for I have myself been cooked through and through by one; and yet, because I had so much fortitude as not to scream out for help, no one seems to think I need help. But God has helped me get out of his hands, and now I intend to help other sufferers out of their tortures, without going through this hell either, as I have had to. This asylum has its altar always smoking with the living sacrifices of American wives and mothers. God grant that mine may be its last victim!

Freedom! Yes, our husbands have it all, and we wives have none at all, except freedom to suffer for our husbands' sins.

It is said that Christ suffered for the sins of the whole world; but he was not a wife, so he couldn't have suffered for these devils' sins. He left spiritual women to redeem the devils, by enduring the punishment of their sins in their own sensitive bodies, I guess. A perverted man *is* a personified devil, and Christ has not told us that he came to redeem devils, but men. Therefore, if these devils are redeemed, somebody must be their redeemer.

Haven't I got the argument, George? Doesn't Christ redeem men, and women redeem devils?

But I do wish these devils only knew that freedom was as dear to their wives as it is to them. But somehow they don't seem to think of it as we do. We often think, " Do to others as you would wish to be done by." I only wish they would. But it won't do to tell them so; we should be dictating to them; and this, you know, or rather *I* know, is an almost unpardonable sin in their eyes.

If we quote Scripture, we must be very careful to let them put their own construction or interpretation upon it, for they must have all the freedom. We may be free, too, if we only will think just as suits them, and be free to lose our identity *in theirs!*

We may echo their interpretations of Holy Writ to the children as much as we like, but woe be to us if we utter our own, if it differs from theirs!

If the devil happens to be a minister, look out! Ministers ought to know, for they have been to the theological seminary! But I don't think much of these Calvinistic seminaries neither. I think they do more harm than good. It makes the priest feel so bigoted to be able to bring up President Woods for his authority. Now I don't think President Woods knows any better than I do, what the Bible means, and I don't feel willing to yield my private opinion to one of these theological professors, or even the doctor himself. I am rather self-conceited on this point, I must acknowledge. I do think my conscience and my opinion are of more importance to me and my practice than Dr. Woods' are to me. I don't say it is more important to him, but to me. Neither do I say that my opinions are of so much consequence to him as his are.

I haven't to look out for his opinions, only my own ; and I am glad of it. What a bother it would be to have to think for other people. It is as much as I can do to have to think for myself, especially when I have such a hard time to do that. I own up, my benevolence doesn't stretch so far as that, in that direction. I will work for anybody, but I can't afford to think for them.

Thinking for myself is my own exclusive privilege. God did not tell me to do others' thinking for them ; only do my own, and he would clear me as a loyal citizen. I trust I shall stand muster there. I wasn't made to be an idle dreamer, I *think*.

Neither do I carry on my thinking business altogether on borrowed capital, I assure you. I borrow some, but I am sure to pay well for it. I return back principal and interest both, and am not slow about it either. I hate to be dunned, so I forestall it by not giving my creditors a chance. But, mind you, I think only for myself. I don't lend my thinking apparatus either. Although husband used to find a good deal of fault with me for being so accommodating to my neighbors in that line—I mean the line of natural things—not spiritual.

But these daggers ? Don't you think my ideality must have become considerably excited by my running off from the main track so often ? But you know "switches" are of some use on the main.

Nothing in vain—only these daggers ! I think they are worse than useless. If the whole armory of Calvinistic weapons were destroyed, I don't think it would be any loss to the world worth putting on black for. I should feel more like putting on pink than black, should the dagger-user be buried with them.

Now I do not think it is so bad a wish, to wish a man

dead, after all; still, I would not try to make him die; that is God's work, not mine, nor anybody else's work, but God's own exclusive right,—the right to take the life which he alone gave. And do we not pray every day for God to kill men,—the secessionists,—by "God prosper our armies"? And now these men never harmed us in particular, and they are not in the way of our particular line of business.

But it is not so with me. I want to get married again! and so do my children need a good father, for my oldest son is now almost twenty-one, and he has not had that article yet. And I hope, if one would marry me, he would love me well enough to be good to my children. I would be good to his if he had any, and set him the example.

And now, what is the harm of wishing a bad man dead, when he has lost his good name, and is seen in his own drapery,—not borrowed drapery from his wife's wardrobe,—and lost his influence and respect by his own vile conduct, and sees nothing but disgrace and scorn before him in this life?

Now, I really think it is a benevolent wish to have such a dead* man buried out of sight, at least long enough to get a better body, and try his chances again at life. I do not fear meeting him up where you are, when I go; or not, at least, till after I have got another husband! Then I will risk his daggers!

The lion-hearted man I mean to get next time will make him stand off, if he claims me as his again. And I shall look out about my saying "Yes," if he asks me for my company. I will tell him I have got other fish to fry,—I have fried his fish long enough for him, and got no thanks for it, but instead,—a prison,—for my good, kind, forgiving behavior to him.

Yes, now, after he has robbed me of everything I ever

---

* Dead in trespasses and sin.

had, and imprisoned me, he comes and asks me if I want my clothes and children! It is provoking! If I ever got mad, I should feel like blowing out to him. But I do not get mad; it does not pay. But I hate evil like the dragon, mind you. It is the Calvinism I hate, not the men or women who are Calvinists; and neither he nor anybody else can make me love it. The more practical Calvinism I see personified in one person, the more I hate it,—not the human who is thus possessed with this hateful demon.

And I manifest my indignation also,—but in a lady-like manner. If I did not show it, I might as well love sin and oppression, so far as I or anybody else is concerned.

I tell you, Mrs. Packard is no hypocrite. She has seen enough of this trash in her husband. I do not like to be an imitator, or an automaton, at all. I like original simplicity, purity, openness, and candor.

Yes, I candidly say, that, instead of thanking my husband for his offered, robbed treasures, of my own, as he seems to expect I will, I feel like saying, " Yes, I do want my things; but this is not the way thieves and robbers are to restore them, when I am their victim! No, they must be treated as thieves and robbers deserve to be treated, with justice." Let the highway-robber turn and ask his spoiled victim if he wants his watch, money, and treasures, and will thank him, as his benefactor, for restoring them! is he not adding insult to abuse? Calvinistic benefactions! Calvinistic obligations!

Now, I ask, Brother George, if in a firm where equal rights and privileges are the conditions of joint capital, and one of the partners usurps all the capital, rights, and privileges, and all, what is the ousted partner to do? Is he to beg, cringe, pray, and thank, for all the use he does make of his capital? or is he to claim justice, or a dissolution of the firm?

Let your and my instinctive sense of right and justice, in our God-given natures, reply.

Neither can a wife maintain her self-respect, and yield to such despotism. And must she do it or become an outcast from society, from home, from all that makes life desirable, because the government will not defend a single inalienable right of her God-given nature?

Yes, she must do it, and run the risk of being cast off into an insane asylum, among the filth and offscouring of all things, with no judge or jury in her defense, and all on the simple testimony of her usurper, as I have been!

Now, shall I acknowledge all these usurped claims as legal, and on this ground, return as a legal wife to this unrepentant usurper? Nay, verily, I will do no such thing! I have yielded to this rule of hell, to this Beelzebub whom government protects, for the last time. On the law of my nature, on the law of God, I take my immovable stand of resistance. If our government will not protect spiritual woman in her rights, may they not be protected in their rights!

Fowler says my self-esteem is too small; and I think God thought it had been crushed long enough; so he took measures to increase it, by putting me where I must defend myself, or go undefended. And small as this bump is, it is too large for me to do the mean, contemptible act of being put off twice by the same man, or devil, by giving him an opportunity to do so.

You won't see Mrs. Packard asking, or consenting to let the Rev. Mr. Packard be the protector of her identity again! " No, sir! I can protect myself—thank you—your services are a gratuity, entirely. I have a body of my own, and a head of my own, and a heart of my own, and a will of my own, and I do not consent to share this capital with you again." No school-like experience. A burnt child dreads the fire, if he is not a fool. And I am not a fool, mind you.

You will find I have sense enough to keep out of the fire, and old Packard's hands, too.

And, George, I do say it is an axiom, for I have proved it out, that a man who breaks his marriage vow—to protect his wife's identity—and does not do it, but tries to annihilate it, has no longer any claim upon the woman, as his wife. And I say further, that she has an inalienable right to leave him and seek another protector. Such a husband is, in reality, "dead" to the wife, as her husband, for the protection she sought, and he promised, is not only withdrawn, but he has become her persecutor, and the law of self-defense forbids us to lie passive in the hands of any persecutor. We not only have a right to escape them, if we can; but it is our duty to do so; for our happiness is as dear to God, as that of any other being.

I tell you, George, I won't bear from another man anything like what I have borne from Packard; I will take up with the advice his sister Marian Severance gave me fifteen years ago, viz.: "Sister Elizabeth, before I would bear what you do from brother, I would leave him, if I had to walk the streets and hang my clothes on the trees!"

Yes, Marian, I would *now*. The fortitude of bearing the persecution of a despotic husband is expended. I then feared the "speech of people;" I now fear God, more. I am now the Lord's freeman—or free-woman, rather—free to obey God, and keep his commandments. No man, or devil, shall ever put me off a second time.

And, I say moreover, a man who will put his wife into an insane asylum to be taken care of, instead of taking care of her himself, ought never to be allowed, by law, to have a wife afterwards. I say, let the wife be sane or insane, he is a wretch that will do it. If she is sane, as Packard's wife is, and always was, he has no right to treat her so—and if she is insane he certainly has no right to; for she then, more

6*

than in any other state, needs the protection and care of him, who has vowed before God never to leave or forsake her.

Oh, husband! forsake your wife! If you will do such a devilish deed, oh, leave her somewhere, yea, anywhere, rather than in an insane asylum!

My husband will be sure to rue the deed—you'll see if he don't, and so will every other perjured man, or devil. Our Father is such a good man, he won't let his daughters be so trampled upon by their brothers, without punishing them for it. I do say, if ever a man deserved to be punished severely, my husband does. And I do hope and pray he will get his deserts, for I don't think anything else will break up his iron will. I don't think this mulish man will, or can, be better, until he gets a better body—for the "Ethiopian cannot change his skin, nor the leopard his spots," without first dying; and then he must change his species to lose them.

But nature has strange freaks doing her work. But let her have her own way, for she is on the right track, and will bring about the right results, at last; but like McClellan, wants her own time to do it in.

And I, for one, have more confidence in her results coming out right, than in McClellan's—although so great an engineer. And I am not afraid to speak my own opinion of him, nor any other great man. But you must take these opinions as you do the other things I say,—as opinions merely, not truth,—until they appear so to your own mind.

If you do take them as truths, I tell you, you may be called upon to defend them; and you know I don't lend my thinking machinery to anybody; and perhaps you will run against a stump before you know it. I can assure you I have found plenty of them in my track. But what is a stump to an invincible purpose! I shall leave you to dig up your own stumps, as I have done before you; and you can do it; for what has been done can be done again. You must recollect

I told you in my introduction, I was not going to give you my reasons for my opinions in this book—but that I had good and sound reasons for all the opinions I advanced, and could give them, if called for.

But it is best for you to get your knowledge by tugging for it, as I have done. I can assure you, it is no easy business to explore unknown regions, where I have been. I can't afford to give you anything but the results of my own observation. If you cannot take my word for it, you may go and see for yourselves, as Kane did the Arctic regions.

But my daggers! I lose them so often. I believe I left them behind with their owner, or inventor, perhaps. I don't know whether this is an original invention of the old serpent, or whether they are borrowed from Calvin. Neither do I care. It makes no difference; they are so much alike, you can hardly tell them apart.

In the first place, the points are very blunt—they hurt dreadfully, going into the heart, and when they come out, they always leave an awful sore—such a big hole! But the time and manner of using them shows the greatest sagacity. It would generally be in company, in some public place, and just when I thought I was saying something worth saying. There was not much danger with small talk—such as about the weather, or the health of the community, or even the gossip of the day. I was pretty safe here, but I had to look out pretty sharp for the " switches," and shun them—or I might say something that would hit somebody present. Calvin has good ears as well as eyes.

But I guess I shall have to illustrate my meaning by example. This is the way to teach novices, like yourself, brother:

One evening, as we were visiting at Mr. Spring's, of Manteno, an elder—and a ruling one too—in the Presbyterian church, and brother to Rev. Gardiner Spring of New York city, in company with quite a room-full of others, I chanced to speak of, or allude to, the principle of slavery, in one of my "switches," thinking I was all safe; for Mr. Spring is such a good man, so kind and sensible, I, of course, took him for a Christian!

And I think you would too; he seemed and talked so much like one. But I won't tell you how he acted towards me, afterwards; or you will think I am easily taken in by appearances. Husband says I am, and I think he is right, there, for I do expect others to be as honest, simple, and true-hearted as I am myself. I don't think, when I see the long phylactery, but that it is a true sign of loyalty to Jesus. But experience has led me to find that my husband was nearer right, on this point, than I was. He used to insist upon it that *all* were totally depraved. I was inclined to doubt it, until he and his church gave me unmistakable proof that some were—well nigh a demonstration!

However, I don't believe anybody is totally depraved, except my husband; and I know he is, if anybody is in God's universe. And out of his own mouth, often, proceeded his own condemnation. He either had got into such a habit of lying unto God, in the form of confession, or he must be a desperate transgressor. I really used to think, sometimes, he was too hard upon himself. If I believed all the terrible stories he used to tell God about his secret practices of wickedness, I should hardly have dared to stay alone with him. But I knew him so well to be a liar, that it was nothing more than what I might expect, that he would tell God lies, also! He used to tell God awful lies about the wicked hearts I and my children had, but I knew God didn't believe his representations of us, because they were false; and, therefore, I didn't trouble myself much about them.

I used sometimes to tell him that if he was half as bad as he told God he was, he was not fit to be a minister. His first work was to repent himself, before he urged others to do so.

But my story. Well, I was talking, on what I supposed was safe ground, against the sin of oppression, etc., when I chanced to get a tremendous dagger, all at once. This set me to considering what I had been, or was, saying, but since I had had the caution to speak in the name of the great Rev. H. W. Beecher—not my own name—I could not, for the world, see what was wrong. I thought Beecher might speak anywhere! But no. I saw I had lost my soundings, and was in a dangerous position, from some cause—I could not imagine what. And I knew I must take in sail, or there would be breakers to meet, ahead. So I just sailed off as best I could.

I have a faculty of being able to say something, if 'taint nothing! So I got through, as I thought, safe and sound.

But, alas! the unlucky remark! It caused me trouble when the Sunday-coat was exchanged for the study-gown. Oh! how I dread these after-claps when we get home!

"Didn't you know, wife, that Mr. Spring is a pro-slavery man, and that it would not do to allude to the subject before him?"

"No," said I; "indeed I did not. I thought such a good man must be an abolitionist, of course, although when he made the remark about John Brown being a crazy man, I began to suspect it then; and when I caught your look, I thought it meant to have me stop; and so I did, didn't I?"

"Yes; I was glad you did not pursue it any further, for you know he pays twenty-five dollars to our salary, and Mrs. Dixon brings us many presents, and I thought it best to 'be wise.' We are directed, you know, to be 'wise as serpents.' "

I wanted to add, "and harmless as doves," but I knew that would be ill-timed. But that was not long before I came here, and I had begun to be bold, a little, then ; so I said :

"I think to be 'wise as serpents' means we must be wise to do good, benevolently,—not to do evil, selfishly. And now I think it is not being loyal to Jesus, to be ashamed of his cause before anybody, under any circumstances. The oppressed ought always to find in us a fearless friend, always ready to defend an unpopular cause before the enemies of Christ : and I think if Mr. Spring is not right, it is your duty to try to enlighten him, and thus set him right, and run the risk of your salary. Besides, I think he would respect you all the more, to see you true to your principles everywhere. I should not want to have him suspect that you were afraid of him. This lack of moral courage gives him ground for suspecting your sincerity as an anti-slavery man."

"Well," said he, "I think it would do no sort of good to him, and it might alienate him, and we lose some of his support ; and I have the family to provide for, and it is my business to do it. I think things would go by the board very quick if you had the rule here. I intend to rule my people as well as my family, too, and if you don't look to it, and do as Mrs. Comstock and Mrs. La Bree do, I shall put you into the asylum !"

"Well, I am not Mrs. Comstock nor Mrs. La Bree, and I must be Mrs. Packard, if you do put me into the insane asylum for it."

Well, I can't do impossibilities, even to please my husband ; and God knows a wife never tried harder than I have to do it. I have often said I cared more to please my husband so he could trust and love me, than for the good will of the whole fraternity.

But it is all labor lost! and it is a pity to lose so much, for I am a worker, I can assure you. I don't pretend to do, and not do it. Lost labor! No, that is not right ; nothing is lost, since God oversees things. But, you know, we say a thing is lost if we can't find it. But that's no sign somebody else won't find it; and it might do them as much good as it would us, and so I won't worry about my loss, hoping some one will be bettered by finding the lost article.

Who knows but that the President will find it and advertise it, and then I might find it, and get it again also! I do think our President is an honest man, and he won't claim lost things until he has tried to find their owner.

Perhaps President Lincoln will issue a decree of emancipation to married slaves when he finds it, and then I shall rush to Washington to thank him for finding the lost article, and for returning it too!

Brother Abraham, let me give you a gentle hint, for I don't think you need a strong one to make you do right. I don't like this " colonization " scheme at all, for I have tried it! I don't like to be colonized into " Central America," because it is not home to me here. Still I own up, it is not so bad to be a prisoner among lunatics as it is to be a slave. Yet I don't like either situation.

It is freedom that I am after—and yet I don't want to jump out of the frying-pan to get it. I had rather be free at home, without having my husband domineering over me so much. When I was a young lady I didn't mind it so much, for then I supposed my husband, being fifteen years my senior, of course, knew more than I did, and his will was a better guide for me than my own. But now, since I have outgrown him,— for he has been a drone, and I a worker,—I don't like his superintendence, or rather interference. I have got a mind of my own, now, and a will too, and I will think and act as I please—for I please to think and act right. He is not my oracle, nor standard either, now; God is both to me now, and his will—not my wicked husband's—is my choice and pleasure. If my husband's will coincided with right, truth, and justice, I could serve both wills at the same time. But since they are diametrically opposed, the one to the other, it is a moral impossibility to obey both. Therefore, since they conflict, I choose "to obey God rather than man."

Now, Brother George, if you were the President, you would stop this business of lording it over a wife's conscience under the insane laws of our government, wouldn't you?

I do feel so indignant that this professed Christian government won't afford a shadow of protection to the rights of conscience to the very best part of its subjects—married women—that I can hardly offer my five sons to die for it, without grudging the sacrifice!

What's the use of fighting to support a government that won't protect the wives and mothers of the soldiers?

If, after all our indefatigable training to make our sons loyal and patriotic, we are allowed only the rights of slaves to despots, what have we to sustain us in our self-denying toil and efforts to train our daughters, while subject to such liabilities?

True, all men are not Calvinists, but all are liable to become so. 'Tis against these *liabilities* that we want our government to protect our daughters. Supposing the spiritual or millennial age should overtake us, with our insane laws and our Calvinistic government, what would be the fate of spiritual woman, the ready recipient of spiritual knowledge and spiritual gifts? The Calvinism of our laws would render them all *liable* to be immured within the horrid prison-walls of our insane asylums! I shudder at the prospect of this arrival of spiritual illumination while the American government stands on its present basis. God grant that I and my lovely daughter, Elizabeth, may never live to see that day! The martyrdom I have already suffered for the gift of wisdom and knowledge which God has imparted to me, above that of many of my contemporaries, is so keenly painful to my spiritual, sensitive nature, that my heart sickens at the thought of my daughter, or any other daughter, experiencing like torture.

Oh, America! you do sustain a persecuting government! Is Christianity shielded by your sheltering arm?

Nay, verily, it is not! The wail of our insane asylums testifies against you. And so does the persecuted Christ, so often entombed there, witness against you. Down with these inquisitions! Down with the worshipers of Baal! Let Christ reign. Let Calvin be beheaded.

Behead Calvin? I thought you, Mrs. Packard, didn't go in for taking life. You said that was God's exclusive right.

Yes, but I want evil beheaded! That evil power which domineers over spiritual woman is what I want cut off or destroyed. That is all I want you to do. Remember, I can take care of myself. I ain't a baby! I'm a full-grown, strong, healthy woman, and know as much as two male Calvinists put together! and I tell you I can take care of myself. And more than that, I can take care of my children, too, better than half of the Calvinists can; and I can cast interest, too, and even correct Dr. McFarland's mistakes in that rule, for I have done it here. So I can take care of my money, too,—if I can get any to take care of. I can take care of my housework, too, and direct my own servants. I didn't marry a man to train me. My parents trained me long before I consented to identify our mutual interests.

If I hadn't thought he considered me competent to be his wife, I would not have consented to his proposal. I made no bargain to be his slave. I consented to be his companion, or helpmeet, but not an underling, to be trained into an automaton. I have a personal identity of my own—an individuality of my own, and all the Packards and McFarlands combined can't destroy or annihilate it!

But Packard is such an inveterate Calvinist, there is no

such thing as setting him right on these points. His wife must be subjected or she must be sent to Central America—the insane asylum—and I won't go back to be his slave again if he lives to the age of Methuselah!

Brother George, I think Lincoln is just about as wrong in his "Central America" project as my husband is in his asylum business. Packard is obliged to look after me here, or rather get the State to, when I can take better care of myself than the State does—a great deal; and Lincoln would have to look after his slave colony there, when they could take care of themselves alone at home, if they were only free. I say charity begins at home, but it mustn't stop there.

Besides, we want our slaves for servants at home. I tell you I don't think my husband would be in favor of colonizing again. I guess he has wished, before this time, that he had his kind, faithful slave back again, to polish his stoves and mend his stockings and make his study-gowns, and take care of the baby, especially nights, when it is sick and cross so as to disturb him. I guess he finds by this time that slaves ain't the worst sort of people in the world yet, especially such slaves as Packard had!

I know some people dislike slaves on account of their color and odor; and there is an odor about some people that is very disagreeable, I acknowledge. Yet the odor which Calvinists so very much dislike is very agreeable to me—the odor of Christianity. I don't like the Calvinistic smell at all. What an unfortunate proximity to have a black and white union! I don't go in for amalgamation, I assure you, and I guess no one would after one fair trial. But since the wearing of masks and artificials has become so common, one has to be very discerning to discover the fictitious from the real down here.

I as really supposed I had married a white man, when I

married the Rev. Theophilus Packard, as I supposed a Calvinist could be a Christian.

But it was not a month before I discovered the black odor! and then, as our laws now are, it was just one month too late for the discovery to be of any practical utility to me or my descendants. I do say, it is a hard case for the believing wife, when she is legally tied to an inveterate Calvinist.

Can't our government so fix it, that she can be as easily untied as she is tied? I am sure our compassionate God wouldn't object to such an enactment, especially if he had once been so tied to a Calvinist himself!

I do go in for freedom—and if a man won't let his wife be as free after she is married as she was before, at least, she has an inalienable right to take her freedom without buying it even. I expected I should be all the more free to do right, by getting a protector to defend my womanly rights, until I found out his unmanly or devilish character. Indeed, that is what I wanted a man for—to defend and protect me, in serving his interests. But I have defended and served him both, while he has been, constantly, bent on my destruction. And he has put up with a share of my Christianity, for the sake of the advantage to himself.

We women know how to work through the ugly weapon of selfishness, if we can't work with anything else, and I would have served his interests until death, had he not put me off for my good behavior. The truth is, the Calvinist wants his wife, and the slave-holder needs his slave, and all parties could be satisfied if all could be free—where they are.

I am sure I should be just as likely to be kind, faithful, and obliging under kind, gentle, loving treatment, as under abusive treatment. And I'm pretty sure the slave would work full as well for cash as for lash.

The slave-holders don't want their slaves sent off to Central America. And the men want their wives, and servants, too, to make home complete. What is a home without a wife! and I think a servant is a good thing too, if we need one. But if you send off the wives and servants to Central America, what will the Calvinistic fraternity do? They want wives as well as Christian men, and I don't go in for robbing any one.

Now, Father Abraham, just apply your conservative feet to their proper use, and not go to smashing up things in this style! Just walk straight into our families, and set things right there; oil up these little wheels, so as to prevent friction there, and you may rest assured the great government wheel will be repaired where repairs are most needed. And when you once get on the right track, I warrant you will walk right into Rebeldom and straighten things up there, also.

We women want our husbands also—for a poor man is better than none at all. And when you whip the Calvinism out of them, we couldn't ask for better men.

I'll tell you a secret. These women-haters, when they get right, make the best sort of men, after all. They have got the grit in them, and if it only takes the right turn, they are just the defenders women want. We don't like gentle-women for husbands near so well as we do gentle-men—strong to protect, as well as love us.

I have the Bible for it, too, as well as for my other hints; but I am in such a hurry to get home to my children, I can't stop to give my Bible reasons or common-sense reasons, either, for my opinions in this volume. I can only just give glances and glimpses in that direction.

The Gentiles had to be cut off from the old wild stock before they could be grafted into the natural olive-tree. And you know that grafts bear the choicest fruit, even superior to the natural fruit. But a good Jew is a first-rate article. The natural fruit will answer my present purpose. it takes so long for grafts to grow!

But God is not in such a tearing hurry as I am about things. My husband used to say there was "no hold back to me—when once in the traces, away I went—and what lay in my way on the track had to be removed, or a smash-up would ensue." I prefer a "cow-catcher" on my engine for safety. I don't like impediments nor "collisions." But I do like safe speed.

I don't like long wars either; I fight it out and done with it, and go to my business. Fighting is not my business. It is only a painful necessity, imposed by circumstances upon me against my will. But I do say, when we must fight, go at it in good earnest, and make a business of it, as we do other things. I believe in thorough fighting as well as thorough cleaning. But neither I nor my husband like the cleaning time. But we both like to be clean. And I, the cleaner, go in for keeping clean. One keep clean, is worth many make cleans.

I guess our government will think so, too, after this. If they don't burn up the Calvinism before they get through, I shall be mistaken. I don't think any will be left to bind into the new government stack with the wheat. And I think it is high time for Lincoln to begin to bind up the little bundles. This assorting time has seemed very long, because 'tis such littering times. He needn't send off his Cabinet, for he can set them at work—there is plenty of the assorted wheat for them to bind up.

But for the gallantry of their noble natures, I might fear that the woman's right question might be put off as a second-class business. But, you know, Christian men are gallant to the ladies, and I don't believe Abraham will employ any more Calvinists to do his business for him; at least, until they have been well grafted into a natural olive-tree.

American citizens must take care of their own business, first; and then they can take care of foreigners. They will naturalize very quickly, when we get rid of the Calvinistic part of our government. As it now is—a splendid inutility! they think it hardly worth fighting for. They want a government that can and will protect them here from Calvinistic intruders.

Never mind! Father Abraham will teach them how this can be done up—you just be patient until he has read my book, and you see if he don't have the woman's right question on the docket in quick time! You will find that the government will protect the rights of your mother as well as your father, after this! But, you know, the men must have their rights before they can have power to protect us.

But they have kept a pretty good lookout for number one, in Congress, so I think it won't take a long time to straighten out the business, before our turn comes. But you see if they forget us, in their reconstruction of things on Christian principles! We mustn't tease him, nor drive him. Men don't like either way.

They are made to rule themselves—not us—and they don't want us to rule them. And I don't want to, either. I have little things enough to attend to, without superintending their business. Besides, you can't drive men—and I shouldn't like a man I could drive. I like those men who know enough to drive their own team.

But some men we can draw, like thunder, with the magnet of love! Cupid's love-darts do great execution in the hands of those who know how to use them skillfully. I think I am pretty expert in the use of this weapon of defense.

For all we want at present is defensive armor. You know the present customs of society forbid our commencing an attack. But we stand ready to repel one we don't like. A man never offered, or tried, to insult me. I believe they respect and love me too well to do such mean things. I hold them at arm's length until I see and know whether they are Christian or Calvinistic men.

A Christian man you needn't fear even to kiss, if you want to! They like to be kissed with the pure lips of charity. Such a kiss don't offend them at all. Besides, Paul kissed the women, or sent kisses in letters to them, and I don't think it hurt him to bestow, or them to receive his kisses. I say kissing has been tainted with Calvinistic prudery.

So, Father Abraham, don't throw them overboard, in your new rules for us, because Calvinism has perverted them. I go for the sorting-out process—keep the good fish, and cast only the bad away—not the whole netfull. I say we have as good a right to draw the honey from promiscuous flowers, as the bee has. But we, like this insect, may leave the poison where God put it. I let the thorns, too, remain unmolested. Thorns won't hurt us if we will let them alone.

Another thing, Father Abraham—don't exclude us from dancing, and going to theaters, with our husbands. They will protect us. 'Tis only the Calvinism that you have to exclude from these amusements, to render them sources of virtue and happiness, and efficient aids to symmetrical development of Christian character. I go in for perfection of graces as well as virtues, and no part of our complex organization was made but for use. And I am sure there cannot be a more refining amusement than a Christian dance. But, mind you, a Christian dance does not trespass on any of Nature's laws. This trespassing is all Calvinistic.

I go for Nature! I approve of no infringement on her sacred laws, under any circumstances. Her laws are as sacred to me as the moral law; for both are Divine codes, and equally binding, so far as we know.

Nature is my best friend—my body-guard—and if I have

to dance when I ought to be in bed, sleeping, I rob her. I can't rob my best friend to please any man, or woman either. I know I am singular, here, but when I come to be plural, you see if my husband don't say I was right! Men like healthy wives, as well as we like healthy children—and we can't have either, unless we take the right means to obtain them. Nature is very arbitrary in her laws. You can't compromise much with her in these things.

And I don't go in for this compromise business, any way. Toe the mark, and risk the consequences of right doing to God's providence! I do think 'tis always safe to do right.

And what if we are ridiculed for it? what hurt does that do us? I have been laughed at for lying in bed one whole day, once a month, when nature called for repose and quiet; but the strong nerves which nature gives me as a compensation for defending her practical rights, enables me to bear this ridicule unharmed—and I am uniformly cheerful and happy—while my tormentors are sad and low-spirited, and discontented. And as Isaac says of his father's daggers,— " He only opens his eyes at you—looking at you can't hurt you!" And if the devil should grin, as well as look at you, what harm could his grinning do you?

I would give more to have the look and smile of Jesus upon me, than I would to shun them all. 'Tis enough for my confiding heart, that Jesus approves and loves me, if devils don't, now.

But they will, by and by, you see if they don't! The devils don't like me much, these days; still, it is only because they don't know I am their best friend, after all, if I couldn't compromise with them, in the long run. It takes time to do great things—such as conquering the old dragon himself!

Remember, it took God himself six days to make the world, and as one day is with him as a thousand years, so, who knows but that he was six thousand years about it?

We must not think we can beat him in doing things up quick, for we can't. We have seen the folly of trying to be quicker than God is, in our government troubles. If we had just taken time to sort out, clean, and be thorough, at first, it would have saved us all this trouble we have now got into, by guilty compromise with Calvinistic principles, for the sake of present peace and quiet. I go for peace, now, as soon as we can get it—based on purity. But purity, first, is God's advice; and if we take it, we can then hope for lasting peace.

This American daughter has been awfully bit in this compromise business!—she ought to dread the fire—for she is well scarred with her burns. I hope she won't be afraid to be singular now, amid devils!

I am not! But I have to make large drafts upon the bank of faith to do it. I am so sensitive, and do so want to please everybody, that I am tempted to displease myself, sometimes, to do it. But I have made up my mind this don't pay—and when I have tried one line of business long enough to know for myself that it is unprofitable to me, I just quit it. I am just so selfish as that.

And I go in for the right to be selfish, if we avoid the Calvinistic part of this article. It is as much my duty to protect my interests as it is to protect others' interests—and I say again, that charity begins at home. Christian charity, I mean—not Calvinistic. And when I have got myself well housed, and secure from molestation, then I can begin to look out for my neighbors—not before.

What good could our government do in shielding us from harm, if it could not protect and defend itself?

I wouldn't give much for a husband who couldn't take care of himself. I want a man to take care of me. I don't want to take care of him all the time! I have got my own duties to see to. But, should he get into danger, from a con-

7

test with wild beasts, I would leave all, and rush to his defense. But when we have driven the wild beasts back to the wilderness, I want him to tend to his own business, himself—that is, to take care of himself, and me too.

And besides, I should expect some extra marks of attention from him, when I have exposed my own life to save his —and if he is a gentleman, he will not suffer me to be disappointed in my expectations. I think he will feel pledged, by this act of heroism on my part, to be all the more watchful over my future happiness and success.

I believe Lincoln is a philanthropist of the right sort, and when he once gets out of the lion's den, I warrant he will show you where he has been, and what sort of company he has been in, in his den. I have caught a glimpse of his lion-heart already, through the bars. His firmness is not milk and water, you'll find! You'll see if Jeff. Davis don't try to run away from him as quick as he would from a lion, or as my husband would from me!

I guess when Lincoln comes to protect the slaves' interests —instead of the slave-holders', as he has been doing hitherto,—you'll see what stuff he is made of, and so will my husband!

The bigoted Calvinist will be as afraid of him as a lion, as he will *do* something besides roar at you, and look daggers at you! It is my opinion he will be the one to do the roaring. Lincoln will do the acting part of the drama. Let a patient, forbearing temper but reach the limits of endurance, and then you may prepare to see the " wrath of the lamb" manifested. When the Good Man's patience has been stretched to almost dangerous tension, without breaking, then is the time for you to look out for yourself, if you can, and if there is a rock or a cave to flee to, to hide yourselves, 1 guess you'll see clipping for it! But you can't hide. He'll find you, and he has long legs, and can run faster than the fleetest of you. Even Floyd will find he is not slippery enough to escape his eagle eye and lightning speed, as his pursuer.

Oh, they'll be hard-up, then, some of them! Yes, up as high as Haman's scaffold was for Mordecai! Never mind; let him have time to let Noah and his family, and beasts, out of the ark first, and we'll be fixing things up against he comes back.

He'll want a nice, clean home to rest in when he comes back; for he must find it hard, tough business for his humane soul to do such sort of things. I do pity him from the bottom of my heart, and all the more because he hates this hanging work himself so bad!

But I go in for thoroughness as well as dispatch, and sometimes dispatch is the way to thoroughness—the only road.

I don't pity the traitors much—scarcely at all. It was a self-moved act wholly, and now they must see where these self-moved acts lead to. In fact they are the ones who slay; it is not our good Lincoln who slays them. They have slain themselves. They have killed all their own manliness already, and all that Lincoln has to do is to kill the old animal it used to tenant! God used to call for sacrifices of animals, not men.

Lincoln just burns up the house after the people are all out of it, and a pest-house is dangerous after the tenant has left it. The safety of society demands its destruction. I guess Lincoln is getting the tar and pitch ready now, in secret; he doesn't say much about it, any more than I do to my husband about this book I am writing, that will burn up his house, I guess, right over his own head, if he doesn't get out of it first!

I told my sons, Theophilus and Isaac, who came to visit me just after the trustees met, about what I had concluded to do in the line of authorship, and also told them not to tell their father of it, for fear he might try to stop my writing, as he had my thinking.

But it is not long we shall have to be so careful about what we write, or speak, or think, for I think Lincoln will let us speak, and write, and think, just as we please, and I don't think he'll let our brothers bother us so much about such things any more. I do hate to be bothered! and those brothers who have been bothering me so long and so unmercifully, I fairly hate; and I don't like this hating business any more than Lincoln does this slaying business; but I can't help it; God made me to hate evil; he does himself; and I am trying to be like him in hating as well as loving. He even tells me to be angry as he is, without sinning. But I have been very loth to obey this command, lest I should not know how to avoid the sinning, to which it makes me liable.

But since God forbids my punishing or revenging my injuries, I venture to let my resentment rise to such a pitch as to ask God, in sincerity, to punish and destroy my enemies *for me*, as he says he will. The way God punishes is the way to bring them to repentance, but my way might only make them worse, instead of better. That is the effect human punishments almost always have upon their victims. Christ didn't try to punish his enemies. He asked God to punish them, though, when he prayed for their forgiveness, for he knew God did not forgive without repentance; and a father's chastisements always lead to repentance—the only condition of pardon.

I can now feel angry or resentful feelings without changing my treatment of my enemy. I can " do good to them that hate me," and at the same time be praying, as Christ did, that God would punish them; and more than that, I can rejoice in their punishment, or the destruction of the evil that is in them; for I know they will be all the happier when this destruction is accomplished, just as I can rejoice to see a stubborn child under the discipline of a wise, judicious, loving parent.

Before I came to this asylum I was too charitable to the rebellious sinner, just as the North have been to the South; but I see now that it is not gospel charity to cover sins—either in ourselves or others—with the mantle of charity. It is best to expose them and conquer them.

I guess the North are of the same opinion. Is it charity to cover corruption? or, is it charity to cure corruption?

I know it is easier to cover it than to cure it; but I know it is the best way to cure it—not to cover it.

I know it is easier for Dr. McFarland to cover the oppression which he sees exercised by cruel kindred over their afflicted relatives than to expose it and cure it. It is easier to say to Mrs. Miller, in reply to her request, " Don't you receive me here the third time if my husband does make application for my admittance on the false charge of insanity;" " keep out of his way!"—than to expose Mr. Miller and put him out of his wife's way.

'Tis easier to let the South rule the North with despotism, than to assert their own rights. But 'tis best for all parties to let right, not despotism, rule.

'Tis easiest to let the strongest, bullying party rule; but 'tis the safest to let justice rule—even if the weak party is the right party—for the right party is the strongest party—if it is the weakest!

I want God to subdue my husband as soon as possible, for I do want to love him; and this I can't do until I see something in him to love. And my Father knows so much, he'll do it! for he can bring good out of evil. We can't. And when he brings out the good—then I can love it—just as readily as I could when he brought the least bit of good out of Dr. McFarland.

I couldn't see the least bit of manliness in this great man, until he took my part as protector against the ridicule of some Calvinistic women, who had become so fallen, as to hold up to scorn and contempt the persecuted disciples of Christ, here!

How I do wish I could see more of such genuine manliness in him, so I could love this protector until God gets me a better one! I do sometimes think I can see Jesus Christ in him, quite plainly, but somehow the mirror gets dirty very easily, so it don't reflect distinctly. But as the negro said of his fiddle, " The music is in it, if it could only get out; " so I say of this " old man of sin," that Christ is in him, if he could only be got out!

I don't believe in going on trust in these matters. A profession of goodness is not worth much, somehow, with my disposition. If people love me, I want them to show it in a natural, rational manner—not as my perverted husband does, by saying, for example, " My dear! will you allow me the privilege of putting you into an insane asylum ? "

No, I won't! He forced me in, and he will have to force me out, if *he* takes me out. I told him when he put me here, to protect me, as he said, that I should ask the government to protect me against such a protector! And I keep my word. I say, and I *do*. I never lie. My conscience won't consent, nohow, to do such business. And he's my Major-General. I don't know what would become of me, if I should be court-marshaled by him! Yes, I do. I should be put into hell fire, where there is " weeping and wailing and gnashing of teeth, for ever." But I should not consent to be for ever in punishment. I would repent, and then my endless torment would terminate.

I know how I could escape this asylum endless torment. But I shan't do it! for I think the remedy would be worse than the disease. I don't believe in curing one disease by inflicting a worse one. And I say, the displeasure of God is worse than the displeasure of men. And if I got out of this hell, by consenting to obey man instead of God, as I ' could, if I would, I should be only getting an incurable disease for a temporary ailment.

Old Packard will find his Elizabeth has got the grit in her : but I don't think the discovery will afford him much satisfaction. But it does me, anyhow ! I am not the one to be trifled with, *always*. I bear, like Lincoln, a great deal before I show my strength ; but when I do show it, you may look out for me, as well as for Lincoln. If I am a woman, I am not afraid of ghosts !

Father Abraham, there is another thing I want to tell you about. I must tell on some of my bad brothers, or you won't know what to do to protect the sisters from them. Mind you, I don't ask you to punish them. That's God's business, not yours .

But 'tis your business to protect the good, not to punish the bad. Don't forget this principle in your reconstruction work. We have a great deal too much punishing done, and a great deal too little protecting done.

Evil will slay the wicked, as it has the inveterate, Calvinistic slave-holders of Egypt. But these are not the worst men in the world, after all.

Making slaves of black people, as servants, is not near so bad as to make a slave of a wife ! and what is worse yet, put her into an insane asylum where the doctor calls all insane, as a matter of course, so that all the sane ones are his passports afterwards. I, for instance, could show what a wonderful cure had been effected—being so sane a person—and he could have the credit of having cured me of insanity that I never had at all !

My husband's lies being credited, and endorsed by him, many of the parasites, and some of the devils of society would believe this double and twisted lie, sooner than they would the truth.

The truth is, Dr. McFarland don't cure any one of insanity.

Those who get better here, could and would get better just as well at home. Those who don't, ought to be taken care of by their natural guardians.

I can tell you the secret of the cure of insanity, as practised here, for I have observed, with both eyes wide open, for two and a half years; it is, "to do nothing at all for the insane, except to attend to their physical wants."

And anybody could do the same for them, anywhere else, just as well, if they had a room, eight feet by seven, with a lock and key upon the door, and a screen before the window, where they could be confined, when the excited times were on them. Or, what is better, enclose a part of a room where there is no window to screen, with a strong wire partition, with a wooden door in it, and a lock and key upon this door; thus, neither the light nor air are excluded, and the patient is never out of sight, nor are his friends out of his sight, yet both are protected.

I never saw the sick doctored or nursed *less* in all my life, than they are here. I never saw such reckless exposures of life and health in all my life, as I have seen in this asylum. A person's life and health are less exposed, as a soldier in our army, than it is here!

President Lincoln, the afflicted in America *do* need the arm of government to protect them against the insane laws of our country. No class need protection so much as the occupants of our insane hospitals, if this is a specimen of others.

In the name of God, I utter my protest against the treatment of the insane and the sane, who are occupants of the insane asylums of America.

Friends should be made to take care of their dependent relatives, and not be allowed to put them off on to strangers, who care no more for them than they do for the brutes. It is the most devilish practice the government can uphold.

I have a volume of facts in detail which support these statements. I hope they will never be called for, as proof. Believe and act, without the horrid detail.

Our insane laws! I guess, Lincoln, our legislature were all Calvinists, the term they were enacted. Therefore, to exclude the Calvinism, the whole code must go overboard.

Just think of a man saying to his wife: "I have you entirely in my power, wife; and now, if you do not look out, and do just as I say, I can, by our laws, put you into the insane asylum, where you will be a prisoner, with none to protect you from abuse, and where you cannot even write to us and tell of your hard usage—for the doctor will not send such letters—and you must stay just as long as the doctor and I can agree to have you, without your voice in the matter, even if it is all your lifetime! I can keep putting you in as often as I please, and you and your children can intercede, in vain, to prevent it; and none can release you, except the one who put you in."

This legal license reads thus, as found on the Illinois statute book, session laws fifteen, 1852, page ninety-six, section ten: "Married women and infants, who, in the judgment of the medical superintendent, are evidently insane or distracted, may be entered or detained in the hospital, on the request of the husband of the woman, or the guardian of the infant, *without* the evidence of insanity required in other cases."

Is it not enough to drive a sensitive woman frantic, to realize the dangers to which her marriage vow renders her liable? "Capital punishment!" without judge or jury, if her husband chances, from any cause, to want to get rid of her!

If there is a country on earth where a woman's identity is so trifled with, I know not where it is, as it is under the American flag!

7*

The slave code, South, furnishes the calaboose, where the slaves can be dressed down on certain terms; and the insane laws, North, furnish an inquisition, where a man can get his wife dressed down on his own terms!

Yes, I can testify, from experience, that this dressing down means something more excruciating than the slave endures under the lash at the calaboose. No agonies,—except the agony of Gethsemane's garden,—can compare with it!

Dr. McFarland understands his business, I can assure you. No man can beat him at "woman-crushing" business. He knows how to work his machinery so as to do execution. If his equal can be found, he must be second to none but Beelzebub himself.

But there are some "niggers" that even the most energetic and skillful calaboose-man cannot subdue, except as Legree did "Uncle Tom,"—with death. So there is one wife in this house, that even the great and knowing Dr. McFarland cannot subdue, except as Christ's murderers did him,—with death. And the chances at death are pretty dubious yet. I keep well in spite of them. They do not seem to understand that there is one, "like to the Son of God," walking at my side in this furnace, so that not even the smell of insanity can be found upon me.

But, what is very singular in my case, this woman-crushing machinery works the wrong way! I guess the engine is reversed, for the true woman shines brighter and brighter under the process, instead of being strangled.

Rev. Mr. Bedell, of Philadelphia, remarked once, during his afflictions, "Gold loses nothing by the furnace, but its dross." I second this statement from my own experience. The spiritual woman in me has suffered no loss by this asylum furnace, but old Eve has lost considerable in me. She has lost her complacency or charity for the unrepentant transgressor. She has lost her fear of the sinner, in her daring to expose his guilt. These lion devils used to frighten old Eve in me, when they roared at me, but since I have seen that they all have got a chain on them, too strong for them to break, their roaring only makes me all the more dauntless in attacking them.

Lincoln, 'tis a fact that despotism and a free government don't chime at all together. The one obstructs the other. So if you are for upholding freedom, I advise you to hunt up and destroy all the despotism of our free institutions.

I would suggest that you make a thorough search for this old devil, and when you have found him, put him directly into the bottomless pit! There is the only place where he is safe, for he can get out of any pit that ain't bottomless. He's used to climbing, you know. But if the pit is bottomless, I don't think he could reach heaven again from it.

Lincoln, I'm pretty sure I can tell you where Despotism's seat, or den—I don't know which to call it—is. It is somewhere about these buildings, I'm very sure! He is certainly within hearing distance, at least, for a whisper or a note brings him to my side very often; and he is in such a rage to put down free speech and free writing that all the secret springs of this great machinery are put into requisition by him to effect his purpose.

Don't you see how great advantage you give him by giving him *irresponsible power* over all the humanity herein entombed? It is an indispensable necessity to his existence here that the patients be prisoners, and that they be cut off from all outside communications, except through censorship.

Lincoln, ought not husbands and wives to be allowed unrestricted communication with each other when they are separated by affliction as when they are well? Is it right to intercept and read this correspondence of bosom friends? Is this a free country, where a parent cannot hold pen-intercourse, by letter, with his child, or a husband with his wife, under any circumstances? Is it right to allow one man to dictate what relatives shall say to each other about matters and things that concern their most vital interests?

Lincoln, it is the height of despotism to place a censorship over asylum correspondence.

The letters of the afflicted should be as sacredly guarded from interference as the letters of the prosperous citizen. And he who will consent to be the censor, and stand between man and wife's intercourse, must certainly commit suicide of his native manliness to do it.

It is through fear that the treatment of the patients will be exposed, that this rule was made and is so tenaciously adhered to. Let the insane write what they please, and if the institution cannot stand before the truth, let it fall! the sooner the better. If the pen of the patient can destroy it, let it be destroyed! but don't try to sustain it by defrauding manhood or womanhood of their inalienable rights to written speech.

I, for one, shall speak and write just what I please from *within* these asylum walls, and if that cannot speak for itself before the public, I shall write what I please after I get out, and get it printed, too.

Now, Father Abraham, in view of all the wrongs which a wife in Illinois is rendered liable to suffer, through this unparalleled despotism, how can a human being—so tender and sensitive as a woman—stand all this without becoming a maniac, as Mrs. Wood did, and many others, solely from this cause? I think the devilish husband who makes use of this machinery to destroy his wife's identity, and succeeds in making her a maniac, ought to be compelled to take care of her himself, and not put her off on to Dr. McFarland to take care of. For, to be called to take care of one whom nobody else cares for, is to some people a temptation not to care for their comfort themselves.

Such cases run a poor chance here of being kindly cared for. Now, for you to pay Dr. McFarland for abusing such women is bringing the crime pretty near home!

, And I say 'tis abusing one to shut them up in prison for being insane, just as if they had done some guilty act.

Dr. McFarland don't punish them so much as he used to for their being insane. I have had some influence at headquarters here. The fact is, Father Abraham, a woman of character and ability does command influence. She always did and she always will command an influence. You can keep a cork under water only while it is held down. I think my persecutors will get tired trying to hold me down, by and by, and then I expect they will brand me "Hopelessly Insane," and I, like the liberated cork, will rise to the surface of society, where I belong. I'll risk their branding—although 'tis burnt in—and you see if I don't live down their slanders, and them, too! Perhaps some will be lifted up, Haman high, through my influence yet!

I am cultivating my influence these days by use, and there is no knowing to what a pitch of power it will rise yet. I say it's felt here already at headquarters, some. I have given the superintendent some gentle hints, and some strong ones, too, that I could write, and he might have some proof of it which he would not like to see if he did not protect God's oppressed children better; and I always stand up for the oppressed, those who need help, not for those who can take care of themselves, and others, too.

The doctor has not liked this trait in my character, much, because he has a Calvinistic side in him—good as he is. But I have pricked it a good deal since I've been here, and I think the irritating plaster has done some good! I don't go in for blisters—only a little irritation on the surface to draw out the inflammation from the vital parts. The skin has looked very red, sometimes, so I see they took hold, and were doing their work. I do think the patient is improving, and there are some symptoms of a convalescent state! I even hope my patient may yet recover his long-lost health and reason—for he is insane, as well as sick!

I think he must have had a very good constitution, or he would have broken down under such an accumulation of diseases, unless I had been sent for just in the nick of time, as I was. I quickly saw—not at first sight, however—that his disease was of a very dangerous type and character, and required most stringent and powerful cathartics, as well as plasters. The stomach and bowels were so coated over, yea, even loaded with mucus, that the natural action of these important organs was almost paralyzed. I don't go in for calomel, only in desperate cases. I never take any, nor do any of my children. We don't obstruct nature to need it; and if you don't obstruct nature, she will do by you as she does by me—do up her own work right.

It is this interference that does so much mischief in the world, and in the body, too. But when the natural action or life is so nearly destroyed that it cannot act of its inherent agency, it needs help to recover this, its vitality.

So I intend to help Dr. McFarland recover his vitality, by removing the Calvinism out of him, to the best of my medical skill. For I think he is too good a man to carry the Calvinistic taint about with him. I intend to be very thorough in his case, since 'tis a very important one. For the truth is, I don't intend to marry him, until I can see Christ's image in him a good deal plainer than I can at present! I don't intend to marry a mongrel stock, again, lest the seed be contaminated.

Well, I "switched off" on to the McFarland "switch," this time. He is so near the insane track, that I have to keep a pretty sharp look-out, or I shall destroy him with the asylums! I want to separate the precious from the vile, but when the proximity is so very close, it is like splitting a hair to do it! And as I go on the main track, I take things just as they happen to come in my way.

You see we are moving from one home to another, and getting the new one ready, and tearing down the old one, disposing of our old trumpery,' and sorting out the valuable from the useless, packing, etc., so I can't help but jumble up things a good deal.

But now I'm in for it, I say, go ahead, David Crockett-like! don't mind trifles! If the knives and forks do get in with the silver spoons, and all together get into my bureau drawers, never mind. I can sort them out, when we get to our new home. I have a place for things, and a good one, too, when I keep house. I don't go in for having things jumbled up, I assure you!

If you can't sort out ideas which are already formed, and packed, and put them in their proper places, just send for me, or my children, and we will help set them up in their proper places. For there is a suitable place in every house for all the valuables—the truths of Nature—if you will only dispose of the artificials—the falsehoods—first. This fictitious, artificial, perverted life we have been living so long, must be broken up, even if it does smash up old and established usages, and customs, and institutions, and governments.

I am for breaking up—sorting out—and getting ready for the establishment of the "new heavens and the new earth, wherein dwelleth righteousness." And I'm sure that everything that is not right, and just, and true, is to be broken up, sooner or later, and I don't care if I am a pioneer in a good cause!

I know I get a good many bumps, in tearing down, for the buildings are so rotten that they come down on to me before I get time to escape the crash, sometimes! But, then, I

trust Providence to protect me, as it did our Deacon Peck of
Shelburne, Mass.—our neighbor—in tearing down father
Packard's old barn, which was so rotten that it came down
of itself, while he was standing in the center of the ruins,
unharmed. He told me, afterwards—for I was an eye witness to his exposure—that when he saw the old frame totter-
ing, and knowing his danger of being struck by the falling
timbers, his first thought was to run from the center, where
he then stood, to the outside of the building; but before he
had time to obey this impulse, the· shower of timbers commenced, and he could do nothing but stand still, and run his
risk of life, where he was; and as the building fell apart,
rather than together, the center was the only unexposed spot.

So, in tearing down our old Calvinistic institutions, I think
I won't run, if the old insane asylum does totter over my
head, while I am prying away at its timbers, but, like Deacon Peck, stand still at the center, and risk my life amidst
its ruins.

But if I, Samson-like, perish with the worshipers of Baal,
I shall count it all gain, in that I slay more Philistines at my
death, than in my life! So be my fate Peck or Samson-
like, I intend to go ahead with this demolishing business.

I'm very sure my Calvinistic or orthodox friends will wish
me no good wishes, when they read my book ; and if I was
not so strongly fortified in this castle of Beelzebub, I might
get some missiles from them, that might hurt my tender flesh
some.

But I'll risk them, while my strong friend, Dr. McFarland,
stands with his great shield to ward them off ! He won't let
me see letters that will hurt my feelings, for Uncle Sam, you
know, has appointed him the censor of all my communications ; and he is so tender of my feelings !

I do wish he would keep his promises to me, and publish
my first volume, while he is my protector, so that this castle

can afford me a shelter from the merciless storm and fury, which it will generate amid the Calvinistic elements of the community!

But that is not my business. Dr. McFarland may be as conscientious in breaking his promises as I am in keeping mine. I am not the guardian of Dr. McFarland's conscience. He can take care of his own conscience. If he can't, I shan't let him take care of mine. I go for entire freedom of conscience, as God does. I don't want to be trammeled by Dr. McFarland's dictations, and I don't think he wants to be by mine.

At any rate, I'll do the writing of my book without his dictation, and he may do the printing of it without my dictation, or not do it at all, just as he chooses, and I'll try to be satisfied.

One thing does comfort me ; and that is, that nothing takes place but what God permits. He does permit people to sin. So must I. If he lets people kill themselves, I must submit to lose some of my fondest hopes in their suicidal death!

But I must return to the main track again. I think I referred you to my children for help in locating my ideas, if you needed help. I must here give them one recommend, so you can confide in them, and that is, they all have a place for everything they have, and more than that, their mother sees to it that they keep their own things in their proper place, too.

But in moving, when we get well under way, things do get into a tumble, and we can't help it. I think, at first, when we agree upon a reconstruction, or a new move, " Well, I will make an orderly move this time, and I commence to the entire satisfaction of my big bump of order. But it is not long before some one more in a hurry than I am, comes, and just upsets all my order, and in comes confusion and disorder in its place. But I find that what can't be cured must be endured by me, at least, patiently.

I don't think all can be as patient as I am, for all are not made just like me. God made but one Mrs. Packard, and she is a pattern for no one but herself. No other's organization is just like mine, so no one's duty is just like mine. So of every other human being. It may be no virtue for me to be patient, any more than it is to have black eyes. It may be a great virtue to a quiet-tempered organization, to be as quiet as I am, naturally, under provocation. Indeed, I do believe I have sinned more in being too patient and forbearing, than in resenting injuries.

So has the North.

But I am made for my place, and no one can fill it but me. God has so fixed it. We must fill our own place, or it is empty for ever.

I said, I bear what I can't help, patiently—but, I tell you, I don't bear what I can help, at all. No, not I. But I wait, sometimes, to get the right aim, a great while, before I fire— but when you see the flash, you may be sure it is not all smoke that my gun carries! No, I put in the paper pellets of my brain for a wad, and I ram down my ball, tight, with them, and keep it ready loaded, till the right time comes, and then the ball goes whizzing through the air to get to the mark on the old Calvinistic carcass, and then I load up again ready for another aim! I have been shooting small game some time ; but I never used the cannon before. My time had not come to write a book.

Papers and journals were all I could afford to write for, and that was precious little, at best. But now I have got hold of a public cannon, I mean to improve my chance, and use it well, for I don't know as I shall get another chance to demolish the Calvinism of our government.

I think all ought to do their part in our moving, and not

let the volunteers do it all. I believe in division of labor. I don't go for burdening some at the expense of others. I want all to do their part, and then none will be too much burdened. None ought to be idle. God did not make drones. They make themselves. I detest drones. They are a disgrace to our race. I shouldn't think of making a queen of a drone! But bees have their own views of things—and so have I.

Bees make good honey—I like that in them. All have some good things about them, if you only have your spectacles clear, to look at them. But these Calvinistic spectacles blur the eyesight I think. The glass is so dirty in them, they do more hurt than good. It is dirt in us that makes us see so much dirt in others, who are pure and clean. So they believe lies and don't know it. And this makes a sight of trouble for themselves and others, too.

I do say that those who believe I am an insane person, are believing a lie, and I can prove it, when I get ready. The dirt or insanity is in these Calvinists, not in me. No Christian believes me to be insane, who knows me. Some Christians pretend to think so, to some people, from policy—but 'tis only pretense. I would no more recognize a human being as a Christian brother or a sister who called me insane, than I would a devil!

But I will let these hosts of Philistines go for the present, and dispose of their champion, Goliath of Gath, first. 'Tis strange how much influence one terrible giant can wield! He can keep all the hosts of Israel in terror and amazement, so that no one of all their armed hosts dare attack him, lest he overcome them. I am ashamed of God's people to be so afraid of this vaunting Goliath!—this vile enemy of God and his true people. His coat of mail—or coat of lies, rather—will answer to shield him from attack, for a time; because he has laid them on so thick that a ball can't break through!

but a stone will make him bite the dust, by and by! Yes, the stone he despised so intensely, will yet be his destruction. The stone of truth wielded by the sling of faith, is a weapon before which all his hosts will yet fall.

This giant has tried to train me to use his armor, in my own defense ; and he has even offered it me, repeatedly. He would say often in his reflective moods: " Now, wife, you just try and treat me as I do you, awhile, and perhaps that will bring me to my senses." I did once take his advice, and thought I would try the experiment—but my courage failed. I couldn't use it. It didn't suit my nature. I like the little stone of truth better, if 'tis small. In fact, I do like to tell the truth much better than he likes to hear it, a great deal. When I see anything that looks crazy or Calvinistic, I just load my sling, and go at it in solemn earnest. I have got pretty well used to my armor. I guess I shall aim straight at the falsehoods of Calvin, with this stone-book—not table—and you'll see if I don't hit—when his shield is off to look after my movements! He may find that little David, though he don't vaunt as much as he does, yet does quite as much service to the Union cause, in putting him low, as he could do to prattle, simply.

I shan't try to aim at his heart, for that is ossified, and the stone will bound off; and besides, he keeps that part covered with his armor. Useless encumbrance! He don't need a shield for his heart, any more than a mud-turtle needs an umbrella!

But I suppose he wants to tantalize us, and make us think he has a heart by shielding it.

But he has got an intellect, and I find that, with some hard-hearted fellows, the only way to reach the heart is through the intellect. I have got to shoot Calvin there, of dire necessity. All other parts are encased, you know, with a coat of mail. And if I shouldn't hit, you know

I run a great risk, for he is so strong, and so protected all over by the laws—and I have not got anything protected to me—not even my thoughts! I am all exposed, as naked as I was born, except my clothes I have on, and some few more in my trunk. Well, I must "trust Providence, and keep the powder dry," too. So I will shoot one of my five stones, and see what game it brings me—that is, if I can find one who can trust Providence long enough for the pay,—to publish it for me. The carnal part is of some consequence as the world now is.

But if the first volume sells well in market, I may write the others and sling them too, at the discomfited hosts of the Calvinists, when they see Calvin himself is down, floored too by a woman! How men hate to be beat by a woman!

I really think they would prefer suicide to being killed by one.

Well, if they do, I shan't object. I shall only have the less shooting to do to dispatch the great hierarchy, or oligarchy rather. You see I can use big words if I could only stop to write them. And I am in such a tearing hurry to get this book to Father Abraham, to read, so I can get out of this asylum quick and see my baby again before he entirely forgets me, that I must be excused if I do write in simple style.

I can dress, I assure you. I've got taste as well as other women. But I don't go in for dressing until the dirty work is done up. I don't get mine done until about noon, and then I have to wash my dishes after dinner; so I don't dress up nice until then. But when I get moved into our new home, and have my rights of property and womanhood protected to me, I shall hire a girl—a black girl, if our government don't know what else to do with them but to send them to Central America—and then I can dress and bathe me at 11 o'clock, and be in good time for my husband's guests to dine with us.

I love to see him bring home company with him. But I can't say how it will be when I get a Christian husband! He may be all the company I want to talk with. But Calvin and I used to get talked out oftentimes.

The fact is, we grew apart, instead of together.

But a Christian husband and I should grow together, I know. We are just made to fit, dovetail fashion, and this union makes the boards as smooth as if it were only one board, and besides, boards thus joined don't warp as easily as a single board. "They twain shall be one flesh." That was so short a cut I could stop to prove it by the Bible.

But I ain't like the Calvinists. They think nothing but the Bible can serve as proof for any point.

I say that nature is as good as the Bible, if not a little "gooder!" Men wrote the Bible, and men printed it, and men sometimes make mistakes. They ain't infallible copyists. But nature and science can't lie. No chance for a mistake here, if you get the real, true thing—nature, not Calvin's nature, but Christ's nature. And so does science tell us just as real truths as the Bible does; only get a Christian Fowler, not a Calvinistic Fowler to interpret it.

And so can Copernicus and President Hitchcock tell us about astronomy and geology as correctly as the Bible can, and a little more so. Professor Snell can tell us the reason why the sun stopped, and Joshua couldn't. He didn't know as much as Professor Snell does. He had not seen his apparatus to learn his astronomy by. It wasn't made then. We should think Joshua was a fool, now-a-days, to tell us the sun stopped till the battle ended in Israel's victory. He would be just such a fool as a steamboat captain would be to tell his passengers on his boat, sailing up North river, "I am going to stop the next village twenty-four hours on its flying journey past us." They know he is only speaking according to appearances, not according to the truth, for they know that the way, and the only way, to stop the village flying by is to stop the boat.

Now science is a book, one of the books John saw in his apocalyptic vision; and Nature is another. This book of science tells us, since the Bible book was written, that it was the earth that stopped on its axis once round, and thus they could see the sun all the time on the side toward the sun, and, of course, the opposite had just as much added to the length of its night as they had to the day. So he robbed one side of light to accommodate his neighbor.

But that sounds too Calvinistic to be true! Christ don't so rob one to enrich another. Neither do I. But I don't think God is any less just than we are, both put together, as they put man and wife together. So I don't go in for that; I go in for reason; but, mind you, no reason which has injustice in its composition is of any account to me. Calvinism is about as good as that kind of reason. Well, there must be some way of getting round all God does—some way straight through. He can't quirk and turn as Calvin has to to carry all his points. God's points carry themselves.

Well, I've guessed how it is. Have you? If you haven't, I can't wait for you, for I must get my book done, so Lincoln will protect me at home. I guess these brave Israelites thought, since worse had come to worse, they'd put in for it right smart, and so fought two days' battles on one day's time—and so took a shorter cut home.

Now I like that. It suits me exactly; and no law but the law of bravery infringed upon; and I go in for such infringe-ments—when nobody is hurt by it—I suppose the rebels were hurt more, but that was what they were after—they only hurt them all at once, and were not a whole year about it.

Now, Lincoln, imitate good Joshua, and put it through in

double-quick time—that is, do a double day's work in one day's time.

Now, try it! won't you? And then we can get to reconstructing all the sooner. I don't like laggards; and I shan't like you if you lay still too long. But I do so want to like you so much! so let me have a chance. It is so easy when we once get started, to go ahead.

But I guess the toes will answer, and perhaps there is more iron inside than outside. Use is the only test of virtue. Who knows but that Calvin has been daubing on miry clay on the outside, just for a bugbear? But let him see you, Abraham Lincoln, are not afraid of bugbears! You'll let our soldiers see that you are not a mere image-man, but a real live man—a lion man—one whom God fitted for his place, and then put him in it.

Remember, the difference between an image and a man is, one moves, and the other does not, without being pushed or drawn. The image has no pluck inside.

And, besides, I want to tell my sons: "Just see how our good President grapples with evils, and how fast he disposes of them." I think when Lincoln does show his strength, he will drive all before him—like a thunder-cloud. I don't know but we shall mistake it for the last trumpet to come to judgment. I guess lots of secesh will find it is even so to them! But I don't like this killing business; although it seems the sword is God's appointed instrument in this case to settle our difficulties; and if so, he takes the responsibility of its use. It seems that we were driven to it, by the force of circumstances, as much as I am driven to defend myself against my persecutors by the sword of truth. The sword slays its thousands, but truth its tens of thousands. At first, it looks as though we didn't love our neighbor as we do ourselves, to kill him to save us.

But then I don't call such folks as the rebels neighbors,

any more than I call such folks as Calvin my husband. It is sacrilege to call him by such a loving title after he has blasphemed it by his perjuries. The rebels are neighbors in the same sense that robbers and assassins are neighbors to their victim.

Duty to ourselves and them, too, demands that we treat them according to their real character, as developed by their own actions. I go in for this Bible principle—treat people according to their deserts—and I agree with God in this thing, that the unrepentant, persistent transgressor deserves punishment; and when God appoints us his instruments to do it, we have no right to shirk out, as Jonah tried to do. If we should, I fear we might get into as tight a place as he did, in the attempt.

I know this war is bad business, and I once should have felt guilty in approving of this war as I now do; but I know more than I once did. I take a more comprehensive view of a subject, and thus see more relations to it than I could from my low standpoint.

A higher wisdom, guided by a truer sympathy than ours, has said, " I come not to send peace, but a sword." And when God sends the sword to break up oppressive systems, it is doubtless because their iron framework will not crumble except by these heavy blows.

The moral struggles of the race must come to a physical adjustment, and then it often happens that the party weakest in the justice of its cause, is the strongest in external force, as Calvin is, in persecuting me. He has external might on his side, while I have only right on my side. But since right is might, under God's government, I fear not the issue of the battle.

So our country, struggling to break its fetters of slavery and despotism, by the power of the sword, may externally have to contend with forces too strong for them to overcome,

8

yet ultimate triumph is certain in the cause they have espoused. Even in seeming defeat victory is often secured. Opposition and defeat only arouse new energies to the combat.

So, Father Abraham, be manly! Don't be discouraged,— but, Luther-like, let your courage be anchored on the truth and justice of our cause, and then drive it through in hot haste. Let our country, and the world too, see that you have an inflexible will and an unconquerable energy in advancing a good cause.

And it is a good cause to break every yoke and let the oppressed go free. Yes, Lincoln, break even that paper creed—our Constitution—rather than break God's laws, by trying to join together that which God has dissevered—freedom and slavery, right and wrong, good and evil. Slavery breaks every law, both human and divine. So, to destroy it, we may break down every obstacle in the way of the car of immediate emancipation, and God and our country will both uphold you in this fearless onset. American freedom is not yet secured. Man has outgrown the narrow limits in which the Constitution confines us, and they are pressed painfully upwards, against the laws which have held them down.

I won't be held down any longer! I will rise to a higher plane of freedom, even if I have to be called singular, and even insane. And what worse can I be called than insane? Nothing, in all the catalogue of crimes, evils, or misfortunes, can be so insulting and torturing to an upright, sensitive soul, as the kidnapping of our accountability. Yet this infamy I'll bear, rather than spiritual bondage to creeds and educational influences. I will not be a spiritual slave, if I have to be a bodily one, or a prisoner. I will die fighting, before I will not think as I please, and think aloud, too; for I have just as good a right to my own thoughts as I have to my own eyes; and no one has any more right to call me insane, because I do not think as they do, than because I do not look as they do. My thoughts are as much my own right as my eyes; and I would as soon part with one as the other. And, besides, my own thoughts are better for me than the thoughts of many other people. I would not exchange my opinion that I am not insane, for the opposite opinion of the entire insane party, that I am! for I can prove that I am a sane person—and they cannot prove that I am insane.

Now, Father Abraham, only think that from this blackest, foulest of all slanders you do not let me have a chance to defend myself, and no one seems to dare to attempt to defend me in opposition to my husband; and thus I lie here, unprotected, forgotten, unknowing and unknown, year after year, leaving my little ones motherless!

It is enough to drive any woman of sense mad, by opposition, to endure this hopeless torment many years. And, Abraham, you see it's no relief to me to go home, as it now is, for he, my tormentor, could now annoy me worse than before, by having the great Dr. McFarland's testimony that I was insane, so he could be emboldened in treating me as an unaccountable moral agent. Even my own conscience would be utterly unprotected! How could I get to heaven without trying to do right? And, you see, I must, by so doing, run the risk of another imprisonment, if not in this asylum (I've been such a thorn in the Calvinistic side of this institution, I hardly think they would take me in again), in some other, perhaps ten times worse.

And, you see, I should run a poor chance of being well-treated, there, since Calvin would be very apt to tell them that I was so troublesome under Dr. McFarland's care, that they would not receive me a second time. And he might tell them that Dr. McFarland kept me in a ward with the worst maniacs in the house, a good deal of the time; and that it took two men to carry me to this ward, twice; and he himself, once; and that he locked me in a screen-room, once, himself, and told the attendants to treat me as they did the other maniacs—to confine me with a jacket or bolts—if they chose, and all such like! How could my word or representation be relied upon, under such circumstances? Could I expect anything but the reception, and treatment, of a maniac, there?

Now, Abraham, I am a real lady, and I always have treated everybody in the most gentle and lady-like manner. I never returned "evil for evil," and I never resisted brute force in all my life, whether in the human or beast form. I always make love to both kinds of brutes, and when they are not mad, they both make love to me in return. Dogs and cats, horses and cows, and poultry always like me, for I like them, and treat them always kindly. Our pony would follow after me like a cosset lamb, and come to my kitchen door or window, to be caressed by me, and eat his lunch of apple, or bread, from my hands. My children would often say: "What does make all animals like mother so well?" Elizabeth, my daughter, would reply: "It is because she is so kind to them."

And, Lincoln, there never was a biped who can testify of one unkind act from me; and yet I have been, for three years, treated as if I was a maniac. Isn't it too bad?

But we must excuse them on the ground that we do the doctors. They wanted to try an experiment, to see if the adage was a true one, viz., "a person is very apt to become what they are taken to be." So in trying this experiment, by the use of the most effective kind of machinery for this purpose—which you, Abraham, furnish for them!—if it had worked in the natural way, I might have become a maniac, and then my persecutor's object would have been attained. That is, he could thus have destroyed my moral influence as a witness for the truth.

But, thanks to God's grace alone, I am unharmed by this fiendish experiment!

Calvin expressed his chagrin in seeing his failure, on his first visit to my cell, after sixteen months' imprisonment, in these words to my attendant: "I never saw a person bear trouble so well as my wife can." No; nor have many others seen such a case. I doubt if the annals of persecution for centuries past can furnish such a case; for the laws of life and health were never so well developed, before, so that they could be intelligently applied for the victim's safeguard, as I have been able to do.

The spiritual laws of our being are built upon the natural laws of our complex nature; therefore, spiritual health is built upon natural health, and cannot be perfect on a rotten or diseased foundation or constitution.

It is the result of obedience to the natural laws of my nature, that I am still in the full possession of sound health, and strong nerves, so that I have been able to resist the temptations to irritability and impatience incident to the provocations I have received, so bountifully, during this merciless storm of persecution.

But Lincoln, it is no credit to your system of abuse in your asylums, that I have not only passed through them unharmed, but even improved thereby, for it is a law of our moral nature, that the more severe the test of virtue—if successfully passed—the greater strength acquired by the pressure. And I do say, that no human being ought to be subjected to the insults, abuses, and indignities of an insane asylum life, under our American flag. It is an open insult to our Creator, to thus trample under foot the divine image, in human form. This image—humanity—ought to be protected under all governments, especially a professed Christian government! But, as it is now treated in our insane asylums, there could not be a more crushing, strangling process devised, by the arch-fiend himself, to destroy the natural dignity and manliness of our God-like natures.

Yes, I do say, " our God-like natures," for man was made in God's image, and Christ took our natures upon him, and knew no sin; therefore, man's nature is not sinful, else Christ would have had a sinful nature.

Christ's nature was holy—he knew no sin—yet his nature was human, like our own human natures. Therefore human nature is a holy nature, and every human being has a holy nature, through which the divine image will ultimately be reflected in every human being. Christ redeemed all the human race—not part. Holiness cannot be destroyed. No holy nature can be lost irrecoverably.

It may be temporarily lost, by abuse and slander, as my character is, by the influence of slander and malignant abuse, yet, ultimately, God's image and nature will recover its rights, and assert its claims to respect and regard, defiant of all opposition. My reputation may be lost; but not my character—that stands on its own intrinsic merits—nothing but my own evil acts can destroy its claims to God's approbation. So a soul may be lost to human view—but not to God's view. God cannot lose a part of himself! however his image may be covered up, as my real character is, by slanders.

So, Father Abraham, you must see to it that you *protect the Godhead* in every human form—that is, you must see to it, that the inalienable rights of their holy, God-like natures are protected to them, or, you expose the Deity, therein enthroned, to insult and abuse!

Oh! Abraham, can you not see that, as our laws now are, a wife is the most defenseless, unprotected of all human beings, in God's universe?

And yet she is the mother of her country! I don't think there is one black slave, even on Legree's plantation, near so cruelly treated as these defenseless wives are ; and are just as far off from the protection of government and community as they are. Community don't like to step between a man and wife, even if they think she is abused.

And besides, the laws afford a shield to the conscience of those who respect the " powers that be." The higher claims of a common brotherhood are lost in our paper constitution or statute laws, which profess to be based upon it.

All men and women are not as dauntless in defense of Christ's government as I am. I say, that any law which conflicts with the divine, is of no binding force on my conscience. Even here—while in the absolute power of unlimited despotism—I fearlessly and boldly assert, even to Dr. McFarland himself, that I shall take the part of the oppressed, here, even if he puts me in irons for it! I never was disloyal to Jesus, through fear of man or law, and I never will be, so long as I have a life to lay down in his defense. Christ tells me to defend his oppressed ones, and I will do it, even if I have to expose the oppressor's secret acts. I am down on all oppressors of humanity, high or low, rich or poor. There is " no respect of persons " in my judgment of wrongs and abuses to God's children, anyhow or anywhere.

And I shall just as soon be down on you, Mr. President of the United States, if you prove, by your actions, to be an oppressor, instead of a defender of the weak and despised human being, as I shall on Dr. McFarland or any of his satelites, if they oppress humanity.

I do say, it is no part of Christianity to " cover sins," and I won't do it, either in myself or any other human being— I love them too well to do so. I know if a human being attempts to cover his sins, instead of abandoning them, he is in danger of not prospering in his interests. I go in for prosperity,—and I go in also for using the proper means for securing it. So, if the hardened sinner will not abandon his sins, I will expose him, lest his blood be found on my skirts.

Dr. McFarland knows what I mean!

So will all others know in the same way, if they lie across my track, in the progress of my "car of universal emancipation" from the bondage of sin and Satan! This car is to be pushed through from the Atlantic to the Pacific Ocean, when the government has laid the track for it!

I tell you, Lincoln, I am fierce for emancipation, for I have been fiercely oppressed, for want of freedom to do right. I will break every fetter of my spiritual bondage, if you won't give me and my sister slaves natural freedom. My energies in behalf of the married slave have been wonderfully sharpened up by the grindstone of abuse, so that I can speak, confidently, from experience. If there is any kind of abuse from a husband that can be told of, that I don't know how to understand, from experience, then I will give in.

To be sure, Brother Calvin never whipped me with a cart-whip, but his asylum rod hurt worse. He never kicked nor struck me,—not because he had not been mad enough a thousand times to kill me!—yet I carry a talisman about with me, which shields me from such manifestations of bitterness and revenge. *It is love.* My husband used to say often: "You are the greatest witch I ever saw—you will love a man out of himself!" But I couldn't love the man out of him into a practical principle; for he hadn't benevolence enough in him to love, even himself, right,—much less could he love any one else, only as they could administer to his gratification. On this principle, I do think he loved me better than he did himself; for I made him happier, by my love influences, than he could make himself.

Yes, this "bewitching" art is of service to women who know how to use it. God knew they would need it, before his son, Calvin, got too old to die. How could the wives of

Calvinists live in peace without it? Love covers a multitude
of sins, as well as exposes a multitude of sins. And, best
of all, it forgives a lot of transgressions, on the terms of
repentance. And I do believe the more it forgives, the more
it loves. I mean the more it forgives the penitent, mind
you. I don't believe in forgiving the unrepentant, at all;
and God don't, either.

But God, like me, gives them a long day of grace. I
wonder if he *always* will pardon the sinner, on this condition? If "he is the same yesterday, to-day, and for ever," I
should think he would. What does he send his children to
hell for, then? To punish them. What does he punish
them at all, for? To make them repent; just as I punish
my child, to make him do as I tell him to do.

Do people repent, then, after they die? Yes, if they don't
before. They have to be sent to the reform school first,
though, and some of them have to serve a pretty long term,
before they can be brought to accept of the discharge terms,
—gospel repentance. I think one thousand years term will
subdue the most inveterate Calvinist; and if God's promises
and terms of salvation are the same then as now, he has a
chance at salvation on the same terms that the Christian has.
I don't believe dying affects the moral character, any more
than eating or sleeping does; therefore, I think the moral
character is governed by the same laws, at one period of its
existence, as at another; just as my physical being is under
the same code of law in my morning dress, as it is in my
afternoon dress.

Well, if I cannot love my Calvinistic husband into repentance, in my morning dress, perhaps I can in my afternoon
dress, after he has been to the reform school a term or two!
I think my afternoon dress will be more attractive than the
one I now wear,—my morning dress; for the spiritual body
is more refined and beautiful than the natural body.

8*

But in both, love is the chief attraction. I therefore aim to cultivate the principle both in myself and my daughter, whom Fowler says is just like me,—"a bundle of affection." And she knows, too, how to use her shield, now I am away from her, to protect her from her father's abuse. I asked Isaac how she got along with father,—if he was as "cross as a bear" to her, as she used to say he was, when I was away from home? He said, "She gets along very well with father, —she is so kind, he can't abuse her,—and she has learned to keep her feelings to herself. She knows it won't do to talk about you to him,—he might flame up to have mother pitied, and do no good at all,—only harm."

Yes, she understands, I see. I wonder if she does as she told me, one day, she should do, if ever pa took off her kind and faithful mother, and hid her in an asylum. She said: "When pa blames me, when I am not to blame, and speaks cross to me, I shall do as you do,—just say nothing, till I have gone and told Jesus of it,—and then come and try to return 'good for evil.'" I hope she does so. Practice takes with some children, more than precept alone, does. But when both are united, the old devil finds it hard to catch the little ones. But if he don't look out, they'll catch him!

Isaac says: "Pa already begins to find that his children are the best friends he has got in the world, after all—except Samuel, a son in his own likeness—a 'woman-hater;' he has now turned against him, and speaks disrespectfully to him, and of him, and don't mind all he says neither. Pa knocks him about more than he does all the other children together, and it don't seem to do any good either."

Calvin's discipline don't seem to train them as mine did. It makes Samuel all the more fierce and revengeful.

By the way, I must own up, I was the occasion of Samuel's being a woman-hater, but his father was the cause. I got mad at his father when I was carrying his son Samuel for

him, because he teased me beyond even my powers of endurance about a hen which was eating up all my nice melons and
cucumbers in the garden, and I could not make him shut her
up, instead of letting me chase after her every hour of the
day, and leave my baby and work, too, to do it. He pre-
tended to try,—but I could see the careless action, whereby
the hen escaped his attempts to confine her,—he just seemed
to try, to tantalize me. I thought it was well for his garden
that his wife was quick enough to save his melons! He could
see how quick I was at chasing her off, from his study window,
and I guess it was fun, too, to him, to see me running so hard
for his benefit, and mine too. I like melons, especially at
times—proper times!

But I thought these vines cost me more than all the melons
were worth. But tried and tired as I was, with ironing all
day, running after the hen, and nursing a crying baby, I
stood it until most night, when the demon, fatigue, overcame
me, and I " blew him up " with a hurricane of words, such
as expressed my mind, in full, upon the subject. He was
scared half to death! If the judgment trump had sounded, I
don't think he could have been more astounded! "The wrath
of a lamb " will scare a wolf—even without his biting him a
bit. I didn't bite—but I scolded; and this " new song "
nearly drove his wits out of him. I haven't tried to chant
this song since—I don't approve of scolding. It don't pay.

I won't tell what he did; it is too bad to write on paper.
But God has got it written in his book, and I think he will
have to own up it is " all straight."

It is said figures won't lie. I guess there are some other
records that won't. My Father's accounts are kept by a
superior bookkeeper. They don't need auditing. How many
more officers we need to do our business than God does to do
his business !

Well, I can tell you, I know from this fact in my experience

(sad ! and oh ! how sad ! to Samuel,—the unborn child !),
that it don't pay to get mad.   Yes, it pays—but in *such* coin
as I would choose to reject as useless plunder.

But God works by rule, or law, and we must be ruled by
it, too, whether we wish it or not—and " as we sow, so we
must reap ;" and I have reaped sorrow enough in training
my flock, in consequence of this black sheep—not a wolf yet—
but there is no telling what changes or metamorphoses of
being sin renders us liable to undergo.

Well, if we do have a black sheep in our flock, it is our own
fault, and so we must do the best we can.   It is not God's
work, but ours—and therefore we must put to all the greater
effort, and make the black one a white one, as God intended
it to be.   No, I can't do that ! and God doesn't require impossibilities of me.   So I must only make a good black sheep of
him.   Black wool is of some use in its proper place.   But it
needs as much dressing as the white wool, and a good deal
more, to make it equally as valuable.

But I don't give up my Judas ! for God didn't give up his
devil, Judas, but sent him to his own place to be cared for.
I guess his place was the grave, where he was gone for a
time, to see if he could get a white fleece by the next mother
who bore him.   I hope his next mother didn't have a Calvin
for his father !

So you see God has laws to change the Ethiopian's skin,
and the leopard his spots, by changing bodies.

But how, in all reason, he can do it in any other way, I
don't see ; for if the slaves become the master in his white
skin, he might detect his owner.   And some masters, like Legree, wouldn't like to have Sambo, or Quimbo either, for his
master, for fear he should get some of his thrashings back
again—some interest he would wish to have discounted—
rather than have it paid in his own coin !

But God oversees the entries on both the debit and credit

side of the account-book, and no mistake has ever yet occurred—and I don't want any to; for I have made large investments in this book on the credit side, and I don't want him to lie, or break his promise either. For, I think, breaking a promise and telling a lie are about equal to six and a half-dozen.

He don't swear, either. Yes, I forgot, he does—by himself. But since he knows why it is best and right for him to swear, and not us, I mustn't ask to know—it is none of my concern. He has told me not to, and I have no disposition to disobey. I couldn't curse him if I tried—he don't give me the least chance to do it—he is always so kind.

Neither Calvin nor Samuel ever cursed me, and I don't think they ever felt disposed to do so. And I am not afraid of it in the least, for my Father says "the curse causeless never comes."

So when I hear a child curse his parents, I think of that. But when I hear them curse God, I know it cannot be my Father they mean, but Calvin's father—the old dragon—and I think the "curse causeless" don't come upon him!!

But I liked to have forgotten these wives with wolves for husbands, who put them into asylums.

I want to give our President one hint upon this subject. I do say that you imprison the wrong animal when you put the sheep in this den and leave the wolf to run at large. Wolves are a great deal more dangerous animals than lambs are—and the lambs need protection, but the wolves don't— you see, don't you? It is the women that want your help, not the men. If I be a woman, I can tell you that you have got the cart before the horse. It is the cart that needs stabling, not the horse. The horse can graze, and won't rot with the dews and rain of heaven, but the cart will, unless you shed it. And even a cart is worth saving.

Yes, if these wolves were all denned up in your great jail,

I do think they would have got home at last—where I think they ought to stay for life—for the lambs and sheep are not safe abroad—with liberty, I mean—liberty to do right, speak right, write right, and think right—unless these terrible animals are confined within proper limits.

Oh! if you could only see the scars these innocent, defenseless lambs carry on their bodies, where the wolves have scratched and bit them—especially those great big wolves in sheep's clothing!—you could not help pitying them, I know. I try to comfort them by telling them to be patient as they can, for I am going to tell of their husbands to Father Abraham, and I expect it won't be long before we shall hear his big key in our key-hole, and then he'll let us out, and won't let our husbands put us in prison again, or compel us to be their slaves any longer. Oh! when our asylum doors are thus opened, we need not fear they will be shut upon us any more. Our spring locks will spring upon our tormentors! and we, like the three worthies in the furnace, shall escape unharmed.

Oh! what glorious times we shall have when all these ravenous wolves are shut up and confined by the government key, as we have been!

We will do just as we please then, and we shall choose to please our Christian brothers, I assure you. They shall never regret that we are allowed to be true women—true to our instincts and to our loving natures. I don't think men have any real objection to being loved by the women. I'm sure I haven't any objection to being loved by the men. I am not ashamed to own up, even now, before the wolves are denned up—that I do worship a true man,—they are so much like Christ I can hardly tell them apart!

Well, Lincoln, I am an economist as well as a good calculator, in my line of business. I don't know how I should succeed in your business, if I should undertake it. Still, since we are now so stirred up, it don't matter much if we do men's work, especially when we can't get it done in any other way; therefore I am going to act as counselor and give you advice, even without being asked—although it is contrary to my principles to govern the men—they know enough to govern themselves, for God made them to rule their own passions. So if you get mad at me for dictating to you,—you can't rule yourself—and then, of course, you are not fit to rule the nation, and we shall give you only one term of presidential honor!

I tell you, President Lincoln, it won't pay for you to fall out with the women! It is best, for your interests, to keep in their good graces. For the fact is, it is dark times now, so much like night that we cannot tell it from midnight, and, you know, night or darkness is woman's time to rule, and we intend to use our privilege well. I want to get out of my prison quick, and so do all the rest of my fellow prisoners; but, lest you hesitate on the principles of economy in the use of public property, I suggest that our insane asylums be immediately appropriated as hospitals for our wounded soldiers until this war is ended, and then, in the meantime, you may find out what God made them for. I am sure God did not intend them for the devil's service, as they are now used! Now, since one body cannot be where another is, just let the soldiers take our beds and we will take our own—and be glad to do so, if you will only watch over our husbands and not let them abuse us any more—I don't like to be abused and scolded for doing right—and it isn't right to let us be so basely treated.

If they do get up some other form of crushing our identity, after you send us home from the " Asylum Inquisition," I shall tell on them again! I hate to be a tattler; but if these Calvinists compel us to tattle, to save our lives and health, won't it be in self-defense? I go on the number one principle, you remember.

I don't think it is any "righter" to let a man abuse me, than to let him abuse any one else. I am somebody! and God wants me protected, as well as his other children. And he has told me to fight for liberty, rather than die in slavery —this married slavery, I mean. I have been loyal to Jesus, and Calvin too, so far as I could serve two such opposite masters, and I don't think it is right to shut up the loyal ones in prison, and let the traitors go free. If they would let them all go free, it would be much better than it is now. But to imprison virtue, and liberate vice, is giving Calvin, or Satan, more than his due. The loyal have no chance at all as it is now.

I find, from my observation here, that lunatics won't hurt folks, if you'll only let them alone, and have pasture large enough.

The horse won't kick you if you don't get too near his heels—it is only because he don't like to be caught, that he kicks you, to get you out of his way. He likes liberty so well, that he runs wildly off, to keep out of the harness. 'Tis liberty the lunatics are fighting for, and that is what they fight here for, so much; and it is a pity so much fighting should be lost! They are too true to their God-like natures, to tamely submit to a trespass upon their personal identity.

I tell you again, Lincoln, these lunatics are the most loyal subjects Christ has on earth, and do you think he will let you imprison them, and abuse them, for being so true to his government, without arising to their defense?

I shouldn't be at all surprised if he should utterly destroy the American government, before he got the case through his court—for 'tis a fact, he is just in his administration, and so are his jury and council. They go strong too; for the bench are all united in sustaining the judge's decisions. Though his loyal subjects have to wait awhile, for their case to come up, yet, they are sure when it is investigated, justice will be done them. I, for one, much prefer to have my case tried at the Court of Heaven, on this account, for I am such a stanch advocate for justice. And, besides, Christ, my advocate, is so tender of my feelings he won't let me be insulted in court! Lincoln, if I were in your place, I would rather be hung than be found to be the one who had imprisoned a lunatic!

It would be a blessing to such a culprit, if the rocks and mountains would fall on him, and cover him from the " wrath of the Lamb ! "

It is bad business. It won't pay to be disloyal to Christ's government! He is too powerful to cope with. I have made up my mind, he shall have one loyal subject on the American continent. I shall defend the inalienable rights of even the President of the United States. He has a right to just treatment, himself, if he will trespass on a lunatic's inalienable rights " to life, liberty, and the pursuit of happiness," *in his own way.*

The lunatic would be the last one to trespass on others' rights, except in self-defense. It is interference,—unlawful interference—that makes maniacs. " Oppression makes the wise man mad,"—it don't hurt a fool, any more than it hurts a rotten egg to pound on it, or even break it!

How benevolent (?) 'tis to deprive a useful, loyal citizen of his liberty, and outlaw him, and shut him up in a cell, or a cage, and feed and clothe him there, "free gratis, for nothing." Yes—for nothing—only because he chose to serve God in his own way, according to the dictates of his own conscience! Or, because he was made a recipient of a spiritual, heavenly influence, and tried to be true to it. Can't spiritual, or heavenly influences find a foothold under the American flag? Yes—in prisons they can. They are not safe, unless bolted and barred down, in this free government, where freedom is protected!

I don't think in Christ's day they knew enough to practice this kind of benevolence on the lunatics. They let them have the liberty I have so often heard sighed after, here,—liberty to lie under a fence, and seek their own food as the squirrel does his, rather than be returned into the hands of friends (!) who had cast him into this prison to protect him! Some try to seek it in this way, when lo! some benevolent (?) soul finds him and returns him to his cell again!

I say the fugitive from slavery runs a better chance of getting his liberty, than the imprisoned lunatic does, under our laws, and humane (?) practice!

I do hope that every individual who has aided in imprisoning a lunatic, contrary to his will, will be furnished with aid enough to be imprisoned himself, in just the very cage he, so benevolently, put the lunatic into! If he thinks 'tis such a blessing to be caged up, let him enjoy the blessing himself—he is not required to love his neighbor better than himself.

It took Calvin's God to inculcate this type of benevolence. He taught that "their good" required that capital punishment, or hopeless, endless torment, be endured, to gratify the arbitrary, despotic will of a cruel tyrant.

Punishing the innocent for "their good"! The devil must have an individuality of his own, in order to have been able to develop this unique principle. I have no fancy for his organization—'tis too Calvinistic. Somehow, the devil and these insane asylums seem to be on the same track! No danger of any "collision," as I see, so I'll put on the steam, and take them both on to my terminus—the bottomless pit.

"Bottomless pit!" What sort of a concern is that? I'm afraid, if it has no bottom, they will come out on the other side! Never mind, if our antipodes do have to superintend this firm awhile; we have more important business to attend to. on this side, just at present. We have a notion of trying Christ's government, here in America, and see how we like it!

I am quite certain there is quite a large class of citizens, here, who will like it better than Calvin's. But I don't think the Calvinists will like it near so well. But they have had a fair chance—I don't think they need to complain of us for not letting them have things all their own way, pretty much.

If they don't interfere with our rights any more than we do with theirs, we shall have no reason to complain of aggressions!

I know they dislike our principles, but our practice they cannot complain of—unless they complain of our allowing them too much liberty to do wrong. But our principles compel us to do this; for "to do as we would wish to be done by," we must let them be as free to do wrong as we desire to be to do right. We want to be our own judges, too, of what is right for us to do. I do go for freedom of conscience, practically, as well as theoretically. I don't care a snap for a theory that can't be applied to practical use. Our government has tried this rule long enough to disgust me with it, entirely. Professing to be a liberty-protecting government, and yet, practically, the most oppressing and persecuting government on earth!

We can't do right, here, without exposing ourselves to capital punishment for it! No—not even speak our own thoughts, or even think them, without being called insane, and outlawed for it!

And I can prove this charge to be a true one, by the knock-down argument of facts. Yes, 'tis a fact; Calvin, or, as he is called in this body, Rev. Theophilus Packard, called me insane, and imprisoned and outlawed me, just because I thought I could see errors in his Presbyterian church creed, and tried to convince him and his church that they were not the "infallible church," on that account. But lo! his creed is so much more sacred to him than his wife's identity, that he can, conscientiously, sacrifice her, whom he has vowed to protect, to save it! Won't his benevolent God reward him for such self-sacrificing benevolence? If he don't, I think he must be incapable of appreciating the character of this act of his devoted subject!

He burned his brother Servetus for the same thing, and thus he paved the way to burning his "better half."

Perhaps his God requires but half of his body as a living sacrifice for his sins. Free-will offering! Oh! how willingly do some devotees lay down their half-bodies to save their creed!

It is said, somewhere, "He that saveth his life shall lose it." Perhaps he feared, if he ventured to save my life, he might be in danger of losing his own life. He was in danger, to be sure. His life devotion to creeds was in peril from my life devotion to truth and duty.

It is a fact, real freedom of opinion and conscience is not a mere humbug! It means something practical. And there is somebody else who has found that these inalienable rights mean something, not very agreeable in their application. But, thank God! I have to "switch off" to find him!

If I didn't, there surely must be a "collision," for his train is going the opposite way. You don't find Dr. McFarland on the track for the "bottomless pit." No! not he— he knows too much to be in such company! He knows it is the nineteenth century, instead of the fourteenth, for I find he has read history before I ever saw him. And I do say that a man who knows beans from corn, knows enough not to attempt to interfere with the rights of opinion and conscience in a woman of the present age.

But there are some mysteries about this "great man," which I can't understand. I do begin to think he is above my comprehension! This is one of his God-like traits. Another trait is, he don't always fulfill his promises as quick as I should like to have him. God treats me just so. I have to " wait—wait patiently " for them both. But since they are both manly, I·don't think either of them will be guilty of " breach of promise ! "

But, President Lincoln, I can assure you that Dr. McFarland is not the only great man under this roof; neither am I the only woman of character.

There are many of the greatest men and greatest women, here, that I ever met anywhere. They can look on both sides of a subject—that is, they have broke the traces, and are free thinkers. Yes, I have met my first truly independent thinker under this roof. These creed-bound thinkers are such common trash, that they are not of much account with me. But when I find one who is ready to acknowledge that " *all* who fear God and work righteousness are accepted of him," of whatever name or denomination, then, I feel sure I have found a kindred spirit—an independent thinker! I seek the companionship of such, for I am sure of some individuality of thought, from this source, worth securing.

Such is the characteristic mark of my asylum companions; and it is this individuality of character that has consigned them here, as patients, to be cured of being as God has made them to be—naturally developed human beings—true to the organization God as given them! Blasphemy! I wonder what sea gave birth to this beast, " which has upon his heads the name of blasphemy ? " I guess 'twas the " sea of Rome."

These finest specimens of God's workmanship are despised and rejected of men, for being so God-like, instead of being devil-like—like their contemporaries. I honestly believe that the sanest people of America are entombed in the insane asylums of our land, or, are bearing the stigma of insanity, assigned them by perverted humanity—the really insane portion of community.   And, furthermore, I'll risk a prophecy, viz., that these now despised ones, who are accounted as the filth and offscouring of all things, will yet be the first in honor and notoriety, as the martyrs of the age, for individuality of thought, feeling, and character ; and our persecutors will be the last in the scale of infamy and dishonor and contempt.

Our persecutors are trying to torment us, as if to punish us for hurting them, when we have not hurt them at all!   It is the truth that hurts them—their own actions—not us, for telling them of it ; as it was Herod's own acts which hurt him, not John, for telling him his sins.   We only want to heal the wounds sin has made, thoroughly—not slightly. We are the most tender-hearted and sympathizing class of human beings.   We only want you to let us help you out of your troubles.

Now, do, Father Abraham, only just try us once, and see if we abuse our liberty to hurt even a fly!   If we do, you can keep the penitentiary ready for us.   We had much rather be thought and proved, by a Calvinistic bar, bad, than insane, for a bad man is entitled to his accountability—and an insane one is not.

Oh ! it is hard to be treated like a wild beast, when we are only doves, and trying to soar out of the reach of all the beasts in creation!   But our time to mount and soar is to come ; and what's to come will take place.

We'll not only destroy the asylums, but the Calvinistic priesthood also.   We don't need them any more.   They have done our thinking long enough for us.   We are twenty-one, and we can oversee ourselves!   Christ is all the teacher we want.   And he can teach us cheaper than Calvin does. He lets us judge for ourselves, what is right for us to do— Calvin don't.

Calvin wants us to go to church and hear what he has thought out; while Christ wants us to listen to our own thoughts—the inspirations of the Divinity "within ourselves."

I don't see the use of going to church all day, and get tired, and cross, and hungry, while the preacher tells us nothing but how bad we are, while we know we are not so bad as he thinks we are—and then he don't even tell us what to do to get better! We have to guess at that. And I can guess at that, at home on my bed, resting, as God told me to do, on resting day. And I think Christ's way to get 'right feelings is to do right. And the way to do right is to do what we think is right, not what any other one thinks is right, if it conflicts with our views of truth and duty. I say, if I go to church when *I* think it is my duty to stay at home and rest, I do wrong, even if I do please the notions of some poor deluded Calvinist.

I believe in Sunday or holy days, but I don't think they come often enough. I try to be just as holy about my work on the other six days, as I do on resting day; and a little holier, if anything, for I am watched and seen more at my work, than at rest. I don't go in for Sunday coats and Sunday faces. I've seen enough of this sort of trash!

I want the right-down honest man, who isn't afraid to speak the truth, in the devil's hearing, too!

I like to shoot a man right in his face and eyes. I feel mean to go to his back, as if I was afraid of him. I am not afraid of any man, nor devil, or fallen angel,—neither am I afraid to shoot a gun at any of them, if I can see any Calvinism in them. You see I'm always watching for this sort of game. Gunning birds, bats, or snakes, is better than gunning men. I can't go that. God save me from killing a human being! for I don't know where one act of disobedience might lead me to. Samuel's case has taught me a lesson, and my memory is good,—especially when his sister and female teachers make complaint to me about his troubling them. Don't you think I hate to punish him, when I know I am the occasion of his needing it? Yes, I do,—but bad acts bring bad recompense;—and I—not God—have to undo or destroy my bad work, on his good work, and God can and will help me; but he must be regenerated or born again, to do it. That is God's work.

But, mind you, to be sure of being born into a better body next time, you must well improve this!—living up to present light, is the only way to a title to future light or help.—In short, all must do the very best they know how to do in this body, and God will take care of the next.

Now, I don't want a minister to keep dinging at me that my conscience is no guide, when I know it is! And I mean to follow it exactly, in everything, in spite of all the clergy in Christendom to the contrary. And you see if I don't come out right, or at least, as well as they who listen to Calvin, instead of Christ, on this and similar subjects!

I do say we never have a right to do wrong, and we never find it wrong to do right. And I do say, it is right for me to stay away from church, and be the priestess to my own children, rather than go with them to hear the doctrines of Calvin taught from the pulpit, by a "wolf in sheep's clothing."

Besides, Christ's doctrines are so simple, that all can comprehend them—and Calvin's are so complex, that children of common-sense can't understand them.

Again, the clergy are so creed-bound that they have to tell us the same thing over and over so many times, that it gets threadbare,—almost worn out to holes in some places! I think, if a minister can't bring out any "new things" out of the Bible, and we have learned by heart all the old things, it is time to stop preaching, and let the people go to thinking for themselves.

I, for one, gained more instruction from the thinking of our Bible-class thinkers, than I have from listening to the reading of Calvin's old sermons for the thirtieth time over. They who dared to speak their own thoughts, gave me light and aid in my search after truth. But they who, through fear, put their own light under a bushel, and just echoed the teachings of the pulpit, were of no account to me, nor themselves either. They are the unprofitable servants of the vineyard,—proving the truth of the adage, " like people, like priest."

Yes, such ministers have been through the "ministers' mill," where all their individuality has been ground out of them, by the grindstones of human creeds; and now they set up a similar mill of their own, to grind out the native manliness of their people. And the process is as sure to make parasites, or parrots, of human beings, as the asylum is to make maniacs of them. But of the two, a maniac is the more noble representative of the Deity, for he maintains his identity, while the other becomes an echo, merely,—his individuality lost in the labyrinth of speculations.

I don't see how Calvin came to think of this way of making ministers! I am sure he didn't get his pattern from Christ. I can't find the theological seminary that Christ went to, to learn his creed by heart, except it was the carpenter's shop.

His creed seemed to be " practical godliness," and it was so broad as to include all the practical duties of every individual being of the whole human family. He practiced religion as much again as he preached it, while some ministers preach it as much again as they practice it. And I think one practical preacher, like Christ, does more good than the entire priesthood of Calvin's oligarchy.

I, for one, would go to a practical Christian to find the way to heaven, as quick again as I would to a Calvinistic

9

preacher,—for I am very sure he knows as much again about
it as Calvin does.

I don't think even King David's dancing and shouting
together, had so much religion in it, as Christ's quiet, holy
life, had.   Doing good,—as Christ did,—is the best religion
I know of.

"THE TERRESTRIAL TRAIN:"

UZZAH.

PREFACE.

The track of " nature " is adhered to on this trip, showing the many radical changes and improvements, the practical observance of its natural laws will bring about in the family, church, and state. This track is laid through the affections and instincts; but in some places we have to "tunnel" very deep to find the " grade" or equipoise we seek in this virgin soil of nature.

To promote our own happiness is our highest ambition, as this is the supreme good, since we are a part of God—whose chief end is his own glory or happiness—and this is the only track where this result is guaranteed. On this track the bogs of selfishness are so thoroughly bridged over with the wrought-iron of self-love as to secure to our train a safe transit; and the gunpowder of truth has blasted every rocky obstruction found on this track; and the blow-pipe of love has melted the iron will of tyranny. These two " surveyors"—truth and love—have already "graded" this track through to the Pacific ocean of universal peace, and our trains are even now thundering through these unexplored regions of prophecy; and our highest national aspirations are, ere long, to be fully consummated.

THE "TICKETED PASSENGERS" ON BOARD THE "TER-
RESTRIAL TRAIN" ARE FOUND IN THE FOLLOWING

LIST OF PASSENGERS.

Queen Victoria of England and her Parliament.

Abraham Lincoln, President of United States.

Dr. A. McFarland, Jacksonville, Ill.

Mrs. E. P. W. Packard and her six children, viz., Theophilus, Isaac, Samuel, Elizabeth, George, and Arthur of
Chicago, Ill.

Lawyer Brown, Chairman of Trustees.

Gen. McClellan, Army Officer.

Goliath of Gath.

Brother Samuel Ware, Batavia, Ill.

The Eclectic Fraternity, Cosmopolitans.

Rev. Mr. Prime, Editor of New York *Observer.*

Brother Austin Ware, South Deerfield, Mass. --

My Sainted Mother—Mrs. Lucy S. Ware.

Rev. Mr. Russell, Asylum Chaplain, Jacksonville.

Rev. Theophilus Packard, Manteno, Ill.

Widow Dixon, Manteno, Ill.

John Brown, the Martyr for Freedom.

Mr. Elliott, Greenfield, Mass.

Cousin Ophelia Fiske, Shelburne, Mass.

Mr. David Allen Fiske, Shelburne, Mass.

Moses, Israel's Leader.

Dr. Woods, Andover, Mass.

Prof. Parks and Mrs. Parks, Andover, Mass.

Rev. H. W. Beecher, Brooklyn, L. I.

Nicodemus, a ruler in Israel.

Abraham, the Patriarch.

Hon. Mr. Seward, Secretary of State.

Lovejoy and Sumner, Congressmen.

"John Bull,"—Old England.

Americus Vespucius, the Usurper.
Columbus, the Discoverer.
Scott, Henry & Doddridge, Commentators.
Dr. Sturtevant, Asylum Chaplain, Jacksonville.
Rev. Mr. Marshall, Jacksonville, Ill.
Dr. Edwards, Andover, Mass.
Rev. Aaron Foster, Charlemont, Mass.
Asa B. Tenney, M. D., Jacksonville, Ill.
Allopathic Fraternity, Cosmopolitans.
Mrs. Forrest, Asylum Patient.
Daniel, the Prophet.
Mrs. Clayton, a Suicidal Patient.
O. S. Fowler, the Phrenologist.
" Harwood & Tucker," Dentists, Boston, Mass.
The New England Ministers.
King David, the Psalmist.
Mr. Tiffany, Mt. Pleasant, Iowa.
Miss Harriet Rumsey, Manteno, Ill.
Miss Sarah Rumsey, Manteno, Ill.
Mr. G. P. Comstock, Manteno, Ill.
Mrs. S. T. Dole, Manteno, Ill.
Mr. Abner Baker, Marshall, Mich.
Deacon Smith, Manteno, Ill.
George Hastings, New Bedford, Mass.
Mr. O'Leary, Phrenologist.
Mrs. Angeline Field, Granville, Ill.
Lawyer Kitchell, Detroit, Mich.

The "Bill of Freight" on board the "Terrestrial Train" is found in the following

List of Thoughts.

Conservatism, as opposed to woman's elevation.
Reasonableness of Christ's theology.
Insanity of Calvin's theology.
Mr. Packard's book.
The Indian's wrongs.
Sinless anger.
Progress accelerated by opposition.
Victoria a model queen.
Natural engineers of thought.
Telegraphic dispatches through conscience.
Nature tends to cure its own diseases.
Calvinistic maxim.
Family scales of truth and honesty.
Is it wicked to laugh?
My spiritual mother.
Feelings the result of our own acts.
Calvinistic logic below the plane of common-sense.
Contrast between Dr. McFarland and Calvin.
Actions form the character.
A woman-hater is rotten at the core.
A woman-lover is loyal.
God makes people good, the devil makes them bad.
Calvin must confess his sins before he gets out of purgatory.
Calvin as a pack-horse.
My maternal joys my only heaven.
Father Abraham in his den.
Manliness should be the qualification for office.
Auction of Calvinistic plunder.
The brimming sugar-ladle.

Children should be made to do right from choice.

Lying parents are Calvinistic.

God's government is the parents' model.

How I managed my children abroad.

How Calvin whipped Toffy.

Why Calvin disliked the West, and why his wife liked it.

The Calvinism of the war.

Lincoln, won't you cut off my husband's head?

Christ's puzzles set people to thinking.

A transition state trying to patience.

Our freight-bill or taxes must be paid.

Sun and Moon should supplant the stripes of our flag.

Columbia the Christian name of our republic.

God's works the best commentary.

Professor Parks a smart colt.

Dr. Wood's total depravity theology.

Christ's nature not sinful, neither is ours.

Dr. Sturtevant preaches universal salvation,—Christianity,
    —but he practices Calvinism.

The Assembly's Catechism not infallible.

The risk of being a natural woman.

Regenerating nature ruins it.

Hereditary depravity.

A holy life in Christ's estimation.

Rev. Aaron Foster, a natural man.

Nature's laws treated as insanity.

A wife's condition worse than the slaves.

Our man-government only a half affair.

A wife's liabilities.

Coral work like character.

Self-love the highest law of our nature.

Good is more contagious than evil.

Drunkards and prostitutes less depraved than consistent
    Calvinists.

9*

To be selfish is to hate our own happiness.

God made woman to soar—the Calvinists make her to crawl.

Women the lightning express—men the freight train.

'Tis natural to love good and hate evil.

Dr. McFarland in a trap.

My book will rise by its own merits.

Dr. A. P. Tenny's compliment to my book.

My compliment in return.

The patient's favorite.

Uncle Sam, won't you protect woman's nature ?

It is not wrong to love people.

Christ-like men inspire trust and do not betray it.

Manliness totally eclipsed by Calvinism.

The unregenerate are woman's protectors.

Woman's way to government should be made easy.

An unmanly government not worth defending.

Shield of faith indispensable for wives of Calvinists.

Resentment of insults a mark of the divinity.

The most cursed institutions of the 19th century.

Culmination of the Calvinistic principle.

Sane abroad, and insane at home !

Sooner sign a death-warrant than an asylum certificate.

Mr. Packard's credit mark.

His discredit mark.

Woman the better-half of the Deity.

Her keenest sufferings.

Why laws are necessary for woman's protection.

Sympathy treated as insanity.

Mrs. Forrest's lament.

Mrs. Clayton's suicide.

Insanity treated as a crime.

Cheerfulness my native element.

My Linen story.

To be judged by our own actions.
" Blasphemy against the Holy Ghost."
Doing wrong impolitic.
A money-hungry wolf.
Dea. Smith's small head.
Catechism on the true and false church.
Government and church must both be winnowed.
Honest dealing commands respect.
Choose no evil that can be shunned.
Law should protect babies.
Retribution and compensation certain.
Christ's kingdom to be established in America.
The New Flag.
Treason one branch of Calvinism.
Little sinners punished, and great ones shielded.
My army sons.
Making prayers is not praying.
My Packard's psychological power.
Kidnapping my daughter.
The lying Misses Bumsys.
Kidnapping my babe.
My condition before being kidnapped.
Protest against Calvinistic contributions.
My parting with Isaac and George.
Samuel, my traitor boy.
Sibyl T. Dole's treacherous conduct.
Defense of my love for Mr. Baker.
" She has burned my valuable papers."
I used to believe a change of heart made one better.
Hating a wife is the result of regeneration.
Church expects spiritual men before natural ones.
Church business to make people healthy.
Must a woman confine her love to one man ?
Or a man to one woman ?

Calvin's God a jealous one.

Calvin's God rightly treated by the swearers.

Calvin's inhospitality.

Our final parting in the asylum.

The new trinity.

God and nature coöperate.

Idleness leads to ossification of nature.

Active toil to development.

Faith a potent shield and defense.

Need carry no burdens of regrets or anxieties.

Our own and God's will should be married.

Heaven found in hell.

Boundary of America and Columbia.

May love and truth kiss each other?

A consistent Calvinist the greatest heathen.

Calvin's God the foulest in the universe.

Calvinism to be buried in the grave it had dug for Christianity.

Christians are the children of nature.

Calvinism and human reason are deadly foes.

The rose which is to be transplanted.

Ignorantly, willfully, conscientiously wrong.

Duty is imperative.

Universal salvation—universal repentance.

God's punishments are reformatory.

'The Terrestrial Train."

Uzzah.

When the Lord sends for me to carry his ark home, as the cows did the ark of God, I do hope I shall not have to go by Uzzah's field! for I hate to have the men interfere with my own especial business. The Lord gave me my business, not Uzzah, and God, not Uzzah, knows whether he has fitted me for it. Uzzah don't know as much as God.

So, Mr. Uzzah, mind your own business! when I go past, for I am in a great hurry to get to my calves, too. Your business is to bind your wheat, and if you look off to watch my movements, your knot may slip, and thus your bundle of wheat may be scattered. If the knot is not tight, it will not bear hard usage. So look out and tie a square knot—the right kind. I don't like to see Uzzah's eyes, for his hands are apt to follow them—fence or no fence.

I tell you, "hands off from my business! or I shall get Father to take them off for you, and then you may wish, when it is too late, that you had taken my advice. I have learned to do business on my own capital, and I understand more than I tell you. I tell you I can stand alone—on my own walking feet—with no man to lean upon—but God—and he lets me lean when I need to."

But here, in this new country, we have to go in a cow-path, so he goes on before to see if the way is all clear for me—not because he is an Indian, or ungallant—it is gallant for a man to go first sometimes. All general rules have their exceptions. But when we get the turnpike built, and the wide sidewalks laid, then we can go abreast, arm-in-arm.

But the ark of testimony, you know, is out of its place. Plague on these Calvinists! to trespass on God's authority as well as man's!

But we women must see to it that nature's laws are obeyed. There is no other rule in the book that can improve the age, except you give the women a chance to be natural women. We don't want any more Calvins to train. Give me the true, natural olive plant, and I don't want any pleasanter business than to fulfill the mission God sent me to do—"to bear children." But it is hard to do right, as things have been, with the ark away down to Beersheba. The testimony must be nearer home—in our houses. Our natures must be respected by the government, and our rights at home must be protected.

Abraham, have you got an Uzzah in your cabinet? If you have, give him plenty of employment. This is the safest way to keep them at home, and from not interfering with this "woman's rights" business. There is plenty of wheat-sprawling; I should think you might keep them busy binding it for the great stack. You'll find reconstruction is no child's play; it is work—hard work—and Christian men ought to work as well as we women. Besides, you are paid and we are not. Our toil is "free gratis"—but I hope for something—not nothing.

Dr. McFarland has got a man in his cabinet who smells rather Uzzahish. Mr. Brown, the chairman of the trustees, asked me a question which smelled a little too "ratish" to suit me. Said he, "Ain't you afraid, Mrs. Packard, that you'll grow too fast?"

I knew it wasn't just right, by my feelings, at the time. I tell you our instincts are worth something, especially these days—for we want to know who it will do to trust—and who not to trust. These instincts help us amazingly in picking out the fellows our votes will go in for!

I acknowledge I was a little taken back by his question at first, but before I got through my answer I hinted at my individuality—just a gentle hint, for he is a man, who, like Lincoln, don't need a strong one. He is smart—no mistake —and can be trusted if you keep a pretty sharp lookout for the Calvinistic rat, and keep a gun ready, as quick as he comes out of his hole, to shoot, at first sight, before he has had time to nibble!

I saw my aim hit. Mr. Brown didn't ask the question the second time.

He may judge for himself—and I'll judge for myself. I didn't return the question—it's none of my business how fast he grows—I think he can take care of his own business without my help. He seemed pretty bright; and I should judge from his head and eyes that he needn't depend upon a woman to beat out a track for him. I guess he can walk and make his own tracks. At any rate—I can go ahead without his help—and I'll trust him to move forward without mine.

But I shouldn't wonder if he had been among the Old School Presbyterians and got his benevolence a little tainted with their Calvinism. You know they are famous for making harnesses for other folks—as well as for themselves. And that is all well enough were it not for this Calvinistic benevolence, which insists upon our using them instead of our own—because they are sure they are better than our own. Well, if they do think they are better for them that's no sign, I think, they are for me. I don't. I like the harness God made for me better than their Presbyterian harness. It fits better and sets easier, and what is more, I can do double the amount of service in it. The conservatism taints

it for my nature. I am for driving right down to the root of
things, and if I find a poisonous root underground, I put the
axe down there and cut it off. I can't shoot underground,
you know—but when I come across a vulture's nest, I pour
in the hot shot until it is too hot for them to conserve any
longer. I hate a "set-still's" nest, especially where they
are hatching!

But to tell the whole truth, I think Mr. Brown did really
have benevolent intentions towards me—he was afraid my
brain would get overtaxed with so much thinking—for it
must have been rather a humane man who asked Paul, " If
much learning had not made him mad ? "

I tell you, it is not learning that makes people mad—but
'tis the want of it.

The clear, sound theology of Christ don't tax the brain to
see into it, as these human creeds do. We can walk right
into it with reason's eye wide open. But it is the unsound,
insane, devilish theology of Calvin which so racks the brain.
The fact is, the more you try to see, the more you can't see.
And as for the reason, that has to be blindfolded entirely,
and so things get all into a tangle ; and I stump Calvin to
answer some of the questions I could ask him on his own
premises.

Another thing with my theology—or rather, Christ's theology—is, that a child can understand it.

By the way, I will tell you, Abraham, this is one cause of
our family troubles ; the children call so much for reasons of
things, and their father is so driven to his wits' ends to put
them easy. His knock-down argument generally is—"I
have reasons, but women and children can't comprehend
them ; it requires too deep and clear a head for you to understand ! " " Fol-de-rol ! " just as if I couldn't understand
as well as he ! I guess that my under-standing is better
than his upper-standing.

This, his vain attempt to escape justice, by putting injustice on to me, will not raise his standing in society to a very high pitch, I guess.

But he is a good scholar—very good. He has helped me in the languages considerably, and Theophilus considerably more. He taught him Latin, when he got too far for me to teach him. Calvin is a good classical scholar, and he excels in dates and names—he is a great antiquarian. He wrote a big book once. It was elegantly printed, and bound in a " go-to-meeting style." It is ornamental, and it wouldn't be a disgrace to any man's library to have it among his other books. But as for the reading, I am not prepared to judge of its merits, for—I am almost ashamed to own it—I never read it. I have very little reading time at home; and, besides, when I do read, I want to read something *practical*, and so dates and statistics are out of my forte, pretty much. The name of the book is, the " History of the Churches and Ministers of Franklin County, Mass."

It took him seven years to write it, and cost him $700 to get it printed, and he has not got near all his money back again. So it was not a very lucrative affair after all. Who knows but that my book, in its every-day clothes and style, may bring me in more of the hard cash than his did? Wouldn't he feel cheap to be outshone by his wife in literary merit—his great forte?

But if I only had time, you don't know what an elegant book I could write! I can paint as well as dress, when I choose to. But a time for all things—it is hunting and shooting times with me now—not party times—and soldiers don't mind their clothes—it is their balls and triggers they mind—so do I. If my balls are not painted, they can do just as good execution. And it is the execution that praises the gun—I don't court any other praise to attend my gun. But I do hope and pray it may demolish Calvinism in America—every fort, arsenal, armory, battery, fleet, and even the hunting-grounds of the aborigines! It was Calvin's spirit that usurped the poor Indian's rights of home and country, and chased him beyond the limits of civilization.

I wonder if some of their spirits have not come back into some of our traitors, to avenge their wrongs on us? I don't think they forget all their old habits and customs in their graves—and I shouldn't wonder if God employed their naturally revengeful spirits, as his agents, in recompensing our cruel deeds. For God says, that "as we sow so shall we reap," and we have sowed cruelty, injustice, oppression, and wrong, in our abuse of the Indian, and if God don't tell lies, then we must reap a harvest of cruelties, injustice, and oppression, and wrong, ourselves—that is, in the same measure that we have meted out to him, so shall it be meted out to us in abundant measure—for seed increases by being sown, sometimes a hundred-fold!

Oh! how I should dislike to sow seeds of injustice to humanity! I don't dare to risk such a harvest; for God don't forget insults, any sooner than the Indian does—He is as sure to avenge them as the Indian is.

I do not know as there is a human being, dead or alive, that I have wronged, without having repented of it, and made restitution. How much happier I feel in prospect of my recompense, than if I had not! If a good spirit—our friend—can administer comfort to us, as God says they do, then, cannot a bad spirit—our enemy—torment us? Dying does not change the spirit—it has new and increased ability and power to harm or help us, by its release from the body. And our friends are those who are like us—not our kindred, always, either. Our kindred are often our worst enemies—most unlike us of any one else.

Again, I do think it is best to make friends of all classes of human beings, by respectful treatment of them, under all circumstances, for God is a tenant of every human soul, and I don't like to be regardless of God—wherever I meet him—either in a white or a black skin.

And I know, too, that there is a devil, also, in every human being who is not entirely sanctified, and I hate him and all his works, as much as I love God and all his works. Yes, I do hate evil, as God tells me to, in my nature, as well as in his word. And I hate it so intensely, that I can't keep it in—I show out my real feelings towards it. And were it not that God had commanded me not to sin in being angry at evil, I should be tempted to attempt to avenge it myself. But as it is, I am not in danger of sinful anger, for I won't disobey God, by avenging my own wrongs—I'll leave that part of angry feelings to God, to exercise for me—I have only to show him that I hate the wicked act, by a manifestation of my hatred, in an open, frank expression of my indignation towards it. For what is the use of a feeling that is not expressed? Who would know that I hated evil, unless I showed my hatred or indignation?

I make no account of a feeling of love or hate towards me that does not show itself, in some sensible manner. And I don't think God does. I judge of a feeling by its manifestation or fruit—not by its professions. I guess God will judge of our hearts by our actions—rather than our words, or our prayers, even. For a prayer is of no account with me, unless it is sincere; and I judge by the actions, as well as words, whether they mean anything by it or not. I guess Satan don't care how angry we feel towards him, if we won't show it out, any way! He can tolerate our ill-will, as long as we don't let any one else know it.

But God won't tolerate us for not obeying his directions—to be angry at sin. I, for one, have made up my mind to "be angry and sin not," and not fear Satan so much more than I do God, that I dare not let it be known that I am loyal to Christ's government, by keeping the feeling out of sight. I know that those over whom Satan has the control of their actions, won't like me for showing this act of loyalty to Christ; yet, I can afford to be unpopular among devils—for the sake of being popular with Christ, when he says he is not ashamed of me, at the judgment—because I was not ashamed of him among devils, on earth. If I am a traitor to Christ, through fear of Satan's power, I can't expect his government will protect me, by its power.

Father Abraham, I want to tell you how my husband slandered our government when he put me in here. 'Tis too bad! And you ought to know it. He said: "Wife, you must not blame me for putting you into the asylum—it is the laws of your country that put you there!" 'Tis a lie—isn't it? You didn't make the laws to imprison such loyal citizens as I have always been to you, and God, too, did you? No. You meant they should protect the good, and punish the bad—and now my husband has just turned the tables, and used the laws to punish the innocent, and shield the guilty. Isn't this a mean, Calvinistic trick of his own getting up?

It took the sagacity of old Calvin, himself, to twist up things in this sort of way. But that is just a chip of the old block—his father knew his trade well, before him. He seems to think he can block up the way to heaven, so that upright souls cannot pass over it! I find it is tremendous narrow—still, I can run on it, when I have such a driver as old Calvin after me. How curious it is, that the very means devised, by Satan—to hinder progress—are used, by God, to increase it! I never ran after truth half so fast in all my life, as I have since Calvin has tried to kidnap my accounta-bility. I not only find it now, but what is better still, I am not afraid to tell the whole world what a Saviour I have found. For he is determined to call me insane—and I am equally determined to become a perfect person in Christ Jesus' estimation—even if Calvin, or the "old dragon," does call me insane for it. We'll see who is the "weaker vessel," by and by! whose head is cracked!

I think it would not be amiss to trepan him even now. But he is so used to setting traps, I guess he'll catch himself before long, and so save others the trouble. For it is a fact, the devils must be caught, if they don't catch themselves. And it does take a crazier head than mine to follow his trail—and I am not going to try to do any such thing. He can hang himself without my help. I have other fish to fry.

My business is to go to the clear stream of truth (translucent stream, if it was not so long), and get me, first, a few smooth stones. I guess three books will answer for the present crisis, and put them into my sling of faith. I don't know whether they will sell or not, till I have tried, you know. If this doesn't sell, I don't write another book for the American market! Perhaps I shall write for Victoria. I like Sister Victoria, because she brings up her children so well. I praise those mothers whose works praise them. So does God. If Victoria neglected her children for her realm, I should fear her kingdom would forsake her, for her folly.

The "kingdom of God" in the family, is the first thing to see to,—and the last thing to be neglected by the Christian mother, whether she be queen or subject,—and no true man or woman can honor any mother who proves a traitor to its interests.

Yes, I do say Victoria is the model queen, for she rules her own children as well as herself; and I believe she lets her subjects do the same thing, as Christ does. I should think Victoria was a Christian, because she seems to imitate Christ in so many things. I wish her Parliament were like her in this respect! then they wouldn't encourage our rebels in overthrowing our government.

But I am getting off the track a little, am I not? No, I think not. You see I have to keep two trains of cars running on two different tracks, and, you know, it requires a little more thought to watch two trains than one. But natural engineers can do wonders, you know. It is these self-made—self-taught—men and women that make tracks for the cars of human progress—and push them on too—with the steam of their own fiery zeal, from the boiling caldrons of their own thoughts. McClellan, for example. He has to engineer his track, and his army too.

I have to engineer the car of Calvin to the grave—and the car of Christ to his throne. But I do hope I shan't be so slow about my work as McClellan is about his! But he's a man—and men are so calculating, sometimes, that they don't do anything else.

I think it's well to be cautious, but I don't think it is best to be too much afraid of treading on the devil's heels, lest he get the start of us, and be at our heels.

I don't stop to calculate what criticisms will be made upon my book—neither do I care—if I can only expose Calvin, and defend Christ. It is not criticisms that I am fishing after—it is to kill Calvinism, and clear the track for the King of Glory.

McClellan is puffed before he does his work—I can wait till mine is done, for mine. But it is not puffing that I am after either; but it is praise—true praise—of well-done work. I wouldn't give a fig for all the false praise of men or devils, if my works didn't praise me. Besides, if men don't praise me when my works do—I know God will—and that will both gratify and satisfy my approbativeness.

Well, I hadn't got through with this government slander. Doesn't it smell strongly of treason? If I believed it, do you think I should feel much interest in supporting it? No—not I—I don't uphold injustice anywhere—and God doesn't either.

I go for and with God—the whole Union against one—if need be. It doesn't scare me. God's justice is more omnipotent than all the Egyptian chariots and horsemen combined in one grand army ; and the Philistines, headed by Goliath himself, in addition to all the rest. But when this great Goliath is your husband—and he sets his great teeth into your heel—it hampers you some, I can tell you !

But, Lincoln, you'll help me get shed of him, won't you ? The fact is, I want you to just use your government axe to just behead the " old Dragon," and then I think I can get his teeth out of my heel myself.

The way he caught me was : I was at work on my fruits, in our grass plot, standing in the high grass, where I could not see the movements of the old serpent, and when I thought he was off yonder, getting up means to send me East, to visit my father, the first I knew, he stuck his old dragon-head up close to my heel ; I tried to run off to Brother Samuel's, in Batavia, but he caught me in the prairie grass and set his teeth in my heel so firmly that I'll risk anybody to unclench them till his head is off.

I can't move a step out of this asylum without running the risk of his claiming me as his wife, and getting me too ! And I won't be his wife again ! Need I be, Father Abraham ? Hasn't he gone beyond the forbearance of the truest woman's charity to forgive—without repentance ? He has gone beyond mine, and whether you think so or not, Father Abraham, I do—and that is enough to decide my duty.

I don't have to ask anybody what my duty is. I know it without asking. I mean men,—I ask God all the time, and he guides me all the time,—by my conscience. I know as quick as a flash, when that brings a "telegraphic despatch" from the upper regions, and I tend to it, too. I don't know all that's going on there, but I think it has some relation to me, or I shouldn't have had anything to do with it. I just get the practical part, and go in for it, and whether it pleases anybody else, or not, I don't stop to ask. I know despatch is one of the prime virtues of the telegraph; and when I am called to put my fingers in the pie, I go in for it!

When I tell my children to hand me pies, I don't always think it necessary to tell them what I am going to do with them. But I don't tell them to put their fingers in the pies, —I tell them to keep them off from the pies,—only to bring them to me. But if I find they don't mind me, and I see a little hole in the top, where their little fingers have been to find a raisin, I just tell them that isn't what their fingers were made for,—and that they mustn't do that thing again, —and they don't. They mind me. But they somehow are tempted to disobey father Calvin. But wife Christian tells them that is wrong. And what Christian mother says is wrong, is wrong for them, at least, and they are as afraid of it as of a rattlesnake. For they know, without trying it, that their bite is fatal, unless you have a pail of new milk handy to put the wounded member into, to draw the poison right straight out. But if the new, fresh, mother-milk isn't all ready on hand, to use right quick, 'tis too late! The child must die, and all the eclectics can't save him from death. No matter if it is my only daughter, "Libby," 'tis all the same thing. The poison don't mind the spirit, nor the person,—it minds the blood,—and spoils that, and when the blood is spoiled, it's death to comfort.

I haven't but one child that's tried this experiment,— thank God! But then Calvin sent me off to the hospital just at the time he needed me most,—and I'm afraid the poison will get so diffused throughout the system,—before I get back home, that new milk won't do. I mean the milk of human kindness. It will take divine kindness. And after two and one-half or three years' delay after the bite of the serpent, traitor, I intend to test the potency of this article.

Eclectics combine the good of all, and discard the evils of all systems. I like them on that account. They don't blister and cut and slash us all up, to make us better. They only take out the evil virus, and let the good blood all stay where God put it,—in the veins! They only want to take out the Calvinism from it.

But what a pity 'tis that a good thing can't be done up in the right way! I can't risk this Calvinistic way of doing up things.' It destroys too much good, in trying to get at the evil. I don't believe in destroying one's nature, or constitution, in order to destroy the disease in it. I say, build up nature, or the constitution, so that it can have strength to grapple with its own diseases, and throw them off, as God designed it to do. This Calvinistic way of doing up things is so savage, it spoils it for me. I don't like savageness anywhere, even among savages.

But it is said, when we are among the Romans, we must do as the Romans do. No,—I won't neither,—if they do wrong. That must be a Calvinistic maxim. It makes society, or organizations, responsible for our sins.

I can't even trust to proverbs without testing them in the scales of the sanctuary,—no, not sanctuary,—I needn't go to the sanctuary to get my scales; I keep scales at home, behind my cupboard door, and I can use them just as well, and a little "weller." And besides, I can teach my children how to use scales, if we have a pair for home use. They learn much faster to see a thing done, than to hear it done. I do believe they might hear honesty preached all one Sunday long at church, and then see the beam slant the wrong way once at home, and they would remember the dishonesty they saw at home, much longer than the honesty they heard at church.

I shouldn't like to keep my scales so far off as the church is, for 'tis so much trouble to dress up so much, to go to church, for fear somebody will see what clothes I cook in. Well, these scales of truth and honesty must test my cooking, whether or no. But I shan't keep mine in the church. I can watch my own beam. I find it won't do to let others eye the beam *alone*, because there are too many Calvinists about,—they may cheat me,—and if 'tis a Christian eye to the beam, it does no hurt to know it, by seeing it myself. I had a little rather trust my own eyes too, rather than another's, even if 'tis a Christian's eye,—for we may differ in opinion on the same subject. If he won't see, I can't make him see. His eyes are his own, and he has no right to prefer mine before them, any more than I have to prefer his before my own. So we must either agree to differ, or to split the difference.

I won't cheat anybody, or "sophisticate" in argument. I can't get a short word for that—I guess it was Calvin who ever made it necessary to use such a word. The shortest cut, and the quickest done, is my way.

But I don't know but I lose something by being so quick, sometimes. I believe I lost a day that way, last week. I really did think that Sunday morning was Saturday morning. For I got up early, as usual, and went to my breakfast, and did not know my mistake until one attendant remarked:

"I did not expect to see *you* out to breakfast, Mrs. Packard."

"Why not?" I asked.

"Because it is Sunday, and you don't usually come to breakfast Sabbath morning."

"Sunday? I thought 'twas Saturday! and I had planned quite a day's work of writing to do for my book, to-day."

I don't get up early Sabbath mornings. I sleep until I get my nap entirely out, before I try to wake up. And here they don't do so, yet. I am the "first person singular," you see, in more respects than one.

So, to meet my own views—that is, to make them practical (and views are of no account to me that are not practical)—I lose my breakfast, but I get my sleep by it. Rest is what I'm after on God's resting day. And my family can rest better on two full meals than on three; so I give them a late breakfast and an early supper, and they can rest late and early too. I don't believe in cheating even the Sabbath of its claims on us, for rest, on that day. I do enjoy our mutual Bible-class, at home, on this day. We have such happy times in it, that we all lot upon it all the week before it comes, and many times I have to answer the question during the week, " Mother, how many days will it be before we shall have our good reading and talking times ? "

Going to church—dressing and undressing—is all the drudgery we find on that day. We have more merry, laughing, social flow of sympathy, and good, easy nature on this day than any other of the six working days, for we let toil go, for that day, and *rest* as God did from his toil.

Our merriment grates rather harshly on father Calvin's ears; for he can hear our shouts of laughter, in his study, with his New York *Observer* before his face and eyes, notwithstanding! I wonder if he ever laughs at Prime's arguments in defense of the Bible institution of slavery? I don't think there would be any sin in it if he should! I believe we have a right to laugh at folly—for God does. And I say it is folly to defend Satan's kingdom at the expense of Christ's kingdom; or to try to make the "higher law" bend to the lower—even the lowest—oppression.

Well, if happy faces and laughing eyes are signs of guilt, then I and my children are great sinners on God's day, as well as on our days.

I know Calvin thinks we are a thoughtless set of incorrigible sinners, by the half-suppressed groans he utters, as he passes through our room, before we get time to straighten our faces, accompanied by such expressions as—"Oh! the doleful condition of my family!" "Oh! that I could see them sorrowing for their sins!" "Laughing! on the brink of hell!"

When pa gets out of hearing, the little ones inquire, "What makes pa talk so?" "Ma, is it wicked to laugh?" "Will God punish us for being happy, when we can't help being so, when mother is with us?"

The children can be cross and cold under Calvin's magnetism; but it is hard for them to be so under "Christian" influence. It is no wonder Calvin is cross; for if he is half as bad as he tells God he is, at our family prayers, I think he ought to go to "confessional" or "anxious seat," and beg for help to get out of "purgatory."

We are not in purgatory, nor don't desire to be; but we are "rejoicing," on God's day, as my brother Austin said he was, when my devoted mother sought his room one Sabbath morning, to inquire after his soul, in the time of a great revival, and found him playing on his favorite flute. To mother's question of surprise, "Why! Austin! what are you doing on God's day?" "I am rejoicing! mother," replied he, in honest frankness.

My mother was an orthodox Christian; and she did fear God, and love him too, and "kept his commandments," so far as her Calvinistic husband would allow her to do so. If she had only been allowed "spiritual freedom," she would have emitted light, as a star of the first magnitude—for she *was one* in reality. Her "spiritual gifts" and spiritual illumination were abundant—beyond the comprehension of her creed-bound husband—so that, had she given utterance to her "visions," her sanity might have been called in question by him; as mine is, by my depraved husband!

Oh! when, when will this bondage to creeds and husbands be broken up?

Well, how is it that creeds and the devils, both, lurk so near my insane track that I don't have to "switch off" to give them a dab, so often?

I said, back yonder, that here I had to lose either my breakfast or my Sunday morning nap. So I do. But, by the way, Dr. McFarland is on the right track, on this subject, only he has not progressed quite far enough on the right track, to satisfy me, yet. He lets the tired help lie one half hour longer, to rest, Sabbath mornings, than usual, and has the supper one half hour earlier.

Yes, 'tis a fact, he is coming right on practical subjects, and you may be sure one can stand muster, when they *practice right*, even if they do speak amiss, sometimes. It is doing right that is to save him. Not thinking—or even speaking right—merely, as our chaplain, Mr. Russell, said last Sabbath; the way to get right feelings was to think right. I say it isn't the way to get right feelings to think right, but to *do* right.

Rev. Mr. Russell did get the cart before the horse, in that sermon. We can't feel right until we do right—and he said we must feel right before we do right. Thoughts don't make our feelings—but actions do. I may think about stealing all day, and even decide to steal, but until I do steal, I can't get the feelings of a thief. I may think I will tell a lie, but until I do lie, I can't have the feelings of a liar. I may think I will be benevolent, but until I do a kind act, I can't feel a kind feeling. I may think I will love my enemy, but I can't do it, until I do him good, as God says, then I can begin to feel good, or kind, to him. Do right, and I feel right. Do wrong, and I feel wrong, and so does everybody else. I only want to know how people act, and I can tell how they feel, without going to "class-meeting" to find it out!

Abuse to man, and love to God, don't grow on the same

stock, any more than a peach grows from a pumpkin-seed.
We shall reap just what we sow, in spite of our hypocritical
professions to the contrary. But if we only think about
sowing our seed, and don't sow any, I don't believe we shall
have any harvest, at all! But if I want to secure a right
feeling, I think if I sow a right act, I shall be pretty sure to
get it. And if I do a wrong deed, I shall feel a wrong
feeling.

Those preachers who tell us that we first must feel right,
in order to do right, are throwing hindrances, or stumbling-
blocks, in the way towards heaven, by encouraging delay in
practical godliness. " Ye knew your duty, but ye did it
not," because you listened to those false prophets, who told
you it would be of no avail to obey until you felt right!

Most of the prosecutions at the judgment, are for "doing
not." 'Tis action—not thought—that determines the character in God's sight, even if our clergy do tell us otherwise.
I don't stop to inquire whether I feel right or wrong,
when I have a duty to do—I *do it*, the best I know how, and
then—not before—my conscience, and God, are both satisfied. God don't require impossibilities of me, nor of any
other accountable, moral agent. It would be a hard case if
he did! What should I do in such a case? I should say, it
is a delusion, growing out of false doctrines—just as it is a
delusion that we can't be perfect, when God tells us to be.
God don't tell me to do anything that I can't do—nor be
anything that I can't be!

The Calvinists do enough of that business, for all the
world. "You may and you must not," "you shall and you
shan't," "you can and you can't," are often the logic of
their sermons. I used to think their reasoning was above
my comprehension; but now I see it was below it. Logic
that is below the plane of common-sense is too low for me to
descend to; for spiritual light comes from above—darkness,
from below this plane.

I have tried to help Calvin around these rough corners of his creed, until I found it was a hopeless case—with reason's eye open—to reconcile their inconsistencies. I can't afford to abandon reason, for any consideration. He won't let me use it in searching after truth, at home—but Dr. McFarland will, here—I like his great, liberal soul! He is not afraid to let others think as they please. He don't pretend to be accountable for the thoughts of anybody but himself!

It is these fragments of men that are so bigoted and intolerant. A whole man is not afraid of the opinions of others. He can stand on his own character—in defiance of opinions. Need Christ circumscribe the opinions of any one, to protect his character? Need any Christ-like man do so? Let us fear sin, or wrong-doing, and we shall have nothing else to fear.

Satan sometimes whispers in my ear: "If you don't withhold the utterance of some of your thoughts, you won't get out of this asylum, at all." Well, I'll stay in it, then! I have found the first man, here, that was not intolerant of opinions! I don't know as there is another, on earth, that is practically in favor of freedom of opinion, except Dr. McFarland! Almost all men are professedly in favor of freedom of opinion, but when this freedom is used in demolishing some favorite system, creed, or custom, or occupation, then they would be very likely to call you insane for using your freedom in that way! I don't think this freedom of opinion is worth thanking for! At least, I don't feel under any obligation to my contemporaries for this measure of freedom of opinion!

I say, if a character, system, creed, or institution can't stand on its own merits, let it fall!—sooner the better. It is too late in the day to try to defend our free institutions by suppressing freedom of speech. It won't do to try to gag Americans, much longer!

I don't think this asylum can hold me, until I recant, or yield my conscience and opinions to human dictation; for I don't expect to die here—a prisoner, for conscience' sake—for our humane government won't let me, if they know my case. And you see if the gallantry of Dr. McFarland don't get my book into print, before long!

Oh! what a comfort it is that one true man has escaped this Calvinistic deluge, without having had his native manliness all drowned out of him! What would have become of me had not God sent me this noble protector, in this, my time of need?

What a contrast between him and Calvin! Calvin professes to be a preacher of righteousness—a defender of Christianity—while practically he is a preacher of wickedness, and a persecutor of Christ's cause. Dr. McFarland is called to superintend a hell—under Beelzebub's rules—and he even protects Christ's cause in the very hell Satan had chosen for its destruction, and had appointed him as his agent to do it. Calvin has proved to be a traitor to Christ's cause—Dr. McFarland a traitor to Satan's cause. Calvin is a traitor to the principles of our free government—Dr. McFarland has proved true to its principles. Calvin has perjured himself, and become my cruel persecutor, instead of my protector; after he had vowed before God and man to protect me, till death part us. Dr. McFarland, without any law or vow to hold him, has been true to his manly nature, and protected the inalienable rights of the weak and defenseless, as Christ protects the church.

And I do say, that the manliness of Calvin, tested in his scales—his own acts—must be like the taper to the sun, when compared to the manliness of Dr. McFarland's, tested in his scales—his own acts.

It is a fact, the "day of judgment," or the day of retribution, has already come to the American nation—the wood,

hay, and stubble is being burnt up—and every man's works
are being tried in the scales of justice; and every one who
can't stand on his own actions, or own character, will have
to fall. Reputation won't survive the fires of this judgment
—but character will. And since character is the result of
actions, the result will show, to a demonstration, whether
they have secretly acted good or bad. Thus secret things
are being proclaimed " on the house-top."

The most destructive kind of rottenness begins at the core,
but is the longest in development, on the outside. So the
basest men—the most hopeless cases—are those who secretly
abuse themselves and their own families. They cannot be
trusted—however fair in church or state circumstances may
have placed them—for their soundness is only skin deep.
Even a frozen and thawed apple is better than a rotten one,
even with a fair skin. Even a whitewashed sepulchre loses
all of its attractions, for me, when I think what's inside of it!
But the painted palace of a king is very attractive, to me,
especially when I am sure its occupant is a defender of
woman's right's—a " woman lover!" And I do love a true
man in a cottage, better than I do a "wolf in sheep's
clothing." The fact is, I can't love wolves, anywhere, outside of their den, for they are so cross and snappish at sheep,
when they can get at them.

Oh! Lincoln, do den them all up, for they don't make at
all good partners or companions for sheep—they don't protect them in any sort of a rational manner! Only let the
lion men we love so well take the field, and the sheep and
lambs will be taken care of—as they like to be.

Let no " woman-hater" find a seat in your cabinet, for you
may be sure he is rotten at the core, and will do more harm
than good to the race of humanity. Shut them all out of
office, and shut them all up with the government key, where

10*

their influence cannot be felt at all, except as beacons or warnings to the race.

A man who will practically protect the rights of a woman and child, will not trespass on the inalienable rights of humanity, anywhere. He is "oppressor-proof"—a subject of Christ's government—whose loyalty is invincible. As you love your country, Father Abraham, put the reins of government into the hands of these loyal ones!

Well, I have switched off again on to the loyal Dr. McFarland " switch ;" for, you see, I have to be true to the good on my track, as well as the bad. When the opposite trains meet, I must "switch," you know, or there would, of course, be a " collision."

I told you I used to help Calvin in his studies some—but the truth is, he didn't like my criticisms at all—for they would clinch so on to his reason and common-sense that he had to become traitor to them or his creed—and no man likes to be proved to be a fool, or a knave either, especially by a woman! I don't like either character, and he didn't like my honest truthfulness; and so there was no love lost between us!

The fact is, Calvinistic preachers must have foolish, insane wives, like themselves—or they can't draw together—it is a moral impossibility; and this drawing apart is very awkward business. For my part, I had rather be a single team than be yoked with such an ass. An ox and an ass ought not to be yoked together, for God says they ought not to be. I guess Calvin thought so when he put me into this hospital, to stable me! I shouldn't be surprised, after all, if God had a hand in it—for God knew how tired I had got, trying to serve his cause with such a yoke-fellow; and he knew I needed rest from toil, as well as abuse, to fit me for service in some other part of his vineyard. So, instead of sending me to the grave, to rest awhile, and then raise me in another body, he perhaps thought this healthy body would answer awhile longer—as a tenant for my soul—by recruiting its energies by rest, and then—by renewing my age—capacitate me for more efficient service.

I am inclined to the belief that God reigns—and that whatever takes place is a part of his wise plan. I don't believe in accidents or mistakes under God's government; and when an event has taken place, I know God planned it to take place. I believe when he made me and my husband he planned to have me live the life of a Christian, and Calvin to be an apostate from the faith of the gospel. Still, I have done just as I pleased, and so has Calvin! and God is going to use us both to advance his cause. But I had much rather be a vessel of honor—as God made me to be—than be a vessel of dishonor—as Calvin made himself to be.

God makes people good, the devil makes them bad. But God is to destroy the devil's works, and the old fellow himself, when he has done up all the dirty work he has for him to do, as servant.

I had rather be a guest at the "marriage supper of the Lamb," than a waiter, for I like the company of the guests much better than I do the society of servants.

So these apostates can find employment if they can't repose in the Lord's service. I have been the Lord's servant, but am now his guest—I am hoping to be his companion by and by! I believe in eternal progression. I expect to be like God some time—and I expect Calvin will be so too, some time. But he has first got to confess that he told a pack of lies on me, to make folks think I was crazy, when I wasn't the least bit; and he has got to own up, that the reason he wanted people to believe I was crazy was, so that they would not believe what I said about him and his creed. And he has got to say that I trained the children in the paths of virtue and holiness, both by example and precept; he has got to say, too, that I never treated him, or any other human being, unkindly, without repenting of it, and asking forgiveness of the injured one; he has got to confess that he made up the slander of insanity wholly out of borrowed capital—that I never exhibited an insane act in all my married life—except the night before Theophilus was born, when I was out of my head a few hours, from three days' agony.

But, unless I am much mistaken in his mettle, he will choose to suffer a pretty long term in the regions of purgatory, first! But that is left wholly to his own choice, just as it was left to his own choice to deserve it.

I like freedom—but I can conceive of even too much freedom to suit me. I should rather be in bondage to a good influence than freedom to destroy myself.

I don't ask for freedom to do wrong—I only desire freedom to do right. I shouldn't like to be a pack-horse to carry one to heaven on, as Calvin has been to me. He has almost forced me there; for he was determined I shouldn't find any comfort short of heaven, if he could undermine it. Well, I have got there at last! the first, or lower-heaven—the heaven of rest from toil—but what will become of my old pack-horse I can't tell, neither do I care, only that he keep out of my sight! I shan't curry him down any more, if his mane does get bushy. I think he ought to be packed to heaven himself, for I am afraid he alone will be one thousand years on the journey before he gets there! I think the Widow Dixon would esteem it an honor to be his pack-horse. But she will have to do the courting, if she gets him; for he doesn't know anything more about courting a woman than a man in the moon!

I should be actually ashamed to tell what clumsy, awkward business he made of it in courting me. I'm glad it's over with—that's one comfort. Indeed, my whole married life, so far as he is concerned, has no greater comfort attached to it!

Yes, God knew how to capacitate me for contentment in my hermit life here—Calvin put me from no joys when he put me off from himself. But he did torture me most terribly, to tear me from my own flesh and blood—my jewels. They do draw most desperately upon my heart-strings. My maternal joys were my heaven—my only heaven, at home. Their memory is pleasure almost unalloyed.

I have tried to do all I can for them in my prison here. I have knit fifteen pairs of stockings, mostly cotton ones. I have embroidered and made sixteen bands and sleeves for chemise—embroidered shirts, pantalets, waists, in abundance, . for myself and my daughter. I expect to need nice under-clothes for myself, for I don't expect to be always locked up in this insane asylum. If Lincoln don't liberate me, God's providence will, I am very sure. This asylum won't long hold Mrs. Packard. I am safe enough with such a Father in Heaven, and such a protector as Dr. McFarland on earth.

I only wish Father Abraham was half as safe as I am, and as sure of getting his liberty again as I am! That old den, or creed, or Constitution he's got into, by his "oath of office," is a tight place—'tis. He can't break the bars himself, for he is on the inside, and if Abraham is ever out of his lion's den, the fact is, we must fight him out. We—the outsiders —we ain't under creeds and oaths and all the paraphernalia of office—to hold us back.

Why can't our officers be free from creeds? Trust men in office to their native manliness! Be sure they are true men first, and then let their individuality raise the office to a higher plane of honor than ever before. Let there be room for progress. God needs no creed or code of laws to control his actions, outside of his own character. Cannot God-like men govern themselves by the same standard?

Men that can't stand upright, without being held by oaths, are not self-reliant enough to fill any office.

A true man should be free—so should a true woman be
equally free—to follow the inspirations of the divinity within
them, so that if, like John Brown, they feel inspired to
strike out into some new, bold, untried path, let them go on
unfettered in it, and be a god unto themselves. Let them
risk the responsibility of their own actions themselves, as
God does.

I intend to have this freedom, and I intend to use it, too,
even before this bugbear—the insane asylum—is demolished.
I'll risk their getting me into one a second time! Satan
finds me a hard case for his cause here. But it has been the
birthplace of my spiritual freedom, and I shouldn't wonder
if the child it has given birth to should show to the outsiders
that we can be our own lawyers, and judges, too. I don't
want any judge over me but God, and I won't have any
other! Isn't that the end of the matter? A woman's
won't is a stumper!—'tis the knock-down argument. If any
one is to judge me, they are the ones to be judged—not I.

God don't allow his inalienable rights to be usurped or
trampled upon. He don't allow one child to control, govern,
or judge another child. God lets them govern themselves,
and so should we. He keeps our records or account books,
and it is to this alone that I pay homage as the infallible
record. My brothers and sisters may tattle on me as much
as they please; it won't change a figure in this book. I
shall just keep on obeying God, notwithstanding all their
slanders.

Father, God, ain't it too bad that my brothers and sisters
do so try to lord it over my conscience? Why can't some of
them, besides Dr. McFarland, let me do what I think you
require me to do? It does seem to me that they trouble
themselves about what is none of their business. Just
think! forty men and women clubbed together to get me
imprisoned just because I chose to think my own thoughts,

and speak my own words, rather than other people's thoughts and words!!

If this isn't usurpation, what is usurpation? How these long words show their origin! Good detectors! ain't they? Detectors again! What made us need detectors, I should like to know? Didn't the Calvinistic clergy make them an indispensable part of the furniture of our counting-rooms?

Well, Father Abraham, don't let us move this useless plunder into our new house—let's have an auction and sell off. I know it won't bring much at auction—but perhaps all it is worth! Ours didn't, at any rate. We might have given them away cheaper. We paid Mr. Elliot of Green-field, Mass., six dollars for coming out to Shelburne, one afternoon, to auction them off. And it didn't pay the cost to hire him to give them away for us. We could have done it cheaper ourselves. I tell you, it is the last time Mr. Elliot is my auctioneer. I like to get a thank-you for my gifts; but when he is my almoner I don't get even that.

I saw how matters were going, so I just took brother Calvin into our parlor, alone, and told him to send him off—I could give my own things to whom I pleased. He didn't know the names of my friends as well as I did. He left out Cousin Ophelia Fiske too often; I saw she was not getting her share, and so I interfered and gave her some things myself. I think a woman may interfere sometimes, in an emergency—(mark the long words—emergency! Scent it! You'll find interference on the same track!) Yes, I gave her my solar lamp, and I got a good price for it, 'twas better than Elliot did for his. I gave five dollars for the one I auctioned off, and I got a thank-you for it; and he didn't get but eleven cents for husband's study lamp; and he paid Mr. Elliot one dollar and thirty-three cents for it just before, and I never knew as David Allen Fiske thanked him for it, as Ophelia did me.

They have got the same name, but I don't know as they are any relation to each other—I don't think they are much alike anyhow.   But names nor looks are not always a certain test of character nor ancestry.   Shelburne abounds in Fiskes.   It seems to be the family name there for our friends on both sides of the house.

We used to have sweet times there, when we visited either side of the house, if it happened to be in sugar time that we went.   And we always like to parochiate in sugar times!   Why couldn't we visit when we chose, as well as other folks?   Well, we did, whether the parish liked it or not.'   But I am sure they did like it—not dislike to have us visit them then—rather than not at all.

They are very generous with their sugar—especially Mrs. Ophelia Fiske.   She could not make us eat enough there, but would insist upon it that we should take some home, to eat also.   I felt almost ashamed to, it looked so much like riding a free horse too hard—for Calvin liked sugar very much himself, and she liked Calvin, and so she was sure never to let his saucer get empty!   But I could see by the ridge around the kettle, that it lowered down pretty fast when Calvin and all his children got at it.   I could see—but I didn't like to let them see I saw it.

So I would just whisper to the young Calvins that mother had had enough.   They understood!   My children are very quick in their perceptive faculties.   I could see it wouldn't do to tell them that *they* had had enough, for I was afraid they wouldn't believe me, and I like to let children be their own judges for their own actions—but I like to have them judge right, though!   But my children are something more than hogs—for they have a conscience—and hogs haven't.   You could see it—or if you couldn't, I could—for the next time Ophelia's brimming ladle was held over their empty saucers, they would, instead of being silent and let her keep on pouring, just say, " No, I thank you, I've had a supply," " I'll not take any more, thank you."

And if Ophelia's generous ladle does continue to pour the liquid sweet into their empty saucers, I can tell you, she does it at her own risk. They don't *choose* to take care of any more of her syrup for her. But, like other human beings, they still kept an eye to see which side the bread was buttered ; for mother don't forget them nor their actions, abroad, after they get home! My children found that it paid pretty well to keep on the right side of mother! Moses had respect unto the recompense of self-denial, and so do I and my children. And God don't forget to give us the recompense, when we get home. Neither do I, when they deserve it. But, mind you, they have to deserve it first.

I always told them to do just as they pleased, at home or abroad—but I looked out, beforehand, to have them please to do right from free choice !

Don't God let his children do as they please? Shan't I take him for my pattern of family government? I am sure there is no better one.

Yes, I do let my children do as they please. They may obey me, or disobey me, just which they choose—and they are just as sure that happiness is the result of obedience, as that unhappiness is the result of disobedience. They have tried the experiment so many times that they are now just as certain of the results as they are that the fire will burn them if they touch it, or that sugar will taste sweet if they eat it.

I don't intend they shall find that I lie in my laws, any more than God does in his.

It is this lying of parents that makes disobedient children. I don't know as I ever told my children a lie, or broke my promise to them. Either practice is too Calvinistic to suit me. And, besides, I should be ashamed to punish them for breaking promises, or telling lies, if I did either, myself. Reform begins at home, with me, but I don't let it end there; if I see seeds of evil sown on the virgin soil of my children's holy natures, I am sure to root it up before it grows to seed. And I don't know of any better way to prevent bad habits, than to form good ones. And no act is a good one unless done from choice—free choice.

My "Toffy," or Theophilus, as he was christened when he was a baby—but so young that he would be likely to forget it, unless we told him of it—but I guess he will credit my testimony about it, and so believe he has been baptized. But if he chose the first-class testimony in this case, and wished to be baptized again all over in the water, I don't see any harm in letting him have his own way, now he is of age, and be baptized as Christ was. I should like to be so baptized, myself, and intend to be, the first opportunity I can get, although my parents tell me I was sprinkled when I was a baby.

Well, this "Toffy" was a very smart boy. He was just as smart to get his own way, as I was to get mine. And I tell you, a boy has to be very smart, for that! I used to like to hear him think aloud, on his way home from our parochial visits, talking to himself, on his little stool between us. He would say: "Well, I was a good boy, to-day, but I did just as I was a mind to—but I had a mind to do right, for I knew if I didn't, mother would whip me, when I got home! But I did right, and now I know she won't. But I did just as I was a mind to!"

No—mother don't punish her children if they do right, even if they are childish in their ways, and do childish or foolish things. But she insists upon it that it is wrong to disobey mother even in one thing—and if they do what I forbid their doing, or will not do what I tell them to do, at once telling them to—they do wrong, and I never fail to notice it at the proper time. I don't tell them they have done wrong, until they have—and it is not wrong for children to be children, instead of men and women. I don't like to see a "little man," or a "little woman." I like to see a little boy or a little girl, much better. But mine must be obedient in all things. But I tell them, "you may do," much oftener than "you mustn't do."

To forbid a child to do what is right and natural for them to do, is to tempt them to do wrong. It is not wrong to be natural, and it is wrong to interfere with nature.

A child is entitled to his rights as much as the mother is to hers—and I have no more right to trespass on my child's rights, than he has a right to trespass on mine. His rights are as dear to him as mine are to me. And I am not guiltless, if a child feels that he is doing wrong—to be natural. It makes them sinners, to do what they think is wrong, and if told an innocent love of theirs is wrong, we trespass on his rights of conscience.

Another thing—I don't carry my rod visiting with me, for I don't go from home to discipline my children; I go to visit, and if they trouble me so I can't, I either train them to do right, or leave them at home. A child whose memory is long enough to remember there *is* a rod at home, is too old to be disciplined in company—and my children know that if the sentence against the evil-doer is not speedily executed, it is no sign it won't be executed in due time. I think God don't punish his children till we both get cooled off, after our transgression—so I don't mine.

But God never forgets the penalty—neither do I mean to. But my children have memories as long as their mother's, and they believe the rod is in its proper place, ready for use when needed, and they think 'tis best not to need it, as they know this is the only way to prevent its getting out of its proper place, on to their bare flesh! But I did pretty good business with my rod on "Toffy," for he was a very smart boy—and the smartest are the ones to need it, I find. But he hasn't needed it scarcely at all, since he was three years old; for I don't like this dallying, half-way business, at all. I say, what's worth doing at all, is worth doing well and thorough. So after that age, I used to find it needed dusting, when I took it for use. He hasn't shown his smartness in the wrong way, since. But it's there! I haven't beat it out of him—the grit and all—for I tell you, if he didn't spring out of his little bed, one night, and seize hold of my arm, when I was using it on Samuel, for his benefit! A rod was in the hand of the arm he gripped, and he held on to it, tiger-like. As it seemed to *him*, his little, hateful brother was being unjustly punished! and, I tell you, let justice be trampled upon—if it isn't—let him *think* so, and if you don't feel his grip, it is only because he hasn't a firm hold!

I tell you, "Toffy" carries the rod, now, himself, and I have to look out for myself, and if I don't toe the mark of justice, I shall feel it, too! Yes, he has a straight back-bone, although I've had a great deal of trouble to get him to hold his head up straight.

I think his father Calvin caused me some of it, too,—for the first time I saw him hang his head, was when I met him coming in from the barn, with head down,—looking as ashamed as if he had been doing something wrong. But he hadn't. But his father had; and thus the little innocent had to be punished for his father's faults—the innocent for the guilty. His guilty father had been treating him as a brute, and he felt brutish.

It's part of my theology, you see,—do wrong, and you feel wrong, do right, and you feel right; and I don't know but to suffer injustice hurts our uprightness or rectitude. And it is wrong for any human being to be made to feel brutish. They are not brutes—they are human beings, and on this account they are entitled to humane treatment—not brutal.

His father Calvin had been treating him like a brute, when he wasn't one. He was as good a little boy at this age, eight years, as the world ever saw. I don't think there ever was his superior, if I do say it. I say the truth, as it seems to me, or I don't say anything. And I now am not afraid to say the truth, even if it does praise me or my children, for we both deserve praise, if we don't get it. But we do get it —God praises us, if the world don't, and that satisfies us for the present. But you'll see if the world don't praise those whom God does, some time! I can wait God's time, and so can my children.

Our business now is, to deserve it. Well, "Toffy" didn't deserve the whipping father Calvin gave him in the cow's-stable! He didn't deserve to be tied up with a rope, by his hands, to a beam, naked, so his father could whip him unjustly, without his power to resist his iron will! No—he didn't. But he had to thus suffer this ignominy, for his father's sins in employing this brutal abuse, under the Calvinistic name of family discipline!

I say it is a cow discipline, not a human family discipline! I've seen his father tie the legs of a cow, so she needn't kick him, when he hurt her sore teats milking her, and I thought it was too bad, especially when my calves hurt my nipples so bad, when they first took hold, that I couldn't help kicking. I only wish all the Calvinists could have sore nipples only once! I think they need them to learn them how to pity those who have.

Well, Calvin did one good thing,—and he shall have the credit for all the good things he does, as well as the evil things. I go for deserts. So does God. Well, the good that he did was, to pour—I can't say how many, for I wasn't there to see it done—pails of cold water on to the whales the whip had made on his naked body!

This took out some of the soreness, you know. Water is

good for that. But Calvin did not mean it for that. He meant to combine the rod and water punishment, so as to do thorough business at disciplining, when he takes the matter into his own hands. He don't go in for "little planting rods," to dress down naughty little boys with! He takes bigger ones. I didn't. But I think my little rods,—well used,—did more good in driving young Calvin out of my children, than his big ones did,—badly used. Christ used a small cord to drive men, and cows, too, out of the temple, and I think if he thinks a small cord will do to drive oxen and sheep with, I think it will do to drive little children with.

But I don't go in for this driving business. I had rather draw than drive. But when young or old Calvin is aboard, I have got to look out, or a free horse will be in danger of being driven to death. And I go in for it,—that self-defense is right, especially when you can't get anybody else to defend you, nor protect you, neither.

I haven't got it in my heart to pound a cow for kicking, when she can't help it; nor do I blame children for crying, when they can't help it. It is enough to blame them for things they can help. And I will help them to do that, rather than prevent them doing it. Because, when there is a will that's worth a sixpence, that will will find a way to show you what it is.

The willing to do, and not doing it, never built Babel, neither will it tear it down!

I can tell you it takes a will to tear down as well as to build up,—and I don't know but it takes a little more of that article to do the latter than the former. Calvin found it harder to leave Shelburne, than he did to build up, out here. Things out here don't suit him, at all. They hurry up things so fast, here. He couldn't make his Uzzah-power felt so much out here as he could in old, conservative New England.

And, besides, he found, to his sorrow, that his wife liked the West. She didn't want to come much, yet she always let Calvin lay his own plans. She only helped him carry them out—that's all. So I didn't care if he thought it best to break up old associations, and start on a new track. I was in for it. Anything for peace,—if it is only the right kind of peace. Peace bought at the price of justice, I never could go in for! I am willing to pay high prices for things, if they are worth it. If not, I don't choose to trade,—that is, if I don't think they are worth it,—'tis all the same to me. What I think is right, is right for me. But, mind you, I don't pretend to keep accounts for anybody else's conscience! It's enough to keep my own straight. God is so correct a cashier, I can't cheat him,—and I don't want to, neither. It won't pay. We Westerners look out for that in our plans.

But we find some things do pay here that didn't there. It doesn't pay to keep two suits of clothing here as well as there. We can't find time to change so often. I wouldn't be seen there with my working-dress on, in the afternoon, for anything, for fear Cousin Ophelia might call and catch me in it. And I don't know but she would think I had been idling away my time in bed—when I hadn't. I was more afraid of folks then than I am now.

I don't care now if Cousin Ophelia does catch me papering my parlor when she calls to see me here in the afternoon. If she can't excuse me, I can't excuse her for interrupting me. But if she would like to sit down in my dusty chairs and rest awhile, I'll let her; but she must tend to her own white crape shawl and kid gloves—I can't be responsible if she does get paste on them. I could not advertise that my parlor was not in readiness to receive, and thus hinting to keep out of it till it was. I had my own business to see to, and it is my business, not any one else's, when I put on my paper. What if they do think or say, " If I were Mrs. Pack-ard—a minister s wife—I wouldn't do such things. I would hire it done, and be dressed after dinner to receive calls"? Yes—you would. You would do just so, if you were Mrs. Packard; but since you are not, you may let Mrs. Packard take care of her own family, in her own way too.

This " speech of people " is not such a bugbear out West as it is East. It don't scare us as it used to in the Old Bay State! It is a Bay State, and the coasts are very rocky, so it is hard to get out of the bay when once in it! But we did get out of the ruts after all—even old Calvin—the last one you would think of starting out of his ruts. Yes, he did start, and come out too, and brought his wife and four Chris-tian children, and one young Calvin, with him. We stopped on the way to rest one year, in Lyme, Ohio. But it didn't hardly seem as though the traces were broken there—it was so very much like Shelburne, Mass.

But when we got to Mt. Pleasant, Iowa, we knew what it was to go West, and found the farther I got from the East the better I liked it. But Calvin didn't. The farther he got the worse it was. He couldn't even hold his own team back, much less others' teams. But he didn't try to hold back the teams which brought our goods from Burlington in the mud a foot deep, in November. No. Teams that did jobs for him were not too fast! They generally were too slow to suit him. He hadn't so much patience to wait for other folks, as he wanted them to have to wait for him—he tried to hurry others—but he didn't like to be hurried himself. Well, the teams couldn't hurry—the mud was so deep, and our stoves were so heavy—and our twenty barrels of apples would press the wheels so into the mud that I thought the kind people who volunteered to cart them up, had the worst of the bar-gain !

Don't you think our soldier volunteers think so too, Father

Abraham? I guess they do. I can't bear to have them blamed for not hurrying to get killed for other folks' benefit! I think such complainers are the ones who ought to be killed.

So it is, this Calvinism always works so—just opposite from what it should be. It is the best of our folks the war is killing off, and the worst are getting the good of it.

Well, these volunteers are Christians. They, like Christ, die for others' sakes and benefit. Oh! what a holy sacrifice God does ask us to give him, as a free-will offering to atone for the sins of the people! And the ones who do the sinning get the good of the sacrifice—and they the evil of it, and nothing more. Not yet. But it will come—and it will come to those who deserve it. But, mind you, we must wait for it. Christ had to. We must. But do you think I ever doubted my Patron's word? No—his simple promise was as good to me as any man's note could be—and I take his word for it, that, if I "suffer with him," as he did, I "shall reign with him."

And now Calvin has offered me up a living sacrifice. Oh! how often I have wished I could die! but I couldn't. And then God says I mustn't kill anybody, and I am somebody. So, what could I do, but to let Calvin do as he chose to, even try to torture the life out of me? He did have things his own way clean through our married life—and you see how he has come out, so far. And I guess Lincoln will see to the rest of the drama! He won't turn off a wife when she asks him to cut off her husband's head for her, I know! Or, at least, I don't think he will, when he has read my book all through, and sees Calvin as he is—a great "wolf in sheep's clothing."

But, Father Abraham, don't misunderstand my parable, as the Jews, your ancestors, did Christ's parables, oftentimes. How he did puzzle them to know what he meant, sometimes! I guess he did it on purpose to set them to thinking. I don't think he approves of Woods of Andover, Mass., doing all

11

the thinking for the country. 'Tis too much for one man, even with Professor Park to help him to do it. And I don't thank him or Park, for thinking for me. I prefer to do my own thinking, sir, and talking too, and I shan't ask your liberty to do so, neither—for Father Abraham will see to it that you can't imprison me for it again after 1863 comes in! You see if women can't speak their own thoughts without a handle to them, by that time!

They need not hold out the handle to Beecher, to hold on to. No, Beecher, you may think just as you please, and you may preach just as you please. I will give you full liberty to do so!—and when I give you this privilege, do you think anybody will dare to trespass upon my authority over you? If they do, I think a woman's power don't scare them—that's all.

But God can scare them, and hurt them too, if they make light of his family government.

Beecher, don't you like Christ's way of giving puzzles and riddles to his disciples? I guess there are some such sort of people in the world, now, for most all papers have a puzzle corner in it. And I see they don't give the answer until next week. I don't—I like to see how many of my readers can hit upon the true meaning. I ain't responsible for their mistakes. I give you the sum; that's enough without the key—I hold my own key, now. I can get any secret unlocked I choose to get; but I don't choose to want any that God don't choose to tell me. I must do as I teach my children to do, or they won't think much of my sincerity or honesty.

Christ's "new birth" sum puzzled Nicodemus to get the right answer straight, without making a mistake. I have got the sum out myself, alone—and you don't know how proud it makes me feel to think no key helped me to a figure or a hint. I do like to do my own thinking. I wouldn't accept of the offer of Dr. Wood's brain now, to think with.

I like Mrs. Packard's better. So does God, or he wouldn't have made me Mrs. Packard—and Dr. Woods, himself. I let the men plan—and God is a man, and I just let him make his own plans. It is as much as I know how to do to follow them, and help him carry them out for the good of others.

I love others as well as I do myself, and some folks better. No—I don't neither, come to think—I do love myself best. I go on the No. 1 philanthropy principle, you recollect. I never saw a man yet that I think could think better, for me, than I can think for myself. And, of course, I never did a woman, for I love the men the best—one man excepted, brother Calvin.

Father Abraham, you see I want you to cut off brother Calvin's head, because he troubles me so much—and it ain't because I am selfish, either; it is for his " own good" to have it done. I am sure it is, or I wouldn't ask you to do it. But since this is rather a delicate request for a wife to make to the government, I must be sure you understand my parable. It is not the head that he wears his hat on, that I want you to cut off—it is that old dragon head down in the grass, that has got such a grip at my heel. You have studied Latin, I suppose—I have, if you have not—and I know that head means power.

It is his power to abuse me, that I want you to behead, or amputate.

I don't believe in this amputating of the human frame. We haven't got any too many heads or feet. But the dragon has a great many on one neck—and that is contrary to nature! I go for nature, as our infallible guide in all things—and when we find a man with two heads, I do say he has got one too many. I don't apply my new birth theory to the " old dragon." I doubt if he is really killed, he will rise again. But you must be sure he is really dead. Some snakes you

can't kill without chopping them to pieces. The tail, especially, will quiver when it has only a little snake on it.

It has bruised my head long enough, ain't it, father? Now,
do bruise his heel so he can't run nor crawl any more, and
hurt other women as he hurts me.

I love my sisters as I do myself—and since I love myself
so well—I think that is well enough. But stop! I have run
against a stump without seeing it! How is that? I just
said I loved the men best, and now—if this is true—I love
the women best! Now, here is a sum to get out. Two
opposites can't be true. I can't love the men best, and not
love them best too; I must own up—"I've got stuck!" The
cars do run into a stone wall, sometimes, with the best
kind of engineering. Well, I don't believe McClellan could
get out of this bog alone! I want help, and so I will advertise for it. "Who can see how a woman can love the men
best, and yet love herself better than she does the men, and
still love the women as well as herself? I wish you would
come on and tell me the answer, and help me out of my
quagmire hole." This is for the puzzle corner of my book.

Well, I hardly know where my old track is, I've got so
perplexed myself! Wasn't I moving our goods from Burlington when I "switched" off on the ministers? Yes, the
ministers take me back to the main track, where we moved
on more slowly, with the clergy aboard to remark upon.
Things fly by us in such a hurry when under steam, high
pressure, that you can hardly count the posts to a rail fence
before it is gone for ever, so far as counting it is concerned.
But the next train may be a "freight train," and then we
can have time to count to our satisfaction.

But I go in for the "express train," full power—high
pressure—lightning express! Although we can't see so
much, we can get home quicker.

Our heaven is our home, and home is heaven, if it holds

the objects we most dearly love. Then they are both one and the same thing, for things which are equal to the same thing are equal to one another. A good home is equal to heaven, and heaven is equal to a good home; therefore they are one and the same thing. But we must get settled first to make it heaven. While our goods are in the carts on the road from Burlington we are not as well off as before we broke up in Shelburne.

Moving times are the worst times in the world for one's patience. We have to think how it is to be to keep patient. So we must think, while Lincoln is reconstructing things, to set up our new home, how it will be when he gets it all straight and right again. I hope he will leave all the old rubbish at home, as we did—for Calvinism ain't worth moving—and we've got so many other things so much better, we are no losers to leave these behind.

Another thing, a rich man has so much more to move than a poor man, and our government is so rich and great, it takes some time to get moved. Little governments, that haven't got much power or territory, can do it quick; but those that have as much as we have cannot do it in a minute, nohow, even if they do work like split—I hope they won't split, though!

I tell you, we had so many things to move to Mount Pleasant that the people thought that old Abraham and all his possessions had come, or was trying to come as fast as he could get on through the mud. The carters thought so before they had carted thirteen thousand weight through the mud, as they had to before they got the whole! Do you wonder they thought it must be old Abraham back again?

But it was not Abraham, as they called Calvin,—it was the "old dragon" himself! with all his trumpery with him, good and bad. They only made the Calvinistic blunder of calling things by their wrong names. But the "old dragon" thought a freight bill was something besides a name before he got it paid, I can tell you!

I guess our tax-payers will find war-taxes mean something before we get through paying them!

Well, he couldn't shirk his freight bills, and he didn't try to. Calvin was good to pay his debts (money debts, I mean—not love debts); he had that good trait in his character. But I guess he found it no use in trying to shirk out—for Uncle Sam carries the bag out here—not Judas, as he does at Washington.

I don't think the locality of our government is a healthy one. The atmosphere isn't good there. It is too hot—so hot they can't work in August—but have to adjourn and go home just when we need Congress most to work for us. Besides, the Southern spirit seems to run in the blood down there, and they get so hot among themselves that they act more like dogs and cats than Congressmen! I mean the Calvinists do so—not Seward, Sumner, Lovejoy, and such like Christian men. I don't know as it would be the greatest misfortune, after all, to have the rebels take Washington, for there are other places as good, if not better, than to remain at Washington. I think the atmosphere of Cincinnati is good and healthy—it is cooler—and I don't see the harm of our government coming North, where the power is—instead of staying at the South, where it is not.

But I know this moving is costly business—very. It cost Calvin a lot of the hard cash to move out West. But I am afraid he hasn't paid his heaviest freight bill yet—his character! I hope it won't cost our government their character to move Northwest!

But I advise them to leave the old plunder, what they can't sell off at Mr. Elliot's auction—for I do say that old things don't pay the cost of transportation. Even our beautiful flag has its useless stripes upon it. What does the

nation want of stripes? They are only fit for the backs of
fools!

And I don't think fools are worth carrying North—that is,
not till they have been whipped into docility to the family
government. If our war-stripes can't make their backs
smart enough, we will just get John Bull to help us put it on
to them. At any rate, beat the folly out of them, so they
won't dare to whip any more slaves. I go for thorough discipline, Calvin-like, when we have a fool's back to whip.

I say our stripes can be left out with our other Calvinistic
plunder, at our old stand, and we shall never miss them,
especially when we get the moon on there, in among the
stars. But if you take the moon, I go for the sun, too, for
I do like the men's company the best! And I can't consent
to separating the sexes anywhere; for God don't often send
only one sort of children in a family, merely—he mixes up
the boys and girls as though they were made for each other.
I guess they were.

It is so lonely for me to be at a woman's party, alone—
something is wanting—it is the men. I wonder if the men
miss us at their men parties? I think they wouldn't be so
rude and rowdy-like at their caucuses and at the polls, if the
ladies were among them. I shouldn't want my husband to
go to any place where he would be ashamed to take me. I
do go for the "Union" of the Sexes.

It may be this war is the result of secession—the secession or separation of the sexes in governmental affairs, I
mean. I say it is not safe to trespass on God's authority or
laws! And he says that what he has joined together, no
man has any right to put asunder. He has joined men and
women together, and we have no right to separate them, anywhere. It is contrary to nature!—and that is the knock-down
argument with me, you know. I say these parties without
men are not worth much. I lot upon the time when our

doors are open to them, in the evening, when our societies meet—for, you know, that's the time our time to rule comes on—at dark. I think it is about time now—I am sure it is dark enough to need moon and stars, too, to navigate the ship of state safely through her coast breakers—these American breakers!

Well, it is time America was all broken up into fragments. It is Columbia we want to save. America is our Calvinistic name and character. But Columbia is our Christian name and character. How Calvinistic Americus Vespucius was, in usurping, so meanly, Columbus's well-earned laurels! Well, Columbus, your sons and daughters won't forget your name in our new government home. Some of them can pronounce it right already—" Hail Columbia ! happy land!" it is not Hail America, happy land ! only on Calvin's side of the house !

Some children can't seem to speak as we want them to. I found it almost impossible to get my first child, "Toffy," to speak plain. He would leave out sounds and put in the wrong ones. Frock he would call frog. And I could not make him see the difference in sounds, until God helped me to, by accident. No—not accident—as I look at things, there are no such things as accidents under God's government—but as Calvin does, I mean. "Toffy's" father used to train him, by getting him to tell him what the animals said, such as—the cow, moos—the horse, neighs—the cat, mews— the dog, barks—the frog, booh, etc. I didn't try to teach them to be brutes or birds, but to be like men, and talk like men. But I didn't interfere with Calvin. They were his children as well as mine ; and I didn't want him to tell me how to train my boys to be men, and I don't think he would like to have me help him to train them to be animals. He understood this kind of business well enough. He didn't need help in this line, any more than I did in mine. But I had a better chance to see the practical part of his system than he did, for they were more with me than with him. Thank God!

God knows how to care for the little foxes. He could make Calvin care more for the "Bibliotheca Sacra," and the *Observer*, than for his children. So, if I couldn't find time to read—he could. But I found time to read every new book sent me, by the printer, fresh from the press of heaven! But Calvin was antiquarian in his habits. (Antiquarian! scent it!) I was Christian in mine. Nature's book didn't wear out, neither could the children tear it when in my arms. I looked out for the book first—maternal nature— then for the baby. I had heard that it was better to lock the horse in the stable, not lock him out!

But I don't like locks for anybody. I like freedom; and I guess horses and birds do. I hate cages. They are too Calvinistic. They smell of slavery and imprisonment too much to suit me. I know too much about these places to like them. I do say, if any one is in favor of enslaving folks or animals, try it then yourself!

We have no objection to locking you up tight and strong. I think a pretty tight place wouldn't hurt them for awhile. I think they would come out abolitionists, as all democrats do, here, before they get out of this asylum, after staying here long enough—and Dr. McFarland is not stingy of time in that line, I can tell you! They begin to think and ask themselves, "I wonder if slaves like liberty as well as I do? If they do, they ought to have it—and if ever I get mine again, I'll go in for their freedom!"

Asylums do some good, you see, after all. They make abolitionists of their patients. I wonder if we can't put the South into so tight a place as to make them practical abolitionists? But I don't like to have these tight means tried *on me.* I can be an abolitionist, without, and always was—

11*

by nature. And what is in the bone stays long in the flesh, if Calvin don't get aboard. If he does, look out for your emancipation principles! Prevention is better than cure, or reform, either.

But to the track again. I began to tell you how children mistook things for names, or rather, names for things. My "Toffy" used to help me pick up my clothes from the grass, and put them into my clothes-basket, to help mother—his best sugar-plum!

He would work smart, I can tell you, when I would tell him how much help he was to his mother! how she couldn't get along without him!—and I couldn't. It did seem that I should die of sorrow, to lose my darling boy. All my children are darling ones, and always have been, until my Samuel became a "Judas"—and lied on his mother, for money from his father, to get her into a prison, by lying! I didn't tell lies to my children when I told them what a comfort they were to their mother.

He would pick up faster than I could, myself, especially with little baby Isaac in my arms. He would drag what he couldn't lift, so that, unless I looked out, the little things would all be picked up before I had done my part—the big things. But no stopping these young colts! They are as free with their hands as Lincoln will be, when we get him on to the track. He will drag what won't come without, you'll see if he don't! His halter won't break, either.

Well, "Toffy" got hold of his father's frock I had made for him, out of bed-ticking, to milk his cow in, when I didn't do it for him.. He liked to change pulpits—he seemed to think it was easier for him, than to change sermons! and I liked to have him, all but the milking part. The baby would wake up before I could, in the morning, so often, that I was put to my wit's end to know where to leave him, safely, while I milked the cow. The baby would milk me all night, and get all my wake out of me into his bright eyes, and mine would keep shut, so I would not think of milking my cow! But I found out his wagon could be made my servant to hold the baby by my cow while I milked, so I used it for one in that way. I never kept servants, or hired help, in Shelburne, or anywhere else, except in Ohio, for nine months.

Well, "Toffy" got hold of his father's frock, and commenced bellowing—"Booh! booh!" I could not imagine what he meant, so I found out. He thought this frock of his pa's was the frog, himself, his father had told him about! He had never seen a frog, and how could he tell the difference between a frog and a frock? They sounded alike—why not the same thing! I tried to teach him the difference between the sound and the animal itself. So I think Columbus's mother should teach her sons the difference between the American sound and the Columbian thing! We shall fix "young America" right, yet.

He's almost old enough, now, to be christened. I don't believe in christening too young—they forget it, unless we keep telling them of it. I guess when Columbus was carried to the christening bowl, that his father was so frightened he couldn't think of his right name, so he thought, as his father did before under similar circumstances, when the right one wouldn't come, he would take the one that did come—namely, "Beelzebub!" The priest could not, of course, interfere in the father's naming his own son—it wouldn't do—so he had to go in for it, and "Beelzebub" had to be baptized " into the name of Father, Son, and Holy Ghost!"

Professor Park, what is the common-sense meaning of this common form of words?

I hope you haven't been held down by Dr. Woods so long that you are all Woodsy. I want the Park in you (if there is a Park in the Woods), to tell your own private opinion—

not Woods's opinion. I can ask him when I want to know.
Or, I can ask Dr. Scott, or Henry, or Doddridge—but I have
heard theirs, and they don't meet my case. I am not satisfied, yet, what it does mean. And I have just as good a
right to be satisfied, before I accept one as my own, as
Dr. Scott has. Dr. Scott is not my commentator, now—out
West. He used to be, in New England. I have found one
out here, I would recommend to all the States in the Union,
as the best commentary extant. It is "God's works," commentary.

Well, parks are God's works, but not a large part of them,
though. However, I go in for Parks! He *is* smart. Or
rather, he *was* a very smart colt—when at Amherst college.
I liked to hear him preach: so did a good many others, I
should judge, by the difficulty my beaux used to have in
finding me a seat, in College Chapel, when Park was in the
pulpit.

Yes, he was a smart colt—but not quite smart enough to
hide his sheep's-eyes from my eye. I remember the morning
he called to see my mother—not me!—now I listened to their
talk about his sermons.

I could see that mother did not get but one of his big eyes
at a time ; I felt a little sheepish, and I guess he made me
feel so! Sometimes sheep's-eyes make sheepish faces in a
bashful girl. I was very bashful then. But I am not afraid
of men now. No. Not all the men in Christendom can
make me halt now, when I know I am on the right track—on
an errand for my Father! for I can stand on my own feet,
alone, now. I don't have to be running round to find some
tree to climb upon. I am a tree myself, and I expect to be
transplanted, some time, into my Father's garden. I like the
virgin soil. It suits my womanly nature.

Well, Brother Park, could Woods hold you by the halter?
If he has tried to rein you, I guess he has had to saw the bits,

some, to do it! I wouldn't submit to it, Brother Park. You
have just as good a right to jump fence, and be free to think
your own thoughts and speak your own words, as Brother
Woods has. He has no right to saw the bits on *you*.

You are made to run, and he to sit still in his old arm-
chair, and assort out and arrange his lectures for the press.
Some of his thoughts will have to be pressed tremendous
hard, to keep them from gassing! They make gas these days
out of charcoal—and it is as black as total depravity is! But
I am not going to be lectured by *him*. I don't like his theology. It knocks my own right in the head, or rather in the
back. My father used to say that the back-bone of Woods's
theology was—total depravity! and that is enough to spoil it
all for me.

I can see depravity enough without seeking for it in lectures
and sermons. I don't like it when I find it either. Depravity
is not my God! The Calvinists and the devils are welcome
to this false god. Their homage to him don't make me like
him any the better. I actually hate the demon depravity, and
all his devotees—that is, the depraved part of them. They
insist upon it, there isn't anything else in them! But I don't
believe it. I can see something besides devil in them if
they don't own it themselves! And more than that, I know
they all have got some of God in them, for God has put his
nature in all human beings—and his nature isn't devilish or
depraved, I know! for Christ didn't act as if it was. I can't
for my life see what depravity there was in Christ's nature!—
and he said he took *our* nature. So I know our nature can't
be a bad article. It can't be a sinful one—that's certain—for
if it had been, Christ must have had a sinful nature, and know
what sin was. He didn't do wrong, or sin, because he acted
natural—any more than other people do, when they act natural. It is the *unnatural* ones who are the sinners, or the
law-breakers. God doesn't give us laws, and then tell us they

are wrong, and we must act contrary to them, or break them, to do right!

It is the devil's theology which tells us that the laws of our holy natures are bad laws—not God's theology. I do say it is right to be natural—and it is depravity to be *un*natural. Old Calvin, my husband, had the most unnatural or perverted nature I ever saw; and yet, he is not totally depraved, for he would bring in my wood and water!—and that is not bad, I am sure. I think it was kind in him. So here is a little of human nature left. It is not devilish to be kind, even to a woman, or a brute. I know the devil sowed lots of tares on the field of his heart, where God had sown only wheat. Still there are some stalks of wheat here and there that are worth saving for seed.

I never did see a wheat field where there was nothing but cockle on it!—totally depraved! I never saw a flock of sheep where there were nothing but goats in it!—totally depraved! But I have seen many fields of wheat with some tares among it; and many flocks of sheep with here and there a goat in among the sheep.

So have I seen a great many people who were not totally perfect—there were some tares to be found amongst the wheat, if you examined very closely. But it is not my business to be looking after the tares—it's the wheat I am after! The tares in us all are fit only for the flames; but the wheat is all worth harvesting.

I don't think the separation of the tares from the wheat means the separation of different classes of human beings; but the division of the good and the bad in the same person. As no person is entirely evil—so no one is entirely good. But since good is indestructible, so all have something in them to redeem them from destruction. But since evil is all to be destroyed, all have to experience " hell fire " to consume it. But I rejoice that God won't be for ever about it! for he tells us that death and hell are to be destroyed some time. So, of course, sin is to cease when it is destroyed; just as the fires die out, for want of fuel to feed the flames.

Oh! how glad I am that this Calvinistic doctrine of total depravity isn't true! for if it was, I could not love anybody, for I can't love evil—I hate it. I could not love a totally bad person—a devil. But I do love everybody I ever saw, except Calvin; so I know the devils are not very common!

I could love Calvin if he'd repent,—but it is a moral impossibility to love him without. I don't believe God can. I like this love principle too well to hate people,—and I couldn't help hating, if I believed they couldn't help speaking anything but lies. For I won't speak lies, and I don't think anybody has any right to. If Calvin says God made them so, they can't help it! I say he didn't. And my opinion is just as good as Calvin's, and a little better, *for me.*

I don't believe my babies are little devilish fiends, if Calvin says they are. I couldn't love them if they were,— for I can't help hating evil any more than I can help loving good. 'Tis a slander to call my children "liars,"—for they are not—nor never were. And I've had as good a chance to know as he,—for he never was a mother. And mothers see into folks farther than men do. We women look through the crust or shell to the meat, the kernel, and there I can see God's image in all God's children—the whole human family! Some are very obstinate children—but God can train them! He has got good family government. A model for any family or country. I think the very worst cases—those who resemble God the least—are those who think they are God's favorites, and others, the greater part, are to be lost. This is such a mean, selfish, contracted spirit,—so unlike to God's expansive, world-embracing benevolence!

Dr. Sturtevant, our chaplain, told us in one of his sermons

here, that " God was so benevolent that he *intended* all
mankind for a life of virtue and happiness." " Very well,"
thought I, " that is complimentary to our good Father,—just
as it is." Now, thought I, there is a clincher,—it holds *all*
the human family to a title to heavenly bliss!—tor if God
" intended" all men for happiness, it is certainly guaranteed
to all men,—for it is certain that God's intentions can't be
thwarted—by men, women, devils, or fallen angels ; for
there is nothing more inflexible or obstinate than God's will
or intentions. He will have his own way about things.

I am so glad the devil isn't omnipresent! because if he
was, he might get some out of God's hands, and so, in some
cases, conquer God, or overcome his will or intentions
concerning them. It is my honest opinion, that God is
stronger than any devil in the universe! therefore, I do
believe he will overcome and destroy the devil and all his
works. But in some cases he has more devil to destroy than
in others, because some have depraved or perverted themselves more than others.

Yes, I do go in for the soul-cheering doctrine Dr. Sturtevant preaches,—" universal salvation ! " Dr. Sturtevant
knows a great deal. His head is very clear. He can make
you understand his meaning, too,—no mistake. In fact,
Dr. Sturtevant, President of Illinois College, located at
Jacksonville, in sight from my asylum window, is the very
best preacher I ever heard preach. He gives God his proper
place—as God—and evil, or the devil, his subject,—not his
sovereign. And he prays universalism, as well as preaches
it. I have often heard him ask God to convert the whole
world to himself,—and, of course, he believes they will all
be converted, or he wouldn't offer such a prayer! He says,
" we must pray in faith, nothing doubting," and he isn't the
man to tell us what to do, and not do the thing himself!
He says, too, that Christ died for all mankind,—that he

came to redeem all from the power of sin. And, of course, what he came to do, he will accomplish, because his plans can't be defeated or thwarted,—for his power is omnipotent. Indeed, Dr. Sturtevant paid God so many compliments, and such just ones, too, in his sermons and prayers in our chapel, that my faith in him grew very rapidly under his preaching. I never before could believe he was so benevolent, that he would save *all* mankind. I thought some were "dead in trespasses and sins,"—and to be dead, I thought was the end of them. But now I see it isn't! Nature, my commentary, teaches us that dead or rotten substances pass through a chemical process, by means of which all the particles of matter of which they are composed pass into a new form of vegetable, mineral, or animal life, and so are saved from destruction or annihilation. In fact, science teaches that there is not a particle of matter lost. So I don't believe there is a particle of soul lost.

But there are some things about Dr. Sturtevant's spirit that I don't think 'twould hurt him to lose,—and these are, his bigotry and intolerance. I hope this part of him will be for ever and eternally lost, so that he, nor nobody else, can ever find it again! I hope that "eternal fire" will be their portion. For if anything can be destroyed, fire can do it. And since fire is to test every man's work, to see of what sort it is, I do hope and pray that this part of him will be burned up! If it isn't, I do hope he will go to Rome and be interred with the pope. We don't like popery in America. We prefer to do our own thinking,—for we have just as good a right to our own thoughts as the pope has to his. And I do say that Dr. Sturtevant did act the pope when he tried to dictate to his brother Marshall, his minister, what he ought to preach, and what he ought not to preach. Mr. Marshall has just as good a right to preach his own thoughts,—even if they are different from Dr. Sturtevant's,—as Dr. Sturtevant has to preach his own thoughts, that differ from Mr. Marshall's. They are both God's children, and they have no right to dictate to each other.

God is the pope in America, and every man's individual conscience is his vicegerent. And one vicegerent, or sovereign, has no right to dictate to another sovereign. Dr. Sturtevant preaches Christianity—but he practices Calvinism.

Brother Park, since I feel a deeper interest in your welfare than I do some others, I want to give you a little sisterly advice. I know you won't dislike to be cared for by a woman! It is this—if they do try to hold you—a full grown, strong, fleet horse—with whip, and bridle, and halter, and all combined, don't be scared off the turnpike! while listening to Delilah's talk, but dash, and leap, and run, just in the right place to save her and the children from harm. These Jehus that do upset, do make a smash-up that is worse than the dray-horse makes. Be sure that wife and children are cared for. I don't know as you have any children though. But I suppose you have, of course. It ain't any more wrong for ministers or professors to have children than it is for farmers!

By the way, don't you tell Delilah all your plans to upset Calvinism, for I am afraid she'll betray you to the Philistines! If I am rightly informed, she is of Calvinistic ancestors, who believed in the "Assembly's Catechism," as an infallible creed. I don't. I don't believe that assembly knew any more about the truth, than our assembly in this asylum do with Dr. McFarland for our chairman. In fact, I don't think they knew so much. For one man of the present age knows more than a great many together knew, so long ago as that catechism was written. We, thriving, growing ones, feed on the fresh-mown grass of the present age instead of the dry husks and stubble of past ages. This fod-

der has lost its virtue *for us*—it was good enough for them—
as rich as they could digest well. Infants and children don't
need so strong meat as full grown men do. The race grow in
capacities, as well as individuals. "Conic sections" ain't
adapted to a child's intellect, so well as Colburn's Arithmetic. Colburn's Arithmetic is good—but I don't want to be
drilling over it, all my life-time—especially when I have got
it all by heart! I am for dropping it then, and taking written arithmetic, and then algebra, and euclid, and trigonome-
try, and conic sections. I want to progress in the sciences,
as my mind progresses or develops. So does our progressive race need advanced truths adapted to the present and
future times.

These Edwardses have such a great name, we hardly dare
differ from them in opinion on any point. But, Brother Park,
if your wife believes in total depravity and election I am not
afraid to say I differ from her in opinion, even if she is Dr.
Edwards's daughter and Professor Park's wife! I have more
respect for my own reason than I have for her father's or
grandfather's, or any other father but God—and I am not so
man-fearing as to yield it up to human dictation. What I
see to be truth—with my organization—is truth to me, if it is
not to any one else. And I am willing others should differ
from me, in my views, as much as we differ in individuality.
For it is a moral impossibility for any two persons to think
alike, as much as it is to look alike. And I, for one, am willing God should make people as he pleases, even if he pleases
to make them different from me.

I won't call God's well-done work "insanity," if the whole
world does call a natural woman an insane woman! I will
go for nature still; and be true to it—if I do have to suffer
a life-long imprisonment for it. I shall get my pay for it in
another life, if I don't in this, for my spiritual body—under
a natural development—will be strong and symmetrical, just

in proportion as it is naturally developed. My hopes are not
all centered in this body or life. I am looking out to shine,
by and by, in another body—and the way to do that, Paul
says, is " first the natural, and then the spiritual." So the
truth is, we have got to—whether we want to or not,—live a
natural life before we can live a spiritual life. So if I don't
live a natural life in this body, I must try it again and again,
in different bodies, until I can make out to live one natural
life, then, and not till then, can I have my spiritual body to
live in. The cupola can't be built until the house is built to
rest it upon.

So I have made up my mind to *try it*, even in this evil and
adulterous generation,—but Calvinism has so corrupted it,
that I have to fight for it like a tiger, to do it ! But I think
I shall conquer the Calvinism that is in me—by actual star-
vation—if I can't by force of arms. I won't practice it—
nor I won't praise it in others !

This condemning nature, and telling us they must be
renewed *before* they can do right, is like telling children they
mustn't eat until their appetite is made to loath their food,
because nature is wrong or depraved ! I say eat when you
are hungry,—and drink when you are thirsty,—and sleep
when you are sleepy,—and obey the calls of nature—because
she knows her own wants better than I do. I don't approve
of interfering with God's laws of family government.

I should not like to have any one come into my family and
tell my children that all mother's rules are wrong, and you
ought to go contrary to them to honor her ! No, they don't
need renewing, or changing, or perverting—but only obeying. So 'tis with the laws of our moral natures—obedience
to them is all that is needed to gain God's favors. God is
the backbone of my theology. But the devil is the backbone
of Calvinism !

So, Brother Park, look out ! or your theology and your

wife's relations, both, will trip you! for this ancestral blood runs through many generations, unless it's purified. Don't let any Calvins spring off from your stock. Cross the breed and go clear! Don't tell Delilah that you never have been shaved!—for I fear she will call on the barber for his services before you want them.

I don't approve of shaving men—nor of cutting women's hair, either. I think razors are too Calvinistic! I don't think Abraham or Christ used them. A man looks too smooth to be shaven—too womanish! God knows where to make the hair grow, and I don't think Delilah has any right to interfere, and take away men's power of self-defence, for she loses by it if she does! He can't help her so well when she needs it, if she has made him weak. I go for men having their own way, especially if that way is to shield *me* from harm! And I believe Christian men are protectors, by nature, of the weak and defenceless.

It is one of Calvin's worst perversions to pervert this straight out of its natural channel, and lead men to oppress where they ought to protect. Oppression will cease—so will Calvinism. God and nature both say so. "Evil slays the wicked." God don't. God makes nothing but good. The perversion of good makes evil. If we could only give up trying to "regenerate" God's well-done works, we should find it much easier getting on with life's duties. I think if God could be regenerated, he could be converted into a devil! So, if beings made in his image could be regenerated, I think we should know how to manufacture devils, and could do it as fast as the Calvinists have long been doing!

I won't go into this business, for I am certain it will not pay! for this regenerating work will not stand the test of fire; for evil, or this regenerated devil part of us, is to be burned up, or consumed. And I don't want to prepare fuel all my lifetime to keep up "hell-fire" with. I don't like to

work for the devil—it don't pay! I don't want anything to
do with "regeneration." I had rather have my nature like
God's!—as he has made it to be—rather than like all the
devils in the universe. And this doctrine—of regenerating
our natures—has made a mighty host of them, I can assure
you. But the more of a bad thing, the worse it is, I think.
The more a wheat field is regenerated, the worse it is for
practical use—for all the regenerated part of it isn't fit for
anything but the flames. God sows the field wholly to
wheat; the devil does all the regenerating on his own capital entirely. He didn't get his tare-seed from God's granary!

God don't make devils. He makes human beings, and
they make themselves into devils by trying to "regenerate"
themselves!

I am willing to be born again, but I want to be born in a
natural way! This interfering with the laws of the mater-
nity makes hard cases for the mother, and offspring, too.
For if I ain't born right in this body, that is, if my mother
broke the laws of her nature, so as to pervert any law or
part of my nature from its natural course, I shall find it very
hard—if not impossible—to live a natural life—which is a
holy life. If my parents were drunkards, and had perverted
my natural appetite into a craving for unnatural stimulants,
I might find it very hard to control this unnatural longing,
with my reason, so as not to become a drunkard myself.
Thus the sins of my parents would be visited upon me.
But God don't blame me for having this perverted or
depraved appetite, for I couldn't help having it! and he don't
blame people for what they are not to blame for. All that
he will blame me for would be for yielding to the temptation
to drink beyond what my own reason and conscience approves
of. It is much harder for me to control this unnatural appetite—by my reason—than it would be to govern a natural
one; yet I must do it, or I don't live a natural life, and so I

must run my risk and be "born again" before I can live a natural life.

Christ says he came to restore the lost image of the fall; but he does it only by working in us a will to do right ourselves. He compels us to work out our own salvation—just as he worked out his own—by living a natural or a holy life. We must live a holy life, or we cannot get our spiritual bodies like his. He tells us to be holy as he is, and I intend to obey him, for I think it is best to obey all God's commands.

I am a sinner—but Christ was not—for I break the laws of my nature without knowing it—but I am a pardoned sinner as soon as I repent—and a repentant sinner is holy in God's sight. Christ was holy without repenting, but we are not. I don't sin wilfully or knowingly, nor never did, as I can remember. I always have done just as well as I knew how to do, and I don't see how I could do any better than that! I don't know but that is living a holy life in Christ's estimation. But I know it isn't in the opinion of the Calvinists. However, if God accepts me—through Christ's advocacy—I can get along without their help—or in defiance of their slanders.

I like the humanity and reasonableness of Christ's government so much better than I can the inhumanity and insanity of the Calvinists.

This regenerating doctrine of these Calvinists leads to evil, vile, unnatural habits and practices—which kills all the manhood out of them—so then they become only walking beasts—only they can talk like as Baalam's ass could! And he could preach! and give him good advice, too. He needed a good counsellor, and he got one. The sermons we hear from the pulpit are not, oftentimes, half as practical as this ass preached!

I think the best pulpit to preach from is—a life of practical godliness!

Such a sermon is never too long. Calvin's sermons were much too long to suit me. I used to so want to get home, and show him, by getting him a nice, warm, good supper, that I am not so bad as he was saying I was. I couldn't speak out in meeting and tell him he lied! for he was a Presbyterian, and Presbyterian women are not allowed to speak or pray in public. So I had all the more to do at home.

But I couldn't get much time on Sunday for this business, I had so much dressing and fixing-up to do, just as if I were going to a dancing-party. I used to do all I could Saturday night in getting all of us bathed well in the "bake-pan," as my little George told Mr. Foster mother would put him into it, whether or no.

Calvin did get us a nice bathing-pan, but I was responsible for its use. It paid good interest; better, I think, than his four-dollar gold pen did—both the same price.

Yes, Rev. Aaron Foster of East Charlemont, Mass., had his eyes and ears both open, when his time to exchange came. I suspect he espied the track I was on which terminated in this asylum depot—the "track of nature." Mr. Foster, my good friend, is not the man to call this an insane track, neither! He knows too much for that; and what is better still, he is too holy—or natural—a man to believe such a lie. For Christ was not insane, if his enemies did say he was. It was because they were insane themselves, that made them call him so. They had regenerated their natures so completely that they could not even recognize the original—a natural man! So it is with my enemies, they have become so lost to reason, that they think depravity is Christianity—and such Christianity is depravity, or insanity, or devilment—all the same thing.

If Mr. Foster does believe me to be insane, it is only because he believes the lies told on me to make it out.

If Mr. Foster could see me, and shut his ears to the lies told on me, he would be the last person to call me an insane woman. The fact is, I am just such a woman as he likes— a true, natural woman. He would be proud to call me his wife, any day! and no man would want an insane wife. I like Mr. Foster, and he likes me; and you don't know yet, who, of my many lovers, I shall choose for my future husband! I believe in the principle that women have just as good a right to choose their own protectors, as men have to choose their wives. And, mind you, Brother Foster, I'm a practical woman! I don't adopt principles that it won't do to practice upon! Theories are too Calvinistic for me. *Practice is my religion.* So find out, if you can, what I practice, and you can judge pretty correctly as to my principles. Practice makes my principles, just as action makes my feelings.

Brother Foster, I'll tell you a secret if you won't tell anybody in the world of it—not even your wife! I'll tell you who I am going to choose for my husband—for I never have had one yet—and I do say I have an inalienable right to one as much as any other woman has. It is to be the very best man I ever saw! that is, the most Christ-like man I ever saw. I intend to scrape acquaintance with this class of society, when I get out of here, and mingle with them exclusively. I shall cut square off all my Calvinistic associates, lest I become contaminated by their depraved moral influence.

I have found out an infallible secret by which to test all my associates. It is to find out whether they think I am or have been insane or not. I can tell very quick who they are who doubt my accountability, by a few secret tests I know how to employ, and, I tell you, the one who is found wanting in confidence in me—as an accountable moral agent—won't be burdened with my friendship, after that!

12

I'll cut from such an one as quick as I would from a Calvinist—for ever! I suspect the sale of my books, or the liberality of friends, or both together, will furnish me with ample means to journey through the country and pick out my new associates from strangers I have never met; for I have reason to fear that all my old friends and relations are found wanting in this indispensable test of all my future associates.

Brother Foster, I intend to call upon you and apply my test very carefully in your case ; for the truth is, I don't like to drop you off. I have counted a great deal upon your friendship for me! But, dearly as I love you, I must do it, if you believe me to be an insane person. But there is so much of Christ—the natural, true man—in you, that I feel pretty confident of your continued friendship. Who knows but that *you* will be the most Christ-like man I can find!

Well, Brother Foster, although my determination to be a true woman, and live a natural life, has cost me my "life, liberty, and the pursuit of happiness," by landing me in this insane depot, yet, I am not sorry I took ticket in the train of nature! For a Calvinistic life is not worth much, after all. It hardly pays the cost. Selfish life has lost all its charms for me. I shall die living for others, as I have lived, even if I have to die in prison for it! It has already cost me nearly three years of wearisome imprisonment to pay the cost of this benevolent life.

I find more "express trains" to the heavenly regions at this "depot," than any other. It is here, like the "Great Western depot," at Chicago, where the tracks radiate off, like the spokes of a wheel, in every direction. The only thing which troubles me, is to decide on which to take passage. But I am not in doubt, now. I go on my own hook, entirely—"lightning express." It must be it isn't a great way off from the heavenly regions, here, for messages go tremendous quick, back and forth—a great deal quicker than my letters do to friends on earth!

I have but one answer to all the letters I have sent out, to my friends, since the first three months. No, not one child, even, until within the last five months. That is one important part of the treatment here. Keep dark! I suppose our doctors think we have resources enough within to sustain us—light enough there—and you know insane folks are not allowed to judge for themselves, on this or any other subject, where reason could be used! Reason and affection must go to sleep, here, and rest content with dreams of past and future bliss.

It is not a blissful process to go through with, I can tell you! and you had better take my word for it, and not come and try it for yourselves. I say a man or a woman who can be content to be in an insane asylum, can be content to be a hog—nothing more. That is all that is required or expected of them here—just to eat and sleep, like hogs—that's all. No—we wear clothes, besides! We are not so well off as the hogs are, either—for they can have their own little hogs with them, in the same pen.

We can't! Good, Christian mothers are here called and treated as insane, only because they were Christians, and are kept entombed here, until their children forget them! But the mothers don't forget their children. No, she don't in three years' time, at least! Oh! could all the tears I have shed, in that time, for my children's sake—not my own—be measured, I do think the tear-glass would overflow! It has seemed, sometimes, as though my tender, sensitive, loving, maternal nature would break and die! And it has died—stone dead. And I am glad of it—right glad. For now, Jesus Christ, my husband, has no rival in my heart.

But my love isn't dead, mind you. No, indeed! You wouldn't think it was, if you could only see how much I lot upon going home, to them. It does seem to me that, as the square of the distance of time between us decreases, attraction increases. But the truth is, the centripetal and centrifugal forces so draw upon me, that I can't move out of my present orbit. My children draw me home to them, by the centripetal force—and my husband drives me off, from home, by the centrifugal force. So, as the result, I must remain stationary, until our government beheads this centrifugal power.

I do hope the government will so fix it, that these Calvinistic husbands will feel that it is easier, and cheaper, for them to keep their marriage vow, than to break it. I am sure, law and gospel, both, teach that fidelity is more honorable of the two, than perjury! A perjured husband makes a far more tyrannical and despotic tyrant than a Southern slave-holder; for his power is absolute over his wife; for she has not the shadow of law to protect her identity; while the slave is allowed to be protected, as property. And, besides, the slave has some chance of escape, by flight, to Canada, where the crown protects the fugitives. But even the crown of England can't protect me from my slaveholder! Our laws give the husband a right to claim his wife under any circumstances, except she sacrifices her virtue, so she can be divorced!

But I love my virtue as well as I do myself, so I can't afford to lose that, to buy my freedom with. But I do wish I could buy some of my children—if I can't myself! But, no! I can't even buy my children, nor be allowed even to see them, except in defiance of his cruel mandates. Yes, my husband instructs Dr. McFarland not to let me see, or hear from my children—only as he dictates! And his wishes dictate that I be kept from all kind of intercourse with my children during all my lifetime, or, as he says, until he can remove the children to where they cannot be influenced by me—lest I ruin them!

And our laws uphold him in doing all this to a competent, gifted, Christian mother, just because I have embraced, conscientiously, a more liberal Christianity than he advocates! Is this protecting the rights of opinion and conscience to American citizens? Does our government think that because it protects the inalienable rights of the men of America, it protects the rights of *all?* Are not women citizens? Are not their rights worth protecting? How could the government be sustained without them? It is my honest opinion that the government would find it to their decided advantage to protect the rights of the women, as well as their own rights. Our government is now only a man affair. It is only a half affair. Adam wasn't but half made, till he got his Eve associate. So our old Adam government is not but half made, because they leave the women out.

I tell you, we are not in our proper place until we are under the men's wings! We have been under their feet long enough. God took Eve out of Adam's side—where I think she is at home—when she can get back there to her old place. I should so like to be a man's companion! It must be so pleasant to be so respected by these " lords of creation!" I don't like to be trampled in the dust, even if we do make good foot-stools for them to stand upon! I don't think it would hurt the soles of the men's feet if they should stand on the dust they have compelled us so long to lick! I should so like to see how it would seem to be allowed to stand up erect on my own feet, with no man or government pulling me down into the dust! We were not made of dust, and we don't like to live in it. It is not *our* native element! It is the men that we want to live in, or with. They are welcome to their native element, if they will only keep us above it!

I should like a government to stand upon—but I don't want to govern! I want to be protected, so I can lead a Christian life without making such a fuss about it. I want to be at home doing my duty to my children, instead of being off here in the asylum, pleading for liberty to think and speak and do right. I say it is too bad to compel me to do this, to keep spirit life from suffocation! I can't go home to seek that tiger's protection, after he has done all he possibly could do to murder my spirit life. For I know that the more blood the tiger finds to feed upon, the more voracious he becomes, and the less chance his victim has for escape out of his power. Since he has been countenanced in all his outrages upon me, hitherto, both by the whole community as well as government—so far as interference is concerned—what reason have I to expect a still greater outrage might not be winked at, and he be sustained in hiding me in a worse place than I am now in? I have no assurances to the contrary! and it would be the height of presumption for me to attempt to maintain my rights—as mistress of my own household—under these auspices. So until rational protection is offered me I see no other way but to remain in prison—the only safe refuge from my tyrant's persecutions!

Oh! heaven protect! Oh! heaven defend me! And Oh! in mercy protect my little flock of motherless ones—from abuse! Oh! God! don't let them forget the mother who bore them!

I wonder if mothers who are taken from their little ones by death feel as I do? I don't think they can be entirely happy until they see some prospect of meeting them again, any more than I can; for mothers do love their children eternally. Their love is deathless. The natural love is not deathless—the spiritual is.

Mind you, they are two different articles! One is a hog's love, a cow's, a horse's love of her colts—the other is a woman's love!—a mother's love!—a Saviour's love of his children, for whom he died to redeem from the power of Satan! And who knows but my death has accomplished a similar purpose for my children? Do you think I could have got Abraham to have cut off Calvin's head if I had not called to him from my grave to do it? No; he wouldn't have even known that there was any need of doing it if he had not acted so to me—his good wife.

Yes, I have been a good wife to the "old dragon" for twenty-one years, and God saw that it was long enough for my profit. So he let old Satan give me a divorce—without my deserving it, by being untrue to him—for even once—and he took the entire responsibility of the act himself. I didn't ask him to cast me off, and I didn't consent to be put off from my children and home either. I did use to ask him to give me a divorce in a civil manner, as other civil husbands do; but I didn't ask him to put me into an asylum, where he meant to keep me for life, where I couldn't support myself, nor anybody else, and the last place in the world where I could expect to pick up a husband!

Who would think of going to an insane asylum to look them up a wife? And besides, we are not allowed to have beaux in the wards! It would be a poor place to court, if we could; for we see men here so seldom, except as they walk, speechless, through, that if they stopped to make a decent visit, so many would be after them that he wouldn't know which offer to accept out of so many admirers!

It is a fact, I don't think Calvin would consent to my being the wife of anybody but himself, for he would be ashamed to let another man know what a good wife he had cast off. He knows that whoever got me for their wife would get as kind and loving a woman as ever wore dresses! He knows I couldn't change colors and play the hypocrite, even to save his character. I go for maintaining my own character first—on the No. 1 principle—he knows, as well as everybody else who has seen me.

And my character is made up of universal kindness to all

God's creatures—for I have quite an idea of trying the experiment, like the coral in the bottom of the ocean, of building my own spiritual house—myself! by adding particle by particle of little acts of kindness to the continental mass, which is slowly but surely rising to the surface of the ocean of universal love—to vitalize the two hemispheres with its benignant influences.

Christ is laying the foundation for a "new heaven and a new earth," wherein dwelleth the righteous builders of this new continent—new, because each one builds his own house, and not his neighbor's. This immense coral army are all swayed by one universal law—"Judge ye not of your own selves what is right!"

We have given up ministers and doctors for God and nature, and we are each one going to be happy in our own way—the way our instincts and impulses lead us into. But, mind you, our instincts and impulses are all reined by reason and enlightened by conscience. Our animal life is left buried in the ocean depths, to rise no more upon our coral continent. Self-love is our principle of action! Happiness is what we all seek, and find, too, in obeying the laws of our holy natures. We all love our own happiness so well that we won't break one of God's laws to interrupt it.

And we love our neighbors as we do ourselves, that is, we let them have the same liberty to be happy which we ourselves use and enjoy—entire freedom! God don't allow us to dictate or control any one but ourselves, and we have no desire to do so, for such responsibilities would burden us. We carry no burdens—not even our own! We let God carry them for us. All we desire to know is—our duty. Events we know as they take place. We can look after God, but not before his providence.

To pursue our own happiness—in the way God appoints—is our highest aim and ambition. For God is our pattern in everything. And he is seeking his glory or happiness in all that he does. So do we.

It is our happiness to do as he does—do as we please, and let others do the same. And we please to obey his laws. We all seek our own happiness, as the supreme good. And yet there is not a selfish one in our circle!—for we "love our neighbor as we do ourselves."

God tells us to love ourselves as we do him, for we are a part of himself, and so is every other human being. So God is in all, and all our good is in God. We don't have to leave our continent to find God, or see him, for we can see him in every being we meet in human form. There are no human beings too degraded to be our companions! We fear no contamination from bad company, for we know that the good in us is more contagious than the evil in others, inasmuch as good is a more potent principle than evil, and our sovereign tells us to "overcome evil with good." We will not be overcome of evil, for evil has lost its power over us since we consented to give up the process of "regeneration"— and be as God made us to be!

We have no experiences to relate of conquests over sin, for we don't tempt a battle! We have good and kind work enough to do without fighting evil—for we find that fighting evil is only adding fuel to the flame, which would die of itself if left alone, unmolested. We don't have to avoid even the publicans and harlots of society, for we like to go into fashionable company—where they are so common that we meet them at almost every step! still we like their company, for they seem to like ours.

They must be nearer heaven than the Calvinists are. especially the preaching part of them, who live as they tell us to live—for Christ said they would get in before the Calvinistic clergy of his day!

In fact I think, for myself, I would risk myself sooner in

12*

any other company than that of the consistent Calvinistic clergy of our day. I should feel more danger from the contaminating influence of their practice, than from the prostitute or drunkard. I am of Christ's opinion that the last will be the first to enter heaven, and the first the last to get there. The drunkard and the prostitute don't degrade or regenerate but a part of their natures—while the Calvinists strive to regenerate the whole—so as to become totally depraved!

I do wish people would love themselves more! They don't seek their happiness enough. If they would only follow Christ's example, and love themselves—as he did himself—they would not be selfish at all. To be selfish is to hate our own happiness. To seek our own happiness, is, to do right. To love ourselves as we ought—we should be serenely happy.

Brother Foster, don't you think I have secured my spiritual freedom by losing my personal liberty? You see I am not afraid to speak my own thoughts before others besides yourself, as I used to be in conservative New England. I don't know whether they would have imprisoned me in Worcester asylum, had I thought aloud, as I do here, or not. I don't think Packard could have carried his point, and got it done in any other community in the Western regions—but Manteno. It will be no honor, I assure you, to have been a Mantenoite in coming ages! Mark my word, Brother Foster.

Do you know, brother, why I liked you so much better than I did most of the ministers husband exchanged with? If you don't, I will tell you. It was because you are such a woman-lover. You seemed to respect me as your social companion. You respected my thoughts and my feelings. You never seemed to look upon me with contempt, because I was a woman! I felt in your company as if I was under your wing, not under your feet. Thus you drew me out to be more free and frank in telling you my inward experiences—my feelings, as the orthodox say—than I was with other ministers. Another thing, I found you could understand me better than other folks, because you had left the creed in your rear, and become wiser than its teachers. I remember you once told me of your experience, which you said you did not dare to tell to any one else, because they might not understand it as you saw I could do, by my own experience.

Now, brother, there are a great many legions, I may well say, that can't understand me—because so much in my rear. Shall I, therefore, "put my light under a bushel," lest those who can't understand me call me insane? Or, shall I be true and honest to my convictions, and hear this reproach for the truth's or Christ's sake? And how can progress be made in knowledge if *all* conceal the teachings of this inner teacher, because in advance of the present standard?

It is these Uzzahs that we women are so afraid of! We don't like to be held back by the "lords of creation"—when we know we are on the track of nature. You are not Uzzah-ish, Mr. Foster, unless you have been "regenerated" since I saw you! A "woman-lover" is not of the Uzzah ranks. I find the Uzzahs are among the women-haters—these "regenerated" characters. You, the women-lovers, know that women are made to fly and soar—not to creep and crawl, as the haters of our sex want us to. We are made more spiritual than men, by nature,—and, of course, we apprehend spiritual things more readily,—and therefore, God, the greatest woman-lover in the universe, appoints them to carry the ark forward, leaving the men to *follow on* in the slower track of reason. Our instincts don't stop to reason—but they are based on the highest and best of reasons.

We fly to our conclusions, while you plod after, on the legs of reason. We are the "lightning express"—you, the "freight train," so heavily laden with reasons that you drag on at a rate, to us, distressingly slow. However, freight is of some use, after all, especially if it is good wheat.

But be sure and switch quick when you hear our whistle, for we don't like to be hindered in our progress—for our merit lies in our speed. Your merit lies in your strength to drag your own heavy train. But, mind you, don't you try to use it in detaining us! Mind your own business, and we'll mind ours. For we are determined to go on lightning speed, and if you don't clear the track for us, we shall have to clear it for ourselves, that's all.

You can't stop lightning—and it is in vain to try. We can't go at your thundering pace—for thunder and lightning are two as different articles as light and sound—both good in their proper places, but very troublesome out of it.

You may keep on bellowing after us, if you choose, but you can't scare us by your noise, nor stop us from lightning, when we find any gas in our track which ought to be exploded. We are for breathing pure air, and if we can't keep the poisonous miasma out of it in any other way, we intend to drive it out, ourselves. And we do something besides bellow, when we use our artillery!

We can't stop to bellow for you after we shoot you. You may bellow, and howl, and criticise us, as much as you choose; all we have to do is to fire!—then run in search of other game.

It is my opinion there is plenty of game, yet, to shoot in this great American wilderness, and we must not stop for your praises or your blame, until we have hunted it up, and put it out of harm's way by our lightning flash. We believe this wilderness is yet to bud and blossom as the rose: but the Calvinistic roots must first be dug out of it, by the grub-ax of patient, persevering toil. If the devil who planted these ugly, noxious trees would only do the grubbing, himself, we should like it! for we want to get to transplanting the Christian tree into the virgin soil of nature.

I say 'tis natural for men to love good, and hate evil—for

God does, and if he hasn't told us a lie, he has made us like himself. The devil has been so successful in "regenerating" the Calvinistic part of the human race, that he has made them honestly believe the lie, that they do hate good and love evil. But they don't! for it is contrary to nature, and, therefore, 'tis a delusion to think they do. For God and nature will stand their own ground. They can't, either of them, be beaten by Satan and all his agents—any more than the old dragon and all his hosts can make a natural woman an insane woman! Their calling me insane, and believing me to be insane, don't make me so. I am just as sane as I was before they got up this hue and cry against me. So our nature is just as holy and God-like as it was before the Calvinists slandered it so much. And when human beings insist upon it that they hate good, they are deceiving themselves, "believing a strong delusion of Satan's."

Besides, many profess to believe they are bad as the devil, when, in fact, they don't believe any such thing, any more than Dr. McFarland believes me to be insane, when he says I am. He knows he is speaking a lie on himself, as well as on me, when he professes to believe me to be an insane person. He knows the truth. He knows I am a perfectly sane person—still, he is led to say I am not, from the influence of a weak policy by which he hoped he might extricate himself, and the institution, from the trap he has got into, by crediting lying testimony, instead of truthful observation. He can't get out of his trap by defending this lie. So, like a wise man, he has concluded—thank God!—to repent, and submit to the humiliating dilemma of being a fallible man, liable, like the other "lords of creation," to resort to policy, instead of principle, as a means of self-defense. Well, if he can't defend himself, from principle, in the course he has taken, I can defend myself, from principle, against his slander—but I have got to expose some unwelcome truths to do so! But this is a free country, and the doctor has just as good a right to defend himself against these unwelcome truths, as I have to defend myself against his very unwelcome slanders!

Again, Dr. McFarland has led a great many to believe I am insane, because they believed he knew better than they did, who was insane, and who was not. Well, I do say this sort of humanity are as weak in manliness as dishwater is of nourishment—for if they can't give more credit to their own common-sense and reason, in so plain a case as whether a person, like me, knows enough to be accountable for their own actions or not, than to Dr. McFarland's, I say they are too weak trash for me to associate with. I want human souls for my companions, not parasites. Any one who prefers another's reason before his own, must be either a baby in manliness, or an idiotic human, or "regenerated!" Now, the clergy have played just such a game on the credulity of the community, by making them believe they hated good and loved evil—by nature—because they told them it was so; while, at the same time, they, themselves, knew it wasn't true, as well as the doctor knew his slanders were not true. And the unthinking part of community credit these slanders of their nature, because they, foolishly, think the clergy know more about *their* natures than they do themselves!

I say, be your own judge of your own nature, and don't be deluded into the lie that you are bad, by nature, when you are not! .I am not going to believe I am insane, if all the clergy and doctors in the universe tell me I am,—for I know I am not,—and whoever thinks I am, is either a knave or a fool, and their opinion isn't worth minding. I've got enough to do to mind my own business, that God has sent me to do. He knows I am sane, and capable of being trusted with great and important trusts and responsibilities.

And I intend to show God, by my own conduct, that he has not misplaced his confidence by allowing me to be an accountable being. I am accountable to God, but to no other being, how I discharge my duties.

I shan't trouble myself at all to go around and ask any of my brothers and sisters if I have written the right sort of book, before it's published. That's a matter between me and God alone. No brother or sister in the world can tell, as well as I can, what God dictates *to me* to write. God is the only critic I'll allow before it's published. The whole world may criticise it as much as they please afterwards. They may blow at it—but they can't blow it away. They may puff it—but they can't make it any bigger. But it don't need praising—for it praises itself! I say, it's a book worth reading, notwithstanding all the contempt the Calvinists will heap upon it to keep it down. But it won't be kept down, any more than its author can be! It will rise by its own merits without the help of newspaper notices, just as I shall,—when the right time comes. I say a work which has given its author so much pleasure in writing, cannot but inspire a similar sensation in its reader. I tell you it's worth reading, if all the critics tell you it isn't! Now there is no way for you to find out whose opinion is correct,—until you read it for yourselves,—and let your own reason speak your own opinion.

I've got one compliment for it already, besides my own compliments; and that is from Dr. Asa B. Tenny, our assistant physician; and he don't begin to know half the good things there are in it, for he has not been its inspector, as Dr. McFarland has. But from what he did know, and from what Dr. McFarland had told him about it, he made the remark to me:

"Mrs. Packard, I expect that your book will be so popular, and acquire so great notoriety, that it will yet be considered an honor to have a piece of the paper on which 'twas written!" this he said, while storing away in the corner of his wallet a slip of my penciled manuscript, that I was about to destroy.

I replied, "I thank you for the compliment, Dr. Tenny,—but you must not flatter me."

"Oh, no," said he, "I am speaking in earnest."

I returned his compliment a few months afterwards, by telling him that "I thought he carried the handsomest beard, and kept it in the neatest order, of any gentleman I ever saw." But, lest he be flattered at the sight of his soft, full, black beard and mustache in his mirror, I added : "but this compliment, Dr. Tenny, is, in reality, not due you, so much as your Maker, who bestowed it upon you."

He acknowledged the qualification, and thanked me for my compliment.

So I say of his, and all other compliments in store for my book, that the merits of the book, and all the good things which it contains, are wholly due to God—its author. But its demerits and its evil things are wholly due to me and my imperfections.

By the way, I must add, in relation to my literary friend, Dr. Tenny, that I am indebted to him, more than to any other individual in this asylum, for my publications, and knowledge of the world outside of these brick walls. He is an earnest and whole-souled patriot, and has kept me well-posted as to the war news, and governmental matters. He has given me, almost invariably, the reading of his *Independent*, and, occasionally, other papers. Yes, he has made me glad almost every week by these his silent, speaking tokens of his true sympathy for me in my afflictions. I have laid my head upon his sympathizing breast and wept tears of anguish, while he sought to comfort my breaking heart by words of sympathy.

His soft, blue eyes betoken his gentle, sympathetic nature, which he allows to be drawn out in sympathy towards God's afflicted ones, here. Indeed, he is a universal favorite with the patients, for they don't expect he will turn a deaf ear to their tale of sorrow. He leaves joys, instead of sorrows, in the path he almost daily treads, through our desolate halls of almost unmingled sadness and sorrow. He differs from Dr. McFarland, in this respect,--he manifests his sympathy for us patients, while we have to take Dr. McFarland's on trust! I guess he feels sympathy for them, though,—at least, I guess he does for *me*, or he wouldn't let me defend myself against his slander!

I find Dr. McFarland differs from Dr. Sturtevant in this respect. Dr. Sturtevant preaches Christianity—but practices Calvinism, while Dr. McFarland preaches Calvinism—and practices Christianity. Dr. Sturtevant says to his Lord, " I go sir, but went not." Dr. McFarland says, " I go not, but afterwards repented and went,"—the right road to secure peace and happiness. I hope he won't backslide, as somebody he is well acquainted with, has!

Well, I've slid back, or forward, with my train of thoughts so far from the old track, that it's hard hitching my cars together again.

I believe I left the train at the asylum depot, where Theophilus told Mrs. Page, my good friend, here, that his father had written him, after visiting the asylum at the September meeting of the Trustees, that " he feared he should not be able to keep his mother much longer in the asylum!'" What if Uncle Sam should let me out without his consent? Would not the government troops be demanded to keep the peace, to have this great dragon's will so ruthlessly crossed ?

He is not used to such treatment. His will is his law,—I don't know of any one, yet, who has been dauntless enough to cross it. I can't insure the safety of these United States, should they dare to run such a risk ! He is so cross with it gratified, I don't know what he might not be tempted to do, to have it crossed. I shouldn't like to be the one to be exposed in such a case; neither should I like to have my children exposed without governmental protection. When Uncle Sam has got the case fairly before him, I think there is some hope that wife and children, both, may secure protection of their inalienable rights.

Uncle Sam, won't you let wives leave their husbands when they treat them badly,—without committing adultery to do so ?—and may not they go to husband hunting, as any other single woman can ? I am sure a woman has lost her husband, when he ceases to protect her, as much, or more, than if he was dead,—for he can trouble her more, and so make her need a protector to protect her against him, more than if the grave held him from her. Now can't you make such laws as will hold him, as well as the grave does ?

I think, if men held their wives on their good behavior to them, they would be more likely to treat them well, than as it now is. Now a woman has to stay with the man she married,—whether he is good to her or not,—and the bad men know that this absolute power can be used to kill their wives, by inches, and they be all shielded in this secret, brutal abuse, ending in murder. Can't a delicate woman's own person be reasonably protected to her ? Or, must the ungoverned passions of beastly men be allowed to be the destroyers of the health and life of the women whom they vowed to protect ?

Nature—womanly nature—calls for the protection of government. Let her not call in vain, for she is the mother of your country ! And I am myself the mother of six of its citizens, and do so want to be allowed to train them, myself, that they can be sure to be loyal and true to their God and their country. They love me better than any one else in the world ; so I think I could have more influence over them than any one else could—for good. And I think God wants me to train them, myself, or he couldn't have made me to love them so well, that I can't be satisfied to be for ever separated from them, just because one devil insists upon it, I am not competent for the charge. Do let me stand on my own actions, not on his opinion of me ; for God knows more than he does, and he gave them to me,—and the devil has no right to take them from me. I say 'tis interfering with the Almighty's plans to do so. Won't our government stand up for God and his plans, or will they shield the devil in his interference ? Can't our maternal rights—the right to our own offspring—be secured from the devil's grasp ? If Uncle Sam is as afraid to protect my children to me, as the community have been, I shall think he worships the priests of the devil more than he does God, as they do.

I tell you, Uncle Sam, the priests of Baal are not worth minding ! for one Elijah could destroy four hundred of them with the sword of truth. The truth is, they are all hollow—inside, if they do make such an imposing appearance with their black coats, white cravats,—outside. It takes something more than a tailor and laundress together to make a man—but they can make a priest, or an idol for the worshipers of Baal to bow down to, and worship, as the " Lord of lords, and the King of kings !"

It is astonishing how people will be gulled by them! They can make them even believe that it is wrong to love people, and I have heard them go so far as to warn them against loving their own offspring too much ! I protest against forbidding people to love one another. If people don't do anything worse than to love each other, I don't think that God—who don't do anything else but love—will punish them for it ! But the devil will ! He and his priests think it is a dreadful thing for a man to love a woman that

ain't his wife—or for a woman to love a man that ain't her
husband. A woman hasn't got a husband till she finds a
protector in a man, even if she has been legally tied to ever
so many beasts who wear pants! It ain't the pants and the
beast together that make a husband to a woman—it takes a
man to husband or protect a woman—the weaker vessel—as
Christ protects the church.

Every man is another personified Christ, and I love them
as Christ—and I go to them for shelter and protection in
trouble, as I would to Christ, and I am just as confident of
protection from such as I am from Christ himself. Hasn't
Christ said I must just " trust him," and he would show me
I had not misplaced my confidence. Does not every true
man like also to be " trusted ?"—and can a true man deceive
or betray a woman's confidence ? If Christ can—they can.
If Christ can't—they can't. I trust every man I can find—
as my superior in manly strength—whose strength is
pledged in my defense, if needed, to defend me from abuse.

But, somehow, these days, men have hid themselves from
me, as Christ says he does, sometimes, hide his face from us
in trouble for a time.

I wonder why it is so ? I don't know but Christ thus
means to test our love to him, to see if we will trust him—
in the dark. I have trusted him a great while in the dark,
and I don't believe he means to harm me. So I can trust
true men in the dark—for I don't think they intend to harm
me in the dark or light either. Christ never harms those
who love and trust him. So no true man will harm any
woman who loves and trusts him! It isn't love that harms—
it is hate—or want of love, that does all the mischief.

And it isn't any more wrong for a man to love a woman,
than it is for a woman to love a man.

It is no more wicked for a man who is healthy to have an
appetite for a good meal than it is for a natural man to love

a woman. A healthy appetite relishes some kinds of food better than others, and he is his best judge which suits him best; so a natural man likes some women better than others, and he is the best judge which suits him best. I go for freedom! Let each one choose his own food and his own wife, for he knows better than anybody else when he is suited.

Again, it is no more of a sin for a woman to be beautiful and fascinating, than it is for a man to love her charms, and be drawn towards her by them. God made the woman beautiful to draw out the men's love for them—so they would make good protectors of their chastity, virtue, purity, and innocence.

Oh! how I do wish I could find a husband who would dare to *protect* me in the exercise of my God-bestowed womanly virtues—instead of being forced to go to government to plead the protection of my identity—because no man cares for my soul!

I don't know but there are some men who do care for me, some; but if there are, their love is so torpid, it ain't of much account to me in my present emergency. I wonder where the chivalry of manhood has hid itself? If I could only get scent of it, I should like to go hunting, to see if I could find it—to be used as a protective weapon against my legal persecutors' abuse. Every one whom I used to think were men, seem to lack this trait of manhood, entirely. For if they don't, how is it that all seem to *act* as though they had altogether more fear of one of Baal's priests, than they have love for Christian woman?

Is American manliness being now weighed in the balances, and found wanting in its essence—its life? God knows why I am left so long utterly unprotected. I don't!

I know it isn't because I haven't informed those whom I considered the most manly, of my situation, by letters,

written myself and mailed, post-paid, to them. I have
written and sent, by the underground express, all the letters
I wish to send out, in appeals for help from this source.
For if these appeals are fruitless—it is in vain to expect
help from what *I* know of American chivalry! Thus far it
has been nothing but silence, mute, dumb—nothing!

If these number one specimens of manliness have all
become "dumb-dogs" that cannot bark at a wolf, because
they are afraid of him, and thus let him devour the defenseless sheep and lambs—without mercy—I say, I think that
this Calvinistic age is culminating! My only hope is, that
when the meridian is past, the decline of this Calvinistic age
will be total, complete, and rapid.

I begin to fear that Calvin—the persecutor of woman—at
the present day, is not the only victim of "total depravity
and regeneration!" However, since I don't know what
causes have operated to prevent my deliverance, I will hope
"total depravity" is not the only cause of non-interference.
I shall be very loth to believe any one is totally depraved,
except Calvin himself! Still, a man who dares not protect a
woman is scarred with the darkest of all marks of total
depravity. A man who has been so completely the subject of
"regeneration" as to become "totally depraved," has lost
entirely his original holy—God-like—nature, and, therefore,
we women cannot hope for help from any subject of "regeneration."

It is from the *unregenerate*—the holy—the God-like—that
woman's protectors must be chosen; for the "regenerated"—
the unholy—the devils—do not protect, but oppress, the weak '
and dependent. I know this lost, holy nature is to be restored
to the depraved, regenerated victims; still I don't know how
to wait so long for my deliverance,—for, if it takes as long
to make gods out of devils as it has to make devils out of
gods, I shall get tired waiting for them to be "regenerated"
back again!

The fact is, the Calvinists are a terribly hard set to deal with—they do cling to their "total depravity" as if it was the best thing in the universe! It is dearer to them than woman's love is! I don't know as they could love a woman who would not acknowledge that she was "totally depraved." So a true woman must play the hypocrite—or belie herself—to get one of them to promise to protect her depraved nature. It isn't my depravity that I want protected—it is my virtue—my womanly nature—that I am looking after a husband for. But I guess our government will be my husband! I have most despaired of the men ever offering me any protection. Yes, I will marry the government of these United States, if you'll protect me and my other husbandless sisters! We'll be loyal and true to you until death parts us, if you'll only take us under your wings.

I want it so fixed that any woman can run—*on her own feet*—right straight to you for help the minute she wants help, to get out of the power of a cruel husband. You must credit her testimony as well as you do his—and a little more—for she is more helpless and dependent than he is, and her nature is more forbearing, and she is more self-sacrificing, and more modest. So you must pave an easy way for her to walk in to seek your help. If you can imprison women on the simple testimony of one who claims to be her husband, I think you certainly ought to imprison the man on the simple testimony of his wife. It is a poor law that won't work both ways. I am sure, while men can get up any lies on their wives, and have them imprisoned on them, the wives ought to have them imprisoned on their own testimony of the truth. It isn't fair for you to credit their lies—and discredit our truths! You are now only a man-protecting government—a Calvinistic one—and I don't, and won't, like you unless you will protect the women!—the weak—who need your protection.

If you won't marry me, and be my protector—now I have

offered myself to you for protection—I won't marry you, and so that is the end of it! I shall tell my Father your government is good for nothing, and I shall ask him to send on Christ, with his angelic hosts, to overthrow it, and take the throne himself. And my Father is very good; he believes my simple testimony, for he knows I never lie, and my word can be relied upon as verity and truth, so *he* will attend to my case, if you won't! Christ, my brother, is a very strong King, and when he does come, woe to your Calvinism! He hates it as bad as I do, but he is not quite so outspoken as I am in giving his opinions. The difference between us is—he is a man and I am a woman—and we women have a little more of the gab about us.

You'll see if Christian wives are not made as free under my brother's government as Calvinistic husbands now are under your man-government!

You protect the Calvinists in their wrongs—and we are to be protected in our rights—when his kingdom is established. I have been corresponding with him all my married life, so he knows how much I have been oppressed in secret, and how patiently I have borne it, and how trustfully I have committed my case into his hands for a just settlement of it. He has promised me often to come and settle it just right, on earth, for me; and I am not afraid of his breaking his promises. I have been bothered a good deal during my earth life, and I think it wouldn't be fair to suffer wrong *all* the time—never have justice done me, where I have suffered so much injustice!

The truth is, Christ's followers have nothing to fear! but much to hope, from the coming of Christ to establish his kingdom in America. It is only the Calvinists who have need to fear. Goodness and truth are to be established on a firmer basis by his coming—but evil and error are to be overthrown by him, and confined in the pit of destruction—

where I intend to pitch in my insane train—with Calvin and all his hosts of passengers, when I've picked up all the devils on the continent, and ticketed them through!

The tares, or false doctrines, make a mighty heavy freight, hitched to the wicked practices on board the passenger train.

However, my "lightning express" goes quick, and pulls tremendous hard, after the bell rings, telling us: "All aboard!" At least, we'll be ready to go beyond the Rocky Mountains, as soon as the track is laid through the unexplored regions. We shan't be hindered so much in a new country, taking on freight and passengers. Mind you, it's the "regenerated" soil which furnishes the Calvinism—not nature!

Another thing, we haven't got through with the devil's services yet, on our continent. There is work enough for them to do, until the track is laid clear through, to get the throne ready for Christ's inauguration. God knows how to use the devils. He makes servants of them to do his mean, sordid, filthy work of imprisoning, killing, and burying themselves. He makes them do their own chores, and don't pay them for it, either.

This is Bible slavery! It is a very different thing from Southern slavery—altogether different. They buy their slaves—God don't. His slaves volunteer their services, and he accepts them—and he don't keep a driver to whip them to go to their work. They work without being made to. 'Tis all free-labor system. Still, it's forging chains, and twisting ropes all the time for no one—but themselves! to chain them up, so they can't do any more harm to their wives and their children—their slaves.

Oh! I do think my Father is one of the best sheriffs I ever saw!

He lets his whole family be free—children, servants, and slaves. The slave is just as free to do his drudgery, as the

13

child is to do his filial duties. He keeps bull-dogs, or
sheriffs, on hand—but I never had one of them hold of
me—until my persecutor sent one of them after me to track
me to the asylum. But, oh! a bull-dog—a real, trained
slave-catcher—isn't half so fierce an animal as a " wolf in
sheep's clothing!" If it hadn't been for the sheep on the
outside of my wolf, I should have stood a better chance of
getting out of harm's way.

I could see the *man* in my sheriff, at first sight—but he
had to work in his office, because a minister had appealed
to him to help him shut up his " crazy, lunatic wife," as he
calls me!—made so " by sickness," as the sheriff said he
told him I had been.

But 'twas a lie! I had only had an influenza for a few
weeks, and couldn't help coughing a good deal. I knew
when I was polishing his linen I could hardly carry a steady
hand, for I coughed so much—and, besides, my breast ached
so, and was so sore from carrying my baby, 'Arthur, about
the house in my arms—or rocking him in his suttee-cradle
in front of my bed—almost all the time—nights, that I did
venture, one day, to ask him to hire a girl, as he passed
through the room where I was at work, ironing, with my
baby on the ironing-board, and looking so weary at my toil-
some work.

Said I: "I do wish you would hire a girl to polish your
linen, till I get rested enough to do it myself."

"Oh! horrors! his wife asking for a hired girl! She
must be crazy! She didn't use to ask for a girl—she could
do her own work, and wouldn't even let me get a girl if I
wanted to—for she said she had rather do her work, herself,
than have a girl do it for her."

So I had, *then*, when I was only thirty-five, and had only
six in the family to work for. Don't he think that circumstances alter cases? I do, if he don't. I tell you, eight

years of woman's life—house-keeping, alone—and moving three times, before you've had time to get rested from the last—and getting eight, instead of seven, to care for—and getting older, too, every year—makes some difference in the feelings and elasticity of beings made of human tissue!

What does the old fellow mean? Don't iron, even, wear out, especially when the wheels ain't oiled at all with a husband's love and sympathy?

Yes, my iron constitution wouldn't have stood it as well as it has done, had I not looked out for my own health,—by living in a natural, healthy manner,—and had I not had strength to hold up the shield of faith for my defense, I guess his eyes would have made me quail before them more than they did.

Oh! how I do pity weakly, sickly wives, with subjective husbands! I don't wonder they get too discouraged and weak to hold the shield of faith up, and are compelled to fight the old dragon with his own weapons!

Then he ousts them off to an insane asylum, and tells Dr. McFarland they are crazy at home! But he must take their word for it, for he can't see any craziness in them here, until they are so galled by the treatment they receive here, that the "old Adam" will come out as it did at home, by being the defenseless victims of unmerited abuse. Can a worse abuse be inflicted upon human beings than to treat them as if they were insane, when they are not? No—there cannot! It is the most outrageous insult that the divinity within us can be subjected to. And, is it possible for humanity to receive the highest of all insults without feelings of resentment? No—'tis a moral impossibility! And the higher the development of the human soul, the more keenly sensitive they are to this kind of persecution. And yet, the least manifestation of this natural, rational resentment, is called insanity here, and punished according to the laws of

the country with imprisonment—protracted imprisonment—
until this mark of the divinity is crushed out of them!

It is an almost moral certainty that this course, persisted
in long enough, will make either a dunce, or a maniac, of
human beings. The living, breathing facts in our insane
asylums, demonstrate this truth. Now, what is the use of
keeping up this most horrid of all kinds of inquisitions on
our free American soil? A thousand times better were it
for our interests, for both worlds, that the money thus expended were sunk in the unfathomed ocean depths! Rather
than give one cent of my money to support such inquisitions,
I would lay down my life for their destruction,—so help me!
God!

For I have seen and felt the truths I utter, and these
sights affect my heart, because it is a human heart, and
sympathizes in human woes. I will lift up my voice against
these institutions of Satan, and cry aloud for their destruction. It shall not be said on my account-book for eternity,
that Mrs. Packard did not do what she could to destroy them
in her day. Insane asylums are the most cursed institutions
of the nineteenth century; and whoever will not aid in their
destruction, I hope and pray may become one of their
occupants!

Still, these wives are crazy at home,—for husbands don't
tell stories on their own wives! 'Tis contrary to nature,
and reason, and conscience, and common-sense. So they
must have been crazy at home, of course!

But, mind you, our clergy have been trying to regenerate
nature, so that it has come to be another article entirely,—
so different from the original that you wouldn't mistrust its
origin. You know it's the regenerate who are insane,—and
they can't tolerate nature,—so they got up these institutions
to complete the process they had begun at home. And so
they got the government to hire Dr. McFarland to punish

other men's wives for being crazy at home, when they weren't crazy at home, nor anywhere else! Besides, if they were, what's the justice in punishing them for it, with capital punishment—indefinite imprisonment!

Is a crazy person to blame for being crazy, or for doing what he isn't accountable for? Who ought to take care of a crazy person—their friends, who love them,—or strangers, who don't? And if friends won't do it, ought they not to be imprisoned for such brutality? Yes, they,—the guilty ones,—ought to be imprisoned, not the innocent, defenceless victim of their brutality!

Oh! Calvinism! how you do regenerate justice, love, and mercy! We can't even tell the article after its "new birth!"

Oh! if old Satan hasn't had things his own way in getting his hells, or inquisitions, planted on this free-soil continent, then I'm mistaken—that's all. I do hope and pray he may get caught in his own trap this time! I do say it, again and again, that a man who will put his wife into hell with his own hands, isn't fit to have a wife, and he ought to be kept there, for life, himself! for doing such a horrid deed to the woman he had vowed to care for and love, until death us part. If this isn't perjury, I don't know what is. Such kind of perjury ought to be punished with imprisonment, if anything ought to be.

What is stealing a horse—to stealing character and accountability? And if a man or husband is willing to have it known that he has an insane wife, he is not right himself. No *husband* would seek to make others believe that he had an insane woman for his wife. No, he would try to make others think she was sane—if she wasn't. And besides, do you think I can be made to believe such a lie as that a man's wife is insane at home when I see she is not away from home? It don't stand to reason that she can be. No, it isn't possible! and I am not going to have this sheep's wool pulled over my own eyes, if others are willing to submit to it. I will not believe Satan's lies—however strong the delusion may become. I think none but those who have been used to lying themselves could be thus duped. They want others to believe their lies, so they are willing to believe others' lies—since one good turn deserves another!

I will use my own reason and common-sense in such common matters as these have got to be now-a-days—of calling anything and everything and nothing insanity!

But really, it is a very serious matter to pronounce a person to be insane. It is not only outlawing them as witnesses for the truth, but it is placing them below the pale of humanity—on a level with the brutes—lost to that only faculty which connects them with human beings—reason. How would you like to be placed on such a level, and told you were not an accountable being? Remember if you have signed such a warrant you will have such a warrant signed against you! or God is a liar—" for with what measure ye mete it shall be measured to you again."

I would sooner far sign a death-warrant, to consign a body to the grave, than sign a warrant to consign a soul to the oblivion of accountability, and the body to a living tomb! Oh! the horrors of being buried alive, deliberately, by those who ought to be your friends and protectors! Those who have done it for others will, some time in the long vista of their never-dying future existence, have it done for themselves. I shall, ere long, rise from my living tomb, never to enter it again—my persecutors must all enter theirs, and receive the same measure of torment which they have caused me to suffer—an innocent victim to their most cruel delusions. I have suffered—being innocent. They will suffer—being guilty. Insanity is not a sin. But sin is insanity. And to say a person is insane when they are not, is the most insane act an accountable agent can be guilty of! And if any lie can deserve hell-fire—this, of all others, does—because, of all others, it is the most malignant—cruel.

A man or woman might, if they were such arch-deceivers as my husband is, be good and kind abroad, and a devil at home, as I guess some of the wives of the Calvinists know they are—but a Christian is one at home and abroad, too. I was both! and I am a real, true Christian, of God's own pattern and make, entirely. I had nothing to do about making myself, except to just do as God told me to do—that is all the hand I had in the work! So it is all God's work—not my own.

And I say the truth of Calvin, or anybody else, just as soon as I would of myself, for I "am no respecter of persons" in speaking the truth of anybody, fact, or anything else. But to say the truth of Calvin, I have to say things as different as a Christian is from a Calvinist! So, to tell the truth, I must say he was insanely wicked at home, and tolerably decent abroad. I don't mean by that that he has lost his reason yet. He is accountable for putting me into this asylum, and for trying to keep me for ever away from my precious jewels—whom I have tried so hard to make a comfort to him, and me, too. Yes, he is accountable for all the misery I have endured here, and for all my children have endured, too. And God will call him to account for these things. And he will be as speechless as the rebels will be when God asks them what they tried to break up the Union for? My husband can't give one reason, out of himself, for breaking up our married union, any more than the rebels can for trying to dissolve our union.

Oh! the destruction and desolation that pack of hungry wolves do make in society! If I didn't hate to be locked up so myself I should go in for denning them all up tight together. But I can't bear to see a wolf chained. Even the sight of a hencoop hurts my feelings—if a hen is shut up in it. A

cage of any kind is an eyesore to me—only when it is used
for a proper purpose—and it isn't a proper purpose to use it
to confine any living being whom God made to be free. It
is contrary to nature, and therefore it cannot be right.

Nature is as true as the gospel, and a little truer than the
gospel which is preached and practiced now-a-days. I do
think we should be better off with none at all, than such
trash as is palmed off to us on the palms of the " wolves in
sheep's clothing." I told you I thought these animals were
the most hateful animals in the universe, and I can prove it.
Mind you, I don't say anything I can't prove! but I don't
stop to prove them. It's enough for me to make the arithmetic. You must do the sums yourselves, and not ask me
to help you, neither. For when I get my arithmetic printed,
and circulated and sold, my part is done—only pocketing the
money it brings me—to pay my fare home to Manteno.
And if you'll buy books enough, I'll use some of the money
to pay my fare down to visit you.

Cousin Ophelia will buy some for that purpose, I know.
She and I are good friends, and I shan't believe Calvin has
pulled the wool so over her eyes, that she can't see cousin
Elizabeth, without being afraid of her—as a crazy woman!
I don't believe she'll lock my bedroom door at night, lest I
should get up and kill her when she's asleep! I ain't a som-
nambulist. I sleep all night, without even waking up all
night, usually.

How often I think, when I wake up in the morning, feeling so bright and fresh for my duties, " For so he giveth his
beloved sleep!" I am God's beloved. I know I am—or he
would not be so tender of me as all this. Good sleep!
What is better? Nothing—when one is tired and cross.
In fact, nothing else will make you feel cheerful. And I'm
always cheerful—and I always sleep quiet, and good, and
long, too. I go to bed early, and lie late, if my nap ain't
out.

Here I must give Calvin a good, long credit-mark—for I do say the devil shall have his dues—as well as God's other subjects, so far as the truth is his due. I hold on to this anchor, for I've nothing else to make a book out of, and if this anchor don't hold me fast, the fact is, I shall be foundered or shipwrecked! and I don't like either dilemma for my ship of state. The storms of fierce persecution have driven it in amongst the high breakers of blasted hopes of earthly bliss, yet the truth shall pilot it still at sea, as it has always been my refuge and fortress on land. Yes, the old dragon did protect rest to my tired frame, or I could not have done half the service and hard work I did for him. He did let me sleep, undisturbed, all night, and as late in the morning as I wanted to. He did let me be my own judge in these matters, for he acknowledged I was the best judge of what I was able to bear. I could bear a sight more hard usage in the day time, because I did not have hard usage to bear in the night. At night all my sorrows were lost in the deep oblivion of entire forgetfulness—sleep. In truth, Calvin was the protector of my body. He never abused it, either by day or by night—at home or abroad. He provided, in liberal measure, food, raiment, and rest for my body. And, besides, he did allow me to be my own judge in relation to what kind of medical treatment I chose to employ for my own personal benefit; and what kind of food and drink I chose to use for myself, and how much.

So far, well done! Rev. Mr. Packard. As an animal, you took good care of me—and protected my body—as the laws of God and the land required you to do, until you put me off—as a pauper—upon the State of Illinois, for support, as an insane pauper for life. My body is now protected by the laws—the "insane laws" of America.

My food and rest is now provided by the tax-payers of Illinois, and my clothes are furnished me by my friends,

13*

independently of my husband, entirely, except as he is the almoner of their gifts to me.

As a wife, I was long, long since abandoned! But as his slave, I was not cast off, until he placed me on the paupers' list of this State. As a woman, I have suffered the most agonizing of all kinds of martyrdom at his hands. Instead of being the husband of the woman—he has been the persecutor of the woman! He has tried, most indefatigably, to deprive me ruthlessly and entirely of my rights of property—of my rights of opinion—of my rights of speech—of my post-office rights—of my rights as mistress of my household duties—and of my hired girls—of my maternal rights—and of my rights of conscience!

My personal identity, as a woman, he has murdered! so far as his efforts could do it, and then handed my body over to Dr. McFarland for burial, at the State's expense! And not one of these inalienable rights of my womanly nature does my country—my government—protect to me. They protect my body—as a pauper—but my soul is defenceless! so far as human government, or human protection is concerned.

The spiritual government of God is its only refuge, so far as governmental protection extends,—and Dr. McFarland is the *only man* on God's footstool, who cares enough for my soul, to offer any protection to one of my soul's inalienable rights. So far as *I* am concerned, he is the *only* representative Christ has on earth—as a protector of the innocent. May he wear the crown of universal homage as his well-earned trophy!

Dr. McFarland honors God's law,—the law of his own manly nature—above the Calvinistic statute of his country's government, and God will honor him above the government. For, " they that honor me, I will honor: but they (or the government) who despise me, shall be lightly esteemed."

The age has so regenerated its human nature, that a man needs the moral courage of a lion to withstand the obloquy Calvinistic influences will try to heap upon that man who dares to be a man now-a-days. If he defends the oppressed, especially the rights of women, he must do it at the risk of losing his popularity with the devils—his contemporaries.

Well, Christ is going to run this risk, for he is going to protect his church, or be its husband, rather, and the church is the most defenseless creature in America, without it is the inalienable rights of married women. I shouldn't be surprised if the church should be found to be his soul in woman! I shouldn't think men would dare to disregard woman's identity, lest they be found to disregard the purest image of the deity on earth!—or rather the better half of the deity. For a woman is the most spiritual or God-like of the twain. I won't object to your protecting, or husbanding our bodies, if you won't leave our souls out entirely; for the truth is, we do like to have healthy bodies, while they are the tenants for our souls: but if you can't protect our souls—our inalienable rights,—I, for one, had rather you would kill my body outright, rather than keep it alive, only, so you can torment my soul through its life, for I have died a thousand deaths trying to live one natural life, in this way! Our soul-life is our real life, and when our feelings suffer, all the members of the body suffer.

The fact is, you men have not the slightest idea how sensitive we are to insults to our moral or spiritual nature! And you can't know, because you can't be women. But we do know, and your gallantry ought to lead you to credit our testimony on this point. We do suffer most excruciatingly where you might not see cause for any uneasiness,—judging by your own feelings. And what is more, we can't help it— God has made us, so as to need husbands on that account. We don't need husbands so much to protect our persons, as we do our rights—for if we can't earn our food and clothing, we can get them both,—as paupers,—for the government has looked out for that part of us. And God has left the men to look out for the better part: and he made them just like himself, as he thought they could be trusted with his church, —as its protectors,—as he is. If Calvinism had not "regenerated" the manly natures of men, so terribly, and rendered them, so nearly, "totally depraved," we never should have had to appeal to the "government to protect the church!"

I can get along without a husband well enough, if the government will only defend my inalienable rights from trespass. But to have no husband—no government—no nothing—to protect my spirit-life, I tell you, 'tis a hard case for the Holy Ghost within me, to live any external life! The Holy Ghost ain't satisfied with a merely animal life. It pants for a natural, womanly life! Christ-life—or man-life—is protected by our government. But the Holy Ghost—or woman's life in me—is not, in the least, protected—only so far as Dr. McFarland protects it. He is the only man who has ever been a husband or father—to me. I hope he will be as good a husband to as many wives as King Solomon had! for I think his manliness would not be overburdened with such a charge. Any man who protects a woman is the husband of that woman—as Christ is of the church. I don't think one man ought to try to protect the person of but one woman— his legal wife—but he may husband or protect the *rights* of all the defenseless women within his reach—as his Christ-like nature prompts him, instinctively, to do. The more women my husband protects, *spiritually*, the better I shall like him; for I do love my sisters as I do myself, and I can rejoice, almost as much, to see a defenseless woman protected, as I should to be protected myself, in exchange of circumstances.

Through the manliness of Dr. McFarland, this hell on

earth has become an asylum of refuge from the spiritual persecution of my contemporaries! I have concluded to spend my days here, rather than go forth to the world to have the work of the Holy Ghost derided as insanity! A prison life, with all its horrors, to any liberty-loving nature, is less aggravating than these insults to *God within me* are. I feel them more and more keenly, every day, as I progress in spiritual knowledge and attainments.

To very many married women this is a refuge from the personal abuses of their beastly husbands. They have destroyed the health of their wives, to gratify their own ungoverned passions, and when they themselves have thus capacitated their wives only for a life of misery, they have pitched them into this hell, to die of neglect, as human beings! I do say, a man who cannot, or will not, govern his animal passions—by his reason and his conscience—is fit only for an insane asylum, where he will be treated as he deserves to be treated—as a brute! If insane asylums would only imprison the murderer—instead of his victim—they would not be quite so insane institutions as they now are. A woman who cannot be allowed the rest her nerves demand, by sleep—nights—cannot help feeling cross, any more than a man can with a severe toothache. And a man would think it hard to be sent to prison for doing what he could not help doing, with a severe toothache—acting cross and ugly. He needs relief from the toothache—not abuse and capital punishment—because he has such a terrible affliction to bear!

To send one to an insane hospital to get cured of nervous diseases, is like sending the neuralgia or inflammatory rheumatism into the system, to cure it of the toothache! or like putting a person into a furnace of fire, to cure him of a scald or a burn!

The sympathy which suffering human nature needs to

sustain it in trouble, is, here, scrupulously withheld, as an indispensable part of the treatment. That is, they must be treated only as animals, and the spiritual or human must be crushed—or the spiritual may gain ascendancy over the animal! Has not insanity itself run mad, under our Calvinistic teachers? To make insanity, is the cure of insanity! Like the allopathics, who profess to cure disease only by inflicting a worse disease—that is, to break down the constitution, to give it power to rally and throw off its diseases by its own inherent agency, or vitality! To take away life, to increase it—to kill, to cure! If any system of treatment can extinguish the reason and all humanity in a human being, it is the present system of treating the insane. I am certain humanity descends to its lowest grade or level under this process; or, the other extreme is reached—by the omnipotent powers of resistance of temptation—with which our systems are endowed—but which is used effectually only by the mightiest spirits in the universe.

Whoever can leave an insane asylum without a feeling of moral degradation, and a self-loathing, debased feeling of himself, as a human being, must have attained to the highest plane of divine influences. His human nature must have been sublimated into the divine.

Not one in a thousand escape, unharmed, this process! Their moral natures receive an indelible scar, from these wounds—so barbarously inflicted on their humanity. Every natural feeling is stifled. I have seen mothers mourning for their children, condemned to a lower ward, simply for this natural manifestation of maternal tenderness! And what is worse, they are told they cannot go home until they stop grieving and talking about their children and home. And I have been represented as insane—simply for express-, ing for them the sympathy my heart felt. An intelligent occupant of the lowest ward, Mrs. Bell Norton, told me, after

I had been here several months, that she had often heard that all the insanity Mrs. Packard exhibited was—her sympathy for the patients, and her prayers for them! Yes, I do still pity them, and pray for them, even after enduring the chastisement the asylum assigns to these offenses, for more than two and a half years; therefore I am condemned as a hopeless case of incurable insanity!

Notwithstanding, I have felt the full, deep meaning of what Mrs. Hosmer told me, when I first came, and established, with the doctor's full and free consent, a social prayer-meeting in my room, held every morning, that "if you ever wish or expect to get out of this place, Mrs. Packard, you must give up praying. So long as you hold these morning prayers in your room, you can never get out of this asylum. I know more of this place than you do, and I tell it for your good, alone." Yes, you did then know more than I did of asylums—but I now do know they are hells upon earth—and nothing else!

And I know, too, *I* shall never give up praying, nor regenerate my sympathizing nature, to get out of this hell. I prefer to give the Godhead a reception in the prison-vaults of hell, rather than try to crush the divinity out of me, to get out of it. Yes, "Though I make my bed in hell, thou art there," and I find it my only solace, here, to cherish the divinity within me—by being true to my kind, sympathetic, womanly nature. I do comfort the disconsolate prisoners, by assuring them I will do all that lies in my power to get them out of their horrid prison, by telling the world of their wrongs and abuses, hoping, as one patient said to me this morning, that:

"If there is one drop of humanity left on earth, I do beg that they would take me out of this place, and let me go to my little boy and girl." "And, oh!" she added, with all the pathos of her maternal nature, "Oh! I would give millions of money, if I had it, for my liberty! Why am I locked up in prison? Why can't I be with my children? I have never harmed any one! why am I punished as a criminal? Do but unlock the door and let me be *free*, and I will fall down and worship you!"

I replied, "Mrs. Forest, I have no power to open the door, I am a prisoner as much as you, and I have six children from whom this prison has kept me for years—and I have no prospect of ever getting out, unless the book I am writing is published—so that the country may know what 'inquisitions' they are supporting in these insane asylums. Then I am sure our prison doors will be opened, and we shall all be free! I may have been sent as God's chosen deliverer of his afflicted people, from the most cruel of all kinds of bondage."

"Yes, good lady! you are kindness itself—but, oh! they won't publish your book!"

"Oh! yes, sister, I think it will be published—for 'tis God's book—and he can and will protect it, and use it for his glory. And it is for his glory that the afflicted, the oppressed, the prisoner—be set free."

While I, with my arms encircling her neck, and my cheek against hers, trying to kiss away the fast-falling tears of maternal anguish, am thus trying to keep her bleeding heart from breaking, others about us are exclaiming: "Mrs. Forest, you are getting worse!—you'll have to be put into the lower ward!—you'll never get out of here so long as you show you want to see your children!"

True, it is no place to be natural—for 'tis nature—human nature—which the devil is here determined to destroy. I see his stratagem—I defy his skill on me! I will be natural even in an insane asylum. I will honor God through my God-given nature—and I will daily ask him on my knees to teach me how to do so, while here. But if I, Daniel-like, thus expose myself to the lions' den, I'll trust to Daniel's God to deliver me out of their power.

Another mother, Mrs. Clayton, became inconsolable when she found she was a prisoner—in the absolute power of others—from whom she could not escape. The horror she felt at the fact that she had come to a prison—instead of a hospital—where she was to be treated like a criminal, overpowered her powers of endurance, and she sought and found the only relief within her reach, which was—a suicidal death! She threw herself from the sewing-room window upon the brick basement beneath, and broke her neck. I could not but rejoice for her, that she had thus escaped the ten-fold greater horrors and agonies of a prisoner's life, as a brute, in this hospital. She had been here only a few days when she killed herself, because the terrible fact of hopeless imprisonment was too great for her freedom-loving nature to endure. Oh! this *limitless* imprisonment is worse—ten-fold worse—than death to a human being, whose humanity is developed to any extent. And yet, this worst of all punishments, this nominally Christian government deliberately imposes upon the most afflicted class of human beings in God's universe, as if the greatest affliction deserved the greatest punishment!

Let those who plead that it is for " their good " to be thus treated, be thus treated themselves, and I can vouch for their pleading to be exempt from being made subjects of such benefactions, ere long! Oh! when our government has learned to treat our afflicted brothers and sisters as unfortunates—not as criminals—one step towards civilization will have been taken.

Insanity is not a crime. It is a misfortune—and yet a criminal, in a penitentiary, is far less severely treated than are these innocent ones—for their term of imprisonment is not indefinite. They know, when they enter, what to rely upon as hope of future liberty. The insane have no hope whatever of deliverance, and it is most scrupulously kept from them, that there is any hope for them! This is one very important part of insane treatment—discipline or punishment. That is, to put upon those the least able to bear it, the heaviest of all human burdens—hopeless torment!

Oh! how my engine will "switch" off in sight of an insane asylum! I can't meet one without stopping my whole train, to fire my heaviest guns at it, to demolish it utterly, if possible, for they are the very culmination of Calvinism.

I believe my main train stopped on my cheerful spirits, being the result of good sleep at night. Yes, I do think you'll find it to be the universal testimony of all who have known me, to be,—"Mrs. Packard was always cheerful and happy, when I saw her, and she was always striving to impart it to her visitors and associates." Yes, I am in my native element when I am carrying others' sorrows, and adding to the comfort of all. Children always like me because I'm always so patient. "Ma isn't ever cross! Ma never gets mad!" my Judas Samuel says. Isn't that a compliment, coming from him whom his father had hired to tell lies about me, to back up his own slanders? And I do say, if a person never gets mad, she ought not to be locked up; even if her husband says she does, when she does not. To show how hard up he is for capital to carry out his point, that I'm insane, I'll tell you the way he took to get up his proof, and this is just of a piece with the rest of his proofs. Just to show what a big lie he can make out of a little bit of truth,—and if you don't give him credit for being an economist of the truth, it is because you haven't worked on my new arithmetic principles,—that's all.

It is a linen story,—not a cotton one. You see I look out for number two, first, when I have a plural to look out for. I never, but once, gave my husband reason to complain of neglecting to look out well for his pulpit linen. But once I did, and he gave me my full due, I can tell you! When he keeps such accounts, they are kept, I assure you. He is a good accountant. He seldom makes a mistake in figures, and he wrote a great many of them, too,—for nothing was ever bought at our house that was not put down in his account-book. "Look out! Mrs. Calvin, you can't elude his eagle eye." "Yes, but I don't like the use the eagle makes of his eye when he is looking into my purse with it." "I think he has perverted it, then, to an owl's eye." Perverted eye! abused eye! I don't mean an owl's eye is a perverted or abused one; it is as good as an eagle's eye, when it is used for the use 'twas made for,—to see in the dark,—but when he tries to see in the light, he can't, for God didn't make it for that purpose. But he did make the eagle's eye for that purpose, and when he tries to look where he ought not to,—into the dark,—he sometimes finds something he don't like to see—a woman's account-book! He didn't see mine, though. He wouldn't let me keep one. He kept it himself, and so saved me the trouble of doing so. But I kept his linen polished, to pay him for it.

Well, one day, when I was carrying his last boy for him, and been seven or eight months about it, I tried also to carry the smoothing-irons over his linen, to make it shine. I did not just smooth my husband's linen as some minister's wives do,—I *polish it,* in addition. I like to do it, too, better than I like to eat, unless I could get a beefsteak to eat. I used to find that nature required the beef-strength to keep me from scolding back. I do go in for oxen for Calvin's wives to eat!—but Christian wives don't need them. They have meat which they like better. "Love eaten in secret, how good is it, Christian wife of a Christian husband?" I do wish I could answer my own question from experience. But I can't,—and I can only guess it would do me good,—for I

have an affection for men's love. And I think I shall have
it, too. God hasn't made one thing in vain, not even the
owl's eyes; and I know he hasn't made my great, conjugal,
loving heart in vain, or for nothing to set it upon. No, he'll
give me a true man to love yet, you see if he don't,—before
I die, too! And I'll warrant you he won't put me off,
neither! At any rate, I'll see to it that he find no cause to
do so, any more than Calvin has had. I never gave him the
first cause, and I never will.

But he took occasion to say he had when he hadn't.—
because I forgot to iron his false wristbands, which Christian
wife had contrived for his express benefit, so he could look
superior to his brother Calvins from the pulpit. I don't
know whether all the clergy have wives who make their
husbands false wristbands, besides the linen ones on the
cotton shirt. But that's none of my business. It's only
mine to see that my Calvin is well served. And I find that
is enough to take almost all my time and spare energies.
Not spare energies, I don't mean. It's the spare energies
that my children get, to serve them, when Calvin has no
more coats, or vests, or pants, to mend, and dress over with
logwood, so that *they* will shine as well as his linen.

And I didn't patch them up neither. You couldn't find a
patch in sight on my Calvin's coat-sleeves or his pants-knees.
No,—I didn't like to see ministers in patched clothes!
Farmers can wear patched clothes, and it looks all right.
But patches don't become a minister's wardrobe, as I think.
And what I think, shows itself in my practice. But, mind
you, I don't think for other folks. 'Tis enough to cut out
my own patterns. I do cut most all my patterns. I seldom
borrow even a pattern. I loan them, sometimes. And I
have them offered to me. But I just say, " No,—I thank
you," for I cut my own dresses by my own patterns. I am
self-reliant,—independent.

Independent! where does this long word belong, to Calvin's or Christ's car? Judge ye.

The way Mrs. Packard mends her husband's knees and elbows is, to cut off the pants below the pockets and turn them, before they need a patch,—and she cuts off the lower part of the sleeves, and puts in a new one in its place, when 'tis threadbare, before the white lining shows. You can't think how I laughed in my sleeves, one day, as we were riding out with his three sisters, just after we were married, in our two-seated buggy, when they were scolding their brother for wearing his wedding suit, so common. They thought his second best would do to ride out in on Shelburne hills. So did his wife, so she had made it look so much like it, that they couldn't tell them apart!

Mrs. Packard did have the talent of metamorphosing before she wrote this metamorphosical book, you see. But one thing she was not perfect in. She would sometimes forget—not often though. I kept a good eye to the beam of justice to all parties.

So, when I was looking out for the constitution of an unborn child, as well as the born ones, I found it hard to honor nature, like other human beings. And I could get tired, especially when both baking and ironing came together on Saturday. I put my clothes out for a few past years to be washed, and I couldn't iron them till they came back, of course. Thus I had both of these unfortunates to meet me on Saturday. And, with all my great dinners to get (I always get good dinners—two courses, too), I got so tired before three o'clock that I did hurry up, at the last, to get a chance to lie down a short time before tea-time, on my unborn baby's account—not my own. I didn't mind how tired I got, one night's sleep would drive it on the scape-goat to the wilderness, never to return to trouble me more. Still, my babe was more tender, and I cared for the little innocent's well being more than I did my own. So, amid my long sum, I just left out one figure—the wristbands.

Oh! what a pity we can't be perfect! But I shall be by-and-by. I shall not miss a figure in my calculations, for God does help those who help themselves. And I do try to help myself and others to do right in everything.

And I don't think it was right in Calvin to blame me, when I always tried to do the very best I could do. And I did do *well*, for I could do well—for God had made me so I could. And when Calvin did blame me, Christ told me, through my conscience, *he* didn't. So I tried to please both husbands as well as I could. But when their interests clashed, as rivals will, of course, oftentimes, I did find it a match to please them both, when they often called me to do opposite things! And that I couldn't do. And because I couldn't, Calvin locked me up in prison for life! I say it is too hard to require impossibilities, in the first place! and then to be locked up for not doing impossibilities isn't right! is it, Abraham? You'll straighten out the Calvinism, won't you?

But don't do so hard with them as Calvin did by me for not ironing his false wristbands, will you?

The next morning he got up first—a great exception to the general rule—and, on dressing himself for the pulpit, he found his wristbands were not in his drawer with his linen. He told me of this fact, which suddenly awoke me to entire consciousness. "Oh! heaven! what have I done? I find I have forgotten to starch and iron them! What shall I do?" And springing up, said I, "Husband, I have forgotten to iron them. I do beg your pardon—I didn't mean to neglect you—but I was so tired before I got through ironing yesterday that, fer the baby's sake, I lay down to rest myself and forgot all about it."

Oh, how I could see the eye flash with indignant wrath as

1 heard him mutter, "Fowler's infidelity! If it wasn't for this cursed villain I might have had my wristbands, as I ought to have them. I do wish Fowler would tend to his own business, and not be filling my wife's ears with his infidelity!"

But confession is only one small part of gospel repentance, and I always knew it. So I said, "I will get right up and build a fire and starch and iron them now, before I get breakfast, so you can have them in due season for the pulpit."

But he, seeming to catch some of my magnanimity of spirit, replied, "No, you needn't be to that trouble—I'll let these clean shirt ones answer for to-day. But they ought to have been done,!"

"Oh! husband," thought I, "how I do wish you could have spared the last remark!" But no, the arrow of neglect must rankle in my tender, sensitive heart, until Christ extracted it for me. "Oh! how much rather I would that he neglect me, rather than have him feel that I had neglected him—even if I hadn't done it."

His jealousy was aroused! I had cared more for his rival Christ than for himself—God's maternal laws had been a barrier to his selfish indulgence, and now the innocent must suffer for the guilty. It wasn't just that I should suffer the reproach of neglect of his interests under these circumstances—the just suffer for the unjust. Christ so suffered. No, he didn't *so* suffer. He didn't know how a wife longed to favor her husband, and how bad she felt when she found she had displeased him—even without having, in God's sight, given cause for the displeasure. No, he wasn't a woman—a wife—or a mother—and, of course, he couldn't tell how much more I suffered than he did in his own agony.

But, Park, is this right? Wasn't Christ "baptized into the name of the Father, Son, and Holy Ghost"—all three? Now, is a woman—the mother of this Son—God's wife?

How can one person be baptized into the name of another person? I want a little of brother's help here to get out this sum—I can't see the solution of it just yet. But I am in school yet. The Teacher can tell me—if the scholars can't.

Well, God, my Father, knows, if nobody else knows, how bad I did feel when, a few days after, in passing his study table, I chanced to see a letter written, directed to his mother, in South Deerfield, and I opened and read in it, to my horror, the following sentence: "I feel very sad indeed. I fear Elizabeth's mind is getting out of order. She is neglecting her duties. My linen has not been properly prepared for the pulpit!"

Well, he knows that they know if Elizabeth had got to neglecting her husband, she must be a different woman from what she used to be in New England! Yes, he could base a suspicion on the truth, and trust his sagacity to supply the deficiency of proof from his own fabrication; and when one has made such a sinner of his own conscience as to believe his own lies, he is pretty likely to make others believe them too. He did so! The lying defamation of insanity has been honestly believed by many of my best friends, because of the arch power which God has permitted the "Arch-deceiver" to wield for my destruction.

One fact is certain, that that was the last, and the only time, when he had reason to complain of my neglecting him. I saw then that his deep determination was to get me into an insane asylum! And he has accomplished his devilish purpose. But he has had to do his business entirely and wholly on borrowed capital. I stump him, or any other human or divine being, to bring forward the first proof of my ever having been an insane person, from the testimony of my own words and actions! Reason, love, kindness, and truth are not insanity, and God knows that whoever dares to say that I am an insane person—after seeing me for themselves—dares to "blaspheme the Holy Ghost!"

It is Christianity personified in a true woman which they are calling insanity, and God himself will be their judge and jury. The laws of our government allowed me no jury or judge, neither has the manliness of native Americans allowed me one. But God will allow me one, notwithstanding! Yes, at his just tribunal I stand or fall on my own actions—not on the actions of other people.

And so will my persecutors, one and all, stand, in single file, before this same tribunal, and be judged on their own actions also; and whoever is found wanting will be wanting in that grace on which he impiously relied for pardon for willful transgression. No. Willful sins are unpardonable sins. Nothing but justice will atone for them. Mercy is extended to the thoughtless child, who did not mean to disobey, and who is sorry as soon as he knows it,—yes, as soon as he knows it—he does not suffer the " sun to go down on his wrath."

How often has Calvin complained of me for being in such a hurry to repent, when I had done wrong. I didn't dare to delay—lest it be too late! I do not allow my children an indefinite time for repentance, and I find God doesn't his children. Besides, I don't like hell, at all, as a place of abode—I am not at home there! And when I go to a place where I am as homesick as I am in prison, I try to make my stay in it as brief as possible. I don't like to be under a cloud. The sunny face of joy, and the sunlight of heaven, are from the same author, and I don't like to make believe laugh, for it don't satisfy me, nor my children either. They can see deep into my soul—little mirrors of truth as they are. I do so love to be to them *only* a sunbeam of joy—and I can't do it, if I am under a cloud myself. These little instinct angels will even see before I do myself, that the sun is going down, and remind me of it by saying: " Ma, don't feel bad."

" What makes you think I do feel bad ?"

" 'Cause you don't laugh."

14

I'll then laugh, and thus try to scatter the sadness of my little angels. But that won't do—for the next I hear is: "You don't laugh, mother; you are only making believe laugh."

So my forced smiles won't do. It is not mother till she is happy—not when she tries to seem to be happy—when she is not. So, for their sakes, I am so benevolent, I must repent quick, or the sunbeam is gone, or eclipsed.

But it is not because I do wrong that I suffer the most for; it is because others do wrong, and I can't get them to see it, and repent. Oh! I do bear the sins and sorrows of others as Christ did! I carry my children's sins, all of them that I know of, in my own body, and bear the burden, until I can cast it off by their repenting and doing right. Till then, there is no atonement for my sorrows. Yes, there is none so great punishment my children can feel, than that it makes mother feel bad—and to relieve my sad, full heart, they will do any-thing and everything I ask of them. Oh, love! nothing but love's magnet do my angels need, to draw them to the paths of righteousness and peace!

Another thing, I won't do wrong. It won't pay. What has taken place it can't change; and what is to take place, it can't prevent. Wrong-doing is the most useless trash in the world. No—one thing is more useless, and that is—Calvinism! and the "wolves in sheep's clothing," who preach it!

A wolf is a good thing, so is a sheep. But they don't agree at all well together, especially when the wolf is hungry, and the sheep wants to live! And I say, there is just as good a chance of one, as there is of the other, when the sheep of a minister's flock want to live a life of faith, to have a money-hungry wolf come to them. The chance is small, in either case, for the poor sheep! But let the wolf get into a sheep's skin, and the chance lessens still more.

I tell you, the souls such animals have eaten up, no arithmetic can calculate! The wolf not only eats the flesh, but
he gnaws the bones, and then makes them into soap-grease,
as Webster tried to Parkman. He means to make a clean
sweep—just as clean as he did of me. He is terribly afraid
I shall get out of the potash, or show him up by the gold in
my teeth, that won't burn up, even under a blowpipe. (I
guess the gold in me will show him up when my book is
printed!) He perhaps recollects the thirty-three dollars he
paid to the firm of "Harwood & Tucker," in Boston, Mass.,
for their filling fourteen cavities in my decayed teeth, twenty-
one years since. Perhaps I shall apply to them for a new
set of teeth, if my book sells well.

Now if the Manteno flock of "sheep-heads" had known
that their shepherd was a wolf, would they have shot him to
save my life? I don't think they would. They had not
sense enough left to do it, because the wolf had been so
ravenous upon them.

Poor "sheep-heads!" how I pity you! and your shepherd,
too! You haven't sense enough to save your own wives—
how could I expect you could protect your shepherd's wife?
Mind you, she never asked you to, either. She can take
care of herself, and you, too, with Lincoln to help me! I
wonder if Deacon Smith's wife wouldn't thank me to get the
government to cut off her husband's head, too? He has got
one too many, as well as his shepherd—though the head he
carries his hat on, is a very small one, yet, I think God
thought it was as big as he knew what to do with. I guess
his children would have liked God to have added a little to
the bump that would make him buy them some more apples
to eat. "Oh, no! we must save our money for Christ's
cause—not squander it on things to eat!"

There is no sense in it—nor in his head, either! I don't
think he knows what the cause of Christ *is*. I can tell him

what 'tis *not*. It's not getting up subscriptions, nor paying them, neither, to *his* shepherd. It is to take care of his own children, and rule himself—not his wife.

My children, especially George Hastings, thinks that because God sent him here without his leave, that he has a *right* to something to eat, and he don't want to thank any one for it, either. And I think if his father would have a boy, " whether or no," the boy ought not to run the risk of supporting himself—until he could support himself, at least. Calvin often tried to get his children to feel thankful to him for giving them something to eat. George is smart, and so is his namesake—George Hastings, of New York city—a " lard-oil merchant," there. George would, at six or seven years old, inquire of his father, with all the pomp of Gen. George Washington, " Haven't I a *right* here, pa?" Yes, he had, and so had his mother; but his pa didn't think so. " Like priest like people." Yes, he made his people just about as mean and sheepish as he is.

How does a lion look when his mane is sheared? Sheepish.

How does a man look with his beard shaven? Sheepish.

How does a man look with his manliness shaven off? Sheepish.

How does a human being feel to see a wolf carry off a lamb in his teeth, and not shoot him? Sheepish.

How does a man act, who sees a man forcing his defense-less wife into an insane asylum, and don't offer her any protection? Sheepish.

How does a man feel to hear the tender lambs bleat for their mother, and not try to hunt her for them? Sheepish.

How does a man feel to hear the motherless cry for their mother, and not try to restore her to them? Sheepish.

How does a woman feel to see a little, tender girl of twelve years, trying to fill the place of mother, hired girl, and sister, to four brothers, and one Calvin father, and not try to restore the mother to her own, true place, which God gave her? Sheepish.

How will such a flock of Calvins feel, when Christ, the great Shepherd, calls them to account for thus letting Mrs. Packard and her little ones go undefended three years? Sheepish.

God will not let the Presbyterian church stand on its rotten timbers of false doctrines, always, already so rotten that even the breath of a woman may shatter them!

Well, I am glad Calvin couldn't pervert me nor my children by their false doctrines. We had too much sense to be gulled by his sophisms; and loved nature too well to disregard her laws of love and kindness. We had rather be natural, —like Christ,—rather than be " regenerated,"—like the devil, —or Calvin. Somehow we are too up and down honest to suit Calvin! He used to say to me, " Wife, you keep a looking-glass in your breast, so people can look right into your heart." So I do, because there ain't the least thing there that I am ashamed to have seen. I know the more one sees of me, the better they will like me; unless they have met with a " change of heart!"

I bet, now, that Dr. McFarland likes me well enough to marry me, even if I have saved his soul from ruin, by my fidelity! A true man respects plain, honest dealing, even if it does deal out unwelcome truths. I mean people shall have reason to like me if they don't. I know we don't like the process by which an ulcer or cancer is removed, to save life. But we like life.

I say, of two evils choose the least, if both cannot be avoided. But I choose no evils which can be avoided. I don't choose to be suffering a living death for twenty-one years, but it could not be avoided by doing right, so I had to suffer, patiently. I don't like to be three years on this cross, suffering crucifixion, in this American inquisition. But I can't get out, and no one seems to care whether I do or not, except my children; and so I telegraph to heaven to get me out. Husband Calvin has mighty power over my destiny!—but, husband Christ has Almighty power! So I am safe, in the long run. Christ protects his wife—Calvin don't. Christ loves his wife—Calvin don't.

I guess Calvin finds it's of some use to have had a wife, once, when he puts on his long, scarlet flannel night-gown, she made for him in New England, so his feet needn't suffer in the cold beds he found when he exchanged. He don't always find his bed warmed with a warming-pan, and a foot-stone in, in place of the wife's feet, as his partner in the exchange did.

Oh! I did love to take good care of Christ's minister!—for Christ has now and then an honest man to preach now-a-days; and since I couldn't tell who treated their wives well at home,—and who did not,—I treated them all alike—though I was pretty sure I "smelled the rat" in some of those old New England ministers! But I don't know of any "wolf in sheep's clothing," but Calvin himself. But their wives can expose them if they are, and they are called to do so in self-defense, as I am. Oh! how sorry I should feel to find another such bad man as Theophilus Packard's own actions prove him to be, in the ministry! I hope he is all alone!

Well, I did love the ministers so well, that I did not care if I did have to be on the jump all Saturday morning getting up something nice for them to eat; even if I did have to take care of the juvenile sewing society in the afternoon at our house; and then carry away forty chairs to their proper places when they were gone. But I didn't have to do that often,—the girls would do it for me before they left—and they would help take care of my baby while I was cutting and planning the work, and reading aloud to them, and sometimes they would stay, at my request, and take care of the baby until I had milked the cow. And sometimes the minister would do it—and sometimes I would wait until my baby went to sleep, and milk by starlight or a lantern. Well, 'tis good business, after all! It does pay to have children, if they love them, as I can't help loving mine. Love is my native element, and these innocent angels are so pure and good, fresh from the throne of God, I would not dare to offend or abuse one of them, lest God would abuse me for it, and he would—for he loves the little blessed angels as well as I do, and is just as tender of them. They ain't fiends and devils, as Calvin says they are, when they cry and keep him awake when he wants to sleep! They don't cry when they can help it, neither do I; and I don't like to have Calvin spank them with his great hard hand on their bare flesh, to make them stop crying! How can they stop, when it smarts so? I know it hurts them, awfully, or "Toffy's" flesh wouldn't have been black and blue three weeks after it, so that he would scream when I changed his diaper, from pure agony! Can our good, kind, tender Father submit to let Calvin always so abuse his babies?

No, I don't think he will, for I have prayed so earnestly to him to help me to protect the babies from harm—through Calvin's brutality! O God! don't let another Calvin abuse a little baby!

Won't you, Lincoln, make a law to shut up such men in the penitentiary for it, instead of the man who steals gold or a horse? It looks as though the government cared more to protect its gold than its babies—and one baby is worth more than the whole continent. What is law? It can't be benevolent unless it protects somebody—not something.

Our property don't need protecting so much as our persons, especially our spirits—our inalienable rights! If our rights are protected, we can take care of our property ourselves.

We only want a right to do just what we please with our own things, that's all. Wives are not mere things—they are a part of society—*they ought to be citizens*—they feel as men do, and want to be allowed to be free moral agents as much as they do. I say it is a shame not to recognize woman's identity in law when she gets married! Does marriage disqualify her for a citizen? Must she lose her individuality to become a slave?

I often wish a subjective husband had to be a wife one year (I shouldn't care if he had a baby in that time, and had sore nipples, too), and see how they'd feel with the tables turned. I guess they will feel it some time! For, mind you, this is not the only life we live in our long existence, which began with God, and dies only with him. The tables will turn! and they can't help it—and, for my part, I don't want to—for I have no sorrow to turn up for me, as a measure of just desert.

You see if Calvin's next wife isn't a termagant.—and my next husband a Christian!

We may lose track of his soul, if he should die first—but God will not. We may both die and rise again, or be born again, in other bodies, before we are either of us married again—and I guess—from what I can learn of God's government and laws—that I shall rise to a better life than I have had—as Calvin's wife—and he rise to a worse life than he has had with his Christian wife. God will track him until he has put him into a body where he will feel all the pangs he has made me feel.

Oh! how I pity him! What a long, black catalogue of guilt stares him in the face—and he can't elude its dreadful doom! He must be spanked by his father, just as hard as he has spanked his "Toffy"—and perhaps his mother will approve of it, too! Interest is apt to accumulate on such debts. So does interest accumulate on my credits—God says an hundred per cent! That's good rate—isn't it? I am glad I have invested so large a stock of unrequited kindness. The vaults are deep—no customer has yet found the bottom of them—and the cashier is never "gone to tea!"

But I do hope Calvin is not to receive his deserts under the American flag—for I hope Christ will be established on the American throne before he has had time to die and be born again in another body! And when Christ's government is established no baby will be allowed to be abused under his laws—nor no mother, or wife, either. So I don't see but that Calvin, in order to get his just desert, will have to be born in some uncivilized part of God's earth, where barbarities are protected by the laws—as they have been here—under our Calvinistic government. He may live one life—as a slave—to punish him for enslaving his wife—and trying to kidnap her accountability. But where can he find a footing, where *such* cruelties are protected by the laws, as he has been protected in, in his abuse of me? I don't know as there is another place on God's footstool—God knows—I don't! I don't know how God will fix it, but this I do know, that with what measure he has meted out to me, in that same measure will he receive again in his own body; for I don't believe God will lie—if he is a man!—and if David said: "All men are liars."

So, to have all the slaveholders in America born slaves, and thus get their just deserts on earth, there must be slavery somewhere besides in America, for the border states won't hold on to it long enough for that, I'm sure. And I'm very sure God has begun the purging process in America, by which *all evils* are to be removed from this continent, and Christ's true church is to be planted in this "garden of the Lord"—in this wilderness—which is soon to "bud and blossom as the rose."

The kingdom of Christ is the kingdom of America—and
14*

here his throne is now being established on the ruins of Antichrist—or the ruins of Calvinism. Here the marriage of the Lamb is to take place—the church and state are to be united, in defending and protecting the *rights of humanity* under all conditions and circumstances.

Our government has hitherto only been the useless fig-tree, which only bore the green leaves of promise of protection to humanity—but has not yet perfected its fruit by keeping these fair promises! Property has been protected by the American government—but humanity has not been protected! Hereafter, the rights of men, women, and children are to be shielded beneath the folds of its celestial flag—on which the sun, moon, and stars radiate their splendid promises of protection to men, women, and children! Our old fig-tree, indicating by its flag of bloody stripes, that it was fit only for the rule of fools, has been only a shadow of protection to the rights of humanity, and therefore, has not answered the divine purpose, and the ax, alone, could remove the incumbrance—"Cut it down!" is God's order.

There is no place for useless trees here in Columbia—happy land! Yes, Columbia's sons call for practical utility, not merely useless splendor. Useless splendor will do for Old-America—but it won't do for New-Columbia. Does the use of the bloody, useless stripes make brothers love one another better? Does killing folks make us love their children?

Is anything useful that does not excite and promote love?

Is not hate the most useless trash in the world, except Calvinism?

Shall we love our Southern brothers and sisters any better o have murdered their fathers? No.

Will they thank us for doing it? No.

What good does killing human beings accomplish? None

at all—after the sacrifice has been offered, which God demanded, as a free-will offering to himself.

Did God make a free-will offering for our sins? Yes. His Son volunteered, and God consented to give him up to fight the rebel Calvinism, and he has accepted the sacrifice, and has now come to redeem his people by destroying treason—or Calvinism, rather—for treason is only one branch of this great Upas-tree!

Has not the American patriotic parent offered its first-born and only son as a free-will offering on the altar of our country, as an atonement for its many sins?

Will not God accept the offering, and spare our Isaac—our country; and make of him a great nation—through whom all the kingdoms of the earth shall be blessed?

Father Abraham, spare our Isaacs! and sacrifice the property of the traitors—instead of our darlings!

Oh! emancipate the slaves! and let the rebels see that you have more respect for the rights of humanity than for their rights of property.

'Tis right to protect humanity. 'Tis wrong to punish it. God, alone, is to avenge or punish his children, and all the human family are his children—the traitors as well as the Calvins. We must keep the traitors and the Calvins from abusing humanity—but God alone has the sovereign right to punish the children. One sinner has no right to punish another sinner—nor one child to punish another child.

God himself is now preparing a rope with which to swing our Calvinistic government into the bottomless pit. The "old dragon," himself, will commit suicide! and the great giant, with all his hosts of Philistine oppressors, is about to be cast into the Red Sea of destruction.

But, mind you, they rush into it themselves—in their fiendish attempt to pursue our government into destruction. We have escaped from their power!—but they are in hot haste pursuing us, only to be engulfed in the Red Sea of—perhaps, a bloody slave insurrection!

Yes, the Calvinism of our government has culminated, and has dug its own grave, as well as taken its own life. No disloyal Columbian will be eligible to office here again. Good is to rule over evil—and evil, alone, is to be our slave. God speed the day!

The true men and the true women in Columbia have washed their hands in innocency, and they can't love sin and injustice any more.

My sons said to me, on their last visit, on their return from service in the Nebraska Regiment, as sutlers, "I can't kill a man, for God says, 'Thou shalt not kill;' and I don't know what the curse is, which God has attached to murder."

But their mother does. "Life for life," God says. If a man kill another, evil shall slay him—not men. Men must not kill, or take away a life they cannot restore—for God says evil shall pursue the wicked to their destruction. To kill a human being is to kill ourselves for him—and thus we, in killing another—commit a suicide on ourselves.

The only object of government is to restrain the bad, to defend and protect the weak. One sinner must not punish another sinner—'tis God's exclusive work. 'Tis unjust to punish the little sinner, and leave the greater sinner unpunished—as our government does. The poor man is not protected from the aggressions of the rich man. The poor man is punished for taking only his lawful rights from the rich, monopolizing Naboths! while the rich Naboth can bear the expense of prosecuting and imprisoning him, yet, he can't afford to give him employment to supersede the temptation to steal bread for his starving wife and children's sake!

Oh! God of justice! is the sacrifice of our first-born sons too costly an offering to lay upon the altar, for this heaven-daring—legalizing oppression of the little ones—of that very poor, weak, dependent class, who, of all others, most need protection—but who have the least? How many a poor, honest laborer, who has earned his living by the sweat of his brow, has been imprisoned by some great governmental *thief*, who has, all his days, been living in idleness—on others' toils and earnings—while he, by his wealth, monopolizes the means and sources of the poor man's income; and then takes from his poor, *honest* neighbor even his personal liberty, because he, forsooth! ventured to take, unasked, some of his hoarded treasures which, *by right*, belong to him, and appropriated them for the supply of his necessary wants! The rich man who has accumulated his treasures by the toil of the poor, and the monopoly of his sources of income, and then imprisons him for stealing an armful of wood from his huge pile—is a Calvinist, in practice! and deserves to be put where the traitors are to be put—as the government's servants. He should never be honored, either by Church or State promotions to office. He should be kept down, where he has tried to keep the poor man. For he is the monster thief! notwithstanding our Calvinistic government protects him in his wholesale robberies of families and communities, while the poor man's *rights to his living* are entirely unprotected to him!

Oh! Abraham! we have come with our Isaacs to the mount, to offer them as a sacrifice for our government's sins. Abraham! Abraham! again I ask, does not God call thee to stay thine hand, and spare these Isaacs, "thine only son—Isaac?"

Oh! can Sarah spare him? Can God spare him? No— God spared Abraham's Isaac, and he will spare my Isaac! Yes, God did bring him safe from the army, with no blemish upon his pure soul. He fed the soldiers, but he did not kill a son of God.

No! no! Theophilus and Isaac, God will not require a

man's life at thy hands—for you have not slain a man! Pies and cakes you sold to them, but not rum. Theophilus sold for Tiffany—but it was not his own act. 'Twas Tiffany's! He protested against it, and Tiffany insisted that he should sell it, as a condition of clerkship. Providence dissolved the connection between him and his agent; and then he and Isaac went into partnership alone, and established a Christian sutlership, excluding all Calvinism from it entirely. They did not lie, nor cheat, nor extort, nor oppress one human being. They dealt justly, loved mercy, and walked humbly with their God. They can meet all they dealt with at God's judgment bar, with an open, unblushing face—for they wronged none—not even themselves. Amidst drunkards—amidst the impure—amidst the profane swearer and blasphemer, they lived, but were entirely separate from them, as partners in any of these, or any other vices. They were saved—and delivered from the power of temptation, because they resisted evil indulgences—as a sin against their own pure natures! And God helped them, because they helped themselves, as their mother had always taught them to do—to "trust God by doing right in everything." Though many bribes were offered them, yet nothing could tempt them to touch, taste, or handle the accursed thing!—intoxicating stimulants of any kind.

They use no tobacco in any form—because their mother has taught them it is a worse than useless herb for man to use. They, like me, never used tea or coffee at home, and I hope, like me, they do not use it away from home. Cold water and milk are our only beverages. And all my children, like me, are healthy.

Yes, thank God! my sons, Theophilus and Isaac, have been weighed in the balances, and have not been found wanting in honesty, integrity, temperance, or virtue! God grant that other American mothers may find their Theophiluses

and Isaacs thus shielded from the crocodiles and serpents
of the Ganges, to be nestled again in her fond embrace,—
never to part more! Has not God heard my prayer, from
this dungeon of hell, for me and mine? Yes, he has—he
can and will hear the prayers of other mothers for their
sons' safe return.

But, mothers, I prayed—I did not merely make prayers.
My George could easily detect the difference between a
make laugh and a real laugh; and none but the real smiles
could satisfy him. Only the real prayers can satisfy God.
One prayer I made for the soldiers was, to make ten thousand
yards of bandages for the wounded; and a just God accepted
a willing mind for other prayers, such as nursing them, etc.,
for the deed. And we have had many social prayer-meetings
here, while at our work—not on our knees—but when reading and talking about them, we have jointly, simultaneously
and earnestly, wished they could be spared this bloody work.
These are God's social prayer-meetings. God saw we were
united in our desires, without making a formal thing of it,
at all. I've got most sick of forms,—for they are so often a
mere substitute for the thing itself.

These real, social prayer-meetings are not much like those
we had at Mr. Spring's, in Manteno, when the sisters could
not conscientiously pray with such a heterodox sister as
Mrs. Packard was!

Oh! orthodoxy! where hast thou wandered to? We can't
find even thy tracks.

But if they did exclude me from their praying circles, my
children didn't. I did have their loving hearts to fly to for
refuge from my persecuting sisters. Oh! how they did fold
their wronged and injured mother to their tender hearts, and
say, If harm comes to her, it shall pierce me first! Yes,
God heard their prayers, and the incense is sweet before his
throne. For when all others did forsake me, my children

did take me up above harm's reach,—for they gave me what my soul needed most,—*sympathy.* Oh! could I have lived without it! God knows how a true woman needs it, to live, and he meant I should live, and so he sent it to me,—through my children.

Now I can live without human sympathy, for the divine is so tangible and real,—through faith's potent power,—that I am wholly self-reliant. With such a bodyguard of divine influences, invisible,—and my darlings, visible,—I am invincible to harm! And Calvin well knew it, too,—and he feared them as his foes.

But Calvin's sagacity is almost omnipotent; and, moreover, he can psychologize his victims, and thus unman them, yea, all those who bear the mark of the beast upon them—those who do not follow their conscience as their guide are entirely under his control. Only the God-fearing can resist his psychological influence,—these are saved by faith alone. His power over the community seemed, apparently, to be omnipotent! thus verifying James's predictions, "that in the last days, I will bring upon them a strong delusion, that they should believe a lie." Yes, the community did "believe a lie," in believing me to be an insane person, on the strength of his testimony,—in opposition to their own observation of me,—which flatly contradicted this slander! I don't think another Sodom could be found in America, who could be so gulled by Calvinism, as to credit the "old dragon" so implicitly, as if they could lick the very dust of his feet, in homage, as to a superior intelligence! Indeed, Satan can make quite an imposing appearance in his "celestial livery!" He is as sanctimonious—prayerful—tender, and sympathetic in "crocodile tears," as any true man can be towards his wife! They therefore coincided with his plans and wishes to help him separate me from my children, by stratagem.

Mr. Rumsy, one of our society, therefore concluded to take

my daughter, Elizabeth, home with them in their carriage after
meeting, Sunday afternoon, before the Monday morning I
was kidnapped, on the plausible excuse of visiting their
daughter, a girl about her own age. The mother's instincts
distrusted foul play.

Said I, "You don't propose this to get her off from me,—
to send me off, do you?"

"No—no, indeed. We only suggest it for her own gratification, and pleasant recreation."

The mother says,—"Go! my daughter! and enjoy yourself
as well as possible, and get well rested, and then come home
by the first opportunity."

She had carried my sorrows in her sympathizing heart so
freely, that I felt that my duty to her compelled me to make
this temporary, voluntary sacrifice for her good. Her health
had already suffered much from her living sympathy in my
sorrows. A brain fever,—attended with some aberration of
mind,—had been the result, and I felt that an entire change
of scene might rest her brain, and thus the better fortify her
for coming trials. With this view, I consented, not suspecting, in the least, that the crisis was so near,—which was to
separate us!

My daughter exclaimed, "Oh, mother! you won't let pa
carry you off, while I am gone; will you?"

"No, my child! Mother will never go without bidding her
darling Elizabeth good-by first! You can depend upon it, my
child. I will send for you the first signs I see of their sending me away from home."

Thus assured, we parted in peace—she trusting to mother's
word—and I to Miss Rumsy's. But, alas! the Misses Rumsy
are liars! They can't be trusted any farther than they
can be seen! Look out for them! If you don't, I shall—and
so will my children, if they live as long as Methuselah, I can
tell you!

We know one thing, if you don't; and that is—a woman who will tell a lie cannot be a true woman—any more than lies can be truths!—a lying or a deceitful woman is not a true woman any more than a fallen angel is a true woman. Such angels will do for a Calvinist's wife ; but it will be an ox and an ass union, to yoke them with a Christian man.

David didn't say all women were liars; for if he did, he would be a liar himself! for, to my certain knowledge, there is one true woman who never lies,—and that is, Mrs. E. P. W. Packard,—and God has employed her to write this—his book—because he knows she is truthful, and won't tell a lie, under any pretext whatever.   Some of my contemporary devils have tried hard to convince me it is right to lie in self-defense; but I say it is not right for *me* to do so,—for if I can't be defended on the ground of the truth, I prefer to go undefended, rather than use Satan's armor in my defense.

The Lord's deliverance don't come in Satan's livery !   But Satan often comes in the Lord's livery.   And, I tell you, it takes a pretty keen eye to detect the cloven foot, with the study slipper on it !

My babe was sent off to Brother Dole's a week or more previous, under the pretext of relieving me.   I did consent to this arrangement for a few days, so that I might get a little more chance to rest nights, and get recruited from my watching the babe during his and my sleepless nights—when our influenza, or lung fever, was upon us.   But when I wanted my little cherub again to comfort me with his loving caresses and innocent prattle, no entreaties nor tears of mine could induce Calvin to let me have the comfort of my angel-babe to cheer my loneliness, when all others had forsaken me and fled !

1 fled to Jesus—my only refuge !—and on his sympathizing breast I laid all my sorrows, and he kept my soul in " perfect peace."   I just submitted, without a murmur, to all the

crosses which were so ruthlessly laid upon me, and with a cheerful and light heart addressed myself, most indefatigably, to the practical duties of my house and fruit garden. I was systematic, as I always am, about all my duties; working two hours in the open air, on my strawberry beds and my asparagus bed, and my other small fruits,—after I had done up my morning duties in the house,—and then I would take a cold bath—wash me all over, and dress me up clean and nice for the parlor duties,—before dinner. In the afternoon I was no more idle than in the morning—reading, and writing some, but sewing diligently for my family, almost all the time. My husband's and children's wardrobes were left in good repair, by my indefatigable exertions to keep them so. I always did my own family sewing, except what societies did for us, through their kindness to me—with but an occasional exception.

Under these circumstances Calvin prepared a cage, or a prison, for me, by nailing down the windows to my nursery and bolting my door—not to keep me from running off—but to keep others from running in to see the crazy woman of Manteno! as his strategics and lies had led community to believe I was, when, in truth, I was, *uniformly*, just as I always had been—a consistent, exemplary, practical Christian woman. Any fancied deviation from this line of conduct is a slander, or a lie, made up entirely out of borrowed capital. It was not found in my own words or actions! but was concocted by his perverted, devilish, hypocritical nature. Thus, for three weeks, I was kept from observers as far as possible, knowing that my sane conduct might betray his falsehoods to those who dared to use their own reason in the case.

During these last three weeks of my home life he did not sleep with me. I asked him why he had forsaken my bed? He gave me no reply. I asked him "if I had ever wronged him, or treated him unkindly?" He said, "No; never."

"Why, then, do you leave me?" He gave me no reason, only—" he thought it best to sleep alone!" He had no reason for thus treating me, outside of his own black heart.

My prison was my nursery, where we had slept until this time. It was a nicely painted and papered room, in the north wing of our house. Two windows fronted the road and opened upon a piazza. The third window, on the north side, was shaded by a creeping cucumber vine in summer, with no other outside blind. The two front windows had green blinds on them, with slats on the lower half, which turned to let in more or less light. The room was five yards square—nicely carpeted all over—a nice curled maple bedstead, with white counterpane and valance. The window curtains were one Turkey-red cotton and one white embroidered muslin. I had an elegant wardrobe in one corner—a nice mahogany bureau in another—a good table under a gilt-framed mirror—a washstand, a large rocking-chair—an embroidered ottoman—with several cane-seated chairs, completed the furniture of the room. I kept my capacious bathing-pan under the bed. I had a two-leaved light stand also in my room, and a suttee-cradle, which I used in place of my crib at night, for my baby. Twelve framed pictures hung upon the walls.

We were not poor and destitute of household comforts, as Calvin used to delight to represent us to be to the Eastern contributors to Home Missions, to draw out their funds and boxes of clothing for his especial benefit, so he could get funds to speculate upon. I often protested against this lying means to get benevolent contributions for his family! But the only good it did, except to relieve my own conscience, was to fortify him in a more determined purpose to resist my interference with his own especial business. He said it was his business to provide for the family, and he—not me—was responsible for the manner in which it was done.

I did not like to write to the American Home Missionary Society and tell them that my husband was lying about us, so he might get more of their funds than rightly belonged to us! for I didn't want anybody—out of our family—to know what a wicked man he was. So our Missionary boxes accumulated to such a superabundant amount of clothing that I found it difficult to store it all safely. There are boxes piled on boxes there that we cannot use in a long lifetime! while other ministers' families, to my knowledge, are suffering for these very comforts which we had hoarded from them—as their just due. I tried to get Calvin to divide with them. But no, the suggestion was met with scorn and abuse on his part. I presume he thought it might be a money-making affair to get me put off into an asylum—*as a pauper*—so that he could then get a new argument to plead his claims to charity.

I find, from what my sons tell me, that this is the way he is now amassing property. He has so managed that his honest wife is no check now upon this mode of *stealing* the charity funds, but is an indirect help towards getting them into his coffer! Can any devil beat this "old dragon"—in sagacity—in making money—by making lies? Did lying ever bring a higher premium?

I do say that a healthy minister, with five hundred dollars salary, and four thousand dollars' worth of property, bringing interest, with a healthy and competent wife to do all the work for a family of eight—besides educating them nearly fit for college—and having an elegant home and house well-furnished from garret to cellar—is not a poor man, and ought not to present himself as an object of charity! I now publicly enter my protest against it. In God's sight I hope I am guiltless in this thing. I could not prevent it, and I did not think it my duty to expose him. Wouldn't he have written on to the Missionary Society and told them his wife was "crazy" if I had? And wouldn't they have believed his representations rather than my own? as Rev. Henry Seymour, of Hawley, Mass., did under similar circumstances. Yes, but God is just!

"I move that Mr. Calvin—the father of Calvinism—be made the chairman of the 'Beggars' Association!' You can't find his equal in this line, I'm very sure. I wait for my motion to be 'seconded' before I call for the vote. I must leave you to count the votes, for I must hurry back to my prison, or they will be sending me off to the asylum before I get ready to go."

I could see through my blinds—which were nailed close before my prison windows—the guests who called, and knocked at our reception-room door, which opened from my piazza, and I could hear their inquiries for me and Calvin's replies. He seldom admitted any to see me, as he told them he thought " my good demanded that I be kept quiet." I heard him tell one minister, " She is not quite so raving or excited to-day!" God knows—I do not—what he meant by my being raving or excited! But·this I do know, I was quietly and peacefully employed at my duties all the time, with no more excitement than I ever had had in all my married life. I was lady-like, calm, and self-possessed as any strong-minded, rational, sensible woman could be—under any circumstances—and under all circumstances. But he knew how to talk about a crazy person, and so he talked about his wife, as if what he said was true—when 'twas all lies, and nothing more nor less !

His deception was in some cases suspected. Then, "he was master of his own house, and he should admit only those he chose to admit!" Those whom he could completely psychologize into his delusion, he would admit into my room, and they would pay for the " sight-seeing," by intimating that they could see insanity in her! The bill was then receipted !

I couldn't think what I had said or done which he could call insane. Was making his bed—doing his mending—polishing his linen—keeping the front rooms in order—etc., acting insanely? These practical duties was what I did, and all I did in the raving or insane line!

Isn't it queer how these Calvinists can twist things to suit their particular fancy? Yes, it suited Calvin's fancy—but not mine—to have his wife looked upon as a wild beast of prey, to be shunned as a pestilence.

Well, the Monday following the Sabbath Elizabeth was kidnapped by the Misses Rumsys, things began to look scary, and I called Isaac to my room and told him I suspected all wasn't right—and, " for fear sister may feel bad if she isn't at home, I want you to get a team this morning, and take me to ride to Mr. Rumsy's and bring her home."

He left me with this intention—and I never saw him again! until he visited me last September, by stratagem. He wanted to enlist, and I had consented, through a letter Theophilus had brought me clandestinely from him, about a year since. I said, " You may join the army if your father is willing, but if he forbids you, you must not disobey him by going." His father would not consent to this act of loyalty, and, to compromise the matter, he consented he might join his brother as sutler. This was all he wanted—he only wanted to get where he could earn money to go and see mother with. He did so, and he and Theophilus spent forty dollars of their hard-earned wages to come and see mother with, and never was a bill more cheerfully paid. His tender, confiding heart was gratified and soothed, and he now felt that he could wait patiently God's time to give him his own dear mother again.

He told me on this visit how he was disposed of after he left me, Monday morning, and told me the following facts:

George Hastings, my fourth son, had to be disposed of ; for he was the mother-boy. He could not live away from his darling mother, and I did not know as I could live away from him. So his father took him to walk down to Comstock's store, where Isaac was clerk, to get him some sugar-plums! Comstock's sugar-plums were all ready for him, and so was the horse and buggy to take them both to do an errand for Comstock, which demanded great dispatch. There was not a moment allowed for them to go and take mother to ride with them! No, she was to have her ride in the cars at ten o'clock.

And now all the band of jewels, except Judas, was disposed of, and he could take care of himself. This was the only one, in Calvin's estimation, who was fit to say " goodby " to his mother. The others had been too true to me to enjoy that privilege. His wife didn't think Samuel was the only one to deserve it. She thought he was the only unfit one to receive the parting kiss. So Samuel's tears and cries, in addition to the entreaties of the Rumsys, could not buy one kiss from his Christian mother; for she knew that *repentance* was the only gospel term of reconciliation—and Samuel had not repented of lying against me, to get his father's bribes. I hope I have received my last Judas kiss—and I hope I have bestowed my last one upon Judas.

The cars were gone, and the crowd dispersed, before Isaac and George got back to that treacherous depot. He was hailed before he got there by a man calling to him from a distance :

" Isaac, your mother is gone ! "

" No she ain't—she is at home in her own room."

" No, she is not. I just saw her start off on the cars," replied the informant.

Poor, disconsolate children ! The story is told. The generous sugar-plums and the gallant attentions of his groom, are all now understood and explained. They hasten on, only to find it too true.

"Yes, George, our dear mother has been stolen from us. We have no home—no mother! Oh! where is the boastful magnanimity and chivalry of the Manteno manliness, which had pledged itself *to me* that your mother should never leave this depot?

"Has it fled with our own dear mother? Yes, gone—gone all confidence in human kind—except my mother! She—she is true—and she alone. Oh! mother! mother! can I see thy sweet face never more? Can I go to thy loved room, and find thy chair empty?

"Oh! can I?—can I?—must I weep alone?—no gentle mother near to soothe and calm my troubled soul!

"Yes, so it is, for they would not protect to me the mother God gave me. They let her go undefended, uncared for, even after they had vowed this scene should never be suffered to take place!

"Oh! that I had been there to get one parting kiss! Oh! how can I go to bed at night without mother's good-night kiss? I never could be willing to go to bed without it; and now, must pa cut me off, also, from seeing that best-beloved of all others—my mother?

"But can't I write and tell her all? No, no, pa won't let me have even this solace. Oh! can I live through it all?— God help me! There is no one now to sympathize with us, George. 'Twill not do, pa won't like it to have any one pity us. Oh! my mother!—my own dear mother!"

George mingles his tears with Isaac. The mourners enter the village. No gentle hand is extended to comfort these two weeping brothers. All flee from them as from tigers. Why do they run? Oh! 'tis guilt that pursues them. Why does Mr. Comstock, as Isaac enters the front door to give his verbal message to him, run to the back store? Why does he run to the cellar? Why does he pursue his flight to the back cellar? Why to the darkest corner of that?

15

'Tis guilt—guilt at the sight of Isaac's innocent face of agony, that drives him to seek the shield of darkness to veil his guilty face.

Oh! Mr. Comstock! the darkest corner of your darkest cellar is not dark enough for your purpose. Isaac, like his mother, and my natural children, can see guilt's glaring eyes in the dark recesses of the human heart. Its image is there, and its reflection cannot be concealed from God, nor those made in his image, who have not defiled this image by their own sins. "The pure in heart shall see God," in their own spirits.

Mr. Comstock, have you a mother? Did you love her? Does Isaac love his mother? Yes, you know he does, and you know how bad he feels, by the reflection of your own loving heart. Oh! how could you, then, thus imprint this mortal agony upon my dear, my tender-hearted Isaac? Was it that you cared more for gold than you did for human feelings —the holiest and the purest of nature's group—that of a son for a mother? Were you afraid Mr. Packard would not cash your note for borrowed money of his Eastern friends, if you did not help on this sad drama by your influence? Did you think that gold bought by human sobs and tears could help on your business in trade?

No, Mr. Comstock, it will not yield your manly heart the interest you want, and most need—the sympathy of the good, the pure, the true. Mr. Comstock, your good, kind heart could not thus be untrue to itself,—without a pang. Yes, your pangs, your regrets are all that is left for me to hope for, for you. Your guilty shame showed your manliness was not dead within you. May God heed your anguish, and heal your guilty soul by the balm of repentance!

Mr. Comstock, don't you ever again tear open a human heart, with agony, as you did my Isaac's, in the part you acted in this sad drama. Don't leave a kind and true mother and children again, at the beck and mercy of a human despot. Oh! my kind friend, Mr. Comstock, I cannot extend to you my forgiveness, unless you will pledge yourself never to desert the defenseless again. I know you feel penitent, or you would not have gone out of your way to meet Isaac, on the prairie, and try to persuade him to return to your employ—and tried to apologize by saying, that it was not because you had gone on to Mr. Packard's side, that you sent him away,—but because you knew it would only be a grievous scene for Isaac to witness, to see me torn away,—with none to rescue me, adding: "You could not have rescued her alone,—and those who were her friends were so cowed by your father's despotism, that they would not dare to interfere in your behalf. It was to save you from a greater scene of anguish that I sent you away."

Isaac accepted your apology and returned to your store and family; but he did not find your wife,—his tender, sympathizing mother. May she never have a son to need the sympathy,—she so scrupulously withheld from him—and from his mother! May her son receive what she withheld from my gentle, sensitive Isaac!

Why did Miss Rumsy and Mrs. Dixon flee from our house, at sight of the return of the mourning brothers, as sheep would flee from a wolf's approach? Because they dared not meet their downcast look,—for it told them that they had a share in the guilty drama which caused it.

Why did Samuel, the traitor,—flee like a bear chased by a tiger,—up to brother Doles, at sight of the wronged brother's approach? Because he felt that he had acted a guilty part in making them motherless.

Why did Sister Dole hurry home before the weeping brother's return? Had she no pity for my desolate children, whom she and her brother had deprived of a loving, faithful mother? Can she cut up human hearts as unfeelingly as she can cut up animal food for the spider or the griddle? Yes, sister, we have by you been deceived,—abused,—slandered, and your seditious attempts to destroy our family has brought upon our innocent,—defenseless heads,—a more merciless storm of persecution than that Romish church, which you so deeply hate, can boast of. Oh! the horrors of the Romish Inquisition are humane, compared with the horrors *you* have subjected your loving, and ever true sister, Elizabeth, to, by encouraging your guilty brother in his fiendish plans to destroy my moral influence,—as a witness for the truth. You know, sister, I never wronged you. I never harmed you, or yours. I even took your part,—even against myself,—to defend you from slander and abuse! No, I never gave you the shadow of a cause for your inflicting on my fair and unblemished character the blackest of all slanders and defamation,—the kidnapping of my accountability! Your heart must be that of a beast's,—it can't be human, and glut itself on human wrongs—on human gore —as unfeelingly as you have done to me and mine. Oh! sister, when your heart of stone is exchanged for a heart of flesh, then,—and not till then,—can you know the agony you have caused, by feeling, in your own susceptible human heart what we have felt.

I don't thank you for taking care of my own, dear, little Arthur. No! I don't! I prefer to take care of my own children—for I know I can take *better* care of them than you possibly can. I excel you in family government. My children mind me better than yours do you. They love me better than yours do you, and they have reason to do so. I am more deserving of their love and confidence, than you are of the love and confidence of your children. My children's habits are better than yours are, and I don't thank you for taking my work out of my own hands, without my leave! No—I don't, Sister Dole! You may ask your own

Calvinistic God to reward you for such devilish benevolence.
The Christian's God—my God—has no rewards to bestow
for such acts of mistaken *un*-kindness—this most brutal of
all abuses!

Let this Calvinistic kindness go with that kindness which
first *makes orphans*,—and then builds orphan asylums for
them—and then forces them into them—against their will
or consent. Yes, I think you, Sister Dole, will do well for
their matron! I can recommend you as an adept in the
business of orphan-making. You could listen to the orphan's
cry of anguish to go to its mother, unmoved—because you
are making its clothes, and cooking its food! No! I say,
food and clothes won't buy a *mother's love*, nor atone for the
loss of it.

Away with your food and clothes! "I prefer the state of
nudity in which I was born, to *this* way of getting them,"
says the mother and orphan, too.

No, sister, 'tis a thankless task you have undertaken to
perform. I, and my children, ain't dependent on your benefactions for support; they can support themselves, and their
little Arthur, too, until he can support himself; and we
would be thankful if you would let my family alone; and not
let your seditious influence extend beyond your own magic
circle. We have no thanks to bestow upon you for destroying our happy family! I would be thankful if you would let
my children alone, and not teach them any of your children's
vulgar habits. I feel above associating with you, or having
my children do so. I fear contamination. I feel conscience-
bound to leave you *for ever*, and to forbid my children from
any future association with you, or your children.

My children may catch some of my Christianity—which
you vainly try to make them believe is insanity!

Sister, you have fought against the better feelings of your
womanly nature, ever since you resisted your sister Jane's

spirit warning: "to look out for Elizabeth; for a snare was being laid for her!"

The snare was not Mr. Baker's writing me, but 'twas your brother's determination to ruin me, by it. It was your *brother's snare*, which he had long been deeply plotting to ruin my influence—by the slander of insanity—that the pure spirit of Jane undertook to warn you against. But your carnal mind could not interpret the message she sent you, on the basis of truth, so you were taken entirely into the old dragon's power,—and became his willing accomplice in his deeds of hellish darkness; and instead of shielding Elizabeth—as Jane wished you to—you just put her into the power of him from whom she was so anxious you should shield me! Instead of trying to shield and defend me, you entered into secret partnership with my husband, and tried to make use of the Baker correspondence as a means of undermining my husband's confidence in my virtue. You not only read the Baker correspondence without my consent—but you helped your brother copy a part of it—and then gave your affidavit that the whole was a true copy of the original. And then you encouraged him to read them to six men—and in asking $3,000 of Mr. Baker for the privilege of writing to his wife—and instructing her in the Swedenborgian views of truth and duty! Yes, you wanted Baker to pay $3,000 for his letters, while he (Mr. Packard)—unbeknown to Baker— kept an affidavit copy of the whole—hoping still to use them for the devilish purpose of defaming his wife's virtue!—and thus help him in getting his wife into an insane asylum. And all this category of guilt and crime on your brother's part, you sanctioned—when you *knew* I was as pure, virtuous, and sane a woman as the world ever saw.

Oh! guilty sister! the blood of lacerated hearts will be required at your hands. You have trifled with the divinity within me,—that high and holiest part of my pure nature,—

the *love of man,* as Christ's representative,—you have tried to debase, as a carnal, sensual love,—such love as your low, animal nature alone knows not how to understand. My tender, pure heart has bled in secret, at this, your wanton outrage upon my *rights of womanhood.*

Sister, it was my right, my privilege, my God-given right, to love a true man,—God's representative on earth,—and, true as the needle is to its pole, so truly does my womanly heart turn instinctively to the *manhood* for protection. I was defenseless,—husbandless,—without protection,—without appreciation,—without love,—without confidence,—and how could my loving heart live and breathe out of its native element? Unlike your carnal, sensual nature, my nature calls for a *higher* than a mere animal love,—it calls for, and cannot live without, a spiritual love,—such as Christ bestows upon his beloved—the church. I have been, all my lifetime, seeking, but never found, that true, Christ-like man, who could love and care for my unsheltered soul,—my inalienable soul rights,—as their protector. And when I hoped I had, at length, found one who did love my soul,—could I help loving him in return? Can the thirsty, famishing soul help loving the pure, cold water? Neither can I help loving a pure man! I did love Mr. Baker! for I believed Mr. Baker loved me,—with a Christ-like, or a manly love.

No man was ever loved with a purer, truer, deeper love than was Mr. Abner Baker, of Marshall, Michigan, by Mrs. Packard. And all the gold of California I would not give in exchange for that pure love he bestowed upon me. How could I have lived through these fiery persecutions, did I not know that one true, manly heart loved me still? I believe Mr. Baker has loved me,—and I know I have loved him,—and God, alone, knows how pure that love is! 'Tis such a love as I feel for Jesus, and it was called out into exercise because I felt that his love for me was *such* as Jesus bestows upon me. We,—the dependent church,—love him because he first loved us,—and showed his love for us,—by bearing our burdens,—and willingly suffering in our behalf. And when a man is willing to defend the inalienable rights of a woman,—at the hazard of his own reputation,—then, and then alone, does he love the woman,—as Christ loved the church,—that is, with a true, manly love.

And God has made it as morally impossible for a true woman to withhold her love from such a man, as it is for the sun to withhold its light and heat. And if it is a sin for me to love the true men on earth,—Christ's representatives,—then it is a sin for me to love God, or Christ,—for they are both men, and have manly hearts! And a woman's nature does, instinctively, pay homage to true manliness,—however embodied,—and whether married or unmarried. The heart knows no legal restraints, no bondage. 'Tis *free*,—as God, —its parent,—is free.

To me, it is of little or no present consequence whether the protector of my soul rights is married or single, if he only will see that I am protected in my inalienable rights,— 'tis all I want! I don't need a husband for my body, for I have a legal one now, and he is as likely to outlive me as I him, so far as I know,—or, if he never repents, so as to never be my natural husband again, I can take care of my body,—alone. Only let my inalienable *rights* be secured to me,—and I have all I want, or can desire,—under present surroundings.

Mr. Abner Baker, God will reward you,—the Christian— not the Calvinistic God,—for this heavenly boon of love, which you have bestowed upon me,—a worthy recipient of it. Your reward will be exceedingly great and glorious. I never could have burned those precious love-letters, had I not known Calvin had determined to use them for our mutual injury. And since Calvinism is not yet all buried—deep as hell!—I felt, instinctively, that there would be danger in trusting them in his polluted hands. I tried to commit their contents to memory, first, and God gave me a good time, when he was gone East, the winter before he incarcerated me here. I read them every day, almost, for my solace and comfort, and then when, like Moses' mother, I could no longer hide them,—I forced myself to cast them into the cruel flames. Oh! 'tis cruel to burn even paper love! 'Tis so precious! and 'tis so rare,—and yet, being a type of the original,—it seems almost a cruel sacrilege to burn it,—even in this frail form.

But God will forgive me, as self-defense against the Calvinistic hate of the present age demanded it. Yes, I had to destroy love tokens, lest the devils of the nineteenth century would pervert them to the injury of a God-loving woman! But I am almost sorry I did it, for there are none but devils and fallen angels who could pervert their true and holy meaning to suit their corrupt, impure, vicious souls—who basely fancy that, because *they* know no higher, purer love than the sexual, therefore there is none. Yea, there is none for them! But there is such a thing as a pure, spiritual love—if the devils do insist upon it that there is not; for I *know* there is—by my own blissful experience—and what I know, I know—notwithstanding all the devils to the contrary!

I don't now court popularity among this class of intelligences, for the simple reason that I don't like them—and can't like them—and what is more, I don't wish to like them—or, at least, so long as they possess nothing but evil or hate in theory and practice both. I can't love evil—and I don't think God can either; for God and I are love! and birds of a feather flock together. I love God, and God loves me, even if the devils do make such an awful fuss about it, and I am not ashamed to own it—even if God *is* a man!

Now, do you know, my beloved Abner, how this old Cal-

15*

vinist—the old dragon—used the cinders of these love-letters to my injury?

I will tell you; and if you don't give him full credit for being an economist of his capital in proof of his wife's deviation from the Calvinistic chalk-line of rectitude, then it is because you do not see the subject in the light I do. You see, he is determined to make me out a crazy woman—for how could it be possible for a sane woman to love a married man! better than she did the persecuting devil to whom she was bound by no ties but the ties of legality—or *il*legality, as it ought to be? So, to establish this point to a demonstration, and finding his greatest proof—the love-letters—were destroyed, he concocted this form of words as a proof of insanity as a *dernier ressort.*

"She has burned my valuable papers!"

Mind you, he doesn't tell *how* he got possession of these his valuable papers, nor in *what* their value consisted, but he is indefatigable in his efforts to send this startling fact all over the country where I am known.

What! Mrs. Packard burned her husband's valuable papers?

Yes, she has burned the most valuable papers he ever had, for he never had, in his estimation, so good a chance as these papers gave him to destroy all the confidence in community in his wife's reputation and character. Oh, how valuable is the reputation of the wife of a perverted husband! I guess *such* husbands have met with "a change of heart"—or, at least, the husband part of them must have been "regenerated!" I won't believe God made men to hate their wives! I think that is all the devil's work of regenerating God's well-made love principle. I find that men who haven't "met with a change of heart" love their wives, and protect their character and reputation, and are even indignant at any attempt made to destroy it. They feel insulted as quick at a slur cast upon their wives as they would upon themselves—and a little quicker; and they feel quite as much inclined to resent an insult offered to their wives as to themselves.

Oh! how I should love and honor such a manly protector, who treated me as if I was his "better half"—his companion—entitled to the same protection as himself! If I ever get another man to take care of me, I hope he will be a natural man—not a converted one. I don't believe in converting God's image into a devil!

But when I married Mr. Packard, I didn't know so much as I do now. I was so green then as to believe that a "change of heart" made people *better*. I didn't know but that they could improve God's work, by remodeling it, or regenerating it. But I am now convinced that God makes a great deal better men than the Calvinistic church does. Still I grant that it is possible for a good man to belong to the church—yet, I do say, the natural man has to be *smuggled* in, to get there, and he has to keep a pretty sharp lookout or the light under the bushel will shine out of some crack, and then he has a poor chance of keeping his place. The only safe way for him to retain his church standing is to put out his light, and not depend upon the half bushel to cover it!

Natural men and natural women are the Church's great antagonists.

The Church has got the cart before the horse—for they aim to make spiritual men *before* they make natural ones—whereas God says "first the natural, then the spiritual," and I am sure God has got the right of it, in spite of all christendom to the contrary—for it stands to reason that a cupola can't stand in its proper place—on the top of the house—without a house to stand upon. I think the Church's great business is to make people healthy; for I am sure they will slay more devils in this way than in any other. It is by the neglect or abuse of our physical frames that almost all our evil demons get access to us, and the way to cast out these devils, and keep them out, is—to give the house a thorough repair, and then keep it in good order. God has so constituted us that, in order to attend to all the laws of our physical natures—properly and thoroughly—takes almost all our time and attention; and, therefore, our natural lives are—in these bodies—our *chief concern*, or God wouldn't have made us so. God knows what he has made us for—and he has a good reason for our living natural lives in these bodies; and I have no disposition to call the wisdom of his arrangements in question. I only wish to fall in with this divine arrangement, and not be found to be resisting his will, by acting contrary to law or nature.

To obey the laws of my God-given nature is *for me* to obey God.

I did obey the love-law of my nature when I loved God, or goodness personified in God's image—a man—and Mr. Packard disobeyed the law of his manly nature, when—instead of loving and protecting the good, kind woman he vowed to do—he did all he could to ruin her character for virtue and sanity. His chief aim and study seemed to be, "How can I accomplish this purpose? I am afraid people won't believe my testimony that she wrote 'love letters' to a married man in Michigan, without the proof—and now the letters are destroyed, I have 'none but testimony to bring against her—and perhaps the six men to whom I read the letters, and my sister Dole, who has seen them, will not like to break their promise never to tell of the fact—not even to their wives—and now give a certificate of their contents! So what shall I do, as a substitute? Oh! I will so represent the thing as to give the impression that she has destroyed some of my notes, or deeds, or receipts—by calling the burnt letters 'valuable papers'—and thus, possibly, I may so make an impression of her being insane that the burning

of the letters may help my cause more than the letters themselves could."

"Yes, your plan is very adroit, Mr. Calvin. I guess you
will succeed very well in your new colors."

Mr. Community says: "Of course Mrs. Packard must be
insane, or she would not burn her husband's valuable papers
—no woman in her right mind would think of doing such a
thing—she, of course, don't know what she is about—and I
think he is right in putting her into an asylum, to keep her
from doing something worse—and, besides, I do think there
is real danger of her doing something worse—for he says
she is very free with the men!—and has even kept up a love
correspondence with a married man! I think he is right in
saying she needs a protector—for she does not know how to
take care of herself, if what he says of her is true—and, of
course, it is true, for he—a minister—would be the last man
who would wish to defame his wife's character, or put an
evil or false construction upon her actions. I think the best
thing that can be done to prevent a greater evil will be to
lock her up in an asylum, as he wants to do, for she may get
cured of her insanity—in this way—and be saved to her
family!!"

"Yes, Mr. Community, you reason tolerably well on your
premises; but let me just tell you your premises are all
false—yes, just as false as the man is who gave you your
premises. For instance, let me catechise you on one point,
which contains the basis of more truth than almost any other
irregularity he attributes to me. He says, "I have burned
his valuable papers." How came my letters to be his letters
or property? By stealing them. In what sense are love letters valuable? As a means of destroying a wife's reputation
for virtue."

Lincoln, won't you please look into this matter, and see if
I can't write to whom I please, and when I please, and as

often as I please. Isn't my tongue my own? Yes. Isn't my
pen my own? Yes. Isn't my love my own? Yes. Are not
my letters my own? Yes. Has Packard, who falsely calls
himself my husband, any right to steal any of these articles
from me? I say he hasn't! whatever your Calvinistic government says to the contrary. Now, Lincoln, protect these
inalienable rights to me, won't you?

Another question: Can't a woman be allowed to love but
one man? Can't a man love but one woman, under our free
government? If you say I mustn't—I shan't mind you, for
God says I may love *him*, wherever I can find him, and I
can find something of him in every devil, but Calvin. I
don't know but I have fallen in love with Jesus Christ! for
just as quick as I see Jesus Christ's image in *any* man, no
matter how he looks—how he drinks—or how he eats—or
how he walks—or how he sleeps—how he dresses—I do love
him, and I want to let him know it right straight off. I do
want to love all the evil demons out of him—and love all the
God-like virtues into him. And all but the Calvinists will
let me. *They* seem to feel that their divinity will be offended
if I love them!

I guess Calvin's God is a "jealous God"—and I don't
like jealousy. I think it looks so mean to be jealous.

What harm in the world can loving do? I don't think it
is half so mean as hating is. And I can't hate anything but
evil. That's the reason I don't like the Calvinists much,
because they seem to feel that it ain't doing right—if I ain't
selfish—and love anybody but myself. But I shall love
them, if they don't like it—even Deacon Smith—with his
little head—has got a little *small* Christ in him; but I guess
he is hungry sometimes. I think he needs a subscription-
paper started for his sole benefit! I'll head it with a dona-
tion of charity for those who differ from him in opinion.
What a pity 'twould be if we all had to believe just as

Dea. Smith does! I am afraid we should next be practicing as he does, if we did.

But I don't get Dea. Smith to do my thinking, I can tell you, nor Professor Park, neither. I can do my own thinking, I hope you'll understand!

Oh! how I do love drunkards and sailors! They have such a *big* Christ in them. And the swearer, too; how I do love him—they have such correct ideas about the Calvinistic divinity—and ain't afraid to let it out, either. I do like honesty! and I like to have people speak out their honest opinions, and speak as they feel. And I go in for the swearer! I do think Calvin's God is of such a base character that he ought to be damned to the lowest hell—and kept there in "endless torment"—if he insists upon it and likes it so well. He is so anxious to get the greatest part of the human family into this pit of despair, I'm sure he ought to have a chance to try it to his heart's content, himself.

But I won't send any of his devils nor angels with him there, to keep him company. I think he can keep bachelor's hall, alone, *there*, well enough—and have none of the hated craft of manhood with him, there—to disturb his lethargy. I guess he don't keep things very straight, there, if he don't succeed any better there than his representative did here, when I left him, once, alone—at his request—to test his house-keeping abilities.

Brother Hastings, when you called on his majesty, in my absence, on my Eastern tour, didn't you find things in a tremendous stew, there, with half a peck of dirt (or less) under his kitchen carpet—and about as much on top—with dirty crockery—thick glass—and unpolished silver, platina, and steel upon his breakfast table? Did his grinded cups and saucers—his salt-cellars filled, in their ridges, with dirt—and casters black with rust and dirt—and his untrimmed, filthy lamps—his corn-cake—and his stewed beans—tempt your appetite beyond your powers of control? I ask you, Brother George, would you like to' keep him company long— under such surroundings? I think not, unless his conversational powers of entertaining his company are greatly improved—his company would be hard up to stand it long, there. I don't think guests will burden him a great while. Good! That would suit Calvin, first-rate. He often has told me " he didn't buy the stores for company to eat up, they are for his own family to eat—not other people's families."

Oh! how ashamed I used to feel for Calvin, for fear his thoughts would come on to his face! But the wool covered up—pretty snug. If I saw the fleece slipping back, I'd just jump on to some other topic—so adroitly that the guests wouldn't suspect the wolf! I have to thank good luck that I was so successful in tucking up the fleece. Oh! I wouldn't have had the world know what a greedy, selfish man he was, for fear they would think that *all* ministers were so. But I was so sagacious and watchful, that I don't think 'twas often noticed when it did get slipped back—I was too cunning for the old wolf to show himself.

But I tell you he did show himself when the company got out of hearing. He would quarrel at me like a tiger! Well, never mind, thought I, I protected his guests, so that they are praising up the hospitality of the " good" Mr. Packard.

" He is one of the very best men I ever saw—so kind and generous—and so devoted a Christian. What a privilege Mrs. Packard enjoys to be under so benign an influence!"

Yes, I got him praised—and I was satisfied to go without. That's all I wanted—to make my husband shine inside and out. I knew there was a well in every rock, and that the gunpowder of truth could blow it into fragments—so that the waters could gush out. And I knew, also, that the blow-pipe of love could melt the iron will of a tyrant. So if truth and love could do the work, I meant to melt his heart into tenderness. But no go! 'Tis lost labor so far as he is concerned; until, perhaps, in some future period, after he has kept bachelor's hall in the lower regions long enough—perhaps he'll let his Elizabeth visit him, and lead him out to a more salubrious atmosphere—where it don't smell quite so strong of brimstone. I promised I'd do so for him when we last parted, when he left me here. Said I, after awaking him from his nap on the sofa, in the asylum parlor, where he had reclined to hear my dying plea! for a life of liberty and some of its clustering comforts—pleading to take me back with him to my precious babe, and little, defenseless, unprotected children—and walking the room in an agony of tears—and my maternal heart breaking in anguish at this most inhuman, unnatural separation, "Well, husband, if you can sleep and snore here—on the moment of our final parting, in this style—while your wife is dying of mortal agony of grief—we may as well say our last words, and separate—for ever. But of one thing rest assured, husband, that, if in the spirit land, where, God grant! our next meeting may be, I find your soul in agony—and it is in my power to help you—remember, that your Elizabeth will cheerfully leave her harp and glory, and descend to you to raise you to a higher plane. Yes, husband, if ever you need a friend—as I now do—don't forget there is a friend for you in the spirit world—somewhere in God's universe—and that friend is *your own*, true, kind, and tender-hearted Elizabeth—and she still longs to bless you."

"THE NIGHT CAR."

Here we must stop to attach our "night car," since the death and burial of a lost soul, in connection with his dismal future, is too dark and gloomy a picture for the sun to shine upon. The "night car" is the only fit place for such a delineation.

The last word was spoken that Calvin ever heard his wife address to him—the parting kiss bestowed—for the last time on Calvin's dry, hard, tearless cheek, and when next I behold him, God grant it may be beneath the coffin lid! May the transparent glass divide our lips and hearts—for ever. I don't like to kiss a corpse. 'Tis too cold—too much of Greenland's icy mountain about it to suit my warm nature. I've kissed this icy mountain to my heart's content. I sigh no more for the embrace of thy loathsome corpse—the whited sepulchre has lost all its claims to my caresses and fond embraces. Your hypocritical heart could utter its symbols of life—in its profuse shower of crocodile tears—when a moment after your tearless cheek had been moistened with your wife's tears of anguish—you entered the doctor's office, to give him your parting directions concerning your wife ; your pantomime was so adroitly acted out, as to lead Dr. McFarland to remark of the scene afterwards, " That he never saw so broken-hearted a man in all his life! "

The wife and children of that man know, to their heart's content, the *black hypocrisy* that " broken-hearted man " can practice!

No, thou base, hypocritical apostate! thy wife has no tears to shed over thy corpse. Calvin, I shan't kiss thy corpse—nor shall I ask your children to do so, either—for I do not ask them to do what I won't do myself. And I won't be a hypocrite! I shall rejoice at your burial, for it is a moral impossibility for a true nature to do otherwise—in my circumstances. Your children may kiss your corpse if they want to—I go for entire freedom. I don't bind or hire my children. I love to do as I please—so do children ; and my children choose to do as mother would wish to have them do.

Calvin, I shan't put on black, neither, at your funeral—I don't mourn your loss, for I have no *reason* to do so. I only

thank God that he has freed me from your anaconda coils—
by snapping the only thread by which you held relationship
to human beings—the form—which enclosed your demon
spirit. Calvin, I do not bid thee fare*well*—fare*evil!* does my
heart say, for you deserve an evil fare—and I, like God, go
in for deserts. Justice reward thee! And as you showed
me no mercy—so may God show you none! Yes, I can
rejoice to see the smoke of thy torment ascending up for ever
and ever—both as a reproof and as a warning—to the rem-
nant of Calvinists on earth, to shun the road by which their
sad doom is sealed—for ever sealed—against a wife's pure
love and children's confidence—because you sealed the door
of your own heart against ours. You would not let us love
you. So God will not let you love them.

Oh! the ossification of a human heart! It is a fatal, incurable disease, by which its action is suspended between life and
death, as Mr. O'Leary said my life was—by my hernia—living
as with a sword suspended by a hair over my naked head.
And Calvin never offered to buy me a truss to save my life.
But Angeline Field, my adopted sister, gave me one, even
while she needed it herself. Yes, sister, your truss has saved
me to be Calvin's faithful slave for fifteen long years more of
unrequited toil. Unrequited toil! did I say? No; he has
given my body rest—at the price of my soul in an insane asylum—for three long years of living death.

But I am dead! I can't suffer more. I am above the
breath of slander. It can't harm me more—I am at rest
in Jesus' arms, doing Jesus' work now—and *he* is my spirit
husband. I am no widow. I am not childless. All God's
sons and daughters are my brothers and sisters. God is my
father; the Holy Ghost is my mother; and all souls are their
offspring. Christ is my elder brother, and now is husband,
sister, and mother to his church—three in one. Two females
in one trio, as there used to be two males in one trio—in the
Christian dispensation.

The spiritual reign of Christ commences with the termination of the Christian, as the Christian commenced with the termination of the Jewish dispensation. Now, three in one. God's perfect order. Jewish, Christian, Spiritual, now blend in one harmonious whole.

"Let there be light! and there was light." Yes, the sun, moon, and stars have now risen upon the "new earth, wherein dwelleth righteousness."

And when Abraham gets ready to begin the reconstruction, or making of his new laws to protect the rights of these minor orbs, the moon and stars—the wife and children—as he has protected the sun in its strength, then will the daughter—mother—wife—form another trio of a new constellation in rejoicing with the sons of God. Earth jubilee has come! for Calvinism is dead and buried; and Christ has arisen from the asylum tomb, to herald the approach of God—the great Conqueror!—over fallen and entombed Calvinism—entombed in his own sepulcher, at Shelburne—his native town.

Yes, Calvin, I, and my group of stars, will follow thy corpse to its last resting place, and see it decently buried, and on your tombstone,—on the first lot, nearest the public road,—shall be inscribed your name, age, and the time of your death, and where.

Here I leave thee, Calvin,—a wide, deep, impassable gulf separates us now—for ever. You must pass down, down through the descending grades of animal, vegetable, and mineral life, only to find it expire in eternal oblivion! "None is lost save the son of perdition." I, your wife,—having lived a sympathetic and true life,—am destined to rise from human to angelic life, terminating in the divine Orb who rules all worlds. Yes, I shall rule you, Calvin, with a "rod of iron," since you would not be ruled with the rod of love. I shall hold you to the laws of your chosen abode, and while you are an animal, I shall rule you with animal laws—and when the animal passes into the vegetable, I shall rule you with God's vegetable laws; and when the vegetable ossifies,—as did your heart into a stone!—I shall rule you still with God's laws. Yes, "I and my Father are one." God and Nature coöperate in bringing about the same results.

Calvin, your road to oblivion is a long one. There are no cars on the underground railroad. The cars of upward, higher progress, are all above ground—and your Elizabeth has long known it. She knows that life succeeds life—and death, death. Oh! the death, Calvin, which your inaction—your torpor—your idleness,—has secured to you—is eternal—without end. God knows whether you are the *only* soul to be lost—I don't! Evil never rises!—but, like water, is constantly seeking the lowest level. "The first shall be last, and the last first." I was below you at home, in my kitchen, toiling to get you some nice luxuries to eat and drink. You were above me, away from the noise of the cook-stove and the children, sitting by your clean, open stove, reading papers. I made your coffee or tea almost every day of my married life—for you alone—hoping that I could stimulate you to study and write some part of a sermon a day, so as to bring out some new truths—and not all old sermons.' You despised my interference. You knew enough to take care of your own duties without my help. Oh, that you had known enough *to do them!* But you didn't. You neglected your sermons.

If Elizabeth can find twenty-one new sermons written out since I married you, twenty-three years since, among your posthumous manuscripts, I shall lose my guess. But I shall not lose the opinion,—until I see the proof that it is false,—in the sermons themselves. Yes, the sermons were false. But the man who wrote them was falsest! If there ever was a human demon personified in human form, it was in the form of Rev. Theophilus Packard, born in Shelburne, Mass., February 1, 1802.

Oh, Shelburne! 'tis no coveted honor to know that the "Old Dragon" found his birthplace in your town,—and was buried in your graveyard,—for "the name of the wicked shall rot."

I and my children shall rise to regions—pure,—where our pure souls shall bask in heaven's purest sunshine. "Be ye pure and holy," has been my own and my children's practical theory. No human being can show that we have wronged, defrauded, or slandered them. Our lips are too pure to speak lies or spread them.

Calvin honored God with his lips,—we with our hearts—by *doing right*. Did I say Calvin honored God with his lips? I unsay it! He did not. He reproached the God of the Bible, and represented him to be just such a demon—as he proved himself to be. No, he did not honor God with his lips, even. In works, he honored Satan,—and blasphemed the Holy Ghost itself,—in attempting to kidnap the accountability of his developed wife, Elizabeth. He did blaspheme the divinity—or the Holy Ghost within her—by placing her on a level with the beasts, as an insane person, and instructing the superintendent to keep her, for life, from the sight of, or even hearing from, her children!

"What God hath joined together, let not man put asunder," I often heard him say over the couples he married. Then they ought not to separate the offspring of such unions from the mother,—without her consent. For this is a union of God's making—not Calvin's. Calvin's unions,—God does not forbid us to break. But God's unions,—God commands us to respect,—and break them if we dare! Calvin dared to defy God's authority in separating me from my children; but God has him in hand for it now. "Vengeance is mine, I will repay, saith the Lord." And the one who makes the law, is the only authorized one to inflict the penalty. Calvin wanted to repeal and defy my laws just so. So he got used to the business,—by this slow process of usurpation,—until it ended in infamy, and landed himself in the lowest hell.

Oh! my brother devils! don't trifle with your wife's inalienable rights! You will rue the day you dare so to do, as Calvin does now, when 'tis too late to repent. He has secured his punishment—so may you. 'Tis trespassing on God's authority, to do so. He gave woman her nature,—and her instincts are God's laws,—by which she *must* be governed, or lie in the grave with Calvin; for her husband, Calvin, would not be ruled by a woman. A woman's rules,—nature's laws,—shall be his everlasting punishment. The laws of nature are imperative!

Mrs. Packard knows,—and so do her children,—that fire *always* burns! and if we forget it, and thoughtlessly pick up a live coal, instead of a cherry,—as we thought it was,—it is just as sure to burn our fingers, as if we did not think it was a cherry. So it is with Mrs. Packard's rules. A law broken, is a certain precursor of hell to the law-breaker! and no cries of "I didn't think! mother," could prevent the child feeling something to quicken his memory, so that he would think,—next time. I know children's memories are short, and I know, too, that God sent them to a mother—to splice them. I do splice them as God told me to, so that they are now too long to ever forget to love the mother who loves them.

Yes, I have borne all my six children,—all alone,—up to Calvary's top, there to be crucified with me, at the sight of the sorrows I am bearing, which they cannot bear for me, nor remove from their dear mother's hard shoulders. I am hard-shouldered,—for nature intended me to carry a very heavy pack of abuse and slanders,—which Packard packed upon me. Still, I am not round-shouldered yet, in the least. I can stand erect—under it all,—for my spirit husband sustains me. I cast all my burdens on to him, for he is so gallant,—he insists upon relieving the weaker vessel,—by carrying my packs for me. Oh! if I had been single all these persecuting times, I do believe I should have drooped, —as Calvin expected I would,—when he locked me up in prison, in addition to all his other abuses,—for he told my attendants, with evident surprise at seeing me look so blithe and happy here, "I never saw a person who can bear trouble so well as she does."

The secret of this lies in the fact that I don't hug my burdens—I hug my duties instead—and the heavier my burdens, the more assiduous I am at my duties. I won't add to my burdens by fretting!—but I will add to my practical virtues, charity,—and to charity, hope,—that they will all work, in the end, for my good. So, to secure this result, "I am diligent in business, fervent in spirit, serving the Lord." I cherish no useless regrets for the past,—for I know what has taken place, God permitted to take place,—and therefore is all a part of his own perfect plan ; and I don't pretend to be wiser than God, by feeling that it would have been better to have had things my way,—instead of God's way. Neither will I carry solicitude or anxiety for the future. I know God can take care of his own business,—without my superintendence,—and besides, it takes all my energies to attend to all my duties. I submit,—if I don't like it,—to God's arrangements, which has made duties mine, events God's.

Verily, Mrs. Packard's head is still on the top of her body, —where God put it—not on my breast, as Calvin has put his own. And Mrs. Packard's head dictates to her dress-maker —her own ingenious fingers,—to cut her dresses with broad fronts and narrow backs, so that the lungs can have room to play in, and not get lapped over into folds, so as to exclude the oxygen or life-element from her blood. Mrs. Packard often sighs—but it is not the sigh of grief,—as when I parted from Calvin, because he would be so cruel as to separate me from my children. No, 'tis the sigh of inspiration,—inflating, to their full capacity, all the air-cells of my lungs, thus invigorating me with new life and hope of getting my book soon done, so I can get to see them once more, this side the grave.

The grave! What is it? 'Tis the tomb of one we love. What do I love? God's will. Can that be entombed? Never! not even in Jacksonville insane asylum. I and God's will are married! and nothing can separate us—not even the bolts and the bars of an insane asylum. I fear no bolts; I fear no bars; I fear no death; I fear no grave.

Calvin thought he put me into hell when he put me in here. He did put me into a living hell—and I have made it a living heaven—for God is here!—and I have been doing his business, in binding up the broken-hearted,—in comforting the desponding,—in bearing the burdens of the weak,—and in scattering the roses of hope upon the graves of human hearts. I cannot go out to pluck them. I have not set my foot on terra firma for nearly two years. But some of my kind sister angels here, think of the caged-up bird, and bring roses to her, for her to scatter as her kind heart dictates.

Indeed, my hell is transformed into an Eden of rest, both to body, and soul, and spirits. I never before found a home among God's angels as I do here. 'Tis a lower heaven upon earth, in rather too close proximity to hell, to suit me, however! It detracts from the bliss of this heaven to come in contact with so much misery, which I cannot help.

"THE PALACE-CAR."

Passengers! here I stop my train for a few moments, to exchange our "Night-Car" for "The Palace-Car,"—the only appropriate coach for the transportation of Columbia's more

16

developed sons and daughters into the higher—or " new heaven,"—of love and truth, "wherein dwelleth righteousness."

Columbia! 'Tis the " garden of God!" bounded north, by the will of God,—south, by God's purposes,—east, by his decrees,—and west, by our deserts. And, Oh! Columbia! toe well the mark of justice,—and eye well the beam,—lest your deserts shoot you in this hollow square!! Here, in the hollow square, erect the temple of liberty, and on its spreading dome, set the flag-staff of universal liberty—let the sun, moon, and stars spangle its uplifted banners! No place left for the bloody stripes, when the sun and moon have kissed each other. The offsprings of truth and honesty need no castigation to make them toe the mark of justice. Let Abraham set in his cabinet none but earnest woman's rights and children's rights-men, to make our protection laws. No tariff to insure their vitality. Their life, is truth and justice!—the living inspirations of our permanent government.

Ancient of days! fit temple for thine abode! come Thou, and make it thy lasting resting-place! Jesus! the first-born Son—come and dedicate our new temple with thy marriage nuptials to the true Church—the Bride—the Lamb's wife. And on Columbia's happy soil, let thy children spread their tents of ease!—no sweat—no thorn shall dim the luster of their unwearied eye. No Calvinism shall enter there, to send the thorn of sorrow to subdue it into docility to right—to obedience.

Here love and truth meet together, " righteousness and peace do kiss each other."

Lincoln, when love and truth meet, may they kiss each other in the open street—and open car—or must they hide behind some tree, or door, to escape a Calvinist's gaze? Lincoln, I shall not obey any law of restraint thrown around my pure instincts! I shall kiss when I feel like it—and I shall let men kiss me when they want to. Too often for me, they cannot—will not. Love is my native element, as water is the element of the fish. In it, I live—breathe—move—and have my inner being. I can no more live in the cold deserts of America, than a fish can live on dry land, or a bird in a cage.

Lincoln, don't let a bird's cage—a relic of Calvinism—be the eye-sore of any ladies' saloon or parlor. Let it be the insignia of disgrace and infamy to the human soul, who will dare to circumscribe the limits God has assigned to one of his creatures—be it beast, bird, fowl, or fish. Oh! how I have repented, with godly sorrow, the act I have so often sanctioned, of cooping up a hen with chickens. I will never do it again—never more, again. Calvin never needed to be asked to make a coop. No, he kept them on hand, as plenty as the slaveholder does his bloodhounds to catch his runaway slaves. I have thought, Oh! did he care as much for the souls of his flock as he did for the imprisonment of the mother hen, his old barrel would not have to be upset—so often—to find a sermon old enough not to have his people know but it had just been written. I should not say barrel—'twas a chest—a college chest—a relic of college life, which was his sermon repository.

His sermons had one striking peculiarity—they were peculiarly depraved! We were goaded almost to death by the goad of the Calvinistic pulpit—"Total depravity." He would "push eastward, westward, northward, and southward," to find some nobleness in human nature to attack—overthrow—and destroy! Amiability was a sin!—desolation followed in its sanguinary track—all the clustering loves of our noble nature were laid upon the track, to be crushed by the progress of the Juggernaut car of devastation. Where are the heathen? In our Calvinistic churches. Nowhere—on the face of God's earth—can be found men and women so far perverted from the original image in which God made them, than these consistent Calvinists are. No race of so-called heathen nations separate the mother and child. This maternal law of our nature is regarded as sacred!—by all *natural* humanity. This barbarism itself—this destruction of human nature—we pay our missionaries for doing—pay them for defaming human nature!—God's own image!—as personified in Christ—and call this Christianizing the heathen! Is it Christianizing the heathen to make demons of them as our Calvinistic religion legitimately does?

I say there is not a falser God worshiped in the universe, than Calvin's God! And if there is a more perverted Christianity than Calvinism inculcates—on God's footstool, I know not where it is.

Oh! England! take thy sword and gird it upon thy thigh, and go forth to slay human beings by its thousands. Calvinism! take *thy* Bible, and go forth and slay thy tens of thousands—on Christian shores! Slay humanity—and let a general resurrection of demons arise from its tomb!

Yes, they have arisen! and are now bent on the destruction of Christ's freedom-loving government—in America! But no. Your legions—though many—are met by a stronger and more invincible host of resurrected humanity—who died in defense of Christ—but who rose before you—and have planted their feet, immovably, upon the principles of universal liberty. And on this platform they dauntlessly defy your power to overcome them! For "Christ *shall* reign King of nations," as he has reigned, and still does reign, over them. Christ! thy bodyguard, in America, is invincible! Thy throne shall here be established, even though it be on the ruins of Antichrist. Yea, Calvinism itself—this hydra-headed monster demon!—shall find its grave on this American soil—deep as hell. Yes, it shall be buried in the very grave it has dug for Christianity.

The heathen of this earth are the American Calvinists.

The Christians are the children of *nature*, found more profusely scattered on every other soil than on our perverted continent. But, as the storm and the hurricane, which rends the forest trees, only to cause them to strike their roots still deeper in their rocky beds, thus rendering them invincible before the tempest's blasts; so the Christianity of America has attained to no ordinary strength, by maintaining its position, amid the howling blasts of persecution! Such Christianity—and such alone—can cope with this monster demon successfully. God has given us a terrible foe to subdue, but he has given us omnipotent strength to meet him. He shall fall to rise no more, for God and our country are one and inseparable.

The purple and the fine linen drapery of the true church are found where nature, reason, and conscience are found—fit badges of honor to the refined and accomplished gentleman and lady. But the trailing dress, which sweeps the streets with a brocade, silk street-brush, and the broad phylactery, are twin children of Calvinism.

Let one's dress be noticed as an index of character, and your mirror is before you, of a Christian or a Calvinist. The Christian stands on the common platform of commonsense, and he uses his own reason and his own conscience as his engineers on this common track of practical duty. But the Calvinist derides common-sense as a Christian basis, and our own reason and conscience are only blind guides—unsafe to follow! Unsafe? Yes, for Calvinism and human reason are mortal, deadly foes.

Calvinism! Calvinism! is there no end to thy hydra-headed perversions of nature—God?

Can we find simple, unaffected nature in the region of thy pestilential mephitics? As well may we seek the rose without a thorn among the lilies and roses of our American

garden.   But there grows here *one* rose—without a thorn—
waiting to be transplanted into Columbia's new Eden.   'Tis
the "Rose of Sharon."   Nature in her simplicity! with no
artistic step or mincing gait, no crinoline subterfuge for that
gallantry which seeks only to protect and shield its object
from harm and abuse.

No Christian, like Comstock or Baker, could insult a
woman!   Even a Calvinistic lady might decoy them to her
den—fearless of danger.

Thank God! the Josephs of America are not all slain by
the wife of Potiphar.   Potiphar may leave his home, for
Joseph will protect his wife's virtue—even at the price of a
prisoner's cell.

Yes, beloved Baker, I begged my husband, with streaming
eyes and bursting heart, with my arms about his neck, sitting
upon his lap—to spare you—the innocent cause—and wreak
his vengeance upon me—the equally innocent occasion of
his brutal wrongs—his unjust suspicions.

But all in vain!   Human love could not break Calvin's
iron will, and, as the hungry wolf seeks her prey, so did my
husband seek to destroy your native manliness.

Oh! Mr. Baker, did your lawyer get my clandestine letter,
begging him to spare you—the innocent, and cast me—the
guilty one of the two—into that awful vortex my husband
was seeking to engulf you in?

Had it not been for that Christian lawyer, Mr. Kitchel of
Detroit, Mich., whose aid my husband sought, in his determination to sue Baker for $3,000 or $6,000 for the love-letters,
I know not where you, now, would have been.   Perhaps your
elegant wife, and your six lovely children, would have had
no husband or father to look to for their daily bread.   You
might have been hid in some penitentiary cell—or what is
still worse, some insane asylum cell—there to linger out the
weary years of your manly life, as Joseph did, until God's
Providence vindicated your innocence.

Thanks! many thanks! to Mr. Kitchel, for his Christian interference and timely warning to my misguided husband, which saved you from the criminal's doom, and left me to be the sole victim of his diabolical hate. He dared not attack you, a man, whose friends might defend you; but he could attack his defenseless wife, whom the law allowed him to shield from defense against a husband's abuse.

Yes, innocent I am! defenseless I am! unjustly I am assailed!—patiently I am enduring the hellish vengeance of the "jealous God" of the Calvinistic priesthood.

But I have been doing God service—and my country service—in so doing.

The devils are God's slaves, and slavery is their reward for doing God's mean drudgery. They are the hewers of wood and the drawers of water for his children to use in getting the family cooking done.

Calvin has been a good, faithful slave to me. He was always good to keep my wood-box well filled, with good, hard, dry wood, and my rain-water pail always filled with water from our cistern, and he gave me good pumps to bring my well-water with. So, brother devil! so far as a hewer of wood and a drawer of water is concerned, you were my faithful slave; and for this service—so well, so kindly and faithfully done—rests your only hope of ever being allowed to assume the responsibilities of a human being, again—as a probationer for the redemptive blood of Christ.

Oh! don't be content, when, in the long vista of the future—after you have received your full punishment for your abuse of me and my children—your God yields to my request to give you another trial for eternal life; I say, Oh! be not content to be a mere slave, for you were made to be a brother!—son!—husband!—father!—all to be used—as God-reflecting mirrors—to see Christ in—in all these various relations, and never, never were filled by you acceptably to

God or man, except the lowest of all—the slave to human lusts. You did love the nice food and drinks your Elizabeth prepared from your wood and water, and these were all you did love—except reading the news, and defending the principles of Calvinism.

Oh! could I have been loved as well as you loved my snowy puffs, I should have been puffed with womanly pride of knowing and feeling that my husband loved me! In words you said you did love me—but in works you denied it.

Poor, deluded, lost soul! You first were ignorantly wrong—in not knowing how to cultivate the love-principle—by showing it in deeds. Your Elizabeth enlightened you on this point; and then you did as well as you could, when you wrote two hours a day on your sermons, and thus got one good sermon ready for use the next Sabbath. Oh! *then* I was loved!—how often did you hug and kiss me, and thank me for getting you to do your duty—for you felt so much happier with a sense of discharged obligation—than you did a sense of neglected duties. This sense of violated obligations—of neglected duties—seemed to so haunt your guilty soul that it found no rest—anywhere—but like the troubled sea, was constantly casting up mire and dirt in your pathway, obscuring the light and peace which the discharge of other duties would otherwise have had attended them. How true is it that it is the little foxes which destroy the vines—the tender vines—and tendrils of love and hope. When you felt the peace arising from doing your duty—instead of shirking it—you often, in all sincerity, asked me " not to give you up, but put you up to doing what you so hated to do "—write sermons.

I did try to, husband, you know I did—but what was the result? You disliked me for it, and seemed to become alienated from me—for this cause alone. I felt that I could not give you up to a life of guilty idleness—of neglect of duties—which you felt conscience-bound to fulfill, for I knew that to neglect conscience's warning voice was to sow seeds for a harvest of tares—and I knew, to persist in this course, the wheat would all be choked out by the more luxuriant tares, and the wheat-field of the human heart become an utter devastation. The result I then so prospectively feared has come—to you and your family's mutual sorrow. As you sowed so have you reaped.

Husband, I did persevere in trying to save you, with all the patience of hope—and all the tenderness of love—until after many sad and oft-repeated failures—and worse than failures—for your sister Mary-Ann told me it would not do to "dictate to brother"—it would estrange him from me, and do no good. Her testimony, coinciding so perfectly with my own observation, led me to feel conscience-bound to abandon my efforts, and leave you, unmolested, to pursue your own chosen way, thorny as it was. My efforts to strew your path with the fragrant roses of hope were thus reluctantly abandoned, and so you were abandoned to a life of restless sorrow. "There is no peace to the wicked." Husband, I did strive and labor for your good until you became willful about it; and then I desisted and let you do, willfully, wrong acts of neglects of duty. And this was the stepping-stone to the last and final act of delusion—conscientiously wrong neglects.

Ignorantly—willfully—conscientiously wrong!! The fatal trio! No human power can break this triune delusion!

Such a sinner—acting as Christ's ambassador—can feel that it is right to get a salary from the people for whom he has promised to labor without earning a cent of it in making efforts for their good. Such a Calvin did neglect his parish and his pulpit, both, to attend to the secular concerns of his family—without any call for it in the facts in the case. His

16*

garden and his secular reading took all his time and energies almost—both physical and mental. Oh! Calvin, the
die was cast! not many years after we were married, and no
subsequent spasmodic efforts at repentance could break the
"spell" by which Satan held you fast in his chains.

Oh! probationer for eternity! don't let the stern demands
of duty ever pass by unheeded, for your deathless soul is thus
jeopardized. Never sleep with a guilty conscience for your
bedfellow. For such a slumber is a treacherous sleep whose
waking is death—death to that vitality which conscience gives
the human soul. A dead or a seared conscience is a certain
forerunner of sorrow!—as endless as the persistent, iron will
is—which caused it.

I believe in universal salvation with all the tenacity with
which I believe in universal repentance. I believe the strongest will will rule. I believe there is no will so stubborn as
God's will ; therefore, no self-willed mortal can conquer God's
determination to make him blessed. All punishment is reformatory, under the government of a benevolent God. God
is not compelled, like human despots, to maintain his authority at the price of justice or mercy. It is a mercy to be just!
Injustice always harms—justice benefits always.

There never was, and there never will be, but one condition
of salvation—*repentance*—and punishments are God's instrumentalities in producing it in the obdurate transgressor.
The parent punishes his obstinate child only for his good, not
to make his power known—as demons do. God subjects the
whole of his human family, not to torment them, but to bless
them. He will bless them all ! "and that right early," to
the great mortification and chagrin of the Calvinistic devils.
Yea more—the very devils themselves will be compelled to be
blessed by him, thus proving their own base slanders of his
character to be false as their endless hell is.

Will a God of love rest content with evil and misery existing under his reign? No! death and hell will be destroyed—for God has said they will be.

LOOK OUT FOR PICKPOCKETS!

Passengers! before leaving this emancipation-car of universal liberty, let me caution you against the " confidence-men" who congregate about this " depot of individuality," ready to seize or grab any injudicious or thoughtless exposure of pearls or gems of thought you may have found on this trip. Be sure and keep them from their evil eye! Or, in other words, do not venture to cast the pearls of truth found on this train, before this swinish or undeveloped class, lest they not only trample them under their feet, but also turn and rend you with the slander of insanity, for endorsing what, *to them*, is incomprehensible,—because above their limited capacity. Hold on to your pearls! for you,—pioneers and volunteers in Christ's army,—must be valiant enough to herald unpopular truths, knowing that, ere long, even these now undeveloped ones will be compelled to enlist, when " drafted in" by the government of popular public sentiment, as will surely be the case in the onward progress of this all-conquering army,—for truth will bear the test of time!—and its defenders can well afford to await its triumphs.

NOTE TO THE READER.

The following trial—although in the order of events in "The Great Drama—is, in its appropriate place, the supplement to my four volumes; yet, since the public ought to know what evidence of insanity the author exhibited before they purchased the book, it is proper that the trial be introduced in the first rather than in the last volume.

It is but justice to myself to say that the testimony of the two great conspirators, Deacon Abijah Dole and Deacon Josephus B. Smith, ought to be taken at a discount—as witnesses—since both of these Deacons perjured themselves openly, upon the witness' stand, while giving in their *manufactured* testimony against my moral character, which, when tested by cross-examination, would not hold together—in fact, was so evidently contradictory and absurd, that I was importuned by my friends to enter a prosecution against them for perjury. This part of these five days' trial was not reported by Mr. Moore, because, as he said, this attack was entirely foreign to the question at issue.

This most wanton attack upon my moral character—made at Mr. Packard's dictation—was evidently an act of desperation, to save their sinking cause; but as it proved, these weapons of cruel slander and defamation were most signally turned against themselves, since by it their testimony—as witnesses against my sanity—was of no account whatever in its effect upon the minds of the jury. In fact, the remark was often made to me :

"We do not believe a word that Deacon Dole or Deacon Smith have spoken against your sanity, now that they have so plainly proved themselves lying witnesses against your virtue."

THE GREAT TRIAL

OF

MRS. ELIZABETH P. W. PACKARD,

WHO WAS CONFINED FOR THREE YEARS IN THE STATE ASYLUM OF ILLINOIS, CHARGED BY HER HUSBAND, REV. THEOPHILUS PACKARD, WITH BEING INSANE. HER DISCHARGE FROM THE ASYLUM, AND SUBSE-QUENT IMPRISONMENT AT HER OWN HOUSE BY HER HUSBAND. HER RELEASE ON A WRIT OF *Habeas Corpus*, AND THE QUESTION OF HER SANITY TRIED BY A JURY. HER SANITY FULLY ESTABLISHED.

A FULL REPORT OF THE TRIAL, INCIDENTS, ETC.

BY STEPHEN R. MOORE, ATTORNEY AT LAW.

IN preparing a report of this trial, the writer has had but one object in view, namely, to present a faithful history of the case as narrated by the witnesses upon the stand, who gave their testimony under the solemnity of an oath. The exact language employed by the witnesses has been used, and the written testimony given in full, with the exception of a letter, written by Dr. McFarland to Rev. Theophilus Packard, which letter was retained by Mr. Packard, and the writer was unable to obtain a copy. The substance of the letter is found in the body of the report, and has been sub-mitted to the examination of Mr. Packard's counsel, who agree that it is correctly stated.

This case was on trial before the Hon. Charles R. Starr, at Kankakee City, Illinois, from Monday, January 11th, 1864, to Tuesday the 19th, and came up on an application made by Mrs. Packard, under the *Habeas Corpus Act*, to be discharged from imprisonment by her husband in their own house.

The case has disclosed a state of facts most wonderful and startling. Reverend Theophilus Packard came to Manteno, in Kankakee county, Illinois, seven years since, and has remained in charge of the Presbyterian Church of that place until the past two years.

In the winter of 1859 and 1860, there were differences of opinion between Mr. Packard and Mrs. Packard upon matters of religion, which resulted in prolonged and vigorous-debate in the home circle. The heresies maintained by Mrs. Packard were carried by the husband from the fireside to the pulpit, and made a matter of inquiry by the church, and which soon resulted in open warfare; and her views and propositions were misrepresented and animadverted upon from the pulpit, and herself made the subject of unjust criticism. In the Bible Class and in the Sabbath-school she maintained her religious tenets, and among her kindred and friends, defended herself from the obloquy of her husband.

To make the case fully understood, I will here remark that Mr. Packard was educated in the Calvinistic faith, and for twenty-nine years has been a preacher of that creed, and would in nowise depart from the religion of his fathers. He is cold, selfish, and illiberal in his views, possessed of but little talent, and a physiognomy innocent of expression. He has large self-will, and his stubbornness is only exceeded by his bigotry.

Mrs. Packard is a lady of fine mental endowments, and blessed with a liberal education. She is an original, vigorous, masculine thinker, and were it not for her superior judgment, combined with native modesty, she would rank as a "strong-minded woman." As it is, her conduct comports strictly with the sphere usually occupied by woman. She dislikes parade or show of any kind. Her confidence that Right will prevail, leads her to too tamely submit to wrongs. She was educated in the same religious belief with her husband, and during the first twenty years of married life his labors in the parish and in the pulpit were greatly relieved by the willing hand and able intellect of his wife.

Phrenologists would also say of her that her self-will was large, and her married life tended in nowise to diminish this phrenological bump. They have been married twenty-five years, and have six children, the issue of their inter-marriage, the youngest of whom was eighteen months old when she was kidnapped and transferred to Jacksonville. The older children have maintained a firm position against the abuse and persecutions of their father toward their mother, but were of too tender age to render her any material assistance.

Her views of religion are more in accordance with the liberal views of the age in which we live. She scouts the Calvinistic doctrine of man's total depravity, and that God has foreordained some to be saved and others to be damned. She stands fully on the platform of man's free agency and accountability to God for his actions. She believes that man and nations are progressive; and that in his own good time, and in accordance with His great purposes, Right will prevail over Wrong, and the oppressed will be freed from the oppressor. She believes slavery to be a national sin, and the church and the pulpit a proper place to combat this sin. These, in brief, are the points in her religious creed which were combated by Mr. Packard, and were denominated by him as " emanations from the devil," or " the vagaries of a crazed brain."

For maintaining such ideas as above indicated, Mr. Packard denounced her from the pulpit, denied her the privilege of family prayer in the home circle, expelled her from the Bible Class, and refused to let her be heard in the Sabbath-school. He excluded her from her friends, and made her a prisoner in her own house.

Her reasonings and her logic appeared to him as the ravings of a mad woman—her religion was the religion of the devil. To justify his conduct, he gave out that she was insane, and found a few willing believers among his family connections.

This case was commenced by filing a petition in the words following, to wit:

STATE OF ILLINOIS, } ss.
KANKAKEE COUNTY.

To the Honorable CHARLES R. STARR, *Judge of the 20th Judicial Circuit in the State of Illinois.*

William Haslet, Daniel Beedy, Zalmon Hanford, and Joseph Younglove, of said county, on behalf of Elizabeth P. W. Packard, wife of Theophilus Packard, of said county, respectfully represent unto your Honor, that said Elizabeth P. W. Packard is unlawfully restrained of her liberty, at Manteno, in the county of Kankakee, by her husband, Rev. Theophilus Packard, being forcibly confined and imprisoned in a close room of the dwelling-house of her said husband, for a long time, to wit, for the space of four weeks, her said husband refusing to let her visit her neighbors and refusing her neighbors to visit her; that they believe her said husband is about to forcibly convey her from out the State; that they believe there is no just cause or ground for restraining said wife of her liberty; that they believe that said wife is a mild and amiable woman. And they are advised and believe that said husband cruelly abuses and misuses said wife, by depriving her of her winter's clothing, this cold and inclement weather, and that there is no necessity for such cruelty on the part of said husband to said wife; and they are advised and believe that said wife desires to come to Kankakee City, to make application to your Honor for a writ of *habeas corpus*, to liberate herself from said confinement or imprisonment, and that said husband refused and refuses to allow said wife to come to Kankakee City for said purpose; and that these petitioners make application for a writ of *habeas corpus* in her behalf, at her request. These petitioners therefore pray that a writ of *habeas corpus* may forthwith issue, commanding said Theophilus Packard to produce the body of said wife before your Honor, according to law, and that said wife may be discharged from said imprisonment.

(Signed)   WILLIAM HASLET,
                               DANIEL BEEDY,

J. W. ORR, } *Petitioners'*   ZALMON HANFORD,
H. LORING, }   *Attorneys.*   J. YOUNGLOVE.

        STEPHEN R. MOORE, *Counsel.*

STATE OF ILLINOIS, } *ss.*
   KANKAKEE COUNTY. }

William Haslet, Daniel Beedy, Zalmon Hanford, and Joseph Younglove, whose names are subscribed to the above petition, being duly sworn, severally depose and say, that the matters and facts set forth in the above petition are true in substance and fact, to the best of their knowledge and belief.

                 WILLIAM HASLET,
                 DANIEL BEEDY,
                 ZALMON HANFORD,
                 J. YOUNGLOVE.

Sworn to and subscribed before me, this }
   11th day of January, A. D. 1864. }

         MASON B. LOOMIS, *J. P.*

Upon the above petition, the Honorable C. R. Starr, Judge as aforesaid, issued a writ of *habeas corpus*, as follows:

STATE OF ILLINOIS, } *ss.*
   KANKAKEE COUNTY.

The People of the State of Illinois, to THEOPHILUS PACKARD:

WE COMMAND YOU, That the body of Elizabeth P. W. Packard, in your custody detained and imprisoned, as it is said, together with the day and cause of caption and detention, by whatsoever name the same may be called, you safely have before Charles R. Starr, Judge of the Twentieth Judicial Circuit, State of Illinois, at his chambers, at Kankakee City in the said county, on the 12th instant, at one o'clock P. M., and to do and receive all and singular those things which the said Judge shall then and there consider of her in this behalf, and have you then and there this writ.

Witness, Charles R. Starr, Judge aforesaid, this 11th day of January, A. D. 1864.

CHARLES R. STARR,   [SEAL.]
Judge of the 20th Judicial Circuit
of the State of Illinois.

[*Revenue Stamp.*]

Indorsed: "By the *Habeas Corpus* Act."

To said writ, the Rev. Theophilus Packard made the following return:

The within named Theophilus Packard does hereby certify, to the within named, the Honorable Charles R. Starr, Judge of the 20th Judicial Circuit of the State of Illinois, that the within named Elizabeth P. W. Packard is now in my custody, before your Honor. That the said Elizabeth is the wife of the undersigned, and is and has been for more than three years past insane, and for about three years of that time was in the Insane Asylum of the State of Illinois, under treatment, an an insane person. That she was discharged from said Asylum, without being cured, and is incurably insane, on or about the 18th day of June, A. D. 1862, and that since the 23d day of October, the undersigned has kept the said Elizabeth with him in Manteno, in this county, and while he has faithfully and anxiously watched, cared for, and guarded the said Elizabeth, yet he has not unlawfully restrained her of her liberty; and has not confined and imprisoned her in a close room, in the dwelling-house of the undersigned, or in any other place or way, but, on the contrary, the undersigned has allowed her all the liberty compatible with her welfare and safety. That the undersigned is about to remove his residence from Manteno, in this State, to the town of Deerfield, in the county of Franklin, in the State of Massachusetts, and designs and intends to take his said wife Elizabeth with him. That the undersigned has never misused or abused the said Elizabeth, by depriving her of her winter's clothing, but, on the contrary, the undersigned has always treated the said Elizabeth with kindness and affection, and has provided her with a sufficient quantity of winter clothing and other clothing; and that the said Elizabeth has never made any request of the undersigned, for liberty to come to Kankakee City, for the purpose of suing out a writ of *habeas corpus.* The undersigned hereby presents a letter from Andrew McFarland, Superintendent of the Illinois State Hospital, at Jacksonville, in this State, showing her discharge, and reasons of discharge, from said institution, which is marked "A," and is made a part of this return. And also presents a certificate from the said Andrew McFarland, under the seal of said hospital, marked " C," refusing to re-admit the said Elizabeth again into said hospital, on the ground of her being incurably insane, which is also hereby made a part of this return.

THEOPHILUS PACKARD.

Dated *January* 12, 1864.

The court, upon its own motion, ordered an issue to be

formed, as to the sanity or insanity of Mrs. E. P. W. Packard, and ordered a venire of twelve men, to aid the court in the investigation of said issue. And thereupon a venire was issued.

The counsel for the respondent, Thomas P. Bonfield, Mason B. Loomis, and Hon. C. A. Lake, moved the court to quash the venire, on the ground that the court had no right to call a jury to determine the question, on an application to be discharged on a writ of *habeas corpus.* The court overruled the motion; and thereupon the following jury was selected:

John Stiles, Daniel G. Bean, V. H. Young, F. G. Hutchinson, Thomas Muncey, H. Hirshberg, Nelson Jarvais, William Hyer, Geo. H. Andrews, J. F. Mafet, Lemuel Milk, G. M. Lyons.

CHRISTOPHER W. KNOTT was the first witness sworn by the respondent, to maintain the issue on his part, that she was insane; who being sworn, deposed and said:

I am a practicing physician in Kankakee City. Have been in practice fifteen years. Have seen Mrs. Packard; saw her three or four years ago. Am not much acquainted with her. Had never seen her until I was called to see her at that time. I was called to visit her by Theophilus Packard. I thought her partially deranged on religious matters, and gave a certificate to that effect. I certified that she was insane upon the subject of religion. I have never seen her since.

Cross-examination.—This visit I made her was three or four years ago. I was there twice—one-half hour each time. I visited her on request of Mr. Packard, to determine if she was insane. I learned from him that he designed to convey her to the State Asylum. Do not know whether she was aware of my object, or not. Her mind appeared to be excited on the subject of religion; on all other subjects she was perfectly rational. It was probably caused by overtaxing the mental faculties. She was what might be called a monomaniac. Monomania is insanity on one subject. Three-fourths of the religious community are insane in the same manner, in my opinion. Her insanity was such that with a little rest she would readily have recovered from it. The female mind is more excitable than the male. I saw her perhaps one-half hour each time I visited her. I formed my judgment as to her insanity wholly from conversing with her. I could see nothing except an unusual zealousness and warmth upon religious topics. Nothing was said, in my conversation with her, about disagreeing with Mr. Packard on religious topics. Mr. Packard introduced the subject of religion the first time I was there: the second time, I introduced the subject. Mr. Packard and Mr. Comstock were present. The subject was pressed on her for the purpose of drawing her out. Mrs. Packard would manifest more zeal than most of people upon any subject that interested her. I take her to be a lady of fine mental abilities, possessing more ability than ordinarily found. She is possessed of a nervous temperament, easily excited, and has a strong will. I would say that she was insane, the same as I would say Henry Ward Beecher, Spurgeon, Horace Greeley, and like persons, are insane. Probably three weeks intervened between the visits I made Mrs. Packard. This was in June, 1860.

Re-examined.—She is a woman of large, active brain, and nervous temperament. I take her to be a woman of good intellect. There is no subject which excites people so much as religion. Insanity produces, oftentimes, ill-feelings towards the best friends, and particularly the family, or those more nearly related to the insane person—but not so with monomania. She told me, in the conversation, that the Calvinistic doctrines were wrong, and that she had been compelled to withdraw from the church. She said that Mr. Packard was more insane than she was, and that people would find it out. I had no doubt that she was insane. I only considered her insane on that subject, and she was not bad at that. I could not judge whether it was hereditary. I thought if she was withdrawn from conversation and excitement, she could have got well in a short time. Confinement in any shape, or restraint, would have made her worse. I did not think it was a bad case; it only required rest.

J. W. BROWN, being sworn, said:

I am a physician; live in this city; have no extensive acquaintance with Mrs. Packard. Saw her three or four weeks ago. I examined her as to her sanity or insanity. I was requested to make a visit, and had an extended conference with her: I spent some three hours with her. I had no difficulty in arriving at the conclusion, in my mind, that she was insane.

Cross-examination.—I visited her by request of Mr. Packard, at her house. The children were in and out of the room; no one else was present. I concealed my object in visiting her. She asked me if I was a physician, and I told her no; that I was an agent, selling sewing machines, and had come there to sell her one.

The first subject we conversed about was sewing machines. She showed no signs of insanity on that subject.

The next subject discussed was the social condition of the female sex. She exhibited no special marks of insanity on that subject, although she had many ideas quite at variance with mine, on the subject.

The subject of politics was introduced. She spoke of the condition of the North and the South. She illustrated her difficulties with Mr. Packard, by the difficulties between the North and the South. She said the South was wrong, and was waging war for two wicked purposes ; first, to overthrow a good government, and second, to establish a despotism on the inhuman principle of human slavery. But that the North, having right on their side, would prevail. So Mr. Packard was opposing her, to overthrow free thought in woman ; that the despotism of man may prevail over the wife ; but that she had right and truth on her side, and that she would prevail.

During this conversation I did not fully conclude that she was insane.

I brought up the subject of religion. We discussed that subject for a long time, and then I had not the slightest difficulty in concluding that she was hopelessly insane.

Question. Doctor, what particular idea did she advance on the subject of religion that led you to the conclusion that she was hopelessly insane ?

Answer. She advanced many of them. I formed my opinion not so much on any one idea advanced, as upon her whole conversation. She then said that she was the " Personification of the Holy Ghost." I did not know what she meant by that.

Ques. Was not this the idea conveyed to you in that conversation : That there are three attributes of the Deity—the Father, the Son, and the Holy Ghost ? Now, did she not say, that the attributes of the Father were represented in mankind, in man ; that the attributes of the Holy Ghost were represented in woman ; and that the Son was the fruit of these two attributes of the Deity ?

Ans. Well, I am not sure but that was the idea conveyed, though I did not fully get her idea at the time.

Ques. Was not that a new idea to you in theology ?

Ans. It was.

Ques. Are you much of a theologian ?

Ans. No.

Ques. Then because the idea was a novel one to you, you pronounced her insane?

Ans. Well, I pronounced her insane on that and other things that exhibited themselves in this conversation.

Ques. Did she not show more familiarity with the subject of religion and the questions of theology, than you had with these subjects?

Ans. I do not pretend much knowledge on these subjects.

Ques. What else did she say or do there that showed marks of insanity?

Ans. She claimed to be better than her husband—that she was right—and that he was wrong—and that all she did was good, and all he did was bad; that she was farther advanced than other people, and more nearly perfection. She found fault particularly that Mr. Packard would not discuss their points of difference on religion in an open, manly way, instead of going around and denouncing her as crazy to her friends and to the church.

She had a great aversion to being called insane. Before I got through the conversation she exhibited a great dislike to me, and almost treated me in a contemptuous manner. She appeared quite lady-like. She had a great reverence for God, and a regard for religious and pious people.

Re-examined.—Ques. Doctor, you may now state all the reasons you have for pronouncing her insane.

Ans. I have written down, in order, the reasons which I had, to found my opinion on, that she was insane. I will read them.

1. That she claimed to be in advance of the age thirty or forty years.

2. That she disliked to be called insane.

3. That she pronounced me a copperhead, and did not prove the fact.

4. An incoherency of thought. That she failed to illuminate me and fill me with light.

5. Her aversion to the doctrine of the total depravity of man.

6. Her claim to perfection or nearer perfection in action and conduct.

7. Her aversion to being called insane.

8. Her feelings toward her husband.

9. Her belief that to call her insane and abuse her, was blasphemy against the Holy Ghost.

10. Her explanation of this idea.

11. Incoherency of thought and ideas.

12. Her extreme aversion to the doctrine of the total depravity of mankind, and in the same conversation, saying her husband was a specimen of man's total depravity.

13. The general history of the case.

14. Her belief that some calamity would befall her, owing to my being there, and her refusal to shake hands with me when I went away.

15. Her viewing the subject of religion from the osteric standpoint of Christian exegetical analysis, and agglutinating the polsynthetical ectoblasts of homogeneous asceticism.

The witness left the stand amid roars of laughter; and it required some moments to restore order in the court-room.

JOSEPH H. WAY, sworn, and said:

I am a practicing physician in Kankakee City, Illinois. I made a medical examination of Mrs. Packard a few weeks since, at her house; was there perhaps two hours. On most subjects she was quite sane. On the subject of religion I thought she had some ideas that are not generally entertained. At that time I thought her to be somewhat deranged or excited on that subject; since that time I have thought perhaps I was not a proper judge, for I am not much posted on disputed

17

points in theology, and I find that other people entertain similar ideas. They are not in accordance with my views, but that is no evidence that she is insane.

Cross-examined.—I made this visit at her house, or his house, perhaps, at Manteno. I conversed on various subjects. She was perfectly sane on every subject except religion, and I would not swear now that she was insane. She seemed to have been laboring under an undue excitement on that subject. She has a nervous temperament, and is easily excited. She said she liked her children, and that it was hard to be torn from them. That none but a mother could feel the anguish she had suffered ; that while she was confined in the asylum the children had been educated by their father to call her insane. She said she would have them punished if they called their own mother insane, for it was not right.

Abijah Dole, sworn, and says :

I know Mrs. Packard ; have known her twenty-five or thirty years. I am her brother-in-law. Lived in Manteno seven years. Mrs. Packard has lived there six years. I have been sent for several times by her and Mr. Packard, and found her in an excited state of mind. I was there frequently ; we were very familiar. One morning early, I was sent for ; she was in the west room ; she was in her night-clothes. She took me by the hand and led me to the bed. Libby was lying in bed, moaning and moving her head. Mrs. Packard now spoke and said, " How pure we are." " I am one of the children of heaven ; Libby is one of the branches." " The woman shall bruise the serpent's head." She called Mr. Packard a devil. She said, Brother Dole, these are serious matters. If Brother Haslet will help me, we will crush the body. She said, Christ had come into the world to save men, and that she had come to save woman. Her hair was disheveled. Her face looked wild. This was over three years ago.

I was there again one morning after this. She came to me. She pitied me for marrying my wife, who is a sister to Mr. Packard; said I might find an agreeable companion. She said if she had cultivated amativeness, she would have made a more agreeable companion. She took me to another room and talked about going away; this was in June before they took her to the State Hospital. She sent for me again; she was in the east room; she was very cordial. She wanted me to intercede for Theophilus, who was at Marshall, Michigan; she wanted him to stay there, and it was thought not advisable for him to stay. We wished him to come away, but did not tell her the reasons. He was with a Swedenborgian.

After this I was called there once in the night. She said she could not live with Mr. Packard, and she thought she had better go away. One time she was in the Bible class. The question came up in regard to Moses smiting the Egyptian; she thought Moses had acted too hasty, but that all things worked for the glory of God. I requested her to keep quiet, and she agreed to do it.

I have had no conversation with Mrs. Packard since her return from the hospital; she will not talk with me because she thinks I think she is insane. Her brother came to see her; he said he had not seen her for four or five years. I tried to have Mrs. Packard talk with him, and she would not have anything to do with him because he said she was a crazy woman. She generally was in the kitchen when I was there, overseeing her household affairs.

I was superintendent of the Sabbath-school. One Sabbath, just at the close of the school, I was behind the desk, and almost like a vision she appeared before me, and requested to deliver or read an address to the school. I was much surprised; I felt so bad, I did not know what to do. (At this juncture the witness became very much affected, and choked up so that he could not proceed, and cried so loud that he could be heard in any part of the court-room. When he became calm, he went on and said), I was willing to gratify her all I could, for I knew she was crazy, but I did not want to take the responsibility myself, so I put it to a vote of the school, if she should be allowed to read it. She was allowed to read it. It occupied ten or fifteen minutes in reading.

I cannot state any of the particulars of that paper. It bore evidence of her insanity. She went on and condemned the church, all in all, and the individuals composing the church, because they did not agree with her. She looked very wild and very much excited. She seemed to be insane. She came to church one morning just as services commenced, and wished to have the church act upon her letter withdrawing from the church immediately. Mr. Packard was in the pulpit. She wanted to know if Brother Dole and Brother Merrick were in the church, and wanted them to have it acted upon. This was three years ago, just before she was taken away to the hospital.

Cross-examined.—I supposed when I first went into the room that her influence over the child had caused the child to become deranged. The child was nine years old. I believed that she had exerted some mesmeric or other influence over the child, that caused it to moan and toss its head. The child had been sick with brain fever; I learned that after I got there. I suppose the mother had considerable anxiety over the child; I suppose she had been watching over the child all night, and that would tend to excite her. The child got well. It was sick several days after this; it was lying on the bed moaning and tossing its head; the mother did not appear to be alarmed. Mr. Packard was not with her; she was all alone; she did not say that Mr. Packard did not show proper care for the sick child. I suppose she thought Libby would die.

Her ideas on religion did not agree with mine, nor with my view of the Bible.

I knew Mr. Packard thought her insane, and did not want her to discuss these questions in the Sabbath-school. I knew he had opposed her more or less. This letter to the church was for the purpose of asking for a letter from the church.

Question. Was it an indication of insanity that she wanted to leave the Presbyterian Church?

Answer. I think it strange that she should ask for letters from the church. She would not leave the church unless she was insane.

I am a member of the church—I believe the church is right. I believe everything the church does is right. I believe everything in the Bible.

Ques. Do you believe literally that Jonah was swallowed by a whale, and remained in its belly three days, and was then cast up?

Ans. I do.

Ques. Do you believe literally that Elijah went direct up to Heaven in a chariot of fire—that the chariot had wheels, and seats, and was drawn by horses?

Ans. I do—for with God all things are possible.

Ques. Do you believe Mrs. Packard was insane, and is insane?

Ans. I do.

I never read any of Swedenborg's works. I do not deem it proper for persons to investigate new doctrines or systems of theology.

Re-examined.—I became a Presbyterian eight years ago. I was formerly a Congregationalist; Mr. Packard was a Congregationalist.

Re-cross-examination.—Ques. Was it dangerous for you to examine the doctrines or theology embraced in the Presbyterian Church, when you left the Congregational Church, and joined it?

Ans. I will not answer so foolish a question.

Witness discharged.

JOSEPHUS B. SMITH, sworn, says:

Am aged fifty years; have known Mrs. Packard seven years. I cannot tell the first appearance of any abnormal condition of her mind. I first saw it at the Sabbath-school. She came in and wished to read a communication. I do not recollect everything of the communication. She did not read the letter, but presented it to Brother Dole. She said something about her small children, and left. She seemed to be excited. There was nothing very unusual in her appearance. Her voice was rather excited; it could be heard nearly over the house. I merely recall the circumstance, but recollect scarce anything else. It was an unusual thing for any person to come in and read an address. I do not recollect anything unusual in her manner.

(At this stage of the trial, an incident occurred that for a time stopped all proceedings, and produced quite an excitement in the court-room; and this report would not be faithful if it were passed over unnoticed. Mrs. Dole, the sister of Mr. Packard, came in, leading the little daughter of Mrs. Packard, and in passing by the table occupied by Mrs. Packard and her counsel, the child stopped, went up to her mother, kissed and hugged her, and was clinging to her with all childlike fervor, when it was observed by Mrs. Dole, who snatched the child up—and bid it " come away from that woman; " adding, " She is not fit to take care of you—I have you in my charge; " and thereupon led her away. The court-room was crowded to its utmost, and not a mother's heart there but what was touched, and scarce a dry eye was seen. Quite a stir was made, but the Sheriff soon restored order.)

Cross-examined.—I had charge of the Sunday-school; am a member of Mr. Packard's church. I knew Mr. Packard had considered her insane; knew they had had difficulties. I was elected superintendent of the school in place of Brother Dole, for the special purpose of keeping Mrs. Packard straight.

SYBIL DOLE, sworn, and says:

I am Mr. Packard's sister; have known her twenty-five years. Her natural disposition is very kind and sweet. Her education is very good; her morals without a stain or blemish. I first observed a change in her after we came to Manteno. I had a conversation with her, when she talked an hour without interruption; she talked in a wild, excited manner; the subject was partly religion. She spoke of her own attainments; she said she had advanced in spiritual affairs. This was two or three years before she went to the Asylum.

The next time was when she was preparing to go to York State. She was weeping and sick. Her trunk was packed and ready to go, but Mr. Packard was sick. From her voice, and the manner she talked, I formed an opinion of her insanity. She talked on various points; the conversation distressed me very much; I could not sleep. She was going alone; we tried to persuade her not to go alone. She accused Mr. Packard very strangely of depriving her of her rights of conscience—that he would not allow her to think for herself on religious questions, because they disagreed on these topics. She made her visit to New York. The first time I met her after her return, her health was much improved; she appeared much better. In the course of a few weeks, she visited at my house.

At another time, one of the children came up, and wanted me to go down; I did so. She was very much excited about her son remaining at Marshall. She was wild. She thought it was very wrong and tyrannical for Mr. Packard not to permit her son to remain there. She said very many things which seemed unnatural. Her voice, manner and ways, all showed she was insane.

I was there when Mr. Baker came there, to see about Theophilus remaining at Marshall with him. She was calmer than she was the day before. She said that she should spend the day in fasting and prayer. She said he had come in unexpectedly, and they were not prepared to entertain strangers. She was out of bread, and had to make biscuit for dinner. (One gentleman in the crowd turned to his wife and said, " Wife, were you ever out of bread, and had to make biscuit for dinner? I must put you into an Insane Asylum! No mistake!") I occupied the same room and bed with her. She went to Mr. Packard's room, and when she returned, she said, that if her son was not permitted to remain at Marshall, it would result in a divorce. She got up several times during the night. She told me how much she enjoyed the family circle. She spoke very highly of Mr. Packard's kindness to her. She spoke particularly of the tenderness which had once existed between them. I did not notice anything very remarkable in her conduct toward Mr. Packard, until just before she was sent to the Hospital.

One morning afterward, I went to her house with a lady; we wanted to go in, and were admitted. She seemed much excited. She said, " You regard me insane. I will thank you to leave my room." This was two or three months before she was sent to Jacksonville. Mr. Packard went out. She put her hand on my shoulder, and said she would thank me to go out too. I went out.

I afterward wanted to take the baby home. One morning I went down to see her, and prepared breakfast for her. She appeared thankful, and complimented me on my kindness. She consented for me to take the child; I did so. In a short time, about ten days after, the other children came up, and said that she wanted to take her own child. I took the child down. Her appearance was very wild. She was filled with spite toward Mr. Packard. She defied me to take the child again, and said that she would evoke the strong arm of the law to help her keep it.

At another time, at the table, she was talking about religion, when Mr. Packard remonstrated with her; she became angry, and told him she would talk what and when she had a mind to. She rose up from the table, and took her tea-cup, and left the room in great violence.

Cross-examined.—I am a member of Mr. Packard's church, and am his sister. He and I have often consulted together about Mrs. Packard. Mr. Packard was the first to ever suggest that she was insane; after that, I would more carefully watch her actions to find out if she was insane. The religious doctrines she advanced were at variance with those entertained by our church. She was a good, neat, thrifty and careful housekeeper. She was economical; kept the children clean and neatly dressed. She was sane on all subjects except religion. I do not think she would have entertained these ideas, if she had not been insane. I do not think she would have wanted to have withdrawn from our church, and unite with another church, if she had not been insane. She said she would worship with the Methodists. They were the only other Protestant denomination that held service at Manteno at the time. I knew when she was taken to Jacksonville Hospital. She was taken away in the morning. She did not want to go; we thought it advisable for her to go.

SARAH RUMSEY, sworn, and says:

Have lived one week in Mrs. Packard's house. I was present at the interview when Mrs. Packard ordered us to leave the room. Mrs. Packard was very pale and angry. She was in an undress, and her hair was down over her face.

17*

It was eleven o'clock in the forenoon—I staid at the house; Mrs. Packard came out to the kitchen. She was dressed then. She said she had come to reveal to me what Mr. Packard was. She talked very rapidly; she would not talk calm. She said Mr. Packard was an arch deceiver; that he and the members of his church had made a conspiracy to put her into the insane asylum; she wanted me to leave the conspirators. Soon after dinner she said, "Come with me, I have something to tell you." She said she had a new revelation; it would soon be here; and that she had been chosen by God for a particular mission. She said that all who decided with her, and remained true to her, would be rewarded by the millennium, and if I would side with her, that I would be a chief apostle in the millennium. She wanted to go to Batavia, but that Mr. Packard would give her no money to take her there; that Mr. Packard called her insane. She started to go out, and Mr. Packard made her return; took her into Mr. Comstock's, and Mr. Comstock made her go home.

I saw her again when Libby had the brain fever. She was disturbed because the family called her insane. She and Libby were crying together; they cried together a long time. This was Tuesday. She would not let me into the room. The next morning while at breakfast, Mr. Labric passed the window and came in. He said that Georgie had been over for him, and said that they were killing his mother. She acted very strangely all the time; was wild and excited.

Cross-examined.—Knew Mr. Packard two years before I went there to live. He was the pastor of our church. I am a member of the church. I did not attend the Bible-class. Brother Dole came to me and said somebody of the church should go there, and stay at the house, and assist in packing her clothes and getting her ready to take off to the hospital, and stay and take care of the children. I consented to go;

I heard that Brother Packard requested Brother Dole to come for me. I never worked out before. They had a French servant, before I went there; Mr. Packard turned her off when I came, the same day. I did not want to take Mrs. Packard away. I did not think she exhibited any very unusual excitement, when the men came here to take her away. Doctors Merrick and Newkirk were the physicians who came there with Sheriff Burgess. She did not manifest as much excitement, when being taken away, as I would have done, under the same circumstances; any person would have naturally been opposed to being carried away.

The church had opposed her in disseminating her ideas in the church; I was opposed to her promulgating her religious ideas in the church; I thought them wrong and injurious. I was present at the Sabbath-school when she read the paper to the school; I thought that bore evidence of insanity. It was a refutation of what Mrs. Dixon had written; I cannot give the contents of the paper now.

I was present when she read a confession of her conduct to the church; she had had her views changed partially, from a sermon preached upon the subject of the sovereignty and immutability of God. I did not think it strange conduct that she changed her views; and never said so. This was in the spring before the June when they took her away.

The article she read in the school was by the permission of the school.

I was present when she presented a protest against the church for refusing to let her be heard; I have only an indistinct recollection of it; it was a protest because they refused to listen to her.

Mr. Dole was the only person who came to the house when she was taken away, except the men with Burgess.

She said that Mr. Packard had deprived her of the liberty of conscience in charging her to be insane, when she only entertained ideas new to him.

I thought it was an evidence of insanity because she maintained these ideas. I do not know that many people entertained similar ideas; I suppose a good many do not think the Calvinistic doctrine is right; they are not necessarily insane because they think so.

When she found I was going to stay in the house, and that the French servant had been discharged, she ordered me into the kitchen; before that, she had treated me kindly as a visitor.

I thought it was an evidence of insanity for her to order me into the kitchen; she ought to have known that I was not an ordinary servant. The proper place for the servant is in the kitchen at work, and not in the parlor; I took the place of the servant girl for a short time.

She wanted the flower-beds in the front yard cleaned out, and tried to get Mr. Packard to do it; he would not do it. She went and put on an old dress, and went to work and cleaned the weeds out, and worked herself into a great heat. It was a warm day; she staid out until she was almost melted down with the heat.

Question. What did she do then?

Answer. She went to her room and took a bath, and dressed herself, and then lay down exhausted. She did not come down to dinner.

Ques. And did you think that was an evidence of insanity?

Ans. I did—the way it was done.

Ques. What would you have done under similar circumstances? Would you have sat down in the clothes you had worked in?

Ans. No.

Ques. Probably you would have taken a bath and changed your clothes, too. And so would any lady, would they not?

Ans. Yes.

Ques. Then would you call yourself insane ?

Ans. No. But she was angry and excited, and showed ill-will. She was very tidy in her habits ; liked to keep the house clean, and have her yard and flowers look well. She took considerable pains with these things.

I remained there until she was taken away; I approved taking her away ; I deemed her dangerous to the church ; her ideas were contrary to the church, and were wrong.

The baby was eighteen months old when she was taken away. She was very fond of her children, and treated them very kindly. Never saw her misuse them. Never heard that she had misused them. Never heard that she was dangerous to herself or to her family. Never heard that she had threatened or offered to destroy anything, or injure any person.

JUDGE BARTLETT was next called to the stand.

Am acquainted with Mrs. Packard. Had a conversation with her on religious topics. We agreed very well in most things. She did not say she believed in the transmigration of souls ; she said, some persons had expressed that idea to her, but she did not believe it. It was spoken of lightly. She did not say ever to me, that Mr. Packard's soul would go into an ox. She did not say anything about her being related to the Holy Ghost. I thought then, and said it, that religious subjects were her study, and that she would easily be excited on that subject. I could not see that she was insane. I would go no stronger than to say, that her mind dwelt on religious subjects. She could not be called insane, for thousands of people believe as she does on religion.

MRS. SYBIL DOLE, recalled.

At the time she got up from the table, she went out. She said, " I will have no fellowship with the unfruitful works of darkness. No! not so much as to eat with them."

Re-cross-examined.—Question. Did you deem that an evidence of insanity?

Answer. I did.

Ques. She called Mr. Packard the unfruitful works of darkness?

Ans. I suppose so.

Ques. Did she also include you?

Ans. She might have done so.

Ques. This was about the time that her husband was plotting to kidnap her, was it not?

Ans. It was just before she was removed to the asylum.

Ques. He had been charging her with insanity, had he not, at the table?

Ans. He had.

The prosecution now wished to adjourn the court for ten days, to enable them to get Dr. McFarland, Superintendent of the State Hospital, who, they claimed, would testify that she was insane. Counsel stated, he had been telegraphed to come, and a reply was received, that he was in Zanesville, Ohio, and would return in about ten days. They claimed his testimony would be very important. This motion the counsel of Mrs. Packard opposed, as it was an unheard-of proceeding to continue a cause after the hearing was commenced, to enable a party to hunt up testimony.

The matter was discussed on each side for a considerable length of time, when the court held that the defense should go on with their testimony, and after that was heard, then the court would determine about continuing the case to get Dr. McFarland, and perhaps he could be got before the defense was through, and if so, he might be sworn; and held that the defense should go on now.

The counsel of Mrs. Packard withdrew for consultation, and in a brief time returned, and announced to the court that they would submit the case without introducing any testimony, and were willing to submit it without argument. The counsel for Mr. Packard objected to this, and renewed the motion for a continuance; which the court refused.

The counsel for Mr. Packard then offered to read to the jury a letter from Dr. McFarland, dated in the month of December, 1863, written to Rev. Theophilus Packard; and also a certificate, under the seal of the State Hospital at Jacksonville, certifying that Mrs. Packard was discharged from the institution in June, 1863, and was incurably insane, which certificate was signed by Dr. McFarland, the Superintendent. To the introduction of this to the jury, the counsel for Mrs. Packard objected, as being incompetent testimony, and debarred the defense of the benefit of a cross-examination. The court permitted the letter and certificate to be read to the jury.

These documents were retained by Rev. Theophilus Packard, and the reporter has been unable to obtain copies of them. The letter is dated in December, 1863, at the State Hospital, Jacksonville, Illinois, and written to Rev. Theophilus Packard, wherein Dr. McFarland writes him that Mrs. Packard is hopelessly insane, and that no possible good could result by having her returned to the Hospital; that the officers of the institution had done everything in their power to effect a cure, and were satisfied she could not be cured, and refused to receive her into the institution.

The certificate, under the seal of the Hospital, was a statement, dated in June, 1863, at Jacksonville, Illinois, setting forth the time (three years) that Mrs. Packard had been under treatment, and that she had been discharged, as beyond a possibility of being cured.

The above is the import of these documents, which the reporter regrets he cannot lay before the public in full.

The prosecution now announced that they closed their case.

DEFENSE.

J. L. SIMINGTON was the first witness called for the defense. Being sworn, he said:

I live in Manteno; lived there since 1859, early in the spring. Knew Rev. Mr. Packard and Mrs. Packard. First became acquainted with them in 1858; I was then engaged in the ministry of the Methodist Church. I have practiced medicine eleven years.

I was consulted as a family physician by Mrs. Packard in 1860. Was quite well acquainted with Mrs. Packard, and with the family. Lived fifty or sixty rods from their house. Saw her and the family almost daily. I did not see anything unusual in her in regard to her mind. I never saw anything I thought insanity in her. So far as I know she was a sane woman. I have seen her since she came from the Hospital; have seen nothing since to indicate she was insane. My opinion is, she is a sane woman.

No cross-examination was made.

Dr. J. D. MANN, sworn, and says:

I live in Manteno; have lived there nine years. Practiced medicine there six years. I am not very intimately acquainted with either Mr. or Mrs. Packard. Mr. Packard invited me to go to his house to have an interview with Mrs. Packard. I went at his request. He requested me to make a second examination, which I did. There had been a physician there before I went. The last time, he wanted me to meet Dr. Brown, of this city, there. This was late in November last. He introduced me to Mrs. Packard. I had known her before she was taken to the Hospital, and this was the first time I had seen her since she had returned. I was there from one to two hours. I then made up my mind, as I had made up my mind from the first interview, that I could find nothing that indicated insanity. I did not go when Dr. Brown was there. Mr. Packard had told me she was insane, and my prejudices were, that she was insane. He wanted a certificate of her insanity, to take East with him. I would not give it.

The witness was not cross-examined.

JOSEPH E. LABRIE, sworn, and says:

Have known Mrs. Packard six years; lived fifteen or twenty rods from their house. Knew her in spring of 1860. Saw her nearly every day—sometimes two or three times a day. I belong to the Catholic Church. Have seen her since her return from Jacksonville. I have seen nothing that could make me think her insane. I always said she was a sane woman, and say so yet.

Cross-examined.—I am not a physician. I am not an expert. She might be insane, but no common-sense man could find it out.

Re-examined.—I am a Justice of the Peace and Notary Public. Mr. Packard requested me to go to his house and take an acknowledgment of a deed from her. I went there, and she signed and acknowledged the deed. This was within the past two months.

Re-cross-examined.—I was sent for to go to the house in the spring of 1860. My wife was with me. It was about taking her to Jacksonville. Mrs. Packard would not come to the room where I was. I stayed there only about twenty minutes.

Have been there since she returned from the Hospital. The door to her room was locked on the outside. Mr. Packard said, he had made up his mind to let no one into her room.

The counsel for Mrs. Packard offered to read to the jury the following paper, which had been referred to by the witnesses, as evidence of Mrs. Packard's insanity, and which Deacon Smith refused to hear read. The counsel for Mr. Packard examined the paper, and admitted it was the same paper.

The counsel for Mrs. Packard then requested permission of the court for Mrs. Packard to read it to the jury, which was most strenuously opposed. The court permitted Mrs. Packard to read it to the jury. Mrs. Packard arose, and read in a distinct tone of voice, so that every word was heard all over the court-room.

HOW GODLINESS IS PROFITABLE.

DEACON SMITH—A question was proposed to this class, the last Sabbath Brother Dole taught us, and it was requested that the class consider and report the result of their investigations at a future session. May I now bring it up? The question was this:

"Have we any reason to expect that a Christian farmer, as a Christian, will be any more successful in his farming operations, than an impenitent sinner—and if not, how is it that godliness is profitable unto all things?" Or, in other words, "does the motive with which one prosecutes his secular business, other things being equal, make any difference in the pecuniary results?"

Mrs. Dixon gave it as her opinion, at the time, that the motive did affect the pecuniary results.

Now the practical result to which this conclusion leads, is such as will justify us in our judging of Mrs. Dixon's true moral character, next fall, by her success in her farming operations this summer.

My opinion differs from hers on this point; and my reasons are here given in writing, since I deem it necessary for me, under the existing state of feeling toward me, to put into a written form all I have to say, in the class, to prevent misrepresentation.

Should I be appropriating an unreasonable share of time, as a pupil, Mr. Smith, to occupy four minutes of your time in reading them? I should like very much to read them, that the class may pass their honest criticisms upon them.

AN ANSWER TO THE QUESTION.

I think we have no intelligent reason for believing that the motives with which we prosecute our secular business, have any influence in the pecuniary results.

My reasons are common-sense reasons, rather than strictly Bible proofs, viz., I regard man as existing in three distinct departments of being, viz., his physical or animal, his mental or intellectual, his moral or spiritual; and each of these three distinct departments are under the control of laws, peculiar to itself; and these different laws do not interchange with or affect each other's department.

For instance, a very animal man may be a very healthy, long-lived man; for, notwithstanding he violates the moral department, he may live in conformity to the physical laws· of his animal nature, which secure to him his physical health. And, on the other hand, a very moral man may suffer greatly from a diseased body, and be cut off in the very midst of his usefulness by an early death, in consequence of having violated the physical laws of his animal constitution. But on the moral plane he is the gainer, and the immoral man is the loser.

So our success in business depends upon our conformity to those laws on which success depends—not upon the motives which act only on the moral plane.

On this ground, the Christian farmer has no more reason to expect success in his farming operations than the impenitent sinner. In either case, the foundation for success must depend upon the degree of fidelity with which the natural laws are applied, which cause the natural result—not upon the motives of the operator; since these moral acts receive their penalty and reward on an entirely different plane of his being.

Now comes in the question, how then is it true, that "godliness is profitable unto all things," if godliness is no guarantee to success in business pursuits?

I reply, that the profits of godliness cannot mean, simply, pecuniary profits, because this would limit the gain of godliness to this world, alone; whereas, it is profitable not only for this life, but also for the life to come. Gain and loss, dollars and cents, are not the coins current in the spiritual world.

But happiness and misery are coins which are current in both worlds. Therefore, it appears to me, that happiness is the profit attendant upon godliness, and for this reason, a practically godly person, who lives in conformity to all the various laws of his entire being, may expect to secure to himself, as a natural result, a greater amount of happiness than the ungodly person.

So that, in this sense, "Godliness is profitable unto all things," to every department of our being.

E. P. W. PACKARD.

MANTENO, March 22, 1860.

Mrs. Packard then stated that the above was presented to the class, the 15th day of the following April, and was *rejected* by the teacher, Deacon Smith, on the ground of its being irrelevant to the subject, since she had not confined herself to the Bible alone for proof of her position.

As she took her seat, a murmur of applause arose from every part of the room, which was promptly suppressed by the sheriff.

DANIEL BEEDY, sworn, and says:

I live in Manteno. Have known Mrs. Packard six years; knew her in the spring of 1860. I lived a mile and a half from them. Have seen her very frequently since her return from Jacksonville. Had many conversations with her before she was taken away, and since her return. She always appeared to me like a sane woman. I heard she was insane, and my wife and I went to satisfy ourselves. I went there soon after the difficulties in the Bible class.

She is not insane. We talked about religion, politics, and various matters, such as a gray-haired old farmer could talk about, and I saw nothing insane about her.

Mr. BLESSING, sworn, and says.

I live in Manteno; have known Mrs. Packard six years; knew her in the spring of 1860; lived eighty rods from their house. She visited at my house. I have seen her at church. She attended the Methodist church for awhile after the difficulties commenced, and then I saw her every Sunday. I never thought her insane.

After the word was given out by her husband that she was insane, she claimed my particular protection, and wanted me to obtain a trial for her by the laws of the land, and such an investigation she said she was willing to stand by. She claimed Mr. Packard was insane, if any one was. She begged for a trial. I did not then do anything, because I did not like to interfere between man and wife. I never saw anything that indicated insanity. She was always rational. Had conversations with her since her return. She first came to my house. She claimed a right to live with her family. She considered herself more capable of taking care of her family than any other person.

I saw her at Jacksonville. I took Dr. Shirley with me to test her insanity. Dr. Shirley told me she was not insane.

Cross-examination waived.

Mrs. BLESSING, sworn, and says:

Have known Mrs. Packard seven years; knew her in 1860. Lived near them; we visited each other as neighbors. She first came to our house when she returned from Jacksonville. I did not see anything that indicated that she was insane. I saw her at Jacksonville. She had the keys, and showed me around. I heard the conversation there with Dr. Shirley; they talked about religion; did not think she talked unnatural. When I first went in, she was at work on a dress for Dr. McFarland's wife. I saw her after she returned home last fall, quite often, until she was locked in her room. On Monday after she got home, I called on her; she was at work; she was cleaning up the feather beds; they needed cleaning badly. I went there afterward; her daughter let me in. On Saturday before the trial commenced, I was let into her room by Mr. Packard; she had no fire in it; we sat there in the cold. Mr. Packard had a handful of keys, and unlocked the door and let me in. Mrs. Hanford was with me. Before this, Mrs. Hanford and myself went there to see her; he would not let us see her; he shook his hand at me, and threatened to put me out.

Mrs. HASLET, sworn, and said:

Know Mrs. Packard very well; have known her since they lived in Manteno; knew her in the spring of 1860; and since she returned from Jacksonville, we have been on intimate terms. I never saw any signs of insanity with her. I called often before she was kidnapped and carried to Jacksonville, and since her return.

I recollect the time Miss Rumsey was there; I did not see anything that showed insanity. I called to see her in a few days after she returned from Jacksonville; she was in the yard, cleaning feather beds. I called again in a few days; she was still cleaning house. The house needed cleaning;

and when I again called, it looked as if the mistress of the house was at home. She had no hired girl. I went again, and was not admitted. I conversed with her through the window; the window was fastened down. The son refused me admission. The window was fastened with nails on the inside, and by two screws, passing through the lower part of the upper sash and the upper part of the lower sash, from the outside. I did not see Mr. Packard this time.

Cross-examination.—She talked about getting released from her imprisonment. She asked if filing a bill of complaint would lead to a divorce. She said she did not want a divorce; she only wanted protection from Mr. Packard's cruelty. I advised her not to stand it quietly, but get a divorce.

Dr. DUNCANSON, sworn, and said:

I live here; am a physician; have been a clergyman; have been a practicing physician twenty-one years. Have known Mrs. Packard since this trial commenced. Have known her by general report for three years and upwards. I visited her at Mr. Orr's. I was requested to go there and have a conversation with her, and determine if she was sane or insane. Talked three hours with her, on political, religious, and scientific subjects, and on mental and moral philosophy. I was educated at, and received diplomas from the University of Glasgow, and Anderson University, of Glasgow. I went there to see her, and prove or disprove her insanity. I think not only that she is sane, but the most intelligent lady I have talked with in many years. We talked religion very thoroughly. I find her an expert in both departments, Old School and New School theology. There are thousands of persons who believe just as she does. Many of her ideas and doctrines are embraced in Swedenborgianism, and many are found only in the New School theology. The best and most learned men of both Europe and this country are advocates of these doctrines, in one shape or the other; and some bigots and men with minds of small caliber may call these great minds insane; but that does not make them insane. An insane mind is a diseased mind. These minds are the perfection of intellectual powers, healthy, strong, vigorous, and just the reverse of diseased minds, or insane. Her explanation of woman representing the Holy Ghost, and man representing the male attributes of the Father, and that the Son is the fruit of the Father and the Holy Ghost, is a very ancient theological dogma, and entertained by many of our most eminent men. On every topic I introduced, she was perfectly familiar, and discussed them with an intelligence that at once showed she was possessed of a good education, and a strong and vigorous mind. I did not agree with her in sentiment on many things, but I do not call people insane because they differ from me, nor from a majority, even, of people. Many persons called Swedenborg insane. That is true; but he had the largest brain of any person during the age in which he lived; and no one now dares call him insane. You might with as much propriety call Christ insane, because he taught the people many new and strange things; or Galileo; or Newton; or Luther; or Robert Fulton; or Morse, who electrified the world; or Watts; or a thousand others I might name. Morse's best friends for a long time thought him mad; yet there was a magnificent mind, the embodiment of health and vigor.

So with Mrs. Packard; there is wanting every indication of insanity that is laid down in the books. I pronounce her a sane woman, and wish we had a nation of such women.

This witness was cross-examined at some length, which elicited nothing new, when he retired.

The defense now announced to the court that they had closed all the testimony they wished to introduce, and inasmuch as the case had occupied so much time, they would propose to submit it without argument. The prosecution would not consent to this arrangement.

The case was argued ably and at length, by Messrs. Loomis and Bonfield for the prosecution, and by Messrs. Orr and Loring on the part of the defense.

It would be impossible to give even a statement of the arguments made, and do the attorneys justice, in the space allotted to this report.

On the 18th day of January, 1864, at ten o'clock P. M., the jury retired for consultation, under the charge of the sheriff. After an absence of seven minutes, they returned into court, and gave the following verdict:

STATE OF ILLINOIS, } *ss.*
    KANKAKEE COUNTY.

We, the undersigned, Jurors in the case of Mrs. Elizabeth P. W. Packard, alleged to be insane, having heard the evidence in the case, are satisfied that said Elizabeth P. W. Packard is SANE.

JOHN STILES, *Foreman,*	H. HIRSHBERG,
DANIEL G. BEAN,	NELSON JERVAIS,
F. G. HUTCHINSON,	WILLIAM HYER,
V. H. YOUNG,	GEO. H. ANDREWS,
G. M. LYONS,	J. F. MAFIT,
THOMAS MUNCEY,	LEMUEL MILK.

Cheers arose from every part of the house; the ladies waved their handkerchiefs, and pressed around Mrs. Packard, and extended her their congratulations. It was some time before the outburst of applause could be checked. When order was restored, the counsel for Mrs. Packard

18

moved the court that she be discharged. Thereupon the court ordered the clerk to enter the following order :

STATE OF ILLINOIS, } 88.
    KANKAKEE COUNTY,

It is hereby ordered that Mrs. Elizabeth P. W. Packard be relieved from all restraint incompatible with her condition as a sane woman.

C. R. STARR,

Judge of the 20th Judicial Circuit of the State of Illinois.

January 18, 1864.

Thus ended the trial of this remarkable case. During each day of the proceedings the court-room was crowded to excess by an anxious audience of ladies and gentlemen, who are seldom in our courts. The verdict of the jury was received with applause, and hosts of friends crowded upon Mrs. Packard to congratulate her upon her release.

During the past two months, Mr. Packard had locked her up in her own house, fastened the windows outside, and carried the key to the door, and made her a close prisoner. He was maturing a plan to immure her in an asylum in Massachusetts, and for that purpose was ready to start on the Thursday before the writ was sued out, when his plan was disclosed to Mrs. Packard by a letter he accidentally dropped in her room, written by his sister in Massachusetts, telling him the route he should take, and that a carriage would be ready at the station to put her in and convey her to the asylum.

Vigorous action became necessary, and she communicated this startling intelligence through her window to some ladies who had come to see her, and were refused admission into the house.

On Monday morning, and before the defense had rested their case, Mr. Packard left the State, bag and baggage, for parts unknown, having first mortgaged his property for all it; worth to his sister and other parties.

We cannot do better than close this report with the following editorial from the Kankakee *Gazette* of January 21, 1864:

The case of this lady, which has attracted so much attention and excited so much interest for ten days past, was decided on Monday evening last, and resulted, as almost every person thought it must, in a complete vindication of her sanity. The jury retired on Monday evening, after hearing the arguments of the counsel ; and after a brief consultation they brought in a verdict that Mrs. Packard is a *sane* woman.

Thus has resulted an investigation which Mrs. Packard has long and always desired should be had, but which her cruel husband has ever sternly refused her. She has always asked and earnestly pleaded for a jury trial of her case, but her relentless persecutor has ever turned a deaf ear to her entreaties, and flagrantly violated all the dictates of justice and humanity.

She has suffered the alienation of friends and relatives ; the shock of a kidnapping by her husband and his *posse* when forcibly removed to the asylum ; has endured three years incarceration in that asylum—upon the general treatment in which there is severe comment in the State, and which in her special case was aggravatingly unpleasant and ill-favored ; returning to her home she found her husband's saintly blood still congealed, a winter of perpetual frown on his face, and the sad, dull monotony of " insane, insane," escaping his lips in all his communications to and concerning her ; her young family, the youngest of the four at home being less than four years of age, these children—over whose slumbers she had watched, and whose wailings she had hushed with all a mother's care and tenderness—had been taught to look upon her as insane, and they were not to respect the counsels or heed the voice of a maniac just loosed from the asylum, doom-scaled by official certificates.

Soon her aberration of mind led her to seek some of her better clothing carefully kept from her by her husband, which very woman-like act was seized by him as an excuse for confining her in her room, and depriving her of her apparel, and excluding her lady friends. Believing that he was about to again forcibly take her to an asylum, four responsible citizens of that village made affidavit of facts which caused the investigation as to her sanity or insanity. During the whole of the trial she was present, and counseled with her attorneys in the management of the case.

Notwithstanding the severe treatment she has received for nearly four years past, the outrages she has suffered, the wrong to her nature she has endured, she deported herself during the trial as one who is not only not insane, but as one possessing intellectual endowments of a high order, and an equipoise and control of mind far above the majority of human kind. Let the sapient Dr. Brown, who gave a certificate of insanity after a short conversation with her, and which certificate was to be used in aid of her incarceration for life— suffer as she has suffered, endure what she has endured, and the world would be deprived of future clinical revealings from his gigantic mind upon the subject of the spleen, and he would, to a still greater extent than in the past, " fail to illuminate " the public as to the virtues and glories of the martyr who is " watching and waiting " in Canada.

The heroic motto, " Suffer and be strong," is fairly illustrated in her case. While many would have opposed force to his force, displayed frantic emotions of displeasure at such treatment, or sat convulsed and " maddened with the passion of her part," she meekly submitted to the tortures of her bigoted tormentor, trusting and believing in God's Providence the hour of her vindication and her release from thraldom would come. And now the fruit of her suffering and persecution has all the autumn glory of perfection.

> " One who walked
> From the throne's splendor to the bloody block,
> Said : ' This completes my glory ' with a smile
> Which still illuminates men's thoughts of her."

Feeling the accusations of his guilty conscience, seeing the meshes of the net with which he had kept her surrounded were broken, and a storm-cloud of indignation about to break over his head in pitiless fury, the intolerant Packard, after encumbering their property with trust-deeds, and despoiling her of her furniture and clothing, left the country. Let him wander ! with the mark of infamy upon his brow, through far-off States, where distance and obscurity may diminish till the grave shall cover the wrongs it cannot heal.

It is to be hoped Mrs. Packard will make immediate application for a divorce, and thereby relieve herself of a repetition of the wrongs and outrages she has suffered by him who for the past four years has only used the marriage relation to persecute and torment her in a merciless and unfeeling manner.

www.ingramcontent.com/pod-product-compliance
Lightning Source LLC
Chambersburg PA
CBHW030820110726

47900CB00006B/1686